BILLY BUDD, SAILOR
(AN INSIDE NARRATIVE)

broadview editions
series editor: Martin R. Boyne

Herman Melville, 1885. Cabinet card by Rockwood.

BILLY BUDD, SAILOR
(AN INSIDE NARRATIVE)

Herman Melville

edited by
Michael J. Everton

broadview editions

BROADVIEW PRESS – www.broadviewpress.com
Peterborough, Ontario, Canada

Founded in 1985, Broadview Press remains a wholly independent publishing house. Broadview's focus is on academic publishing; our titles are accessible to university and college students as well as scholars and general readers. With over 600 titles in print, Broadview has become a leading international publisher in the humanities, with world-wide distribution. Broadview is committed to environmentally responsible publishing and fair business practices.

The interior of this book is printed on 100% recycled paper.

© 2016 Michael J. Everton

Library and Archives Canada Cataloguing in Publication

Melville, Herman, 1819-1891, author
    Billy Budd, sailor (an inside narrative) / Herman Melville ; edited by Michael J. Everton.

(Broadview editions)
Includes bibliographical references.
ISBN 978-1-55481-238-7 (paperback)

    1. Executions and executioners—Fiction. 2. Ship captains—Fiction. 3. Impressment—Fiction. 4. Sailors—Fiction.
I. Everton, Michael J., editor II. Title. III. Series: Broadview editions

PS2384.B5 2016   813'.3   C2016-904899-3

Broadview Editions
The Broadview Editions series is an effort to represent the ever-evolving canon of texts in the disciplines of literary studies, history, philosophy, and political theory. A distinguishing feature of the series is the inclusion of primary source documents contemporaneous with the work.

Advisory editor for this volume: Michel Pharand

Broadview Press handles its own distribution in North America
PO Box 1243, Peterborough, Ontario K9J 7H5, Canada
555 Riverwalk Parkway, Tonawanda, NY 14150, USA
Tel: (705) 743-8990; Fax: (705) 743-8353
email: customerservice@broadviewpress.com

Distribution is handled by Eurospan Group in the UK, Europe, Central Asia, Middle East, Africa, India, Southeast Asia, Central America, South America, and the Caribbean. Distribution is handled by Footprint Books in Australia and New Zealand.

Broadview Press acknowledges the financial support of the Government of Canada through the Canada Book Fund for our publishing activities.

Canada

Typesetting and assembly: True to Type Inc., Claremont, Canada
Cover Design: Lisa Brawn

PRINTED IN CANADA

Contents

Acknowledgements

This Broadview edition is intended especially for students new to Melville or to *Billy Budd*, and my own students, to whom it is dedicated, were never far from mind while I was putting it together. Thanks especially to my ingenious 2014 Melville seminar, which generously volunteered to act as a focus group to work out what non-specialists would need to acquire a foothold in *Billy Budd*. Three students from that course, Josh Hamm, Zahra Mohamud, and Eric Stein, deserve particular thanks for their efforts toward that goal and for their research assistance. Thanks, too, to Amy Flockhart, Denise Khouri, Madeleine Lascelle, Meghan Smith, and Abdul Zahir for test-driving early drafts of the introduction to help fine-tune its pitch. Once the introduction was ready to move beyond the friendly confines of my own campus, David Faflik, Michael Hingston, Mary Liston, Tim Marr, and Bryan Sinche went to work on it from various disciplinary perspectives. I appreciate more than I can express the time and care they put into their feedback. As for the many other Melville scholars past and present whose work and thought inform this edition, I've been trying unsuccessfully to come up with an elegant way of properly acknowledging my debts. The best I can do is say, inelegantly, that if I had the space to note everything that ought to be read about Melville or *Billy Budd*, my bibliography would be considerably longer than it is. What a brilliant community from which to learn. The same goes for the anonymous readers at Broadview, who helped improve the manuscript at every turn.

Thanks to the staffs at the eclectic assemblage of libraries where I worked on this edition alongside other research projects that had me away from home: Free Library of Philadelphia, the Historical Society of Pennsylvania, Richmond Public Library, University of Ottawa Library, and University of Virginia Library. Simon Fraser University Library and Vancouver Public Library played their usual role as local homes away from home, and I'm particularly indebted to Simon Fraser's indefatigable interlibrary loan staff.

Every encounter with Broadview Press has been a pleasure—it's a press to believe in—but Don LePan, Marjorie Mather, Martin Boyne, Michel Pharand, and Tara Trueman in particular made this edition a labour of love rather than just labour. For encouragement and cheer I owe happy debts to my department colleagues, staff, and chair; to John Beatty, Lara Campbell, Pete Cramer, and Eric Wredenhagen; and to my Richmond, Charleston, and Toronto families, most emphatically to my mom and dad, whose tattered 1964 Bobbs-Merrill edition of *Moby-Dick*, with its creepy cover, was my first literary hand-me-down and remains on my office shelf lovingly bound by rubber bands.

Speaking of editions, I am grateful to the University of Chicago Press for permission to reproduce the Harrison Hayford and Merton M. Sealts Jr. copy-text of *Billy Budd* (copyright © 1962 by the University of Chicago) and to Random House for permission to reproduce W.H. Auden's "Herman Melville."

As I entered the home stretch of this edition my wife, Karen Ferguson, and I welcomed our daughter, Tanisha, into our family. My work would not have been possible without Karen, and it would not mean as much without Tanisha, who, as it happens, landed at a school named for Lord Nelson. Finally, a nod to my East Vancouver neighbourhood of Commercial Drive, where arguments over the ins and outs of civil society are the welcome din of everyday life.

Introduction

A strange thing happened to Herman Melville on his way to the grave. In the 1880s, decades after he had been written off, people started saying nice, even extravagant things about his work. Really the attention was modest: a few fawning letters and articles, a publisher query, a reverential poem or two. Still, Melville had grown so accustomed to his books being reviled that even this dusting of praise must have seemed like an avalanche of goodwill. If he cared anymore, and no doubt he did, he did little to show it. When in 1889 a Harvard-educated professor from Nova Scotia sent Melville a gushing letter celebrating his work as "the most thoroughly New World product in all American literature" and asking "the honour of correspondence," the writer demurred (Melville, *Correspondence* 752). "After twenty years nearly, as an outdoor Custom House officer, I have latterly come into possession of unobstructed leisure, but only just as, in the course of nature, my vigor sensibly declines," he replied (519). "What little of it is left I husband for certain matters as yet incomplete, and which indeed may never be completed." *Billy Budd* was one of those matters, and Melville never did finish it. We don't know why—one theory is that he didn't because he couldn't—but we do know what happened next.

After Melville's death in 1891 the *Billy Budd* manuscript ended up in a bread box inherited by a granddaughter, Eleanor Melville Metcalf (1882–1964), who as a little girl would visit the Melvilles at their East 26th Street house in New York, wonder at her grandfather's big bookcases, eat his figs, squeeze his rough beard, and, when he occasionally "left the recesses of his own dark privacy" for her grandmother's room, listen to "wild tales of cannibals and tropic isles," no doubt child-friendly versions of the stories that had brought him salacious celebrity half a century before (Metcalf 283). In 1919, the manuscript ended up in the hands of a graduate student sent to Metcalf's house to dig for gold in her grandfather's surviving papers. Soon the chaotic manuscript was deciphered—not for the last time—and Melville's final book appeared right at the moment Melville was becoming MELVILLE. Then, because he wrote it and because of what it says and especially how it says it, it ended up a masterpiece of world literature, a book that cuts right across disciplinary boundaries, from philosophy to literature to law. Even if *Billy Budd,*

Sailor (An Inside Narrative) was never quite done, it has proven a book very difficult to be done with.

The plot, spoilers and all: John Claggart, master-at-arms (chief security officer) of a British warship, alleges a sailor is talking mutiny. The sailor, Billy, isn't just innocent of the charge; he's *an* innocent, an Adamic character whose fundamental ingenuousness contrasts with Claggart's fundamental depravity. Yet when confronted by his accuser, Billy reacts impulsively, striking Claggart and killing him instantly. The act is unintentional but the timing is unlucky. *Billy Budd* is set against a backdrop of anarchy and revolt. The year is 1797 and Britain is at war with Revolutionary France, its way of life ostensibly threatened from within and without.[1] Already apprehensive about their old, albeit newly radicalized enemy, Britain's military leaders are shaken by two naval mutinies that signal trouble in the ranks.[2] It is on the heels of these mutinies that Billy kills a superior officer, and it is under these circumstances that the ship's commander, Captain Vere, must decide whether to hang a man he knows is innocent in principle or risk even the appearance of lawlessness aboard the ship. Billy hangs at dawn, following a perfunctory trial in which Vere, steeped in a conservatism that prefers the way things are to the ways things might be, persuades the jury it has no choice. Morality and natural rights are all well and good, but they're irrelevant to maintaining a society, much less an empire.

Vere's logic has haunted readers for nearly a century now. It sounds uncomfortably like murder or, worse, like murder "legalised by lawyers," to borrow a phrase from Melville's "Timoleon" (*Published Poems* 253).[3] *Billy Budd* is more than a dense and dazzling account of human life under human law, however. It's a study of terrorism, and of the paranoia of the terrorized; an examination of the logic of slavery, and of the lynchings that outlived it; a debate over capital punishment at the dawn of state-sanctioned electrocution; an exegesis of evil rivalling *Othello* and *Paradise Lost*; a theory of narrative; a chronicle of same-sex desire under an illiberal status quo; a retrospective of a literary career; and perhaps the autobiography of an offending life.

---

1   See the discussion of the French Revolutionary Wars below, pp. 26–28, and in Appendix A.

2   On the Great Mutiny of 1797, see pp. 32 33, and Appendix C1.

3   All references to *Billy Budd* and to work reproduced in appendices list the page number in this Broadview edition. References to poems not included in the appendices cite page numbers in the relevant volume.

It is both like and unlike Melville's earlier work. Mostly, it is unlike it. Werner Berthoff, one of Melville's best readers, reminds us that "a critical thirty years" passed between his final novel and *Billy Budd* (128). What's pivotal about those years? That's partly what this introduction tries to explain. As for what's different about *Billy Budd*, that's easier. There are no shipboard orgies (*Typee*), no cozy coupling with cannibals (*Typee* and *Moby-Dick*) or mothers or half-sisters, implied or otherwise (*Pierre*). Though Claggart dies a violent death, we get no grisly details, as we do in *Redburn*, where the master-at-arms spews "a torrent of blood" before committing suicide as a trapeze artist might (295). "The Great Massacre of the Beards," a scene in *White-Jacket* in which a sailor consents to having his beard shaved only with "consecrated" shears, is too bohemian for this book's decorum (360). *Billy Budd* boasts no Wall Street folk-hero with his show-stopping refusal to work or, for that matter, continue living ("Bartleby"), no devil steaming down the Mississippi duping passengers out of their money and their faith (*The Confidence-Man*). There's most definitely no lunatic Ahab trying to punch through reality to annoy and outmuscle the "outrageous strength" of what's above and beyond (*Moby-Dick* 164). *Billy Budd* has things in common with these works, all of which were published between 1846 and 1857. However, it has as much in common with what came later. The Melville calendar extends well beyond the 1850s, well beyond *Moby-Dick*.

Readers who come to this little book with that big one in mind risk being put off. *Billy Budd* can make *Moby-Dick* look like vaudeville. There are many reasons for this, but one is worth noting right away, because it surprises readers new to the twelve-month Melville calendar. By the time he wrote and rewrote (and rewrote) this book, Melville had spent more years writing poetry than he'd ever spent writing fiction. In fact, *Billy Budd* was a poem before it was prose, which may explain why John Updike found its grammar "tortuous" (xxxiv) and critic Richard Chase even its clear parts blurry (*Herman Melville* 268). *Billy Budd* was written by a poet in the way that Henry James's *The Turn of the Screw*, that other beautiful but baffling novella of the 1890s, was written by a dramatist. (In adapting *Billy Budd*, contemporary filmmaker Claire Denis said her writers and actors "were full of Melville's last poems" [Renouard and Wajeman 21].) Both Melville and James brought back to fiction the murky, sometimes claustrophobic style they refined in other genres. In the book, the result is tightly packed sentences that insinuate much more than they say and do so in discomfiting ways. What they insinuate has proven to be important. James's *The Turn of the Screw* is about the uncanny horror of the self. It's an account of how wrong the mind can go when what's been repressed over the years explodes into view. *Billy Budd* is about the uncanny horror of civilization. It's an account of how wrong a society can go when it follows its own laws.

Melville's Life and Early Work

Melville was born to a Calvinist-leaning, boom-and-bust New York merchant family in 1819. The family moved up and down the economic ladder, but the trend was down. "Things should have gone better with them," biographer Elizabeth Hardwick writes, likening the clan to "certain European families with a fading title, handicapped by the sweep of history or by maladaptation" (10). Both grandfathers were in the Revolution, one in the Boston Tea Party, though over time that grandfather's politics swung from insurgent to reactionary, a distance Melville theorizes in his work and especially in this book. The family trajectory from soldier to merchant to author would seem something to celebrate—America should be "as famous for *arts* as for *arms*," declared Noah Webster—if only it coincided with financial stability, which it did not (4; emphasis in original). There's a reason Melville's letters and fiction read like an extended rant against capitalism, or what he later called the "the thousand villains and asses who have the management of railroads and steamboats, and innumerable other vital things in the world" (*Piazza Tales* 269–70). Melville was a child when his father died insolvent, raving mad from fever, and so young Herman was put to work.

Erratically educated and mostly bad at making money, he went to sea in 1839 and more or less remained there through 1844, first on a trading vessel, then a whaler, then a naval ship. For many young men, going to sea was equal parts responsible and romantic, but the publication of Richard Henry Dana's (1815–82) *Two Years before the Mast* in 1840 made the responsible all the more romantic. Even today it's hard to read Dana comparing the "low and regular swell" of a foggy ocean to the cadence of "the near breathing of whales" and not want to make for the docks (36). When Melville returned home he started writing. His first novel, *Typee* (1846), a semi-autobiographical tale of cannibals as sexy as they are scary, brought notoriety but also typecast him as "'the man who lived among the cannibals,'" a tag Melville came to despise (*Correspondence* 193). Its sequel, *Omoo* (1847), solidified his place in the burgeoning American literary scene. "We trust now that Mr. Melville will consider his life as fixed," one reviewer said, "that he will live and die an author" (Leyda 249). Reviewers were considerably less enthusiastic about his third novel, *Mardi* (1849), a book that's hard to describe and that contemporaries found hard to finish. "Mr. Melville 'feels his oats,'" reviewers sighed (Higgins and Parker 223). In hindsight, *Mardi* does what Melville does best: take characters and "situate them in front of great imponderables" (Bryant xvii). At the time, however, his readers were less interested in pondering imponderables. Melville got the message, if only briefly, and his reputation rebounded with his next offering, *Redburn* (1849), an autobiographical account of his first sea voyage, and *White-Jacket* (1850), another autobiographical treatment, this one of his time aboard a naval frigate.

Reviewers loved these last two books. Melville didn't. He hankered for those imponderables. He wanted to write richly figurative works, what he called "the poetry of salt water," and he was growing impatient with readers and critics who liked books like *Redburn* but not books like *Mardi* (*Piazza Tales* 205). "What I feel most moved to write, that is banned,—it will not pay. Yet, altogether, write the *other* way I cannot," he grumbled to Nathaniel Hawthorne (1804–64) (*Correspondence* 191). In his next book, *Moby-Dick* (1851), he tried to have it both ways. It would have crossover appeal, he promised: *Mardi* meets *Redburn*. While *Moby-Dick* does start out in the *Redburn* vein—the opening twenty-two chapters are fairly reader-friendly—it soon out-*Mardi*es even *Mardi*, perhaps because while writing it Melville fell hard for Shakespeare and even harder for Hawthorne.

Moby-Dick wasn't as poorly received as legend has it, but it wasn't well received either. *Pierre* (1852), a bewildering purée of philosophy, incest, and murder, on the other hand, was exactly as poorly received as legend has it. The book was not disliked so much as despised. Though it contains some of Melville's most bewitching writing ("There is nothing so slipperily alluring as sadness; we become sad in the first place by having nothing stirring to do; we continue in it, because we have found a snug sofa at last") it must have seemed a deliberate provocation (*Pierre* 258–59). Reviewers, his publisher, and members of his family thought and in some cases said publicly that he'd gone crazy. A century later, poet Charles Olson (1910–70) summed up Melville's early career misadventures with exquisite precision:

"Melville took an awful licking. He was bound to" (13). No one knew it at the time, but *White-Jacket* (1850) marked the end of Melville's career as a writer of books that would sell the way publishers require if they want to earn a living.

Magazine fiction kept Melville's name in circulation in the 1850s and earned him a little money, but the damage was done. American publishing was a small world, and word was out that he was rushing through projects. When his final novel, *The Confidence-Man*, was published, in 1857, it looked to the few people who still cared that Melville didn't care at all. One patient reviewer suggested that if he was going to "act the part of a mediaeval jester, conveying weighty truths under a semblance antic and ludicrous," then at least he should try "not to jingle his bells so loud" (Higgins and Parker 492). Melville knew all this—hence the charges of self-sabotage that dogged him—but couldn't help himself. As much as he loved a good sea yarn, he loved the temper and heft of Plato and Ecclesiastes more. He once told a publisher that "some of us scribblers ... always have a certain something unmanageable in us, that bids us do this or that, and be done it must—hit or miss" (*Correspondence* 132). By the late 1850s the misses were taking a toll on Melville, however, and Melville was taking a toll on his family.

Ralph Waldo Emerson (1803–82), New England's philosopher-king, once asked Americans if they really expected to discover something abroad they couldn't find at home. In the margins of his copy of Emerson's *The Conduct of Life* (1860), Melville responded sarcastically that "possibly, Rome or Athens has something to show or suggest that Chicago has not" (Olson-Smith, Norberg, and Marmon 90). He'd long believed that the Holy Land had something to show him, and after *The Confidence-Man* Melville's father-in-law, Lemuel Shaw (1781–1861), financed a pilgrimage of sorts. Shaw wasn't just worried about his son-in-law; he was worried about his daughter's day-to-day life married to a man who was increasingly unstable. As for the son-in-law, he hoped to find "a definite belief" in the Holy Land, according to Hawthorne (163). Hawthorne saw Melville en route in November 1856. Their white-hot friendship around the time of *Moby-Dick* had cooled, and the two writers had not seen each other for a few years.[1] In his journal, the fastidious Hawthorne noted his erstwhile friend was still "a little heterodox in the matter of clean linen," before noting something more substantive: that Melville was in a bad way.

---

1 On Melville's relationship with Nathaniel Hawthorne, see Appendix F6.

He stayed with us from Tuesday till Thursday; and, on the intervening day, we took a pretty long walk together, and sat down in a hollow among the sand hills (sheltering ourselves from the high, cool wind) and smoked a cigar. Melville, as he always does, began to reason of Providence and futurity, and of everything that lies beyond human ken, and informed me that he had "pretty much made up his mind to be annihilated"; but still he does not seem to rest in that anticipation; and, I think, will never rest until he gets hold of a definite belief. It is strange how he persists—and has persisted ever since I knew him, and probably long before—in wandering to and fro over these deserts, as dismal and monotonous as the sand hills amid which we were sitting. He can neither believe, nor be comfortable in his unbelief; and he is too honest and courageous not to try to do one or the other.

Hawthorne was more right about Melville's thoughtful irresolution than even he knew. In the years following his friend's death, in 1864, Melville raised equivocation to an art form, first in his poetry, and then in *Billy Budd*.

If Melville expected places like Jerusalem to make faith real, it did not. He found a sarcophagus. Actually, his metaphor was altogether fouler: "In the emptiness of the lifeless antiquity of Jerusalem the emigrant Jews are like flies that have taken up their abode in a skull" (*Journals* 91). The Holy Land had become a theme park. He notes a guide saying in one breath, "Here is the stone Christ leaned against, & here is the English Hotel" and over there "the best coffee in Jerusalem" (89). These quotations come from Melville's journal, which is a gloomy read, and which would serve as fodder for his long narrative poem *Clarel*. Biographer Andrew Delbanco calls the journal a "document of spiritual exhaustion" (257). Not just his own spiritual exhaustion, though: Melville decided Christians had either exhausted their faith or were exhausted by it. (Both things, as it happens, are the subject of *Clarel*.) Here, in the Holy Land, where religious faith should have been at its most crucial and crushing, it barely registered except as a means to gouge tourists. The journal is also a document of literary exhaustion, and probably an acknowledgment that Melville's life as a husband was spiralling out of control. Imagine the state of mind of a person who upon visiting the Dead Sea would summarize it this way: "smarting bitter of the water,— carried the bitter in my mouth all day—bitterness of life— thought of all bitter things—Bitter is it to be poor & bitter, to be reviled" (Melville, *Journals* 83). Operatic, perhaps, but according to biographers, on the mark.

Things were no less bitter when he returned home. Frustrated by the world of publishing, Melville tried his hand at lecturing, a potentially lucrative career for speakers able to connect with an audience. He couldn't. The fault was less in style than subject. He wanted to talk about antiquity; audiences wanted to hear about South Seas assignations. When a university student made the pilgrimage to his house for lurid tales à la *Typee*, he complained that the "shade of Aristotle arose like a cold mist between" him and the naked women he was hoping to hear about (Leyda 605). The student should have known that dead philosophers had a way of showing up around Melville. (In *Paradise Lost*, Satan says that wherever he goes is hell. Wherever Melville went was philosophy.) Such griping suggests he wasn't entirely playing the misunderstood-artist card when he complained to Hawthorne a year earlier, "we pigmies must be content to have our paper allegories but ill comprehended" (*Correspondence* 212). It was around this time, in the late 1850s, that Melville started telling people he was done with writing.

Life and Later Work

The image of the underappreciated genius laughed offstage so hard that he forsakes art and cowers in an insipid day job before rallying for one last masterpiece is irresistible and mostly wrong. So too is the image of said genius dying penniless and forgotten. A source for both legends may be Melville himself. "Though I wrote the Gospels in this century," he moped to Hawthorne in 1851, "I should die in the gutter" (*Correspondence* 192). The facts are less romantic but important, which is the reason that in the following few pages I go into his later life and career in some detail. These years, so helpful for understanding *Billy Budd*, remain unexplored territory for most casual readers. The short version is that Melville's wife, Elizabeth Shaw Melville (1822–1906), came into an inheritance in the late 1870s, which means that he had plenty of pennies when he died, enough to haunt Manhattan bookstores. And what of the insipid day job at the customs house, the job he performed six days a week for almost two decades beginning in 1866? Just another poet in search of a steady paycheck, says biographer Stanton Garner ("Herman Melville" 283). Even the job itself was not that dreary, though it strained Melville's already strained impression of human nature. (This is the person, after all, who once wrote, "Man is noble, man is brave, / But man's—a weed" [*Published Poems* 90].) Finally, what about that now-famous refusal to write any longer? The truth is, Melville never stopped writing. He just became a different kind of writer. For thirty years, he wrote and wrote and wrote poetry.

Poetry was not some dilettantish genre flirtation for Melville; he brought to it all his manic energy. By 1860 he had enough poems for a book, which was summarily rejected by publishers. He'd never taken rejection well, but he seems to have taken this one particularly hard, perhaps even burning some of his work. In "Immolated," an unpublished poem possibly about this little literary bonfire, the speaker treats his poems—now "Snugged in the arms of comfortable night"—the way people toss kittens into a sack and the sack into a river, as if they were the by-product of an overactive literary libido (Melville, *Tales* 330). Still, he kept writing, eventually publishing four books of poetry: *Battle-Pieces and Aspects of the War* (1866), *Clarel* (1877), *John Marr and Other Sailors* (1888), and *Timoleon* (1891). The final two were issued privately in editions of 25 copies. Even the books that were issued by commercial presses might as well have been so limited, given how poorly they sold. By standard benchmarks, Melville's second career was even less successful than his first.

There are a few reasons for this. We tend to think everyone born before 1900 went around reciting poetry. Hardly. Unless your name was Longfellow or Tennyson, publishers weren't necessarily all that enthusiastic about it, either. Also, no one knew Melville as a poet, even though he had snuck a little verse into novels like *Mardi*, and parts of *Moby-Dick* scan like poetry. Finally, he couldn't escape *Typee* and the legend of his South Seas sexual escapades among the cannibals. Unless he was planning to write poetry about being dinner, and to do so in the style of Longfellow or Tennyson, he didn't stand much chance of reversing his fortunes.

Melville marked this passage in one of the books he studied early on: "the effects of poetry depend still more on the *melody of words* than on the *ideas* which they serve to express" (Cowen 2:633; emphasis in original). The problem was that his idea of melody wasn't other people's. Melville's melody could (and still can) sound charmingly to weirdly off-key to readers used to more conventional poetry. If his work resembles that of anyone from the nineteenth century, it's Emily Dickinson (1830–86). Dickinson is one of the few contemporaries whose melody jars the way

Melville's does, whose diction somersaults the way his does, whose vocabulary surprises the way his does, and who lovingly mocks faith the way he does. ("But in her Protestant repose / Snores faith toward her mortal close?" [*Clarel* 278].) The resemblance may have something to do with the respect both writers had for the unconventional rhythms and metaphor-laden work of seventeenth-century poets such as Andrew Marvell (1621–78). Whatever the cause, the effect was inevitable. Melville had as much luck with the literary establishment as Dickinson probably would have had if she'd published a book in her lifetime. Critics largely ridiculed him: he wouldn't know a true rhyme if he tripped over it, they said. As for regular readers, they probably just thought Melville had graduated to crazy poetry after writing mostly crazy prose.[1]

But in fact, Melville never was all that interested in friendly lines or perfect rhymes. In "A Utilitarian View of the Monitor's Fight" (1866), he compares the sound of mechanized warfare, "The ringing of those plates on plates," to the dissonance of the verse necessary to describe it (*Published Poems* 44). Coming as it does early in his first published collection, *Battle-Pieces*, the poem is a primer for how to read Melville's verse generally. It also redefines time-honoured traditions of poetry in the wake of the Civil War, the subject of the entire volume. Though Melville's poetry is as much in the habit of being as gorgeous as his prose, he is suggesting that poetry's reason for being was changing with the times. Welcome, he says, to "rhyme's barbaric cymbal": a poetry to represent the atrocities of a war that Dickinson characterized as amputating God's right hand.

If to many readers Melville's poetry sounded like fingernails on a chalkboard, there were other problems. His attitude grated, too. William Dean Howells (1837–1920), the writer and influential editor who launched a thousand literary careers, all but damned *Battle-Pieces* for what he saw as its abstraction of a war that was, for Americans living in 1866, anything but an abstraction. Howells wanted literature that was accessible, not Melville's art-house approach. Also offensive was *Battle-Pieces'* refusal to reduce the war to a simple binary of good versus evil. Melville's poetry questions the faux-religious logic famously voiced by Abraham Lincoln (1809–65) in his second inaugural address, where the war is God's way of righting wrongs, as if it were all that simple. (Lincoln knew better; he was practised at rhetorical

---

1 See, for example, "The Portent (1859)," Appendix B5.

sleight of hand.) In poems like "The Fall of Richmond," Melville responded sarcastically to such glosses of the war, wondering if, in the waning days of the conflict, the North's honourable ends justified the ruthless means adopted by Lincoln and Union General Ulysses S. Grant (1822–85):

> But God is in Heaven, and Grant in the Town,
>   And Right through might is Law—
>   *God's way adore.* (*Published Poems* 99)

The poem reads as though it should end with a question mark. Had the North exceeded the rational use of force in its effort to subdue the South? While no fan of slavery—he called Confederates "zealots of the Wrong"—Melville tried to ask dispassionately whether it had to be quite like this (69). Another poem from *Battle-Pieces* pivots on the same questions about the coldly rational versus moral use of force. "The House-top," a poem often mentioned in the same sentence with *Billy Budd*, is about the 1863 New York City draft riots, where disenfranchised groups, especially poor Irish and black New Yorkers, violently protested the implementation of the first draft and were in turn violently suppressed. The speaker awakes to "the Atheist roar of riot" and then seems to welcome the government's heavy-handed response to it. At the same time, however, he describes that response as excessive, tellingly characterizing it as the second coming of Draco, the Roman legislator whose laws were so callous that his name evolved into the adjective *draconian*.[1] Melville's language here, as in *Billy Budd*, isn't so much ambiguous as ambidextrous. The sight and sound of law reasserting itself are simultaneously awful and awe-inspiring; Melville doesn't tell us which. It's what critic Helen Vendler calls his refusal "to pronounce easily upon the whole" (593). William Dean Howells would have none of it: give us the moral straight, he said; make sure it's the one we already agree with, he implied.

Until recently, even most Melville scholars treated his poetry like a rickety bridge from *Moby-Dick* to *Billy Budd*. *Battle-Pieces* has finally ranked the canon, but *Clarel*, Melville's harrowing of faith in the age of Darwin, and harrowing of science by informed sceptics, remains understudied and undertaught. The poem is as smart and prescient an account of debates over fact and faith

---

1 On "The House-top," see Appendix B6. On the rational use of force, see also Appendices B4 and B5, B7 to B10, D, and E.

today as it was when Melville published it in 1876. The problem then (and now, apparently) is that *Clarel* takes a while to make its point—18,000 lines, in fact. 18,000 lines of theology, religious anthropology, science ("Evaporated is this God?"), scriptural allusions, sea stories, travel writing, economics, ethics, and musings on Hawthorne (*Clarel* 267). In a letter, Melville referred to it as "a metrical affair, a pilgrimage or what not, of several thousand lines, eminently adapted for unpopularity" (*Correspondence* 483). The comment isn't untrue. *Clarel* is not always easy on the eye or ear, or even the brain. If Walt Whitman (1819–92) angered readers with his refusal to play by metrical rules, Melville angered readers by forcing rhyme and syntax to do unholy things in a poem about the fate of holy things in scientific modernity. The few reviewers who bothered with it suggested he consider paying more attention to the basic rules of poetry. Imagine if they'd seen a poem Melville didn't publish on evolution, "The New Ancient of Days," where the fossil record, "The vomit of slimy and sludgey sea," yields no end of surprises for the religiously inclined:

> Purposeless creatures, odd inchoate things
> Which splashed thro' morasses on fleshy wings;
> The cubs of Chaos, with eyes askance,
> Preposterous griffins that squint at Chance
> And Anarch's crazed decree! (Melville, *Tales* 322)

Clarel is weird enough, thank you. Three years after it was published, Melville gave the publisher permission to pulp remaining copies. He'd produced another commercial wreck and then, characteristically, went on writing. He was long past caring whether readers could keep up.

Billy Budd, c. 1886–91

When Melville received that gushing letter from the Nova Scotia professor in 1889, he'd probably been working on *Billy Budd* for about four years. Manuscript evidence suggests he'd tried to put it into a semi-final form, or "fair copy," at least three times. Reading *Billy Budd* now, it's difficult to tell. Where so much early Melville feels improvised, this book feels deliberate. Most scholars think it was just the opposite, developing, Robert Milder believes, "epiphanically, as new frames of understanding suggested themselves and returned him to a narrative that he must, on some level, have heartily wished to be done with" (*Exiled* 243). We'll never know for sure what happened every time Melville fouled up a fair copy, but most scholars accept the following origin story, proposed in 1962 by scholars Harrison Hayford and Merton M. Sealts Jr.

In the beginning, there was a poem and a short contextual headnote, typical of the proto-modernist prose and poetry experiments that characterized Melville's writing in the 1880s. Like a volcano, the headnote grew underneath the poem. Eventually a 30,000-word novella buttressed a 282-word poem. As the idea expanded in size and execution, it changed. In the original poem—drafts of which survive, dubbed by John Bryant "The Ur-*Billy Budd*"—Billy has the hail-fellow-well-met qualities of his later self but none of his preternatural innocence (Melville, *Tales* 524). The Ur-Billy means mutiny and gets caught, fair and square. "Our little game's up," he concedes with unflappable goodwill toward all, even those who "needs must obey" the order to execute him (525). However cheerful about his impending death and however obliging toward the system that requires it, this older, Ur-Billy is a sailor whom a law-and-order captain can put to death without a second thought. Not so the Billy of our text, which is weighed down by second thoughts.

Melville accomplished this transformation through a series of excruciatingly focused revisions. He enlarged Billy's victim, Claggart, and complicated the circumstances of his death, absolving Billy of moral if not legal guilt. Billy kills Claggart unintentionally, Vere kills Billy intentionally, and the narrator has trouble explaining why any of it has to happen the way it does. What was left unexplained—Claggart's motive for framing Billy, for example—was meant to be unexplainable, unless you happen to have a couple "Hebrew prophets" on hand (p. 84). As Melville developed Claggart and his character became more mysteriously antithetical to Billy—as he became a kind of seafaring Iago, rebellious without cause—Billy became more mysteriously innocent. Walker Percy once said that "in Dostoevsky's hands" Billy "would have turned out to be a child molester" (203). Melville's gift was that he could take Billy seriously as a physical and conceptual ideal. When the narrator remarks that Billy's "moral nature" is as toned as his biceps, he does so without even a trace of a smile (p. 54). He's the only one. Practically the entire crew smiles every time Billy struts his stuff across the decks of the *Bellipotent*. Billy "Baby" Budd is among the most halcyon killers in American literature, a right-hook artist time-travelled from classical Greece, where gorgeous young men were uncontroversial archetypes of perfection—and sexuality.

Hayford and Sealts don't go into sexuality. We should, because it may give Claggart something like cause after all. In his 1939 poem about Claggart's powerful attachment to Billy, and Melville's to Hawthorne, W.H. Auden (1907–73) introduces one of American literature's great villains with an in-your-face empathy that surprises some readers unfamiliar with Auden's homosexuality or with *Billy Budd*'s sexual context:[1]

> Evil is unspectacular and always human,
> And shares our bed and eats at our own table,
> And we are introduced to Goodness every day,
> Even in drawing-rooms among a crowd of faults;
> He has a name like Billy and is almost perfect
> But wears a stammer like decoration:
> And every time they meet the same thing has to happen;
> It is the Evil that is helpless like a lover
> And has to pick a quarrel and succeeds,
> And both are openly destroyed before our eyes. (p. 204)

To thousands of students who had (or right now are having) to study *Billy Budd*, Claggart was (or is) little more than a hackneyed symbol of evil. Or he was Satan to Billy's Christ the Son and Vere's God the Father. Needless to say, he *is* Satan to Billy's Christ and Vere's terrible God. An imperative frame of reference in *Billy Budd*'s final chapters is obviously the crucifixion, and the book obviously broods on Christianity, as much of Melville's work does. However, Auden calls attention to a less obvious, murmured aspect of Claggart: that in some indisputable way he desires Billy and is helpless for doing so. This is most obvious, and moving, in Chapter 17, where we learn of the "settled and melancholy expression" of the master-at-arms when watching Billy act like one of the boys, his "eyes strangely suffused with incipient feverish tears" (p. 95). "Then," we're told, would Claggart "look like the man of sorrows. Yes, and sometimes the melancholy

---

1 "To say flatly that Melville was homosexual, latently homosexual, or not homosexual is not simply to over-read the evidence," Robert Milder notes, "it is to neglect the problematizing work of recent cultural historians" (*Exiled* 119). Christopher Castiglia and Christopher Looby, summarizing more recent scholars of sexuality, note that "'sexuality' is neither transhistorical nor innate, easily discoverable (either across history or within the individual body) nor conventionally comprehensible" (196). See Appendix F. Auden's poem "Herman Melville" is reprinted in its entirety in Appendix F6.

expression would have in it a touch of soft yearning, as if Claggart could even have loved Billy but for fate and ban." In one fell swoop, Melville marries Christ's experience of grief with a gay man's experience of an illiberal sexual status quo. It's a deft and gutsy gesture for the late nineteenth century. For Auden, who had reason to sympathize with the tragic sexual determinism he saw in Melville's book—the idea that same-sex desire could necessarily condemn—what destroys Billy and Claggart isn't just Claggart's lie about Billy's participation in a mutiny plot. What destroys both is the lie he's forced to live as a man desiring other men but living under a "ban" of that very desire.

In his revisions Melville also went to work on Vere. The captain of the ship had been around in earlier drafts but without much to do. Now he is brought centre stage. Vere is made to play the emblem of the state saddled with a "moral emergency": X, who's morally flawless, is guilty of murdering Y, who doesn't seem to have a moral bone in his body (p. 79). It should be easy enough for a contemplative captain like Vere to find a way to acquit X, but it's not, thanks to the combination of Vere's by-the-book character and the date 1797, a contextual masterstroke of Melville's revisions. Mutiny is one thing; mutiny in 1797, after revolts in the Royal Navy threatened the very existence of the British Empire and everything it stood for, that's something else entirely. Melville made sure readers would know that. He made sure, too, through a series of painstaking additions and subtractions, that while readers would know that Vere is nothing like the tyrannical officers that had caused sailors to revolt in 1797, they'd also know he's a certain kind of Englishman and represents a certain kind of Englishness, and, by the late nineteenth century, a certain kind of Americanness.[1]

Two other characters are instrumental but fly below the radar of many first-time readers. The first is the surgeon, who witnesses Vere's strange breakdown in the moments following the murder and who wonders privately if his captain is "unhinged" (p. 107). He's the book's sceptic, and his incredulity braces readings that find Vere incompetent or insane. The second is the Dansker, the book's folksy philosopher, a sailor who's seen everything except a phenomenon like Billy and who dispassionately views him as little more than an engrossing experiment. "[W]hat might eventually befall a nature like that," he speculates on our

---

1   On the Great Mutiny of 1797, see Appendix C1. On Vere's ideological frames of reference, see Appendices A1, B3 to B10, C2b, and D6.

behalf, "dropped into a world" like the *Bellipotent* (p. 79)? Good question. If Melville's in this book at all, he's in the Dansker, and if he's in the Dansker, it's a self-aware and unflattering portrait. In their "pithy guarded cynicism" (p. 81), both know what's bound to happen to Billy, yet neither lifts a finger to help, making *Billy Budd* feel at times like a Naturalist experiment along the lines of Stephen Crane's (1871–1900) *Maggie: A Girl of the Streets* (1893). The Dansker and Melville feed the mouse to the snake.

Melville never did finish *Billy Budd*, it's true, but it's not as though he keeled over midsentence. By summer 1891 he was tinkering with a story that was probably nearly done, and there's every reason to think he would have published it, perhaps in the kind of private edition he'd used for his final two books of poetry. Nevertheless, the uncertainty over the *Billy Budd* manuscript, which is a mess even by nineteenth-century standards, helps explain the book's colourful publication history. Reconstructing it according to what he assumed to be the author's intentions— Melville left no references to it, much less instructions— Raymond Weaver published *Billy Budd* in 1924 amid the fanfare of a revival of interest in Melville and his work. Over the next several decades other editions were published, each prompting fresh disagreement over what Melville would have wanted and whether that even matters. In 1962, Hayford and Sealts prepared a new copy-text that has been the standard ever since.[1] While the text of *Billy Budd* will always be a moving target, discoveries do happen. After Elizabeth Shaw Melville's death in 1906, a secret compartment was found in her desk with the phrase "To know all is to forgive all" etched into it (qtd. in Robertson-Lorant 597).

Outside of a few sticking points, the biggest being whether Melville intended to include a preface found in the manuscript, scholars generally agree on how *Billy Budd* ought to look. There's much less agreement about how it ought to be read. This has less to do with the fact that the story underwent years of freezing and thawing than with the shading of its language. Befitting his decades writing poetry, Melville's language contracts even as its implications expand: he crowds more and more meaning into

---

1   The manuscript is housed at Harvard's Houghton Library and is available online (http://nrs.harvard.edu/urn-3:FHCL.Hough:4686413). See, too, the *Melville Electronic Library*, which has an interactive application showing both the manuscript and its layers of revisions (http://mel.hofstra.edu/versions-of-billy-budd.html). Two new copy-texts are now in production. See "A Note on the Text," p. 49.

smaller and smaller spaces. It can be frustrating for readers, and not just those new to the text. Some passages give the sensation of having the ladder kicked out from under you, no matter how many times you've read them. *Billy Budd* criticism is refreshingly honest about this dizzying experience. "With apologies to the reader," says Laurie Robertson-Lorant in her 1996 biography, "it is difficult to write about *Billy Budd* without falling naturally into the convoluted, hair-splitting, overly self-conscious style of the novella's narrator. Snakelike, the double negatives, the conditional and subjunctive verbs, the abstract nouns and cautious qualifiers, insinuate themselves into the consciousness" (594). *Billy Budd* is, another critic-victim concedes, "a very difficult work to interpret with both honesty and confidence" (Hunt 273). It's not my fault, Melville seems to say in *Clarel*. "The inventor miraged all the maze" (249).

It's cliché, of course: the oracle writer and his textual riddles that could solve the world if only we could figure them out, like Ahab puzzling over Queequeg's tattooed body in *Moby-Dick*: "Oh, devilish tantalization of the gods!" (481). Newton Arvin once said that "Melville's world is insuperably incomprehensible, and he makes no claim to comprehending it" (297). If *Billy Budd* reads at times like an incoherent argument, or an undecided one, it may be because it's supposed to be. "Truth uncompromisingly told will always have its ragged edges," the narrator observes, partly as justification for his "narration" being "less finished than an architectural finial" (p. 130). Just a few years after it was first published in the 1920s, critic Vernon Parrington noted Melville's weariness with oversimplified categories of right and wrong, good and bad, suggesting that he "smiled ironically at the neat little classification that divides the human animal into sinners and saints" (265). In a crucial passage in Chapter 22, when Vere goes to tell Billy that he's going to die at his command, Melville compares the sacrifice to Abraham catching "young Isaac on the brink of resolutely offering him up in obedience to the exacting behest" of God (p. 118). It's likely he wanted to prevent readers from dismissing Vere out of hand as a lunatic or tyrant, though that doesn't stop many readers from boasting that they would have done things differently. Milton R. Stern found such reactions dubious, however appealing at a gut level. To "dismiss" Vere, he notes, is to dismiss Abraham, who stoops under imperatives he does not understand but must fulfill nonetheless (xxxix). Vere is not a "villain of obedience" any more than Abraham or Job. Søren Kierkegaard, writing about the Abraham/Isaac story in 1843, suggested that the more we think about God's horrible command, and Abraham's horrible obedience to it, the less we understand either (9). That incapacity doesn't make the story any less real or charged. For Kierkegaard, to accept Christianity was to agree to live with the contradiction of Abraham. For Melville, did accepting society mean agreeing to live with the contradiction of Vere?

Vere's Imperial Conscience

Melville could resist a creepy Calvinist metaphor no better than Emily Dickinson, which is to say not at all. It was a blessing and a curse of being raised partly in the Calvinist tradition of Michael Wigglesworth (1631–1705), whose 1666 poem about the end times, *The Day of Doom*, terrified Puritan New England. Melville channels his inner Wigglesworth in his 1888 poem "Bridegroom Dick. 1876" (see Appendix D6). Summoned to witness punishment for drunken insubordination—a flogging at the mast—his sailors emerge from below deck like the dead at Judgment:

> Morning brings a summons. Whistling it calls,
> Shrilled through the pipes of the Boatswain's four aids—
> Thrilled down the hatchways along the dusk halls:
> *Muster to the Scourge!*—Dawn of doom, and its blast!
> As from cemeteries raised, sailors swarm before the mast,
> Tumbling up the ladders from the ship's nether shades.
> (p. 184)

There's plenty to criticize in a crew so brainwashed by naval discipline, but Melville forces us instead to criticize the God that made it that way, the one who, as Jonathan Edwards (1703–58) says in "Sinners in the Hands of an Angry God" (1741), created a world in which we "were *always* exposed to destruction, as one that stands or walks in slippery places is always exposed to fall" (89; emphasis in original). Melville too liked his crime and punishment Old Testament style. When Vere tells the crew he's going to hang the most beloved man on the ship, it takes the news like a "congregation of believers in hell listening to the clergyman's announcement of his Calvinistic text" (p. 120). In the manuscript, Melville actually took the time to write out Edwards's name beside this passage (Hayford and Sealts 184). Though a far cry from a vengeful God and from the predestination- and persecution-happy Puritan magistrates that populate Hawthorne's fiction, Vere embodies a rule of law every bit as rigid, a vested authority as overpowering. Like Edwards's impeccable God, Vere has the power to "crush out your blood, and make it fly" (100). Unlike that God, he doesn't seem to cherish it.

The name Jonathan Edwards never made it into *Billy Budd*. That of another exemplar and whipping boy of eighteenth-century orthodoxy did, however: British statesman Edmund Burke (1729–97). Edwards was worried about the decline of faith in God and Church; Burke, half a century later, was worried about the decline of faith in king and custom. Edwards looked for Satan in the forest and human heart, but Burke knew better: Satan was in France, or at least in the revolutionaries who, in Burke's view, started mucking up civilization in 1789. Burke's response to the French Revolution was to pen a theory of government in which tradition is so fetishized, orthodoxy so right, authority so felicitous that it would become the very definition of conservatism. *Reflections on the Revolution in France* (1790) valorizes "unchangeable constancy" and dismisses new ways of doing things simply for being new (p. 137). *Reflections* pulls no punches. "Atheists are not our preachers," Burke hisses; "madmen are not our lawgivers" (p. 141). "We know," he then says, more measuredly, "that *we* have made no discoveries, and we think that no discoveries are to be made, in morality; nor many in the great principles of government, nor in the ideas of liberty, which were understood long before we were born." It's tempting to dismiss Burke as authoritarian, but this wasn't fascism. Burke made sense, especially to the tradition-happy English. His logic could be so sound that even detractors had to admit he had a point, as when he suggests that the "effect of liberty to individuals is, that they may do what they please: we ought to see what it will please them to do, before we risque congratulations" (10). No doubt Burke grossly underestimated the efficacy and staying power of Enlightenment liberalism. However, he did foresee things would get bloody—even he didn't imagine just how bloody—and by 1797, when *Billy Budd* is set, that was enough to convince most British that he was right.[1]

Most, but definitely not all. Burke insisted that the French Revolution, if allowed to fester, would "pervert the natural order of things" (p. 137). In his rebuttal, *Rights of Man* (1791–92), Thomas Paine (1737–1809) had some fun with Burke's tautology, suggesting that the revolutions of the late eighteenth century

---

1 On Burke's response to the French Revolution, see Appendix A1.

were merely "a *renovation* of the natural order of things" (p. 145; emphasis added). What Burke holds up as unquestionably good and right—respect for authority, for example, or monarchy itself—Paine tears down as a figment of the English nobility's collective imagination. *Rights of Man* likens monarchy "to something kept behind a curtain, about which there is a great deal of bustle and fuss, and a wonderful air of seeming solemnity; but when, by any accident, the curtain happens to be open—and the company see what it is, they burst into laughter" (p. 145). The state spends an obscene amount of energy trying to maintain the ruse that it knows or cares about what's best for its citizens. According to *Rights of Man*, France is the future: a society governed not by dead men and their laws and property but by the living and their inborn sense of right and wrong. Burke believed that tradition was redemptive, Paine that it was damning.[1]

Burke's *Reflections on the Revolution in France* and Paine's *Rights of Man* are not museum artefacts for us any more than they were for Melville. For more than two hundred years they've been touchstones of conservatism and liberalism, respectively. Each epitomizes one side of an argument that refuses to go away: How does a society balance the twin but opposed imperatives of security and change? One of the achievements of *Billy Budd* is that it somehow simultaneously makes each imperative seem the most imperative. Burke might as well be the figurehead on the *Bellipotent*'s bow for all the ways in which the ship embodies the *Reflections*, and if we read its captain un-ironically, Vere is presented with considerable sympathy considering that most readers hate what he does and why he does it. As for Paine, lest anyone miss the relevance of his worldview, Melville just went ahead and called Billy's former ship the *Rights-of-Man* and made it sound like a party compared to the *Bellipotent*, Latin for "mighty in war." Given a choice between the two ships, most readers would be incredulous. We'd choose the *Rights*, where Billy thrives in the absence of Burke's/Vere's much-ballyhooed rule of law. But read carefully Captain Graveling's description in Chapter 1 of life aboard the *Rights* before the arrival of Billy and his fists of lightning. Apparently, Melville didn't think Paine's political dream was all that achievable, either. Like generations of political thinkers before and after, Melville couldn't figure out which vision was less unappealing. Captain Edward Fairfax Vere chose Burke's.

---

1 On Paine's response to Burke and his counter-interpretation of the French Revolution, see Appendix A2.

Vere, whose "settled convictions were as a dike against those invading waters of novel opinion," thinks he has no choice in the matter of Billy Budd (pp. 72–73). He judges Billy by exactly the same code used to judge Ur-Billy and the prisoner in "Bridegroom Dick."[1] He's perfectly aware, and says so, that Billy's case is complicated enough for a jury of philosophers, but he also says there's no place on the *Bellipotent* for philosophers, no time for speculation about why we do the things we do. Leave the speculation to dreamers like Paine and Voltaire and Rousseau, who imagined, for example, the state of nature to be a friendly place, and therefore whose ideas, for Vere, are "insusceptible of embodiment in lasting institutions" and "at war with the peace of the world and the true welfare of mankind." Vere has no patience for theoretical moonshine. He reminds the officers on Billy's jury that on a Royal Navy warship prowling enemy waters far from friendly flags "'private conscience'" yields to the "'imperial one'" (p. 114). Under the military law, it is the officers who must hold a man responsible for rebellion even when he is clearly not. And the crew, well, it must accept that decision. (Remember the congregation-in-hell metaphor.) In all, it is the "needs must" that guides Vere's thinking. Peace and prosperity depend on maintaining the status quo. Maintaining the status quo, in turn, means unquestioned dependence on what Vere calls "forms, measured forms": the laws, rules, creeds, and codes that function like "Orpheus with his lyre spellbinding the wild denizens of the wood" (p. 129). Everything in its place, including you and me. There's too much to lose if things go awry.[2]

Anyone who spends any time with *Billy Budd* scholarship will quickly encounter a question as old as it is inevitable: Does the book resist or accept Vere's logic? Is it revolutionary or counterrevolutionary? And what did Melville believe? For readers familiar only with the legend of Melville, the idea that he might have agreed with Vere seems not just implausible but unconscionable. Melville the great rebel Romantic? Melville who lionized Hawthorne for saying "NO! in thunder" (*Correspondence* 186)? Melville who begot epic Ahab? Melville's work isn't all Ahab all the time, though, or at least not unbridled Ahab all the time; *Moby-Dick* readers know that even raging Ahab squeezes out a tear. It is not apostasy to say that Melville might have agreed with

---

1 On "Bridegroom Dick," see Appendices D6 and F4.
2 For nineteenth-century American analogues to Vere's logic, see Appendices B1 to B7, C1b–c, and C2a. See also Appendix G4.

Vere that Billy must die. Like the officers on the *Bellipotent* who signal "sad assent" to Vere's logic, Melville's work did sometimes resign itself to distressing imperatives (p. 114).

This is the "testament of acceptance" reading of *Billy Budd*. It holds that Melville's final book describes the way things are and his acceptance of the way they must be. Wendell Glick, one of this reading's earliest and most articulate defenders, argues that *Billy Budd* is about the "preservation of the tight little society" that is ship and state (105). If, like the officers on the jury, readers squirm at Vere's coldly rational logic in the trial scene, then they've never thought democracy through to its logical ends. For Vere, morals do not solve moral problems. Conscience does exist in the book; it's just not relevant in what Melville calls elsewhere "our man-of-war world" (*White-Jacket* 186). For all sorts of good bad reasons, it just won't do for Billy to survive. As Charles Olson said, Melville "was no naïve democrat" (64).

In the other corner are readers who find this logic disgusting. Why should custom, law, or expedience trump what seems so obviously right? Why must Billy's death be a *fait accompli*? "Is history, after all, an endless repetition of man's crucifixions of his loveliest hopes?," Milton Stern asked in his superb 1975 introduction to the book (xxiv). Stern's anger is hard to miss and is not misplaced, no matter how accepting one is of *Billy Budd* as an aging writer's testament of acceptance. "Over and over, again and again," Melville wonders in the poem "The Armies of the Wilderness," "Must the fight for the Right be fought?" (*Published Poems* 70, emphasis removed).

This is the "doctrine of resistance" reading of *Billy Budd*. It holds that the book doesn't preach acceptance of a tragic status quo but, rather, inveighs against it. That is, *Billy Budd* is an ironic account of a society that ought to be other than it is. For resistance readers, Melville rails against the same disturbing assumptions that Henry David Thoreau (1817–62) railed against decades earlier. "I think that we should be men first, and subjects afterward," Thoreau wrote in "Civil Disobedience" in the 1840s (358). "It is not desirable to cultivate a respect for the law, so much as for the right." Thoreau wanted to know why we have a conscience if we're not going to use it. Translated into the realm of politics: Why do we have a conscience if we're not *permitted* to use it? Thoreau wasn't just calling out Americans who looked the other way while their government did unconscionable things in their name: safeguarding the rights of some people to own other people, for instance, or hanging people who are better than the state that is hanging them. He was questioning, Paine-like, the idea of government itself. Ultimately people need not subordinate their moral sense to authority, least of all when that authority goes around disregarding human rights. It was such times that had Thoreau writing, in a later essay, "My thoughts are murder to the state" (407).[1]

Thoreau did not see a solution to the predicament Vere faces in Billy, but he saw a start: in the face of a moral problem, act morally. Conscience might be uncomfortable—"takes up more room than all the rest of a person's insides, and yet ain't no good nohow," Huck Finn observes with disarming ignorance—but like Mark Twain (1835–1910), Thoreau believed it was pretty much all you could call on in the face of a society that mistook what's easy for what's right (Twain 290). For readers especially attuned to *Billy Budd*'s irony, this book makes a similar case. How could the writer who earlier asked angrily, "Just God, what's that?," later ask us to accept that things "must needs" be the way they are (*Clarel* 245)? How could the writer who seems to sympathize in *Clarel* with "all the damned in Sodom's sea" not hate Vere and his imperial conscience? For resistance readers, the testament of acceptance has Herman Melville serving the wrong master.

Resistance readings come in various shapes and sizes. Vere's a rogue captain, for example, or he's insane. One of the most compelling is also the most topical, and Vere doesn't need to be insane or a tyrant for it to work. The captain, after all, doesn't play tyrant nearly so well as the captains in Melville's earlier fiction or, for that matter, in most nineteenth-century sea literature. In Douglas Jerrold's (1803–57) popular 1830 play *The Mutiny at the Nore*, a commander is referred to (à la Jonathan Edwards) as a sailor's "captain and his destroyer" (25). In another Jerrold play, *Black-Eyed Susan* (1829), a captain attempts to rape the wife of a sailor who is then sentenced to death for defending her because, in doing so, he violates the same Article of War that gets Billy hanged.[2] In *Two Years before the Mast*, Dana's captain practically pirouettes torture:[3]

---

1   See Appendices B2 to B4, for Thoreau's and Emerson's responses to the brand of conservatism that Vere represents. For Melville's response in *White-Jacket*, see Appendix B1.

2   On playwright Douglas Jerrold, including an excerpt from *Black-Eyed Susan*, see Appendix C1b.

3   The passage from Dana's *Two Years before the Mast* is reproduced in its entirety in Appendix D2.

[T]he captain, swelling with rage and with the importance of his achievements, walked the quarter-deck, and at each turn, as he came forward, calling out to us,—"You see your condition! You see where I've got you all, and you know what to expect!"—"You've been mistaken in me—you didn't know what I was! Now you know what I am!"—"I'll make you toe the mark, every soul of you, or I'll flog you all, fore and aft, from the boy, up!"—"You've got a driver over you! Yes, a *slave-driver—a negro-driver!* I'll see who'll tell me he isn't a negro slave!" (p. 176)

Melville's Vere is not a rapist, not a racist, not an overlord. He's a leader trapped in crisis mode. Though this reading of *Billy Budd* pre-dates 9/11, the state of perpetual crisis characterizing the US since the fall of the twin towers has people once again taking notice of *Billy Budd*'s portrayal of civil rights in a time of civic paranoia.[1] "Struck dead by an angel of God!," Vere nearly shrieks in the long moments after Claggart's death. "Yet the angel must hang!" What kind of society hangs an angel? A society that, one legal scholar wrote after 9/11, tries to convince us "that we must make certain sacrifices in times of crisis," a place and time like England in 1797 (Solove 2462).

Rebellion in Naval Fleets and City Streets

By 1797 Great Britain had been at war with France for four years. Things were not going well. The French controlled much of Europe and most of its southern coastline. The British Navy found itself beaten back to its lair to await an invasion force it knew would come eventually. A kind of national paranoia set in. Even the freakish weather seemed an adversary, and the British people reacted in kind, seeing omens in every gale (Dugan 34–35). About the only thing that could have set the British further on edge would have been the knowledge that a future torment, a young artillery whiz named Napoleon Bonaparte (1769–1821), was at that moment beginning to show his mettle. Or if they had known their own navy was about to rebel.

In the months before *Billy Budd* is set, that's exactly what happened. It was not the first instance of open rebellion in the British navy. The munity on the *Bounty* had occurred just a few years

---

1 For contemporaneous discussions of terrorism, see Appendices A1, B4, B6 to B10, C, and E8.

earlier, but that was a world away. The Great Mutiny of 1797 took place on Britain's doorstep.[1] The navy's ranks had recently ballooned with better educated conscripts who refused to believe that life aboard ship had to be as bad as it was, and who helped their fellow sailors realize it too. They didn't need much convincing: most of them had been impressed into service, just as Billy is, and were none too happy about it. Conditions aboard ships were indeed bad, and had been growing worse for some time. As Douglas Jerrold put it, for too many officers, torturing sailors had become an "hourly pastime" (50).[2] The Admiralty, aware of this fact, chose to do nothing, never expecting that sailors who had scant chances to hold conversation could organize. But organize they did, especially at Spithead, in the fleet responsible for protecting the entrance to the English Channel. Spithead was shocking but ended peaceably. The mutineers won concessions and even pardons, and briefly Britain's famous naval force-field returned to full strength. Then the trouble started again, this time at the Nore sandbank, in the fleet responsible for protecting the Thames, London's lifeline to the world. Insurgent sailors turned from defenders to attackers, blockading London and panicking the British economy at large. With the hated French at the door, Britain's military more or less stood down. In the end, the Nore mutiny collapsed under its own weight and the Crown tried to spin it as the handiwork of foreign subversives—à la Billy's makeover as a foreign terrorist in Chapter 29—rather than admit what it was: a strike by citizens crying foul over un-redressed wrongs. Either way, it felt to many British that civilization itself was under threat. Or collapsing.

After the Civil War, it felt that way to a lot of Americans, too. "To the British Empire, the Nore Mutiny was what a strike in the fire brigade would be to London threatened by general arson," Melville writes at the beginning of Chapter 3, borrowing imagery from Burke's *Reflections* (p. 64). "Reasonable discontent growing out of practical grievances in the fleet had been ignited into irrational combustion as by live cinders blown across the Channel from France in flames." In 1790s Britain, the cinders were republicanism and anti-monarchism. In Gilded Age America, the cinders were socialism and anarchism, and once again they came from France. More specifically, they came from the Paris Commune, the social-

---

1   For background on the Spithead and Nore mutinies, see Appendix C1.
2   For discussions of corporal punishment at sea, see Appendices D1 to D3, and D6.

Fred B. Schell, "The Great Strike—Destruction of the Union Depot and Hotel at Pittsburgh," *Harper's Weekly* (11 August 1877), 624.

ist regime established in 1871.[1] Though the Commune lasted only a few months—it was crushed by the military, and in the chaos Paris burned—it terrified Americans, who worried that their cities had become beachheads for invading forces of political unbelievers, just as the British had worried in 1797.

In the US, things blew up in 1877 when a massive railway strike, aptly tagged the "Great Upheaval," crippled much of the country's transportation network.[2] It began on the B&O in West Virginia, and in a matter of days rail yards from Maryland to Illinois were in full revolt. Rail workers' grievances echoed those in other industries, not to mention those of the sailors at Spithead and Nore in 1797: they were continually asked to do more work for less money, in worsening conditions caused in part by bumptious and incompetent supervisors. Given the rate at which the unrest spread from rail yards to city streets, people began to ask when—and even if—it would stop. (Taunting Burke, Paine had suggested that once "revolutions have begun ... it is natural to expect that other revolutions will follow" [403].) In the 1840s, Melville had lived close enough to the Astor Place Opera House to hear the shots fired by a militia into a riotous crowd (Parker, *Herman Melville* 1:633). It was the first time the military had opened fire on American citizens. Now, in

1 On the Paris Commune and American responses to it, see Appendix B7.
2 On the railroad strike of 1877, see Appendix B8.

1877, in cities like Pittsburgh, troops opened fire again, only this time they used Gatling guns. Soon after this show of force against supposed insurgents, one railroad owner lobbied successfully for the creation of a National Guard to "keep the peace," that is, protect property and keep workers in line (Painter 21–22). New York's *Evening Post* went so far as to recommend that the city build an armoury with semi-automatic weapons mounted on turrets to mow down demonstrators, like medieval archers firing down on invading barbarians (Beatty 207).

In his first inaugural address, in 1861, Lincoln equated secessionists with anarchists. He defined enemies of democracy geographically. Once the Civil War was over, the forces supposedly aligned against democracy were defined economically and ideologically. Historian Nell Irvin Painter notes that the railway strike "fixed the image of the Commune—violence, burning, and bloodshed—on the very idea of organized workers and socialists of any sort" (24). Labour activists were even called "Pétroleuses," a reference to the poor women sympathetic to the French socialists accused of setting the fires that burned Paris in 1871. Just as the ringleader of the Nore mutiny was suspected of having cavorted with Maximilien de Robespierre (1758–94) during the Terror,[1] American labour leaders were suspected of being puppets of foreign, especially French, extremists.

Tensions exploded again in 1886 in Chicago's Haymarket Square, when a national rally for an eight-hour work day turned into a demonstration against police brutality.[2] Someone threw a bomb into a line of advancing police, killing eight officers and injuring others. The explosion set off a chain reaction of rioting and gunfire. No one knows who threw the bomb. Labour activists? Anarchists? Police posing as anarchists? Although most of the police hurt in the ensuing riot were injured by friendly fire, and although some of the defendants weren't even in the square at the time the bomb was thrown, eight anarchists were convicted and four were hanged. (One of the convicted never made it to the scaffold: on the eve of his execution he lit a blasting cap in his mouth.) Initially the press and public congratulated the authorities for securing democracy against terrorism. Over the next few years

---

1 Between September 1793 and July 1794, during the Reign of Terror, tens of thousands of people were executed by the French government, which deemed them enemies to the revolution. Robespierre was a chief architect of the Terror.

2 On the Haymarket bombing and trial, see Appendices B9 and B10.

"The Law Vindicated," *Frank Leslie's Illustrated Newspaper* (19 November 1887), 216.

people started wondering if that's really what had happened. Many Americans were surprised at how easily paranoia could turn into bloodshed, and how easily the law could license all of it.

In Melville's lifetime, the railroad strike of 1877 and the Haymarket Affair of 1886 dramatized the widening gap between rich and poor in a nation increasingly governed by an industrial capitalism less forgiving than the mercantile capitalism that defined the nation before the war. Of course, the America of Melville's youth wasn't some workers' paradise either. Melville knew that all too well, his family having suffered through the Panic of 1837, a half-decade recession that bankrupted people and businesses well beyond the nation's financial centres. Melville's fiction of the 1850s—most famously "Bartleby" but also his novels *Israel Potter* (1855) and especially *The Confidence-Man*—is sceptical of the good deeds antebellum businessmen claimed on behalf of capitalism. Yet the economy that characterized Gilded Age America, and the tactics adopted to maintain it, made its antebellum counterpart appear tame by comparison. Looking back on the nineteenth century from the perspective of the twentieth, Henry Adams (1838–1918), grandson of one US president (John Quincy Adams) and great grandson of another (John Adams), noted that "sooner or later" everyone "would have to deal with Karl Marx" (72). Adams was no Marxist; he just worried about the kinds of inequality he saw in American society, including the development of an economic ruling class on par with Europe's.

The paternalism of the state and its big business shows up in quieter ways in *Billy Budd* than in stories like "Bartleby," but it's there. Melville uses the idea of a natural ruling class so important to Burke to characterize Vere's attitude toward those under him, the rabble whom the French revolutionaries would raise up in order to level society. "Believe me, Sir," Burke warned in 1790, "those who attempt to level, never equalize" (p. 137). "It is said, that twenty-four millions ought to prevail over two hundred thousand. True; if the constitution of a kingdom be a problem of arithmetic" (p. 138). Vere fears the unreasoning crew who, infected by the "contagious fever" of the Nore, may read any leniency on the officers' part as an opportunity to level. "'You know what sailors are'" (p. 116), Vere says to Billy's jury. No, Captain, please tell us. What are we?

In 1842, three sailors on a US naval vessel were hanged for mutiny under the Articles of War. The event became a public scandal for a number of reasons. For one, the ship wasn't in enemy waters at the time; in fact, there were no "enemy waters," because the US wasn't at war. For another, the supposed ring-leader of the mutiny, Philip Spencer (1823–42), was the ne'er-do-well son of the Secretary of War, John C. Spencer (1788–1855). Finally, the official inquiries into the captain's actions looked like a whitewash. For Melville, what happened on the *Somers* was a family matter. His cousin was one of the officers on the ship, and though, like his commander, Captain Macken-zie, he was cleared of wrongdoing, he never recovered from the trauma. Melville, too, was haunted by the events and by what they did to his cousin. In *White-Jacket*, which takes every oppor-tunity to decry the Articles of War as ill-befitting a democracy—it's a critique of the very idea of law on par with Thoreau's—the eponymous, autobiographical narrator holds forth on what came to be known as the *Somers* Affair, reacting to the misconception that the Articles were only in force during actual wartime and thus wondering if the laws themselves were being used not just to curb civil liberties but to legitimize murder, as in the Haymarket Affair and the railroad strike.[1] "What happened to those three

---

1 For *White-Jacket*'s appraisal of the Articles of War, see Appendices B1 and E3. In the latter Melville addresses directly the *Somers* Affair. Thoreau's "Slavery in Massachusetts" is excerpted in Appendix B3.

Americans, *White-Jacket*—those three sailors, even as you, who once were alive, but now are dead? 'Shall suffer death!' those were the three words that hung those three sailors" (*White-Jacket* 275–76). Melville said he wrote *White-Jacket* in two weeks for tobacco money, so it may be that when a few pages later he comes back to the *Somers* Affair—"Three men, in a time of peace, were then hung at the yard-arm, merely because, in the Captain's judgment, it became necessary to hang them"—he'd forgotten he'd already addressed it (284). Or maybe he was just that angry. In any case, it's hard to miss the point: Americans were executed by their leaders out of duty to a security imperative that, from the outside, didn't seem all that imperative.

In *Billy Budd*, a few paragraphs after Vere asks his officers to remember that the hundreds of men working the *Bellipotent* are essentially herd animals—"'all angel is not'ing more dan de shark well goberned'" the cook in *Moby-Dick* says—Melville again raises the spectre of the *Somers* (295). But this time he exchanges *White-Jacket*'s tabloid outrage for the guarded, ambivalent tone of a legal brief, noting only that the "resolution" to hang the sailors "was carried out though in a time of peace and within not many days' sail of home. An act vindicated by a naval court of inquiry subsequently convened ashore" (p. 117). Then with a shrug of the shoulders, as it were, he tosses out this line: "History, and here cited without comment." Nothing anybody can do about it now, so what's the point in protesting, the narrator seems to say. The thing is, people *were* still protesting what had happened aboard the *Somers*, even in the late 1880s, when Melville was writing *Billy Budd*.

In 1889, Gail Hamilton (Mary Abigail Dodge, 1833–96) published a three-part article on the *Somers* Affair, excoriating Captain Mackenzie and the authorities that blessed his actions and all but accusing the state outright of murder. Hamilton went especially hard on a lawyer, Charles Sumner (1811–74), who defended Mackenzie in the pages of the conservative standard-bearer the *North American Review* in the months following the mutiny.[1] Sumner would later become a household name—in 1851 he was caned on the Senate floor by a colleague from South Carolina—but in the 1840s he was just another well-connected Boston lawyer and occasional Harvard law professor. In his article, Sumner used the *Somers* to expound the meaning and

---

1 Sumner's and Hamilton's respective accounts of the *Somers* Affair are excerpted in Appendix C2.

function of law in times of crisis, including the Great Mutiny of 1797 and the *Somers* Affair, lecturing those who would recklessly raise the legal "'anchors'" that keep the ship of state firmly in place because of a little injustice now and again (p. 166). Damn the anchors, Hamilton said. As mad at apologists like Sumner who explained away Mackenzie's actions as she was at the captain himself, Hamilton argued that the imperial conscience, or law, is no conscience at all. Atrocities committed against individuals are no less atrocious for being legal. Her article was titled, pointedly, "The Murder of Philip Spencer."

Sumner's logic is Vere's, his argument a carbon copy of the testament of acceptance. Hamilton, meanwhile, channelling Thoreau, rolls out the doctrine of resistance. To read the two articles alongside *Billy Budd* is to see why many critics today avoid aligning themselves with one side or the other: because *Billy Budd* may live with the possibility of both being right. We need Sumner/Burke/Vere to be right, or we need Hamilton/Paine/the surgeon to be right. The narrator, however, seems to understand that it's not a matter of right or wrong. Both are right *and* wrong. After the narrator tells us at the end of the trial chapter, in reference to the *Somers* Affair, that it's all just history, "here cited without comment," he comments anyway. "Of course, the circumstances on board the *Somers* were different from those on board the *Bellipotent*. But the urgency felt, well-warranted or otherwise, was much the same" (p. 117). "Well-warranted" is the logic of the acceptance argument, "otherwise" that of the resistance argument, and it doesn't matter which one is right or true. Regardless of why what happened happened, it did happen, and it keeps happening. Whether we accept or resist it in 1797, 1842, 1877, 1886, or today, it's "much the same." It's unacceptable, this murder "legalised by lawyers" (that's "Timoleon" again), but there it always is.

The philosopher David Hume (1711–76) said it in his *Treatise on Human Nature* in 1739: it's so easy to slip unconsciously from saying something is this way to saying something ought not to be this way—to slip from the *is* to the *ought*. We can protest all we want that the *Somers*'s Captain Mackenzie should have acted differently, but it's not going to change how he did act. We can complain all we want that Captain Vere ought not to kill Billy, but it's not going to change the fact that he does kill Billy. More than once Melville's narrator calls attention to this tendency to slip seamlessly but illogically from description to prescription. Should Horatio Nelson have been on deck in plain sight of a

French sharpshooter at Trafalgar, he asks in Chapter 4, referencing posterity's habit of second-guessing England's most famous admiral for the decision that cost him his life. The narrator has as little patience for hypotheticals as does Vere: "the *might-have-been*," he warns, "is but boggy ground to build on" (p. 68; emphasis in original). Whether Nelson ought to have been there, he was. Whether Vere ought to talk the jury into convicting Billy, he does—again and again, every time the book is read. Gail Hamilton couldn't change what happened on the *Somers* any more than Melville could when he wrote *White-Jacket*. Charles Sumner and Edmund Burke couldn't make everything okay by telling us, pedantically, that we should just trust in the rule of law and everything will be all right. *Billy Budd* seems to hover above all this, for better or for worse, looking down in acceptance and in anger: "History, and here cited without comment."

Confirmation of the Old Despair

In October 1885, a 66-year-old Herman Melville sat for what would be his last portrait, reprinted as the frontispiece to this edition. He was surprised by what he saw. "What the deuse makes him look so serious, I wonder," he joked with a cousin when he sent her a copy with pressed leaves from his rose garden. "I thought he was of a gay and frolicsome nature, judgeing [*sic*] from a little rhyme of his about a Kitten, which you once showed me. But is this the same man?" (*Correspondence* 490). In his novelization of Melville's life, *The Passages of H. M.* (2011), Jay Parini imagines Melville even before old age as "all scowls and deferrals" (105). It's a fair description. Biographers agree that Melville's "gay and frolicsome nature" wasn't always readily apparent, to say the least.

In "Bridegroom Dick," Melville's old salt of a speaker realizes, while prating on about his seafaring past, that his long-suffering wife is less interested in his endless stories than in getting him to bed. It's a sweetly sad poem that ends with a kiss. It hints, though, that this sweet old man wasn't always so sweet. Melville had been growing increasingly unstable since the early 1850s. In 1856, Hawthorne recognized that his friend was "much overshadowed since I saw him last," but he didn't say by what (170). A decade later things had become so untenable for Elizabeth that her family and minister hatched a plan to kidnap her from her own home. She didn't go through with it; we don't know why. (That's a refrain in Melville biography.) It may have had something to do with the fact that a few months later their oldest son, Malcolm (1849–67), whose relationship with his father had long been fraught, shot himself in his upstairs bedroom. At least one biographer speculates that Elizabeth couldn't leave Melville that way. Later, Malcolm would find his way into *Billy Budd*, where Vere's sacrifice of Billy may suggest that Melville came to understand he'd sacrificed a son—really his whole family—to his art. "Implacable I, the old Implacable Sea," he writes in the poem "Pebbles" (1888): "Pleased, not appeased, by myriad wrecks in me" (247). Like the Dansker, the lines are a fair appraisal of their author.

By the 1880s, however, the Melville of the historical record, such as it is, seems altogether less terrible. His presence could still scare his granddaughters, but they were comfortable enough around him to build houses with the books piled on his floor, even raiding the drab blue pile containing his beloved Arthur Schopenhauer (1788–1860), whose influence on everyone from Friedrich Nietzsche (1844–1900) to Albert Camus (1913–60) has long been logged but whose effect on Melville has only recently begun to be fully appreciated.[1] In one of the Schopenhauer volumes appropriated by the little girls, Melville marked this passage: "He who lives to see two or three generations is like a man who sits some time in the conjuror's booth at a fair, and witnesses the performance twice or thrice in succession. The tricks were meant to be seen only once; and when they are no longer a novelty and cease to deceive, their effect is gone" (Olson-Smith, Norberg, and Marmon 14). Melville may have recognized the erosion of pluck and wonder that Schopenhauer describes. No longer the young man who lived among the cannibals and jumped ship at tropical islands, who appeared on friends' stoops, as one put it, "fresh from the mountain charged to the muzzle with his sailor metaphysics and jargon of things unknowable," Melville was old and sick (Leyda 523). This is what he'd tried to tell admirers in the late 1880s when again there was a critical mass: he had things left to do and little time left to do them. Certainly Melville was talking about his poetry, which his family could hear him reciting as he walked across the floor of his room, but he also likely meant *Billy Budd*.

Melville's popular reputation is that of arch Romantic. Characters like Ahab and Bartleby are, understandably, idols of revolt. But for every hot-head Ahab—"Talk not to me of blasphemy,

---

1 On Schopenhauer, see Appendices E4 and G1.

man; I'd strike the sun if it insulted me"—there's a measured, utilitarian Starbuck (*Moby-Dick* 164). For every anti-everything Bartleby, there's a sad-sack, pragmatic lawyer who believes with no trace of irony that "the easiest way of life is the best" (*Piazza Tales* 14). The fact is, few nineteenth-century American writers so compellingly theorized the repose of the status quo as Melville. Sometimes his take feels like determinism, sometimes fatalism or conspiracy. Contemporaries such as Howells and Émile Zola (1840–1902) might have called it, reasonably, Realism or Naturalism. Whatever it was, Melville wrote about it affectingly, most famously through early characters like Starbuck and the lawyer of "Bartleby," but also in less well known works like *Pierre*, which contains one of his most elegiac meditations on surrender: "For in tremendous extremities human souls are like drowning men; well enough they know they are in peril; well enough they know the causes of that peril;—nevertheless, the sea is the sea, and these drowning men do drown" (303). In the second half of the nineteenth century, the belief that the world is a place of constant striving and constant failure and thus constant suffering had a name: pessimism.[1] Pessimism is Buddhism without the spirituality, existentialism without the atheism. For Melville, it was reality without the nonsense. Schopenhauer was pessimism's most influential theorist, but he wasn't Melville's first pessimist love. That would be James Thomson (1834–82), whose poem *The City of Dreadful Night* (1874) is an *Inferno*-like romp through a London-like city written by a depressive insomniac who, like Melville, was told he was a talentless poet.[2] Melville immediately took to him. This isn't surprising, given that Thomson shared Melville's obsession with Ecclesiastes, that, in Thomson's words, "all is vanity and nothingness" (p. 212).

Pessimism was a welcome corrective for those disaffected by the cloying optimism that characterized the late nineteenth century, what philosopher Charles Taylor calls "the very picture of history as moral progress" cherished by social Darwinists and tycoons (394). Thomson made sure readers didn't mistake his attitude toward such bamboozling:

> Surely I write not for the hopeful young,
>   Or those who deem their happiness of worth,

---

1   On pessimism, see Appendix G. Following discussions of pessimism in literature, this edition does not capitalize the term.
2   For background on James Thomson, see Appendix G2.

Or such as pasture and grow fat among
  The shows of life and feel nor doubt nor dearth,
Or pious spirits with a God above them
To sanctify and glorify and love them,
  Or sages who foresee a heaven on earth. (p. 209)

Melville was not a card-carrying pessimist. Hawthorne had him
pegged when he said back in 1856 that Melville never could settle
into a single belief. But he did stumble upon a way of thinking
about the world that accorded with his own long-standing views
and that would colour much of his writing in the final decade of
his life (Dillingham 47). The pessimism in his late poetry is
almost sumptuous. "Pebbles" describes the sea as an amoral,
meaningless reality on which "Man, suffering inflictor, sails on
sufferance" (Melville, *Published Poems* 246). In "The Berg"
(1888), a ship slams into an iceberg, which barely registers the
shock.[1] The ship sinks, "Through very inertia overthrown" (p.
213). The poem's original final line records the human experience of the whole event starkly and darkly, almost Naturalistical-
ly, as the "dead indifference of walls." In a copy of the published
version, however, Melville changed by hand the ending from the
"dead indifference of walls" to the "dense stolidity of walls"
(*Poems*, ed. Robillard 27). The emendation suggests that reality
isn't uncaring. Instead it's unknowable and unperturbed. The
release of pessimism is its counsel that the "lumbering lubbard
loitering" berg doesn't change, and neither does the humanity
that slams into it. Hence, maybe, *Billy Budd*. Melville may not be
asking us to agree or disagree or even to understand Vere's
actions. He may simply be showing the push and pull of alle-
giances, or "what sometimes happens," as he wrote in a passage
he apparently struck from the manuscript, "in this incomprehensible world of ours," what he calls in *Clarel* "This star of tragedies,
this orb of sins" (qtd. in Matthiessen 512; *Clarel* 100). Or:
"History, and here cited without comment."

    Needless to say, it's all so terribly serious sounding, all this
philosophy and talk of *is*'s and *ought*'s and Burke and Paine and
Gatling guns strafing Pittsburgh streets and capitalism and anarchism and mutiny and revolution. Funny, then, that *Billy Budd*,
Melville's final fiction, the "inside narrative" of the sailor sacrificed to preserve a sick status quo, the book Melville couldn't
quite finish, should end with an inside joke. In "Billy in the

---

1   "The Berg" is reprinted in Appendix G3.

Darbies," which functions as a figurative epilogue, Melville seems to mock himself and his poetry, which he refers to with a wink as the "rude utterance" of a sailor "gifted, as some sailors are, with an artless *poetic* temperament" (p. 133). It's almost too perfect. This swan song of a novella, which would cement Melville's reputation when it was finally published, concludes with a reference to his failed poetic career and a pot shot at critics who labelled him a sailor whose literary reach exceeded his grasp.

Herman Melville: A Brief Chronology

1819   Born on 1 August in New York City to Allan Melvill
        (final "e" added later) and Maria Gansevoort.
1825   Attends New York Male High School (until 1829).
1829   Attends Columbia Grammar School, New York City
        (until 1830).
1830   Family moves to Albany, NY. Melville attends Albany
        Academy (until 1831).
1832   Father dies insolvent; family's fortunes never recover.
        Melville clerks at the New York State Bank in Albany
        (until 1834).
1834   Works on uncle's farm outside Pittsfield, Massachusetts
        (until 1835).
1835   Moves back to Albany, where he clerks in brother's fur
        business; enrolls in Albany Classical School.
1836   Attends Albany Academy (until 1837).
1837   Brother's business falls apart in Panic of 1837; Melville
        teaches school near Pittsfield.
1838   Returns to Albany and mother moves family to Lans-
        ingburgh, near Albany, to reduce expenses; Melville
        works again at farm near Pittsfield before returning to
        Lansingburgh, where he studies surveying and engi-
        neering. Becomes president of debating society.
1839   "Fragments from a Writing Desk" published in the
        Democratic Press. First ocean voyage, New York to Liver-
        pool round-trip on trading ship *St. Lawrence*. Teaches
        school near Albany (until 1840).
1841   Sails from New Bedford, MA, for Pacific on whaling
        ship *Acushnet*.
1842   Deserts *Acushnet* in Marquesas Islands, in South
        Pacific; lives for month among indigenous inhabitants
        reputed to be cannibals. Sails on Australian whaler
        Lucy Ann, where he is charged with mutiny and jailed
        in Tahiti. Escapes and sails for Hawaiian Islands on
        Nantucket whaler *Charles and Henry*.
1843   Enlists in navy in Honolulu; sails on *United States*.
1844   Discharged from navy; returns to Lansingburgh and
        begins writing.
1846   Publishes first novel, *Typee*.

1847	Publishes novel *Omoo* and book review "Etchings of a Whaling Cruise." Marries Elizabeth Shaw, daughter of Massachusetts Supreme Court Justice Lemuel Shaw; couple settles in New York City.
1849	Publishes novels *Mardi* and *Redburn*. Birth of son, Malcolm. Travels to London to deal with publishers and then to France.
1850	Publishes novel *White-Jacket*. Family moves to farm, Arrowhead, near Pittsfield, which Melville buys with money loaned by father-in-law. Begins friendship with Nathaniel Hawthorne; publishes anonymous review of Hawthorne's work, "Hawthorne and His Mosses," as well as other magazine pieces.
1851	Publishes novel *Moby-Dick*. Birth of son, Stanwix.
1852	Publishes novel *Pierre*.
1853	Publishes short stories "Bartleby, the Scrivener" and "Cock-A-Doodle-Do!" Submits manuscript (now lost) for a presumed novel, *Isle of the Cross*, to his American publisher, Harper and Brothers; they reject it. Birth of daughter, Elizabeth. Concerned by Melville's worsening finances and psychological health, friends and family make unsuccessful attempt to secure him government position.
1854	Begins serializing novel *Israel Potter*, which is published in book form following year.
1855	Publishes novella *Benito Cereno* and short stories "The Paradise of Bachelors and the Tartarus of Maids" and "The Bell-Tower." Birth of daughter, Frances.
1856	Publishes collection, *The Piazza Tales*, consisting mostly of previously published works; publishes short story "I and My Chimney." Leaves for Middle East, Greece, and Italy on tour financed by father-in-law; stops in England en route and sees Hawthorne for last time.
1857	Publishes last full-length novel, *The Confidence-Man*. Returns from trip and seeks government position unsuccessfully. Begins lecturing and likely begins writing poetry.
1860	Quits lecturing. Sails for San Francisco on ship captained by a brother. Book of poetry declined by publishers.
1861	Seeks government position from Lincoln administration. Father-in-law Lemuel Shaw dies.

1863	Family leaves Arrowhead and moves to New York City for good.
1864	Visits Civil War front in Virginia.
1866	Publishes poetry collection *Battle-Pieces and Aspects of the War*, some poems from which were published earlier in *Harper's New Monthly Magazine*. Appointed customs inspector at Port of New York.
1867	Elizabeth Melville advised to leave marriage and family and friends plot means for her to do so. Eldest son, Malcolm, dies of self-inflicted gunshot wound.
1876	Publishes book-length narrative poem *Clarel*.
1878	Elizabeth Melville receives inheritance, relieving family's financial stress.
1885	Resigns customs post at end of year.
1886	Probably begins *Billy Budd*; son Stanwix dies.
1887	Receives final royalty check from his New York publisher.
1888	Publishes poetry collection *John Marr and Other Sailors* (printed privately).
1891	Publishes poetry collection, *Timoleon* (printed privately). Dies of heart failure on 28 September in New York City, leaving various manuscripts, including *Billy Budd* and a book of poetry, *Weeds and Wildings*, unpublished.
1924	*Billy Budd* first published in London by Constable & Co.

A Note on the Text

The first fact of *Billy Budd* is that Melville never finished it, so there is no final version to reproduce. This edition follows the copy-text established in 1962 by Harrison Hayford and Merton M. Sealts Jr. and published by the University of Chicago Press. While most scholars consider the Hayford–Sealts copy-text the standard, two projects now underway will likely revise their work. The first is the edition currently in preparation for the authoritative Northwestern–Newbury edition of Melville's works. The second is a digital edition in preparation for the online *Melville Electronic Library* (http://mel.hofstra.edu/versions-of-billy-budd.html). For an overview of the editing and publication history of *Billy Budd*, see the Introduction, p. 24.

Public domain versions of texts have been used in appendices whenever possible. In most cases original spellings and grammatical constructions have been left unchanged.

BILLY BUDD, SAILOR
(*An Inside Narrative*)

DEDICATED
To
JACK CHASE
ENGLISHMAN[1]

Wherever that great heart may now be
Here on Earth or harbored in Paradise

Captain of the Maintop
in the year 1843
in the US Frigate
United States

---

1 Melville's friend and shipmate aboard the *United States* in 1843 and
central figure in *White-Jacket* (1850), where he represents the ideal
citizen: "Though bowing to naval discipline afloat; yet ashore, he was a
stickler for the Rights of Man, and the liberties of the world" (17). The
allusion is the first of a number of explicit and implicit autobiographical
references in *Billy Budd*.

1

In the time before steamships, or then more frequently than now, a stroller along the docks of any considerable seaport would occasionally have his attention arrested by a group of bronzed mariners, man-of-war's men or merchant sailors in holiday attire, ashore on liberty. In certain instances they would flank, or like a bodyguard quite surround, some superior figure of their own class, moving along with them like Aldebaran[1] among the lesser lights of his constellation. That signal object was the "Handsome Sailor" of the less prosaic time alike of the military and merchant navies. With no perceptible trace of the vainglorious about him, rather with the offhand unaffectedness of natural regality, he seemed to accept the spontaneous homage of his shipmates.

A somewhat remarkable instance recurs to me. In Liverpool, now half a century ago,[2] I saw under the shadow of the great dingy street-wall of Prince's Dock (an obstruction long since removed) a common sailor so intensely black that he must needs have been a native African of the unadulterate blood of Ham[3]—a symmetric figure much above the average height. The two ends of a gay silk handkerchief thrown loose about the neck danced upon the displayed ebony of his chest, in his ears were big hoops of gold, and a Highland bonnet with a tartan band set off his shapely head. It was a hot noon in July; and his face, lustrous with perspiration, beamed with barbaric good humor. In jovial sallies right and left, his white teeth flashing into view, he rollicked along, the center of a company of his shipmates. These were made up of such an assortment of tribes and complexions as would have well fitted them to be marched up by Anacharsis Cloots[4] before the bar of the first

---

1 Bright star in the Taurus constellation: the eye of the bull. The name is Arabic for "follower" because its location gives the impression of trailing other stars.
2 Melville visited Liverpool in 1839, during his first sea voyage; fictionalized in *Redburn* (1849).
3 In Genesis 9:20–27, Noah curses his son Ham's descendants, the Canaanites, consigning them to serve the Israelites and, in one particularly problematic and consequential interpretation, turning their skin black. In the US and elsewhere, the story was used to justify slavery.
4 Prussian Jean-Baptiste du Val-de-Grâce (1755–94) adopted France and took the name Anacharsis Cloots; in 1790, he led a group of non-French citizens to France's National Assembly to illustrate and affirm the republican ideals of the revolution. Melville uses him here and elsewhere as a symbol of a worldly democratic feeling.

French Assembly as Representatives of the Human Race. At each spontaneous tribute rendered by the wayfarers to this black pagod[1] of a fellow—the tribute of a pause and stare, and less frequently an exclamation—the motley retinue showed that they took that sort of pride in the evoker of it which the Assyrian priests doubtless showed for their grand sculptured Bull when the faithful prostrated themselves.[2]

To return. If in some cases a bit of a nautical Murat[3] in setting forth his person ashore, the Handsome Sailor of the period in question evinced nothing of the dandified Billy-be-Dam, an amusing character all but extinct now, but occasionally to be encountered, and in a form yet more amusing than the original, at the tiller of the boats on the tempestuous Erie Canal or, more likely, vaporing in the groggeries along the towpath. Invariably a proficient in his perilous calling, he was also more or less of a mighty boxer or wrestler. It was strength and beauty. Tales of his prowess were recited. Ashore he was the champion; afloat the spokesman; on every suitable occasion always foremost. Close-reefing topsails in a gale, there he was, astride the weather yardarm-end, foot in the Flemish horse as stirrup, both hands tugging at the earing as at a bridle, in very much the attitude of young Alexander curbing the fiery Bucephalus.[4] A superb figure, tossed up as by the horns of Taurus against the thunderous sky, cheerily hallooing to the strenuous file along the spar.[5]

The moral nature was seldom out of keeping with the physical make. Indeed, except as toned by the former, the comeliness and power, always attractive in masculine conjunction, hardly could have drawn the sort of honest homage the Handsome Sailor in some examples received from his less gifted associates.

Such a cynosure, at least in aspect, and something such too in nature, though with important variations made apparent as the story proceeds, was welkin-eyed[6] Billy Budd—or Baby Budd, as more familiarly, under circumstances hereafter to be given, he at

---

1 Idol.
2 Reference to Baal, powerful god worshipped in diverse forms in the ancient Middle East.
3 Joachim Murat (1767–1815), Italian/French military and political leader known for his showy fashions.
4 Reputedly untamable horse tamed with kindness rather than force by Alexander the Great (356–323 BCE).
5 Generic nautical term for large poles in the form of masts, booms, etc.
6 Blue-eyed; "welkin" refers to the heavenly sky.

last came to be called—aged twenty-one, a foretopman[1] of the British fleet toward the close of the last decade of the eighteenth century. It was not very long prior to the time of the narration that follows that he had entered the King's service, having been impressed[2] on the Narrow Seas from a homeward-bound English merchantman into a seventy-four[3] outward bound, H.M.S. *Bellipotent*; which ship, as was not unusual in those hurried days, having been obliged to put to sea short of her proper complement of men. Plump upon Billy at first sight in the gangway the boarding officer, Lieutenant Ratcliffe, pounced, even before the merchantman's crew was formally mustered[4] on the quarter-deck for his deliberate inspection. And him only he elected. For whether it was because the other men when ranged before him showed to ill advantage after Billy, or whether he had some scruples in view of the merchantman's being rather short-handed, however it might be, the officer contented himself with his first spontaneous choice. To the surprise of the ship's company, though much to the lieutenant's satisfaction, Billy made no demur. But, indeed, any demur would have been as idle as the protest of a goldfinch popped into a cage.

Noting this uncomplaining acquiescence, all but cheerful, one might say, the shipmaster turned a surprised glance of silent reproach at the sailor. The shipmaster was one of those worthy mortals found in every vocation, even the humbler ones—the sort of person whom everybody agrees in calling "a respectable man." And—nor so strange to report as it may appear to be—though a ploughman of the troubled waters, lifelong contending with the intractable elements, there was nothing this honest soul at heart loved better than simple peace and quiet. For the rest, he was fifty or thereabouts, a little inclined to corpulence, a prepossessing face, unwhiskered, and of an agreeable color—a rather full face, humanely intelligent in expression. On a fair day with a fair wind

---

1   Sailor stationed at the foretop, a small platform on the foremast in the front of the ship.

2   The forced but legal conscription of sailors into the navy. In this era, the Royal Navy was perpetually short of sailors.

3   A type of warship named for its armament of 74 guns and valued in the British and French navies for being a practical compromise of firepower, handling, durability, and cost. In early drafts, Melville called the ship the *Indomitable*.

4   Marshalling of soldiers for the purposes of inspection, accounting, or readying for battle.

and all going well, a certain musical chime in his voice seemed to be the veritable unobstructed outcome of the innermost man. He had much prudence, much conscientiousness, and there were occasions when these virtues were the cause of overmuch disquietude in him. On a passage, so long as his craft was in any proximity to land, no sleep for Captain Graveling. He took to heart those serious responsibilities not so heavily borne by some shipmasters.

Now while Billy Budd was down in the forecastle[1] getting his kit together, the *Bellipotent*'s lieutenant, burly and bluff, nowise disconcerted by Captain Graveling's omitting to proffer the customary hospitalities on an occasion so unwelcome to him, an omission simply caused by preoccupation of thought, unceremoniously invited himself into the cabin, and also to a flask from the spirit locker, a receptacle which his experienced eye instantly discovered. In fact he was one of those sea dogs in whom all the hardship and peril of naval life in the great prolonged wars of his time never impaired the natural instinct for sensuous enjoyment. His duty he always faithfully did; but duty is sometimes a dry obligation, and he was for irrigating its aridity, whensoever possible, with a fertilizing decoction of strong waters. For the cabin's proprietor there was nothing left but to play the part of the enforced host with whatever grace and alacrity were practicable. As necessary adjuncts to the flask, he silently placed tumbler and water jug before the irrepressible guest. But excusing himself from partaking just then, he dismally watched the unembarrassed officer deliberately diluting his grog a little, then tossing it off in three swallows, pushing the empty tumbler away, yet not so far as to be beyond easy reach, at the same time settling himself in his seat and smacking his lips with high satisfaction, looking straight at the host.

These proceedings over, the master broke the silence; and there lurked a rueful reproach in the tone of his voice: "Lieutenant, you are going to take my best man from me, the jewel of 'em."

"Yes, I know," rejoined the other, immediately drawing back the tumbler preliminary to a replenishing. "Yes, I know. Sorry."

"Beg pardon, but you don't understand, Lieutenant. See here, now. Before I shipped that young fellow, my forecastle was a rat-pit of quarrels. It was black times, I tell you, aboard the *Rights* here. I was worried to that degree my pipe had no comfort for me. But Billy came; and it was like a Catholic priest striking peace in

---

1 Raised deck at the front of a ship.

an Irish shindy. Not that he preached to them or said or did anything in particular; but a virtue went out of him, sugaring the sour ones. They took to him like hornets to treacle; all but the buffer of the gang, the big shaggy chap with the fire-red whiskers. He indeed, out of envy, perhaps, of the newcomer, and thinking such a 'sweet and pleasant fellow,' as he mockingly designated him to the others, could hardly have the spirit of a gamecock, must needs bestir himself in trying to get up an ugly row with him. Billy forebore with him and reasoned with him in a pleasant way—he is something like myself, Lieutenant, to whom aught like a quarrel is hateful—but nothing served. So, in the second dogwatch[1] one day, the Red Whiskers in presence of the others, under pretense of showing Billy just whence a sirloin steak was cut—for the fellow had once been a butcher—insultingly gave him a dig under the ribs. Quick as lightning Billy let fly his arm. I dare say he never meant to do quite as much as he did, but anyhow he gave the burly fool a terrible drubbing. It took about half a minute, I should think. And, lord bless you, the lubber was astonished at the celerity.[2] And will you believe it, Lieutenant, the Red Whiskers now really loves Billy—loves him, or is the biggest hypocrite that ever I heard of. But they all love him. Some of 'em do his washing, darn his old trousers for him; the carpenter is at odd times making a pretty little chest of drawers for him. Anybody will do anything for Billy Budd; and it's the happy family here. But now, Lieutenant, if that young fellow goes—I know how it will be aboard the *Rights*. Not again very soon shall I, coming up from dinner, lean over the capstan[3] smoking a quiet pipe—no, not very soon again, I think. Ay, Lieutenant, you are going to take away the jewel of 'em; you are going to take away my peacemaker!" And with that the good soul had really some ado in checking a rising sob.

"Well," said the lieutenant, who had listened with amused interest to all this and now was waxing merry with his tipple; "well, blessed are the peacemakers, especially the fighting peacemakers.[4] And such are the seventy-four beauties some of which you see poking their noses out of the portholes of yonder warship lying to

---

1 Short evening work shift.
2 Speed, quickness.
3 A device that mechanically assists in the raising of heavy objects, such as sails or anchors.
4 Ironic application of Christ's Sermon on the Mount: "Blessed are the peacemakers: for they shall be called the children of God" (Matthew 5:9).

for me," pointing through the cabin window at the *Bellipotent*. "But courage! Don't look so downhearted, man. Why, I pledge you in advance the royal approbation. Rest assured that His Majesty will be delighted to know that in a time when his hardtack[1] is not sought for by sailors with such avidity as should be, a time also when some shipmasters privily resent the borrowing from them a tar[2] or two for the service; His Majesty, I say, will be delighted to learn that *one* shipmaster at least cheerfully surrenders to the King the flower of his flock, a sailor who with equal loyalty makes no dissent.—But where's my beauty? Ah," looking through the cabin's open door, "here he comes; and, by Jove, lugging along his chest— Apollo with his portmanteau![3]—My man," stepping out to him, "you can't take that big box aboard a warship. The boxes there are mostly shot boxes. Put your duds in a bag, lad. Boot and saddle for the cavalryman, bag and hammock for the man-of-war's man."

The transfer from chest to bag was made. And, after seeing his man into the cutter and then following him down, the lieutenant pushed off from the *Rights-of-Man*. That was the merchant ship's name, though by her master and crew abbreviated in sailor fashion into the *Rights*. The hard-headed Dundee owner was a staunch admirer of Thomas Paine, whose book in rejoinder to Burke's arraignment of the French Revolution had then been published for some time and had gone everywhere.[4] In christening his vessel after the title of Paine's volume the man of Dundee was something like his contemporary shipowner, Stephen Girard of Philadelphia,[5] whose sympathies, alike with his native land and

---

1 A simple but long-lasting biscuit rationed on long voyages in the absence of perishable foods.

2 Sailor (slang).

3 Apollo, Greek deity and ideal of male youth, beauty, and athleticism, was often represented artistically as a perfectly proportioned nude.

4 *Reflections on the Revolution in France* (1790), British statesman Edmund Burke's (1729–97) powerful denunciation of the French Revolution as naïve and self-destructive. *Rights of Man* (1791–92), Anglo-American pamphleteer Thomas Paine's (1737–1809) equally famous response, argues that people have the right to rebel when government fails to protect their natural rights. In the text, Melville collapses historically diffuse strains of conservatism and liberalism into Burke (the *Bellipotent*) and Paine (the *Rights-of-Man*), respectively. See Appendix A.

5 Stephen Girard (1750–1831), French-American who helped save the US from bankruptcy during the War of 1812 and then willed one of the largest fortunes in American history to local philanthropic causes in Philadelphia; an emblem of civic love and social virtue.

its liberal philosophers, he evinced by naming his ships after Voltaire, Diderot, and so forth.[1]

But now, when the boat swept under the merchantman's stern, and officer and oarsmen were noting—some bitterly and others with a grin—the name emblazoned there; just then it was that the new recruit jumped up from the bow where the coxswain[2] had directed him to sit, and waving hat to his silent shipmates sorrowfully looking over at him from the taffrail,[3] bade the lads a genial good-bye. Then, making a salutation as to the ship herself, "And good-bye to you too, old *Rights-of-Man.*"

"Down, sir!" roared the lieutenant, instantly assuming all the rigor of his rank, though with difficulty repressing a smile.

To be sure, Billy's action was a terrible breach of naval decorum. But in that decorum he had never been instructed; in consideration of which the lieutenant would hardly have been so energetic in reproof but for the concluding farewell to the ship. This he rather took as meant to convey a covert sally on the new recruit's part, a sly slur at impressment in general, and that of himself in especial. And yet, more likely, if satire it was in effect, it was hardly so by intention, for Billy, though happily endowed with the gaiety of high health, youth, and a free heart, was yet by no means of a satirical turn. The will to it and the sinister dexterity were alike wanting. To deal in double meanings and insinuations of any sort was quite foreign to his nature.

As to his enforced enlistment, that he seemed to take pretty much as he was wont to take any vicissitude of weather. Like the animals, though no philosopher, he was, without knowing it, practically a fatalist. And it may be that he rather liked this adventurous turn in his affairs, which promised an opening into novel scenes and martial excitements.

Aboard the *Bellipotent* our merchant sailor was forthwith rated as an able seaman[4] and assigned to the starboard watch of the foretop. He was soon at home in the service, not at all disliked

---

1 Allusion to the thought of Voltaire (1694–1778), Denis Diderot (1713–84), and likely Jean-Jacques Rousseau (1712–78), all aggressive and influential critics of traditional forms of authority as vested in extant religious, political, and philosophical institutions, and here metonyms for the Enlightenment.
2 Person in charge of steering and/or navigation; helmsman. The bow is the front of a ship.
3 Railing encircling the very back, or stern, of a ship.
4 Upon impressment, sailors were assigned ranks based on experience and other factors: an "able seaman" would have experience.

for his unpretentious good looks and a sort of genial happy-go-lucky air. No merrier man in his mess: in marked contrast to certain other individuals included like himself among the impressed portion of the ship's company; for these when not actively employed were sometimes, and more particularly in the last dogwatch when the drawing near of twilight induced revery, apt to fall into a saddish mood which in some partook of sullenness. But they were not so young as our foretopman, and no few of them must have known a hearth of some sort, others may have had wives and children left, too probably, in uncertain circumstances, and hardly any but must have had acknowledged kith and kin, while for Billy, as will shortly be seen, his entire family was practically invested in himself.

2

Though our new-made foretopman was well received in the top and on the gun decks, hardly here was he that cynosure he had previously been among those minor ship's companies of the merchant marine, with which companies only had he hitherto consorted.

He was young; and despite his all but fully developed frame, in aspect looked even younger than he really was, owing to a lingering adolescent expression in the as yet smooth face all but feminine in purity of natural complexion but where, thanks to his seagoing, the lily was quite suppressed and the rose had some ado visibly to flush through the tan.

To one essentially such a novice in the complexities of factitious life, the abrupt transition from his former and simpler sphere to the ampler and more knowing world of a great warship; this might well have abashed him had there been any conceit or vanity in his composition. Among her miscellaneous multitude, the *Bellipotent* mustered several individuals who however inferior in grade were of no common natural stamp, sailors more signally susceptive of that air which continuous martial discipline and repeated presence in battle can in some degree impart even to the average man. As the Handsome Sailor, Billy Budd's position aboard the seventy-four was something analogous to that of a rustic beauty transplanted from the provinces and brought into competition with the highborn dames of the court. But this change of circumstances he scarce noted. As little did he observe that something about him provoked an ambiguous smile in one or two harder faces among the bluejackets.[1] Nor less unaware was he of the peculiar favorable effect his person and demeanor had upon the more intelligent gentlemen of the quarter-deck. Nor could this well have been otherwise. Cast in a mold peculiar to the finest physical examples of those Englishmen in whom the Saxon strain would seem not at all to partake of any Norman or other admixture, he showed in face that humane look of reposeful good nature which the Greek sculptor in some instances gave to his heroic strong man, Hercules. But this again was subtly modified by another and pervasive quality. The ear, small and shapely, the arch of the foot, the curve in mouth and nostril, even the indurated hand dyed to the orange-tawny of the toucan's bill, a hand telling alike of the halyards and tar bucket; but, above all, something in the mobile expression, and every chance attitude and movement, something suggestive of a mother eminently favored by Love and the Graces; all this strangely indicated a lineage in direct contradiction to his lot. The mysteriousness here became less mysterious through a matter of fact elicited when Billy at the capstan was being formally mustered into the service. Asked by the officer, a small, brisk little gentleman as it chanced, among other questions, his place of birth, he replied, "Please, sir, I don't know."

"Don't know where you were born? Who was your father?"

"God knows, sir."

Struck by the straightforward simplicity of these replies, the officer next asked, "Do you know anything about your beginning?"

"No, sir. But I have heard that I was found in a pretty silk-lined basket hanging one morning from the knocker of a good man's door in Bristol."

"*Found*, say you? Well," throwing back his head and looking up and down the new recruit; "well, it turns out to have been a pretty good find. Hope they'll find some more like you, my man; the fleet sadly needs them."

Yes, Billy Budd was a foundling, a presumable by-blow, and, evidently, no ignoble one. Noble descent was as evident in him as in a blood horse.

---

1 One of the guarded references to Billy's sexual effect on the *Bellipotent*'s crew members. See Appendix F.

For the rest, with little or no sharpness of faculty or any trace of the wisdom of the serpent, nor yet quite a dove,[1] he possessed that kind and degree of intelligence going along with the unconventional rectitude of a sound human creature, one to whom not yet has been proffered the questionable apple of knowledge. He was illiterate; he could not read, but he could sing, and like the illiterate nightingale was sometimes the composer of his own song.

Of self-consciousness he seemed to have little or none, or about as much as we may reasonably impute to a dog of Saint Bernard's breed.

Habitually living with the elements and knowing little more of the land than as a beach, or, rather, that portion of the terraqueous globe providentially set apart for dance-houses, doxies, and tapsters, in short what sailors call a "fiddler's green,"[2] his simple nature remained unsophisticated by those moral obliquities which are not in every case incompatible with that manufacturable thing known as respectability. But are sailors, frequenters of fiddlers' greens, without vices? No; but less often than with landsmen do their vices, so called, partake of crookedness of heart, seeming less to proceed from viciousness than exuberance of vitality after long constraint: frank manifestations in accordance with natural law. By his original constitution aided by the co-operating influences of his lot, Billy in many respects was little more than a sort of upright barbarian, much such perhaps as Adam presumably might have been ere the urbane Serpent wriggled himself into his company.

And here be it submitted that apparently going to corroborate the doctrine of man's Fall, a doctrine now popularly ignored,[3] it is observable that where certain virtues pristine and unadulterate

---

1   Allusion to Matthew's instructions to disciples upon entering the world: "Behold, I send you forth as sheep in the midst of wolves: be ye therefore wise as serpents, and harmless as doves" (Matthew 10:16).

2   A "sailor's Elysium, in which wine, women, and song figure prominently" (*OED*).

3   The first of two times the narrator complains that people have lost a sense of Original Sin, which modulates blind faith in human goodness; possibly a shot at Rousseau and other thinkers who believed human nature was inherently good. According to Hayford and Sealts, Melville marked in his copy of *Studies in Pessimism* (1891) Arthur Schopenhauer's (1788–1860) admission that the Fall is "the sole thing that reconciles me to the Old Testament" (143). On Schopenhauer, see Appendices E4 and G1.

peculiarly characterize anybody in the external uniform of civilization, they will upon scrutiny seem not to be derived from custom or convention, but rather to be out of keeping with these, as if indeed exceptionally transmitted from a period prior to Cain's city, and citified man.[1] The character marked by such qualities has to an unvitiated taste an untampered-with flavor like that of berries, while the man thoroughly civilized, even in a fair specimen of the breed, has to the same moral palate a questionable smack as of a compounded wine. To any stray inheritor of these primitive qualities found, like Caspar Hauser,[2] wandering dazed in any Christian capital of our time, the good-natured poet's famous invocation, near two thousand years ago, of the good rustic out of his latitude in the Rome of the Caesars, still appropriately holds:

> Honest and poor, faithful in word and thought,
> What hath thee, Fabian, to the city brought?[3]

Though our Handsome Sailor had as much of masculine beauty as one can expect anywhere to see; nevertheless, like the beautiful woman in one of Hawthorne's minor tales,[4] there was just one thing amiss in him. No visible blemish indeed, as with the lady; no, but an occasional liability to a vocal defect. Though in the hour of elemental uproar or peril he was everything that a sailor should be, yet under sudden provocation of strong heartfeeling his voice, otherwise singularly musical, as if expressive of the harmony within, was apt to develop an organic hesitancy, in fact more or less of a stutter or even worse. In this particular Billy was a striking instance that the arch interferer, the envious

---

1 That is, a less corrupt time, before Cain kills his brother Abel, is exiled by God, and builds the first city, Nod: "And Cain went out from the presence of the LORD, and dwelt in the land of Nod, on the east of Eden" (Genesis 4:16).

2 Kaspar Hauser (1812?–33), the so-called "forest boy" who one day in 1828 appeared in Nuremberg claiming to have been raised in the woods, though he later said he spent his entire childhood locked away in a dungeon. Among Europeans and Americans alike, the mysteries of Hauser's origins, eventful life, and even death prompted fanciful speculation of, among other things, a royal conspiracy.

3 Epigram by the Roman poet Martial (c. 38–103 CE).

4 In Nathaniel Hawthorne's (1804–64) short story "The Birthmark" (1843), Georgiana is perfect in every way except for a birthmark in the shape of a crimson hand. On Hawthorne, see Appendix F6.

marplot[1] of Eden, still has more or less to do with every human consignment to this planet of Earth. In every case, one way or another he is sure to slip in his little card, as much as to remind us—I too have a hand here.

The avowal of such an imperfection in the Handsome Sailor should be evidence not alone that he is not presented as a conventional hero, but also that the story in which he is the main figure is no romance.

3

At the time of Billy Budd's arbitrary enlistment into the *Bellipotent* that ship was on her way to join the Mediterranean fleet. No long time elapsed before the junction was effected. As one of that fleet the seventy-four participated in its movements, though at times on account of her superior sailing qualities, in the absence of frigates, dispatched on separate duty as a scout and at times on less temporary service. But with all this the story has little concernment, restricted as it is to the inner life of one particular ship and the career of an individual sailor.

It was the summer of 1797. In the April of that year had occurred the commotion at Spithead followed in May by a second and yet more serious outbreak in the fleet at the Nore.[2] The latter is known, and without exaggeration in the epithet, as "the Great Mutiny." It was indeed a demonstration more menacing to England than the contemporary manifestoes and conquering and proselyting armies of the French Directory.[3] To the British Empire the Nore Mutiny was what a strike in the fire brigade would be to London threatened by general arson. In a

---

1 Someone or something that spoils a plan; here, Satan as the serpent.
2 Reference to two areas in the waters off England's southeast coast and to the famous 1797 mutinies in the Royal Navy fleets anchored there. The Spithead mutiny ended peacefully when the crown made concessions to striking sailors; the Nore mutiny was more violent and more treacherous for the British empire, in part because mutinous sailors blockaded London and some even threatened to decamp their ships to Revolutionary France. Both mutinies sent shockwaves through the British military, government, and society at a time when the British were already worried that the Revolution would spread to England. See Appendix C1.
3 Name of the French Revolutionary government in power from 1795 to 1799.

crisis when the kingdom might well have anticipated the famous signal that some years later published along the naval line of battle what it was that upon occasion England expected of Englishmen;[1] *that* was the time when at the mastheads of the three-deckers and seventy-fours moored in her own roadstead—a fleet the right arm of a Power then all but the sole free conservative one of the Old World—the bluejackets, to be numbered by thousands, ran up with huzzas the British colors with the union and cross wiped out; by that cancellation transmuting the flag of founded law and freedom defined, into the enemy's red meteor of unbridled and unbounded revolt. Reasonable discontent growing out of practical grievances in the fleet had been ignited into irrational combustion as by live cinders blown across the Channel from France in flames.

The event converted into irony for a time those spirited strains of Dibdin[2]—as a song-writer no mean auxiliary to the English government at that European conjuncture—strains celebrating, among other things, the patriotic devotion of the British tar: "And as for my life, 'tis the King's!"

Such an episode in the Island's grand naval story her naval historians naturally abridge, one of them (William James)[3] candidly acknowledging that fain would he pass it over did not "impartiality forbid fastidiousness." And yet his mention is less a narration than a reference, having to do hardly at all with details. Nor are these readily to be found in the libraries. Like some other events in every age befalling states everywhere, including America, the Great Mutiny was of such character that national pride along with views of policy would fain shade it off into the historical background. Such events cannot be ignored, but there is a considerate way of historically treating them. If a well-constituted individual refrains from blazoning aught amiss or calamitous in his family, a nation in the like circumstance may without reproach be equally discreet.

Though after parleyings between government and the ringleaders, and concessions by the former as to some glaring abuses, the first uprising—that at Spithead—with difficulty was put down, or

---

1 According to Robert Southey (1774–1843), in his influential account of Nelson, what England expected of Englishmen was that they would do their duty. On Southey, see Appendix C1a.
2 Charles Dibdin (1745–1814), prolific, popular British songwriter and playwright whose nautical works Melville appreciated.
3 British naval historian (1780–1827) and one of Melville's sources.

matters for the time pacified; yet at the Nore the unforeseen renewal of insurrection on a yet larger scale, and emphasized in the conferences that ensued by demands deemed by the authorities not only inadmissible but aggressively insolent, indicated—if the Red Flag[1] did not sufficiently do so—what was the spirit animating the men. Final suppression, however, there was; but only made possible perhaps by the unswerving loyalty of the marine corps and a voluntary resumption of loyalty among influential sections of the crews.

To some extent the Nore Mutiny may be regarded as analogous to the distempering irruption of contagious fever in a frame constitutionally sound, and which anon throws it off.

At all events, of these thousands of mutineers were some of the tars who not so very long afterwards—whether wholly prompted thereto by patriotism, or pugnacious instinct, or by both—helped to win a coronet for Nelson at the Nile, and the naval crown of crowns for him at Trafalgar.[2] To the mutineers, those battles and especially Trafalgar were a plenary absolution and a grand one. For all that goes to make up scenic naval display and heroic magnificence in arms, those battles, especially Trafalgar, stand unmatched in human annals.

4

In this matter of writing, resolve as one may to keep to the main road, some bypaths have an enticement not readily to be withstood. I am going to err into such a bypath. If the reader will keep me company I shall be glad. At the least, we can promise ourselves that pleasure which is wickedly said to be in sinning, for a literary sin the divergence will be.[3]

---

1 Emblem of revolutionary and leftist political movements, including the French Revolution.

2 Famous battles fought by Sir Horatio Nelson (1758–1805), revered British admiral: the Battle of the Nile (1798) dealt a severe blow to Napoleon's North African campaign; the Battle of Trafalgar (1805), on the coast of southern Spain, was a brilliant tactical victory, perhaps Nelson's greatest, though it cost him his life.

3 In the narrative Nelson is the quintessential naval commander; the quality of his abilities and heroism are distinguished from Vere's, who, though a strong commander, simply does not rise to that level. Melville was conflicted about including the chapter, cutting and then re-adding it. On Nelson, see Appendix C1a.

Very likely it is no new remark that the inventions of our time have at last brought about a change in sea warfare in degree corresponding to the revolution in all warfare effected by the original introduction from China into Europe of gunpowder. The first European firearm, a clumsy contrivance, was, as is well known, scouted by no few of the knights as a base implement, good enough peradventure for weavers too craven to stand up crossing steel with steel in frank fight. But as ashore knightly valor, though shorn of its blazonry, did not cease with the knights, neither on the seas—though nowadays in encounters there a certain kind of displayed gallantry be fallen out of date as hardly applicable under changed circumstances—did the nobler qualities of such naval magnates as Don John of Austria, Doria, Van Tromp, Jean Bart, the long line of British admirals, and the American Decaturs of 1812 become obsolete with their wooden walls.[1]

Nevertheless, to anybody who can hold the Present at its worth without being inappreciative of the Past, it may be forgiven, if to such an one the solitary old hulk at Portsmouth, Nelson's *Victory*, seems to float there, not alone as the decaying monument of a fame incorruptible, but also as a poetic reproach, softened by its picturesqueness, to the *Monitors* and yet mightier hulls of the European ironclads. And this not altogether because such craft are unsightly, unavoidably lacking the symmetry and grand lines of the old battleships, but equally for other reasons.[2]

There are some, perhaps, who while not altogether inaccessible to that poetic reproach just alluded to, may yet on behalf of the new order be disposed to parry it; and this to the extent of iconoclasm, if need be. For example, prompted by the sight of the star inserted in the *Victory*'s quarter-deck designating the spot where the Great Sailor fell, these martial utilitarians may suggest considerations implying that Nelson's ornate publication of his person in battle was not only unnecessary, but not military, nay,

---

1 Notable naval commanders from the age of sail, ending with Stephen Decatur (1779–1820), whose exploits during the War of 1812 (1812–15) earned him a place in American naval history.
2 Steam-powered warships with metal-plated hulls were introduced in the 1850s, ushering in an era of mechanized naval warfare and quickly making wooden-hulled ships obsolete. Melville's 1866 poem "A Utilitarian View of the Monitor's Fight" is an account of the first encounter between two "ironclads" at the Battle of Hampton Roads (Virginia) in 1862.

savored of foolhardiness and vanity.[1] They may add, too, that at Trafalgar it was in effect nothing less than a challenge to death; and death came; and that but for his bravado the victorious admiral might possibly have survived the battle, and so, instead of having his sagacious dying injunctions overruled by his immediate successor in command, he himself when the contest was decided might have brought his shattered fleet to anchor, a proceeding which might have averted the deplorable loss of life by shipwreck in the elemental tempest that followed the martial one.

Well, should we set aside the more than disputable point whether for various reasons it was possible to anchor the fleet, then plausibly enough the Benthamites of war may urge the above. But the *might-have-been* is but boggy ground to build on. And, certainly, in foresight as to the larger issue of an encounter, and anxious preparations for it—buoying the deadly way and mapping it out, as at Copenhagen[2]—few commanders have been so painstakingly circumspect as this same reckless declarer of his person in fight.

Personal prudence, even when dictated by quite other than selfish considerations, surely is no special virtue in a military man; while an excessive love of glory, impassioning a less burning impulse, the honest sense of duty, is the first. If the name *Wellington* is not so much of a trumpet to the blood as the simpler name *Nelson*, the reason for this may perhaps be inferred from the above. Alfred in his funeral ode on the victor of Waterloo ventures not to call him the greatest soldier of all time, though in the same ode he invokes Nelson as "the greatest sailor since our world began."[3]

---

1 Here and in ensuing paragraphs, a reference to the debate over whether Nelson ought to have exposed himself unnecessarily to risk ("ornate publication of his person") by standing in the open on the deck of his ship at the Battle of Trafalgar; the decision cost him his life and cost England its greatest naval commander. The narrator seems to approve of Nelson's decision, even if practical-minded observers, whom below he associates with the utilitarianism of Jeremy Bentham (1748–1832), would not.

2 Reference to Nelson's painstaking nautical reconnaissance of the waters around Copenhagen in preparation for the British attack on the Danish navy in 1801, an episode in the larger campaign against Revolutionary France and one of Nelson's most famous, if controversial, victories.

3 From Alfred, Lord Tennyson (1809–92), "Ode on the Death of the Duke of Wellington"; in the course of praising the general who defeated Napoleon at Waterloo in 1815, Tennyson praises Nelson as well, though apparently not enough for the narrator's taste.

At Trafalgar Nelson on the brink of opening the fight sat down and wrote his last brief will and testament. If under the presentiment of the most magnificent of all victories to be crowned by his own glorious death, a sort of priestly motive led him to dress his person in the jewelled vouchers of his own shining deeds; if thus to have adorned himself for the altar and the sacrifice were indeed vainglory, then affectation and fustian[1] is each more heroic line in the great epics and dramas, since in such lines the poet but embodies in verse those exaltations of sentiment that a nature like Nelson, the opportunity being given, vitalizes into acts.

5

Yes, the outbreak at the Nore was put down. But not every grievance was redressed. If the contractors, for example, were no longer permitted to ply some practices peculiar to their tribe everywhere, such as providing shoddy cloth, rations not sound, or false in the measure; not the less impressment, for one thing, went on. By custom sanctioned for centuries, and judicially maintained by a Lord Chancellor as late as Mansfield,[2] that mode of manning the fleet, a mode now fallen into a sort of abeyance but never formally renounced, it was not practicable to give up in those years. Its abrogation would have crippled the indispensable fleet, one wholly under canvas, no steam power, its innumerable sails and thousands of cannon, everything in short, worked by muscle alone; a fleet the more insatiate in demand for men, because then multiplying its ships of all grades against contingencies present and to come of the convulsed Continent.[3]

Discontent foreran the Two Mutinies, and more or less it lurkingly survived them. Hence it was not unreasonable to apprehend some return of trouble sporadic or general. One instance of such apprehensions: In the same year with this story, Nelson, then Rear Admiral Sir Horatio, being with the fleet off the Spanish coast, was directed by the admiral in command to shift his

---

1 Grandiloquent, affected language.
2 William Murray (1705–93), 1st Earl of Mansfield, one of the most powerful and reform-minded jurists in eighteenth-century Britain.
3 Reference to the French Revolutionary Wars and the Napoleonic Wars, conflicts that spanned, temporally, the late eighteenth and early nineteenth centuries and, geographically, practically the whole of Europe.

pennant from the *Captain* to the *Theseus*; and for this reason: that the latter ship having newly arrived on the station from home, where it had taken part in the Great Mutiny, danger was apprehended from the temper of the men; and it was thought that an officer like Nelson was the one, not indeed to terrorize the crew into base subjection, but to win them, by force of his mere presence and heroic personality, back to an allegiance if not as enthusiastic as his own yet as true.

So it was that for a time, on more than one quarter-deck, anxiety did exist. At sea, precautionary vigilance was strained against relapse. At short notice an engagement might come on. When it did, the lieutenants assigned to batteries felt it incumbent on them, in some instances, to stand with drawn swords behind the men working the guns.

6

But on board the seventy-four in which Billy now swung his hammock, very little in the manner of the men and nothing obvious in the demeanor of the officers would have suggested to an ordinary observer that the Great Mutiny was a recent event. In their general bearing and conduct the commissioned officers of a warship naturally take their tone from the commander, that is if he have that ascendancy of character that ought to be his.

Captain the Honorable Edward Fairfax Vere, to give his full title, was a bachelor of forty or thereabouts, a sailor of distinction even in a time prolific of renowned seamen. Though allied to the higher nobility, his advancement had not been altogether owing to influences connected with that circumstance. He had seen much service, been in various engagements, always acquitting himself as an officer mindful of the welfare of his men, but never tolerating an infraction of discipline; thoroughly versed in the science of his profession, and intrepid to the verge of temerity, though never injudiciously so. For his gallantry in the West Indian waters as flag lieutenant under Rodney in that admiral's crowning victory over De Grasse, he was made a post captain.[1]

Ashore, in the garb of a civilian, scarce anyone would have taken him for a sailor, more especially that he never garnished unprofes-

---

1   Reference to George Brydges Rodney's (1718–92) victory over French commander François Joseph Paul de Grasse (1722–88) at the Battle of the Saintes in the West Indies in 1782.

sional talk with nautical terms, and grave in his bearing, evinced little appreciation of mere humor. It was not out of keeping with these traits that on a passage when nothing demanded his paramount action, he was the most undemonstrative of men. Any landsman observing this gentleman not conspicuous by his stature and wearing no pronounced insignia, emerging from his cabin to the open deck, and noting the silent deference of the officers retiring to leeward, might have taken him for the King's guest, a civilian aboard the King's ship, some highly honorable discreet envoy on his way to an important post. But in fact this unobtrusiveness of demeanor may have proceeded from a certain unaffected modesty of manhood sometimes accompanying a resolute nature, a modesty evinced at all times not calling for pronounced action, which shown in any rank of life suggests a virtue aristocratic in kind. As with some others engaged in various departments of the world's more heroic activities, Captain Vere though practical enough upon occasion would at times betray a certain dreaminess of mood. Standing alone on the weather side of the quarter-deck, one hand holding by the rigging, he would absently gaze off at the blank sea. At the presentation to him then of some minor matter interrupting the current of his thoughts, he would show more or less irascibility; but instantly he would control it.

In the navy he was popularly known by the appellation "Starry Vere." How such a designation happened to fall upon one who whatever his sterling qualities was without any brilliant ones, was in this wise: A favorite kinsman, Lord Denton, a freehearted fellow, had been the first to meet and congratulate him upon his return to England from his West Indian cruise; and but the day previous turning over a copy of Andrew Marvell's poems had lighted, not for the first time, however, upon the lines entitled "Appleton House," the name of one of the seats of their common ancestor, a hero in the German wars of the seventeenth century, in which poem occur the lines:

This 'tis to have been from the first
In a domestic heaven nursed,
Under the discipline severe
Of Fairfax and the starry Vere.[1]

---

1   Lines from "Upon Appleton House" by Andrew Marvell (1621–78), published posthumously in 1681 and likely written in the early 1650s when Marvell tutored the daughter of Thomas and Anne Vere Fairfax, to whom "starry Vere" refers.

And so, upon embracing his cousin fresh from Rodney's great victory wherein he had played so gallant a part, brimming over with just family pride in the sailor of their house, he exuberantly exclaimed, "Give ye joy, Ed; give ye joy, my starry Vere!" This got currency, and the novel prefix serving in familiar parlance readily to distinguish the *Bellipotent*'s captain from another Vere his senior, a distant relative, an officer of like rank in the navy, it remained permanently attached to the surname.

7

In view of the part that the commander of the *Bellipotent* plays in scenes shortly to follow, it may be well to fill out that sketch of him outlined in the previous chapter.

Aside from his qualities as a sea officer Captain Vere was an exceptional character. Unlike no few of England's renowned sailors, long and arduous service with signal devotion to it had not resulted in absorbing and *salting* the entire man. He had a marked leaning toward everything intellectual. He loved books, never going to sea without a newly replenished library, compact but of the best. The isolated leisure, in some cases so wearisome, falling at intervals to commanders even during a war cruise, never was tedious to Captain Vere. With nothing of that literary taste which less heeds the thing conveyed than the vehicle, his bias was toward those books to which every serious mind of superior order occupying any active post of authority in the world naturally inclines: books treating of actual men and events no matter of what era—history, biography, and unconventional writers like Montaigne, who, free from cant and convention, honestly and in the spirit of common sense philosophize upon realities.[1] In this line of reading he found confirmation of his own more reserved thoughts—confirmation which he had vainly sought in social converse, so that as touching most fundamental topics, there had got to be established in him some positive convictions which he forefelt would abide in him essentially unmodified so long as his intelligent part remained unimpaired. In view of the troubled period in which his lot was cast, this was well for him. His settled

1   Michel de Montaigne (1533–92), widely read French essayist; "Of Vanity" (1580) asks, in a line that would resonate with Vere, "What is the use of these lofty points of philosophy on which no human being can settle, and these rules that exceed our use and strength?" (756).

convictions were as a dike against those invading waters of novel opinion social, political, and otherwise, which carried away as in a torrent no few minds in those days, minds by nature not inferior to his own. While other members of that aristocracy to which by birth he belonged were incensed at the innovators mainly because their theories were inimical to the privileged classes, Captain Vere disinterestedly opposed them not alone because they seemed to him insusceptible of embodiment in lasting institutions, but at war with the peace of the world and the true welfare of mankind.[1]

With minds less stored than his and less earnest, some officers of his rank, with whom at times he would necessarily consort, found him lacking in the companionable quality, a dry and bookish gentleman, as they deemed. Upon any chance withdrawal from their company one would be apt to say to another something like this: "Vere is a noble fellow, Starry Vere. 'Spite the gazettes, Sir Horatio" (meaning him who became Lord Nelson) "is at bottom scarce a better seaman or fighter. But between you and me now, don't you think there is a queer streak of the pedantic running through him? Yes, like the King's yarn in a coil of navy rope?"

Some apparent ground there was for this sort of confidential criticism; since not only did the captain's discourse never fall into the jocosely familiar, but in illustrating of any point touching the stirring personages and events of the time he would be as apt to cite some historic character or incident of antiquity as he would be to cite from the moderns. He seemed unmindful of the circumstance that to his bluff company such remote allusions, however pertinent they might really be, were altogether alien to men whose reading was mainly confined to the journals. But considerateness in such matters is not easy to natures constituted like Captain Vere's. Their honesty prescribes to them directness, sometimes far-reaching like that of a migratory fowl that in its flight never heeds when it crosses a frontier.

8

The lieutenants and other commissioned gentlemen forming Captain Vere's staff it is not necessary here to particularize, nor needs it to make any mention of any of the warrant officers. But

---

1   For historical analogs for Vere's conservatism and arguments against it, see, generally, Appendices A, B, and C.

among the petty officers was one who, having much to do with the story, may as well be forthwith introduced. His portrait I essay, but shall never hit it. This was John Claggart, the master-at-arms.[1] But that sea title may to landsmen seem somewhat equivocal. Originally, doubtless, that petty officer's function was the instruction of the men in the use of arms, sword or cutlass. But very long ago, owing to the advance in gunnery making hand-to-hand encounters less frequent and giving to niter and sulphur the pre-eminence over steel, that function ceased; the master-at-arms of a great warship becoming a sort of chief of police charged among other matters with the duty of preserving order on the populous lower gun decks.

Claggart was a man about five-and-thirty, somewhat spare and tall, yet of no ill figure upon the whole. His hand was too small and shapely to have been accustomed to hard toil. The face was a notable one, the features all except the chin cleanly cut as those on a Greek medallion; yet the chin, beardless as Tecumseh's,[2] had something of strange protuberant broadness in its make that recalled the prints of the Reverend Dr. Titus Oates, the historic deponent with the clerical drawl in the time of Charles II and the fraud of the alleged Popish Plot.[3] It served Claggart in his office that his eye could cast a tutoring glance. His brow was of the sort phrenologically[4] associated with more than average intellect; silken jet curls partly clustering over it, making a foil to the pallor below, a pallor tinged with a faint shade of amber akin to the hue of time-tinted marbles of old. This complexion, singularly contrasting with the red or deeply bronzed visages of the sailors, and in part the result of his official seclusion from the sunlight, though it was not exactly displeasing, nevertheless seemed to hint of something defective or abnormal in the constitution and blood. But his general aspect and manner were so suggestive of

---

1 Chief security officer.
2 Tecumseh (1768–1813), the renowned Shawnee chief who dreamed of a confederated Native American nation, fought with the British against the United States during the War of 1812, in which he was killed.
3 Fabricated 1678 Jesuit plot to terrorize London and assassinate King Charles II (r. 1660–85) in favour of a Roman Catholic monarch. Titus Oates (1649–1705), Anglican priest who spread rumours of the plot, was initially hailed as hero before being exposed as fraud. In the ensuing panic, 35 people were executed, a historical illustration of the consequences of political paranoia.
4 The pseudo-science of phrenology claimed to account for and predict character based on the shape of the skull.

an education and career incongruous with his naval function that when not actively engaged in it he looked like a man of high quality, social and moral, who for reasons of his own was keeping incog. Nothing was known of his former life. It might be that he was an Englishman; and yet there lurked a bit of accent in his speech suggesting that possibly he was not such by birth, but through naturalization in early childhood. Among certain grizzled sea gossips of the gun decks and forecastle went a rumor perdue that the master-at-arms was a *chevalier* [1] who had volunteered into the King's navy by way of compounding for some mysterious swindle whereof he had been arraigned at the King's Bench. The fact that nobody could substantiate this report was, of course, nothing against its secret currency. Such a rumor once started on the gun decks in reference to almost anyone below the rank of a commissioned officer would, during the period assigned to this narrative, have seemed not altogether wanting in credibility to the tarry old wiseacres of a man-of-war crew. And indeed a man of Claggart's accomplishments, without prior nautical experience entering the navy at mature life, as he did, and necessarily allotted at the start to the lowest grade in it; a man too who never made allusion to his previous life ashore; these were circumstances which in the dearth of exact knowledge as to his true antecedents opened to the invidious a vague field for unfavorable surmise.

But the sailors' dogwatch gossip concerning him derived a vague plausibility from the fact that now for some period the British navy could so little afford to be squeamish in the matter of keeping up the muster rolls, that not only were press gangs notoriously abroad both afloat and ashore, but there was little or no secret about another matter, namely, that the London police were at liberty to capture any able-bodied suspect, any questionable fellow at large, and summarily ship him to the dockyard or fleet. Furthermore, even among voluntary enlistments there were instances where the motive thereto partook neither of patriotic impulse nor yet of a random desire to experience a bit of sea life and martial adventure. Insolvent debtors of minor grade, together with the promiscuous lame ducks of morality, found in the navy a convenient and secure refuge, secure because, once enlisted aboard a King's ship, they were as much in sanctuary as

---

1 A soldier on horseback, or knight; also a reference to an order of French knighthood. According to Hayford and Sealts, Melville may also have in mind a confidence man (155).

the transgressor of the Middle Ages harboring himself under the shadow of the altar. Such sanctioned irregularities, which for obvious reasons the government would hardly think to parade at the time and which consequently, and as affecting the least influential class of mankind, have all but dropped into oblivion, lend color to something for the truth whereof I do not vouch, and hence have some scruple in stating; something I remember having seen in print though the book I cannot recall; but the same thing was personally communicated to me now more than forty years ago by an old pensioner in a cocked hat with whom I had a most interesting talk on the terrace at Greenwich, a Baltimore Negro, a Trafalgar man.[1] It was to this effect: In the case of a warship short of hands whose speedy sailing was imperative, the deficient quota, in lack of any other way of making it good, would be eked out by drafts culled direct from the jails. For reasons previously suggested it would not perhaps be easy at the present day directly to prove or disprove the allegation. But allowed as a verity, how significant would it be of England's straits at the time confronted by those wars which like a flight of harpies rose shrieking from the din and dust of the fallen Bastille.[2] That era appears measurably clear to us who look back at it, and but read of it. But to the grandfathers of us graybeards, the more thoughtful of them, the genius of it presented an aspect like that of Camoëns' Spirit of the Cape,[3] an eclipsing menace mysterious and prodigious. Not America was exempt from apprehension. At the height of Napoleon's unexampled conquests, there were Americans who had fought at Bunker Hill who looked forward to the possibility that the Atlantic might prove no barrier against the ultimate schemes of this French portentous upstart from the revolutionary chaos who seemed in act of fulfilling judgment prefigured in the Apocalypse.

But the less credence was to be given to the gun-deck talk touching Claggart, seeing that no man holding his office in a man-of-war can ever hope to be popular with the crew. Besides,

---

1 A flattering naval sobriquet indicating that a sailor participated in the Battle of Trafalgar, the site of Nelson's greatest triumph and death.
2 Paris fortress and prison, the storming of which on 14 July 1789, in the early stages of the French Revolution, became a symbol of resistance to monarchical tyranny.
3 In the Portuguese epic *The Lusiads* (1572), by Luís de Camoëns (c. 1525–80), Adamastor, the Spirit of the Cape, lords over the Indian Ocean in the form of a storm cloud, menacing seafarers.

in derogatory comments upon anyone against whom they have a grudge, or for any reason or no reason mislike, sailors are much like landsmen: they are apt to exaggerate or romance it.

About as much was really known to the *Bellipotent*'s tars of the master-at-arms' career before entering the service as an astronomer knows about a comet's travels prior to its first observable appearance in the sky. The verdict of the sea quidnuncs[1] has been cited only by way of showing what sort of moral impression the man made upon rude uncultivated natures whose conceptions of human wickedness were necessarily of the narrowest, limited to ideas of vulgar rascality—a thief among the swinging hammocks during a night watch, or the man-brokers and land-sharks of the seaports.

It was no gossip, however, but fact that though, as before hinted, Claggart upon his entrance into the navy was, as a novice, assigned to the least honorable section of a man-of-war's crew, embracing the drudgery, he did not long remain there. The superior capacity he immediately evinced, his constitutional sobriety, an ingratiating deference to superiors, together with a peculiar ferreting genius manifested on a singular occasion; all this, capped by a certain austere patriotism, abruptly advanced him to the position of master-at-arms.

Of this maritime chief of police the ship's corporals, so called, were the immediate subordinates, and compliant ones; and this, as is to be noted in some business departments ashore, almost to a degree inconsistent with entire moral volition. His place put various converging wires of underground influence under the chief's control, capable when astutely worked through his understrappers of operating to the mysterious discomfort, if nothing worse, of any of the sea commonalty.

9

Life in the foretop well agreed with Billy Budd. There, when not actually engaged on the yards yet higher aloft, the topmen, who as such had been picked out for youth and activity, constituted an aerial club lounging at ease against the smaller stun'sails rolled up into cushions, spinning yarns like the lazy gods, and frequently amused with what was going on in the busy world of the decks below. No wonder then that a young fellow of Billy's dis-

---

1 Gossips (Latin).

position was well content in such society. Giving no cause of offense to anybody, he was always alert at a call. So in the merchant service it had been with him. But now such a punctiliousness in duty was shown that his topmates would sometimes good-naturedly laugh at him for it. This heightened alacrity had its cause, namely, the impression made upon him by the first formal gangway-punishment he had ever witnessed, which befell the day following his impressment. It had been incurred by a little fellow, young, a novice afterguardsman absent from his assigned post when the ship was being put about; a dereliction resulting in a rather serious hitch to that maneuver, one demanding instantaneous promptitude in letting go and making fast. When Billy saw the culprit's naked back under the scourge, gridironed with red welts and worse, when he marked the dire expression in the liberated man's face as with his woolen shirt flung over him by the executioner he rushed forward from the spot to bury himself in the crowd, Billy was horrified. He resolved that never through remissness would he make himself liable to such a visitation or do or omit aught that might merit even verbal reproof.[1] What then was his surprise and concern when ultimately he found himself getting into petty trouble occasionally about such matters as the stowage of his bag or something amiss in his hammock, matters under the police oversight of the ship's corporals of the lower decks, and which brought down on him a vague threat from one of them.

So heedful in all things as he was, how could this be? He could not understand it, and it more than vexed him. When he spoke to his young topmates about it they were either lightly incredulous or found something comical in his unconcealed anxiety. "Is it your bag, Billy?" said one. "Well, sew yourself up in it, bully boy, and then you'll be sure to know if anybody meddles with it."

Now there was a veteran aboard who because his years began to disqualify him for more active work had been recently assigned duty as mainmastman in his watch, looking to the gear belayed at the rail roundabout that great spar near the deck. At off-times the

---

1 Billy's terror at witnessing a flogging is often taken to indicate Melville's scepticism of corporal punishment as an effective deterrent or punishment for misbehaviour, an argument substantiated by the vitriol with which he treats the subject in *White-Jacket*. At the same time, however, in "Bridegroom Dick" (1888) and even in *White-Jacket* itself, Melville acknowledges the necessity of corporal punishment within reason. See Appendix D.

foretopman had picked up some acquaintance with him, and now in his trouble it occurred to him that he might be the sort of person to go to for wise counsel. He was an old Dansker[1] long anglicized in the service, of few words, many wrinkles, and some honorable scars. His wizened face, time-tinted and weather-stained to the complexion of an antique parchment, was here and there peppered blue by the chance explosion of a gun cartridge in action.

He was an *Agamemnon* man, some two years prior to the time of this story having served under Nelson when still captain in that ship immortal in naval memory, which dismantled and in part broken up to her bare ribs is seen a grand skeleton in Haden's etching.[2] As one of a boarding party from the *Agamemnon* he had received a cut slantwise along one temple and cheek leaving a long pale scar like a streak of dawn's light falling athwart the dark visage. It was on account of that scar and the affair in which it was known that he had received it, as well as from his blue-peppered complexion, that the Dansker went among the *Bellipotent*'s crew by the name of "Board-Her-in-the-Smoke."

Now the first time that his small weasel eyes happened to light on Billy Budd, a certain grim internal merriment set all his ancient wrinkles into antic play. Was it that his eccentric unsentimental old sapience, primitive in its kind, saw or thought it saw something which in contrast with the warship's environment looked oddly incongruous in the Handsome Sailor? But after slyly studying him at intervals, the old Merlin's[3] equivocal merriment was modified; for now when the twain would meet, it would start in his face a quizzing sort of look, but it would be but momentary and sometimes replaced by an expression of speculative query as to what might eventually befall a nature like that, dropped into a world not without some mantraps and against whose subtleties simple courage lacking experience and address, and without any touch of defensive ugliness, is of little avail; and where such innocence as man is capable of does yet in a moral emergency not always sharpen the faculties or enlighten the will.

---

1 Dane.

2 *Breaking Up of the Agamemnon* (1870), etching by British artist Sir Francis Seymour Haden (1818–1910). The *Agamemnon* was a Royal Navy ship launched in 1781.

3 Merlin, in Arthurian legend, is the powerful political savant, magician, and seer who counselled Arthur and the Knights of the Round Table.

However it was, the Dansker in his ascetic way rather took to Billy. Nor was this only because of a certain philosophic interest in such a character. There was another cause. While the old man's eccentricities, sometimes bordering on the ursine, repelled the juniors, Billy, undeterred thereby, revering him as a salt hero, would make advances, never passing the old *Agamemnon* man without a salutation marked by that respect which is seldom lost on the aged, however crabbed at times or whatever their station in life.

There was a vein of dry humor, or what not, in the mast-man; and, whether in freak of patriarchal irony touching Billy's youth and athletic frame, or for some other and more recondite reason, from the first in addressing him he always substituted *Baby* for Billy, the Dansker in fact being the originator of the name by which the foretopman eventually became known aboard ship.

Well then, in his mysterious little difficulty going in quest of the wrinkled one, Billy found him off duty in a dogwatch ruminating by himself, seated on a shot box of the upper gun deck, now and then surveying with a somewhat cynical regard certain of the more swaggering promenaders there. Billy recounted his trouble, again wondering how it all happened. The salt seer attentively listened, accompanying the foretopman's recital with queer twitchings of his wrinkles and problematical little sparkles of his small ferret eyes. Making an end of his story, the foretopman asked, "And now, Dansker, do tell me what you think of it."

The old man, shoving up the front of his tarpaulin and deliberately rubbing the long slant scar at the point where it entered the thin hair, laconically said, "Baby Budd, *Jemmy Legs*" (meaning the master-at-arms)[1] "is down on you."

"*Jemmy Legs!*" ejaculated Billy, his welkin eyes expanding. "What for? Why, he calls me 'the sweet and pleasant young fellow,' they tell me."

"Does he so?" grinned the grizzled one; then said, "Ay, Baby lad, a sweet voice has Jemmy Legs."

"No, not always. But to me he has. I seldom pass him but there comes a pleasant word."

"And that's because he's down upon you, Baby Budd."

Such reiteration, along with the manner of it, incomprehensible to a novice, disturbed Billy almost as much as the mystery for which he had sought explanation. Something less unpleasingly

---

1 Jemmy Legs is a slang expression for a ship's master-at-arms.

oracular he tried to extract; but the old sea Chiron,[1] thinking perhaps that for the nonce he had sufficiently instructed his young Achilles,[2] pursed his lips, gathered all his wrinkles together, and would commit himself to nothing further.

Years, and those experiences which befall certain shrewder men subordinated lifelong to the will of superiors, all this had developed in the Dansker the pithy guarded cynicism that was his leading characteristic.

10

The next day an incident served to confirm Billy Budd in his incredulity as to the Dansker's strange summing up of the case submitted. The ship at noon, going large before the wind, was rolling on her course, and he below at dinner and engaged in some sportful talk with the members of his mess, chanced in a sudden lurch to spill the entire contents of his soup pan upon the new-scrubbed deck. Claggart, the master-at-arms, official rattan in hand, happened to be passing along the battery in a bay of which the mess was lodged, and the greasy liquid streamed just across his path. Stepping over it, he was proceeding on his way without comment, since the matter was nothing to take notice of under the circumstances, when he happened to observe who it was that had done the spilling. His countenance changed. Pausing, he was about to ejaculate something hasty at the sailor, but checked himself, and pointing down to the streaming soup, playfully tapped him from behind with his rattan, saying in a low musical voice peculiar to him at times, "Handsomely done, my lad! And handsome is as handsome did it, too!" And with that passed on. Not noted by Billy as not coming within his view was the involuntary smile, or rather grimace, that accompanied Claggart's equivocal words. Aridly it drew down the thin corners of his shapely mouth. But everybody taking his remark as meant for humorous, and at which therefore as coming from a superior they were bound to laugh "with counterfeited glee," acted accord-

---

1 Chiron, in Greek mythology, was a centaur renowned for wisdom, and the grandfather and tutor of Achilles.
2 Greek mythological hero whose mother had dipped him (when a baby) into the river Styx, making him invulnerable to injury except at the heel by which she had held him; hence the term "Achilles heel," which suggests Billy's single weakness: his stutter.

ingly; and Billy, tickled, it may be, by the allusion to his being the Handsome Sailor, merrily joined in; then addressing his messmates exclaimed, "There now, who says that Jemmy Legs is down on me!"

"And who said he was, Beauty?" demanded one Donald with some surprise. Whereat the foretopman looked a little foolish, recalling that it was only one person, Board-Her-in-the-Smoke, who had suggested what to him was the smoky idea that this master-at-arms was in any peculiar way hostile to him. Meantime that functionary, resuming his path, must have momentarily worn some expression less guarded than that of the bitter smile, usurping the face from the heart—some distorting expression perhaps, for a drummer-boy heedlessly frolicking along from the opposite direction and chancing to come into light collision with his person was strangely disconcerted by his aspect. Nor was the impression lessened when the official, impetuously giving him a sharp cut with the rattan, vehemently exclaimed, "Look where you go!"

11

What was the matter with the master-at-arms? And, be the matter what it might, how could it have direct relation to Billy Budd, with whom prior to the affair of the spilled soup he had never come into any special contact official or otherwise? What indeed could the trouble have to do with one so little inclined to give offense as the merchant-ship's "peacemaker," even him who in Claggart's own phrase was "the sweet and pleasant young fellow"? Yes, why should Jemmy Legs, to borrow the Dansker's expression, be "down" on the Handsome Sailor? But, at heart and not for nothing, as the late chance encounter may indicate to the discerning, down on him, secretly down on him, he assuredly was.

Now to invent something touching the more private career of Claggart, something involving Billy Budd, of which something the latter should be wholly ignorant, some romantic incident implying that Claggart's knowledge of the young bluejacket began at some period anterior to catching sight of him on board the seventy-four—all this, not so difficult to do, might avail in a way more or less interesting to account for whatever of enigma may appear to lurk in the case. But in fact there was nothing of the sort. And yet the cause necessarily to be assumed as the sole one assignable is in its very realism as much charged with that prime element of Radcliffian romance, the mysterious, as any that the ingenuity of the author of *The Mysteries of Udolpho*[1] could devise. For what can more partake of the mysterious than an antipathy spontaneous and profound such as is evoked in certain exceptional mortals by the mere aspect of some other mortal, however harmless he may be, if not called forth by this very harmlessness itself?

Now there can exist no irritating juxtaposition of dissimilar personalities comparable to that which is possible aboard a great warship fully manned and at sea. There, every day among all ranks, almost every man comes into more or less of contact with almost every other man. Wholly there to avoid even the sight of an aggravating object one must needs give it Jonah's toss[2] or jump overboard himself. Imagine how all this might eventually operate on some peculiar human creature the direct reverse of a saint!

But for the adequate comprehending of Claggart by a normal nature these hints are insufficient. To pass from a normal nature to him one must cross "the deadly space between."[3] And this is best done by indirection.

Long ago an honest scholar, my senior,[4] said to me in reference to one who like himself is now no more, a man so unimpeachably respectable that against him nothing was ever openly said though among the few something was whispered, "Yes, X——— is a nut not to be cracked by the tap of a lady's fan. You are aware that I am the adherent of no organized religion, much less of any philosophy built into a system. Well, for all that, I think that to try and get into X———, enter his labyrinth and get out again, without a clue derived from some source other than what is known as 'knowledge of the world'—that were hardly possible, at least for me."

"Why," said I, "X———, however singular a study to some, is yet human, and knowledge of the world assuredly implies the knowledge of human nature, and in most of its varieties."

"Yes, but a superficial knowledge of it, serving ordinary purposes. But for anything deeper, I am not certain whether to know

---

1   1794 gothic novel by British writer Ann Radcliffe (1764–1823).
2   Jonah, trying to hide from God's wrath onboard a ship, is thrown overboard by fellow sailors. See Jonah 1:10–15.
3   Unknown allusion, if one at all.
4   Another of the narrator's invented acquaintances.

the world and to know human nature be not two distinct branches of knowledge, which while they may coexist in the same heart, yet either may exist with little or nothing of the other. Nay, in an average man of the world, his constant rubbing with it blunts that finer spiritual insight indispensable to the understanding of the essential in certain exceptional characters, whether evil ones or good. In a matter of some importance I have seen a girl wind an old lawyer about her little finger. Nor was it the dotage of senile love. Nothing of the sort. But he knew law better than he knew the girl's heart. Coke and Blackstone[1] hardly shed so much light into obscure spiritual places as the Hebrew prophets. And who were they? Mostly recluses."

At the time, my inexperience was such that I did not quite see the drift of all this. It may be that I see it now. And, indeed, if that lexicon which is based on Holy Writ[2] were any longer popular, one might with less difficulty define and denominate certain phenomenal men. As it is, one must turn to some authority not liable to the charge of being tinctured with the biblical element.

In a list of definitions included in the authentic translation of Plato, a list attributed to him, occurs this: "Natural Depravity: a depravity according to nature,"[3] a definition which, though savoring of Calvinism,[4] by no means involves Calvin's dogma as to total mankind. Evidently its intent makes it applicable but to individuals. Not many are the examples of this depravity which the gallows and jail supply. At any rate, for notable instances, since these have no vulgar alloy of the brute in them, but invariably are dominated by intellectuality, one must go elsewhere. Civilization, especially if of the austerer sort, is auspicious to it. It folds itself in the mantle of respectability. It has its certain negative virtues serving as silent auxiliaries. It never allows wine to get

---

1 Sir Edward Coke (1552–1634) and Sir William Blackstone (1723–80), English jurists whose work writing and interpreting English law, respectively, is inordinately influential.

2 Biblical law.

3 According to Hayford and Sealts, Melville drew this quotation from his edition of Plato's works (Bohn, 1848–54), in which the phrase is defined as "a badness by nature, and a sinning in that, which is according to nature" (162).

4 Protestant faith associated with the theology of John Calvin (1509–64), which stressed, most relevantly here, the idea of total depravity: that human beings are inherently, and powerless to be anything but, sinners, thus necessitating God's mercy.

within its guard. It is not going too far to say that it is without vices or small sins. There is a phenomenal pride in it that excludes them. It is never mercenary or avaricious. In short, the depravity here meant partakes nothing of the sordid or sensual. It is serious, but free from acerbity. Though no flatterer of mankind it never speaks ill of it.

But the thing which in eminent instances signalizes so exceptional a nature is this: Though the man's even temper and discreet bearing would seem to intimate a mind peculiarly subject to the law of reason, not the less in heart he would seem to riot in complete exemption from that law, having apparently little to do with reason further than to employ it as an ambidexter implement for effecting the irrational. That is to say: Toward the accomplishment of an aim which in wantonness of atrocity would seem to partake of the insane, he will direct a cool judgment sagacious and sound. These men are madmen, and of the most dangerous sort, for their lunacy is not continuous, but occasional, evoked by some special object; it is protectively secretive, which is as much as to say it is self-contained, so that when, moreover, most active it is to the average mind not distinguishable from sanity, and for the reason above suggested: that whatever its aims may be—and the aim is never declared—the method and the outward proceeding are always perfectly rational.

Now something such an one was Claggart, in whom was the mania of an evil nature, not engendered by vicious training or corrupting books or licentious living, but born with him and innate, in short "a depravity according to nature."

Dark sayings are these, some will say. But why? Is it because they somewhat savor of Holy Writ in its phrase "mystery of iniquity"?[1] If they do, such savor was far enough from being intended, for little will it commend these pages to many a reader of today.

The point of the present story turning on the hidden nature of the master-at-arms has necessitated this chapter. With an added hint or two in connection with the incident at the mess, the resumed narrative must be left to vindicate, as it may, its own credibility.

---

1 2 Thessalonians 2:7: "For the mystery of iniquity doth already work: only he who now letteth will let, until he be taken out of the way." Here, "mystery" refers to knowledge that can come only from God, i.e., knowledge beyond human reason.

12

That Claggart's figure was not amiss, and his face, save the chin, well molded, has already been said. Of these favorable points he seemed not insensible, for he was not only neat but careful in his dress. But the form of Billy Budd was heroic; and if his face was without the intellectual look of the pallid Claggart's, not the less was it lit, like his, from within, though from a different source. The bonfire in his heart made luminous the rose-tan in his cheek.

In view of the marked contrast between the persons of the twain, it is more than probable that when the master-at-arms in the scene last given applied to the sailor the proverb "Handsome is as handsome does," he there let escape an ironic inkling, not caught by the young sailors who heard it, as to what it was that had first moved him against Billy, namely, his significant personal beauty.

Now envy and antipathy,[1] passions irreconcilable in reason, nevertheless in fact may spring conjoined like Chang and Eng[2] in one birth. Is Envy then such a monster? Well, though many an arraigned mortal has in hopes of mitigated penalty pleaded guilty to horrible actions, did ever anybody seriously confess to envy? Something there is in it universally felt to be more shameful than even felonious crime. And not only does everybody disown it, but the better sort are inclined to incredulity when it is in earnest imputed to an intelligent man. But since its lodgment is in the heart not the brain, no degree of intellect supplies a guarantee against it. But Claggart's was no vulgar form of the passion. Nor, as directed toward Billy Budd, did it partake of that streak of apprehensive jealousy that marred Saul's visage perturbedly brooding on the comely young David.[3] Claggart's envy struck

---

1 Multiple commentators observe Melville's engagement here with both Satan in John Milton's *Paradise Lost* (1667) and Iago in William Shakespeare's *Othello* (1603–04). Hayford and Sealts note that at one point the manuscript title for this chapter was "Pale ire, envy and despair," a direct reference to Milton's Satan (IV.114–17) (165).

2 Thai-American conjoined male twins (1811–74) who gave birth to the term "Siamese twins."

3 David (c. 1040–970 BCE), second king of Israel, following Saul; reputedly deranged and jealous of David's beauty and military prowess—e.g., his defeat of Goliath—Saul tried multiple times to have him murdered. Also perhaps a reference to Italian artist Michelangelo's (1475–1564) statue *David* (1501–04), which emphasizes David's strength and beauty, consistent with Greek ideals of masculinity.

deeper. If askance he eyed the good looks, cheery health, and frank enjoyment of young life in Billy Budd, it was because these went along with a nature that, as Claggart magnetically felt, had in its simplicity never willed malice or experienced the reactionary bite of that serpent. To him, the spirit lodged within Billy, and looking out from his welkin eyes as from windows, that ineffability it was which made the dimple in his dyed cheek, suppled his joints, and dancing in his yellow curls made him pre-eminently the Handsome Sailor. One person excepted, the master-at-arms was perhaps the only man in the ship intellectually capable of adequately appreciating the moral phenomenon presented in Billy Budd. And the insight but intensified his passion, which assuming various secret forms within him, at times assumed that of cynic disdain, disdain of innocence—to be nothing more than innocent! Yet in an aesthetic way he saw the charm of it, the courageous free-and-easy temper of it, and fain would have shared it, but he despaired of it.

With no power to annul the elemental evil in him, though readily enough he could hide it; apprehending the good, but powerless to be it; a nature like Claggart's, surcharged with energy as such natures almost invariably are, what recourse is left to it but to recoil upon itself and, like the scorpion for which the Creator alone is responsible, act out to the end the part allotted it.

13

Passion, and passion in its profoundest, is not a thing demanding a palatial stage whereon to play its part. Down among the groundlings, among the beggars and rakers of the garbage, profound passion is enacted. And the circumstances that provoke it, however trivial or mean, are no measure of its power. In the present instance the stage is a scrubbed gun deck, and one of the external provocations a man-of-war's man's spilled soup.

Now when the master-at-arms noticed whence came that greasy fluid streaming before his feet, he must have taken it—to some extent wilfully, perhaps—not for the mere accident it assuredly was, but for the sly escape of a spontaneous feeling on Billy's part more or less answering to the antipathy on his own. In effect a foolish demonstration, he must have thought, and very harmless, like the futile kick of a heifer, which yet were the heifer a shod stallion would not be so harmless. Even so was it that into the gall of Claggart's envy he infused the vitriol of his contempt.

But the incident confirmed to him certain telltale reports purveyed to his ear by "Squeak," one of his more cunning corporals, a grizzled little man, so nicknamed by the sailors on account of his squeaky voice and sharp visage ferreting about the dark corners of the lower decks after interlopers, satirically suggesting to them the idea of a rat in a cellar.

From his chief's employing him as an implicit tool in laying little traps for the worriment of the foretopman—for it was from the master-at-arms that the petty persecutions heretofore adverted to had proceeded—the corporal, having naturally enough concluded that his master could have no love for the sailor, made it his business, faithful understrapper that he was, to foment the ill blood by perverting to his chief certain innocent frolics of the good-natured foretopman, besides inventing for his mouth sundry contumelious[1] epithets he claimed to have overheard him let fall. The master-at-arms never suspected the veracity of these reports, more especially as to the epithets, for he well knew how secretly unpopular may become a master-at-arms, at least a master-at-arms of those days, zealous in his function, and how the bluejackets shoot at him in private their raillery and wit; the nickname by which he goes among them (Jemmy Legs) implying under the form of merriment their cherished disrespect and dislike. But in view of the greediness of hate for pabulum[2] it hardly needed a purveyor to feed Claggart's passion.

An uncommon prudence is habitual with the subtler depravity, for it has everything to hide. And in case of an injury but suspected, its secretiveness voluntarily cuts it off from enlightenment or disillusion; and, not unreluctantly, action is taken upon surmise as upon certainty. And the retaliation is apt to be in monstrous disproportion to the supposed offense; for when in anybody was revenge in its exactions aught else but an inordinate usurer? But how with Claggart's conscience? For though consciences are unlike as foreheads, every intelligence, not excluding the scriptural devils who "believe and tremble,"[3] has one. But Claggart's conscience being but the lawyer to his will, made ogres of trifles, probably arguing that the motive imputed to Billy in spilling the soup just when he did, together with the epithets

---

1 Contemptuous, insolent.
2 Nutrition.
3 In the New Testament, James expostulates the difference between faith and works: "Thou believest that there is one God; thou doest well: the devils also believe, and tremble" (2:19).

alleged, these, if nothing more, made a strong case against him; nay, justified animosity into a sort of retributive righteousness. The Pharisee is the Guy Fawkes[1] prowling in the hid chambers underlying some natures like Claggart's. And they can really form no conception of an unreciprocated malice. Probably the master-at-arms' clandestine persecution of Billy was started to try the temper of the man; but it had not developed any quality in him that enmity could make official use of or even pervert into plausible self-justification; so that the occurrence at the mess, petty if it were, was a welcome one to that peculiar conscience assigned to be the private mentor of Claggart; and, for the rest, not improbably it put him upon new experiments.

14

Not many days after the last incident narrated, something befell Billy Budd that more graveled him than aught that had previously occurred.

It was a warm night for the latitude; and the foretopman, whose watch at the time was properly below, was dozing on the uppermost deck whither he had ascended from his hot hammock, one of hundreds suspended so closely wedged together over a lower gun deck that there was little or no swing to them. He lay as in the shadow of a hillside, stretched under the lee of the booms, a piled ridge of spare spars amidships between foremast and mainmast among which the ship's largest boat, the launch, was stowed. Alongside of three other slumberers from below, he lay near that end of the booms which approaches the foremast; his station aloft on duty as a foretopman being just over the deck-station of the forecastlemen, entitling him according to usage to make himself more or less at home in that neighborhood.

Presently he was stirred into semiconsciousness by somebody, who must have previously sounded the sleep of the others, touching his shoulder, and then, as the foretopman raised his head, breathing into his ear in a quick whisper, "Slip into the lee forechains, Billy; there is something in the wind. Don't speak. Quick, I will meet you there," and disappearing.

---

1   A Pharisee, here, is a strict observer and enforcer of law. Guy Fawkes (1570–1606) was the main conspirator in the 1605 Gunpowder Plot to overthrow the government of James I (r. 1603–25) in retaliation for its treatment of Catholics.

Now Billy, like sundry other essentially good-natured ones, had some of the weaknesses inseparable from essential good nature; and among these was a reluctance, almost an incapacity of plumply saying *no* to an abrupt proposition not obviously absurd on the face of it, nor obviously unfriendly, nor iniquitous. And being of warm blood, he had not the phlegm tacitly to negative any proposition by unresponsive inaction. Like his sense of fear, his apprehension as to aught outside of the honest and natural was seldom very quick. Besides, upon the present occasion, the drowse from his sleep still hung upon him.

However it was, he mechanically rose and, sleepily wondering what could be in the wind, betook himself to the designated place, a narrow platform, one of six, outside of the high bulwarks and screened by the great deadeyes and multiple columned lanyards of the shrouds and backstays; and, in a great warship of that time, of dimensions commensurate to the hull's magnitude; a tarry balcony in short, overhanging the sea, and so secluded that one mariner of the *Bellipotent*, a Nonconformist[1] old tar of a serious turn, made it even in daytime his private oratory.

In this retired nook the stranger soon joined Billy Budd. There was no moon as yet; a haze obscured the starlight. He could not distinctly see the stranger's face. Yet from something in the outline and carriage, Billy took him, and correctly, for one of the afterguard.[2]

"Hist! Billy," said the man, in the same quick cautionary whisper as before. "You were impressed, weren't you? Well, so was I"; and he paused, as to mark the effect. But Billy, not knowing exactly what to make of this, said nothing. Then the other: "We are not the only impressed ones, Billy. There's a gang of us.—Couldn't you—help—at a pinch?"

"What do you mean?" demanded Billy, here thoroughly shaking off his drowse.

"Hist, hist!" the hurried whisper now growing husky. "See here," and the man held up two small objects faintly twinkling in the night-light; "see, they are yours, Billy, if you'll only———"

But Billy broke in, and in his resentful eagerness to deliver himself his vocal infirmity somewhat intruded. "D—d—damme, I don't know what you are d—d—driving at, or what you mean, but you had better g—g—go where you belong!" For the moment

---

1 Christians—e.g., Baptists, Methodists, Puritans—who refused authority of Church of England after the 1662 Act of Uniformity.
2 Sailors stationed at the mainmast and aft, or rear, part of the ship.

the fellow, as confounded, did not stir; and Billy, springing to his feet, said, "If you d—don't start, I'll t—t—toss you back over the r—rail!" There was no mistaking this, and the mysterious emissary decamped, disappearing in the direction of the mainmast in the shadow of the booms.

"Hallo, what's the matter?" here came growling from a forecastleman awakened from his deck-doze by Billy's raised voice. And as the foretopman reappeared and was recognized by him: "Ah, Beauty, is it you? Well, something must have been the matter, for you st—st—stuttered."

"Oh," rejoined Billy, now mastering the impediment, "I found an afterguardsman in our part of the ship here, and I bid him be off where he belongs."

"And is that all you did about it, Foretopman?" gruffly demanded another, an irascible old fellow of brick-colored visage and hair who was known to his associate forecastlemen as "Red Pepper." "Such sneaks I should like to marry to the gunner's daughter!"—by that expression meaning that he would like to subject them to disciplinary castigation over a gun.

However, Billy's rendering of the matter satisfactorily accounted to these inquirers for the brief commotion, since of all the sections of a ship's company the forecastlemen, veterans for the most part and bigoted in their sea prejudices, are the most jealous in resenting territorial encroachments, especially on the part of any of the afterguard, of whom they have but a sorry opinion—chiefly landsmen, never going aloft except to reef or furl the mainsail, and in no wise competent to handle a marlinspike or turn in a deadeye, say.[1]

15

This incident sorely puzzled Billy Budd. It was an entirely new experience, the first time in his life that he had ever been personally approached in underhand intriguing fashion. Prior to this encounter he had known nothing of the afterguardsman, the two men being stationed wide apart, one forward and aloft during his watch, the other on deck and aft.

What could it mean? And could they really be guineas, those two glittering objects the interloper had held up to his (Billy's) eyes? Where could the fellow get guineas? Why, even spare

---

1 Marlinspike and deadeye: sailors' tools for working with rope.

buttons are not so plentiful at sea. The more he turned the matter over, the more he was nonplussed, and made uneasy and discomfited. In his disgustful recoil from an overture which, though he but ill comprehended, he instinctively knew must involve evil of some sort, Billy Budd was like a young horse fresh from the pasture suddenly inhaling a vile whiff from some chemical factory, and by repeated snortings trying to get it out of his nostrils and lungs. This frame of mind barred all desire of holding further parley with the fellow, even were it but for the purpose of gaining some enlightenment as to his design in approaching him. And yet he was not without natural curiosity to see how such a visitor in the dark would look in broad day.

He espied him the following afternoon in his first dogwatch below, one of the smokers on that forward part of the upper gun deck allotted to the pipe. He recognized him by his general cut and build more than by his round freckled face and glassy eyes of pale blue, veiled with lashes all but white. And yet Billy was a bit uncertain whether indeed it were he—yonder chap about his own age chatting and laughing in freehearted way, leaning against a gun; a genial young fellow enough to look at, and something of a rattlebrain, to all appearance. Rather chubby too for a sailor, even an afterguardsman. In short, the last man in the world, one would think, to be overburdened with thoughts, especially those perilous thoughts that must needs belong to a conspirator in any serious project, or even to the underling of such a conspirator.

Although Billy was not aware of it, the fellow, with a sidelong watchful glance, had perceived Billy first, and then noting that Billy was looking at him, thereupon nodded a familiar sort of friendly recognition as to an old acquaintance, without interrupting the talk he was engaged in with the group of smokers. A day or two afterwards, chancing in the evening promenade on a gun deck to pass Billy, he offered a flying word of good-fellowship, as it were, which by its unexpectedness, and equivocalness under the circumstances, so embarrassed Billy that he knew not how to respond to it, and let it go unnoticed.

Billy was now left more at a loss than before. The ineffectual speculations into which he was led were so disturbingly alien to him that he did his best to smother them. It never entered his mind that here was a matter which, from its extreme questionableness, it was his duty as a loyal bluejacket to report in the proper quarter. And, probably, had such a step been suggested to him, he would have been deterred from taking it by the thought, one of novice magnanimity, that it would savor overmuch of the dirty work of a telltale. He kept the thing to himself. Yet upon one occasion he could not forbear a little disburdening himself to the old Dansker, tempted thereto perhaps by the influence of a balmy night when the ship lay becalmed; the twain, silent for the most part, sitting together on deck, their heads propped against the bulwarks. But it was only a partial and anonymous account that Billy gave, the unfounded scruples above referred to preventing full disclosure to anybody. Upon hearing Billy's version, the sage Dansker seemed to divine more than he was told; and after a little meditation, during which his wrinkles were pursed as into a point, quite effacing for the time that quizzing expression his face sometimes wore: "Didn't I say so, Baby Budd?"

"Say what?" demanded Billy.

"Why, *Jemmy Legs* is *down* on you."

"And what," rejoined Billy in amazement, "has *Jemmy Legs* to do with that cracked afterguardsman?"

"Ho, it was an afterguardsman, then. A cat's-paw, a cat's-paw!"[1] And with that exclamation, whether it had reference to a light puff of air just then coming over the calm sea, or a subtler relation to the afterguardsman, there is no telling, the old Merlin gave a twisting wrench with his black teeth at his plug of tobacco, vouchsafing no reply to Billy's impetuous question, though now repeated, for it was his wont to relapse into grim silence when interrogated in skeptical sort as to any of his sententious oracles, not always very clear ones, rather partaking of that obscurity which invests most Delphic deliverances[2] from any quarter.

Long experience had very likely brought this old man to that bitter prudence which never interferes in aught and never gives advice.

16

Yes, despite the Dansker's pithy insistence as to the master-at-arms being at the bottom of these strange experiences of Billy on board the *Bellipotent*, the young sailor was ready to ascribe them to almost anybody but the man who, to use Billy's own expression, "always had a pleasant word for him." This is to be wondered at. Yet not so much to be wondered at. In certain matters,

---

1   The Dansker implies that Squeak is Claggart's agent, toying with Billy as a cat's paw would a mouse.

2   Equivocal prophecies issued by the Oracle at Delphi, in Greece.

some sailors even in mature life remain unsophisticated enough. But a young seafarer of the disposition of our athletic foretopman is much of a child-man. And yet a child's utter innocence is but its blank ignorance, and the innocence more or less wanes as intelligence waxes. But in Billy Budd intelligence, such as it was, had advanced while yet his simple-mindedness remained for the most part unaffected. Experience is a teacher indeed; yet did Billy's years make his experience small. Besides, he had none of that intuitive knowledge of the bad which in natures not good or incompletely so foreruns experience, and therefore may pertain, as in some instances it too clearly does pertain, even to youth.

And what could Billy know of man except of man as a mere sailor? And the old-fashioned sailor, the veritable man before the mast, the sailor from boyhood up, he, though indeed of the same species as a landsman, is in some respects singularly distinct from him. The sailor is frankness, the landsman is finesse. Life is not a game with the sailor, demanding the long head—no intricate game of chess where few moves are made in straightforwardness and ends are attained by indirection, an oblique, tedious, barren game hardly worth that poor candle burnt out in playing it.

Yes, as a class, sailors are in character a juvenile race. Even their deviations are marked by juvenility, this more especially holding true with the sailors of Billy's time. Then too, certain things which apply to all sailors do more pointedly operate here and there upon the junior one. Every sailor, too, is accustomed to obey orders without debating them; his life afloat is externally ruled for him; he is not brought into that promiscuous commerce with mankind where unobstructed free agency on equal terms—equal superficially, at least—soon teaches one that unless upon occasion he exercise a distrust keen in proportion to the fairness of the appearance, some foul turn may be served him. A ruled undemonstrative distrustfulness is so habitual, not with business-men so much as with men who know their kind in less shallow relations than business, namely, certain men of the world, that they come at last to employ it all but unconsciously; and some of them would very likely feel real surprise at being charged with it as one of their general characteristics.

17

But after the little matter at the mess Billy Budd no more found himself in strange trouble at times about his hammock or his clothes bag or what not. As to that smile that occasionally sunned him, and the pleasant passing word, these were, if not more frequent, yet if anything more pronounced than before.

But for all that, there were certain other demonstrations now. When Claggart's unobserved glance happened to light on belted Billy rolling along the upper gun deck in the leisure of the second dogwatch, exchanging passing broadsides of fun with other young promenaders in the crowd, that glance would follow the cheerful sea Hyperion[1] with a settled meditative and melancholy expression, his eyes strangely suffused with incipient feverish tears. Then would Claggart look like the man of sorrows.[2] Yes, and sometimes the melancholy expression would have in it a touch of soft yearning, as if Claggart could even have loved Billy but for fate and ban.[3] But this was an evanescence, and quickly repented of, as it were, by an immitigable look, pinching and shriveling the visage into the momentary semblance of a wrinkled walnut. But sometimes catching sight in advance of the foretopman coming in his direction, he would, upon their nearing, step aside a little to let him pass, dwelling upon Billy for the moment with the glittering dental satire of a Guise.[4] But upon any abrupt unforeseen encounter a red light would flash forth from his eye like a spark from an anvil in a dusk smithy. That quick, fierce light was a strange one, darted from orbs which in repose were of a color nearest approaching a deeper violet, the softest of shades.

Though some of these caprices of the pit could not but be observed by their object, yet were they beyond the construing of such a nature. And the thews[5] of Billy were hardly compatible with that sort of sensitive spiritual organization which in some cases instinctively conveys to ignorant innocence an admonition of the proximity of the malign. He thought the master-at-arms acted in a manner rather queer at times. That was all. But the

---

1 In Greek mythology, a Titan overthrown by Apollo.

2 Isaiah 53:3: "He is despised and rejected of men; a man of sorrows, and acquainted with grief: and we hid as it were our faces from him; he was despised, and we esteemed him not." The passage refers to a servant of God, but the phrase is often applied to Christ himself.

3 On the narrative's sexual overtones, see Appendix F.

4 Powerful French family that participated in violence against Catholics, most infamously the slaughter of Huguenots in the 1572 Saint Bartholomew's Day Massacre in Paris.

5 Moral habits. Hayford and Sealts note that Elizabeth Melville put a question mark next to this word in the manuscript, and that in earlier texts Melville used it to refer to "muscles or sinews" (172).

occasional frank air and pleasant word went for what they purported to be, the young sailor never having heard as yet of the "too fair-spoken man."

Had the foretopman been conscious of having done or said anything to provoke the ill will of the official, it would have been different with him, and his sight might have been purged if not sharpened. As it was, innocence was his blinder.

So was it with him in yet another matter. Two minor officers, the armorer and captain of the hold, with whom he had never exchanged a word, his position in the ship not bringing him into contact with them, these men now for the first began to cast upon Billy, when they chanced to encounter him, that peculiar glance which evidences that the man from whom it comes has been some way tampered with, and to the prejudice of him upon whom the glance lights. Never did it occur to Billy as a thing to be noted or a thing suspicious, though he well knew the fact, that the armorer and captain of the hold, with the ship's yeoman, apothecary, and others of that grade, were by naval usage messmates of the master-at-arms, men with ears convenient to his confidential tongue.

But the general popularity that came from our Handsome Sailor's manly forwardness upon occasion and irresistible good nature, indicating no mental superiority tending to excite an invidious feeling, this good will on the part of most of his shipmates made him the less to concern himself about such mute aspects toward him as those whereto allusion has just been made, aspects he could not so fathom as to infer their whole import.

As to the afterguardsman, though Billy for reasons already given necessarily saw little of him, yet when the two did happen to meet, invariably came the fellow's offhand cheerful recognition, sometimes accompanied by a passing pleasant word or two. Whatever that equivocal young person's original design may really have been, or the design of which he might have been the deputy, certain it was from his manner upon these occasions that he had wholly dropped it.

It was as if his precocity of crookedness (and every vulgar villain is precocious) had for once deceived him, and the man he had sought to entrap as a simpleton had through his very simplicity ignominiously baffled him.

But shrewd ones may opine that it was hardly possible for Billy to refrain from going up to the afterguardsman and bluntly demanding to know his purpose in the initial interview so abruptly closed in the forechains. Shrewd ones may also think it but natural in Billy to set about sounding some of the other impressed men of the ship in order to discover what basis, if any, there was for the emissary's obscure suggestions as to plotting disaffection aboard. Yes, shrewd ones may so think. But something more, or rather something else than mere shrewdness is perhaps needful for the due understanding of such a character as Billy Budd's.

As to Claggart, the monomania in the man—if that indeed it were—as involuntarily disclosed by starts in the manifestations detailed, yet in general covered over by his self-contained and rational demeanor; this, like a subterranean fire, was eating its way deeper and deeper in him. Something decisive must come of it.

18

After the mysterious interview in the forechains, the one so abruptly ended there by Billy, nothing especially germane to the story occurred until the events now about to be narrated.

Elsewhere it has been said that in the lack of frigates (of course better sailers than line-of-battle ships)[1] in the English squadron up the Straits at that period, the *Bellipotent 74* was occasionally employed not only as an available substitute for a scout, but at times on detached service of more important kind. This was not alone because of her sailing qualities, not common in a ship of her rate, but quite as much, probably, that the character of her commander, it was thought, specially adapted him for any duty where under unforeseen difficulties a prompt initiative might have to be taken in some matter demanding knowledge and ability in addition to those qualities implied in good seamanship. It was on an expedition of the latter sort, a somewhat distant one, and when the *Bellipotent* was almost at her furthest remove from the fleet, that in the latter part of an afternoon watch she unexpectedly came in sight of a ship of the enemy. It proved to be a frigate. The latter, perceiving through the glass that the weight of men and metal would be heavily against her, invoking her light

---

1 Warships built to present maximum firepower in the kind of manoeuvres characterizing seventeenth- and eighteenth-century naval warfare, before the advent of steam power; also called a "ship of the line." With only 74 guns, the *Bellipotent*, though a ship of the line, is faster than other ships built for this kind of engagement.

heels crowded sail to get away. After a chase urged almost against hope and lasting until about the middle of the first dogwatch, she signally succeeded in effecting her escape.

Not long after the pursuit had been given up, and ere the excitement incident thereto had altogether waned away, the master-at-arms, ascending from his cavernous sphere, made his appearance cap in hand by the mainmast respectfully waiting the notice of Captain Vere, then solitary walking the weather side of the quarter-deck, doubtless somewhat chafed at the failure of the pursuit. The spot where Claggart stood was the place allotted to men of lesser grades seeking some more particular interview either with the officer of the deck or the captain himself. But from the latter it was not often that a sailor or petty officer of those days would seek a hearing; only some exceptional cause would, according to established custom, have warranted that.

Presently, just as the commander, absorbed in his reflections, was on the point of turning aft in his promenade, he became sensible of Claggart's presence, and saw the doffed cap held in deferential expectancy. Here be it said that Captain Vere's personal knowledge of this petty officer had only begun at the time of the ship's last sailing from home, Claggart then for the first, in transfer from a ship detained for repairs, supplying on board the *Bellipotent* the place of a previous master-at-arms disabled and ashore.

No sooner did the commander observe who it was that now deferentially stood awaiting his notice than a peculiar expression came over him. It was not unlike that which uncontrollably will flit across the countenance of one at unawares encountering a person who, though known to him indeed, has hardly been long enough known for thorough knowledge, but something in whose aspect nevertheless now for the first provokes a vaguely repellent distaste. But coming to a stand and resuming much of his wonted official manner, save that a sort of impatience lurked in the intonation of the opening word, he said "Well? What is it, Master-at-arms?"

With the air of a subordinate grieved at the necessity of being a messenger of ill tidings, and while conscientiously determined to be frank yet equally resolved upon shunning overstatement, Claggart at this invitation, or rather summons to disburden, spoke up. What he said, conveyed in the language of no uneducated man, was to the effect following, if not altogether in these words, namely, that during the chase and preparations for the possible encounter he had seen enough to convince him that at least one sailor aboard was a dangerous character in a ship mustering some who not only had taken a guilty part in the late serious troubles, but others also who, like the man in question, had entered His Majesty's service under another form than enlistment.

At this point Captain Vere with some impatience interrupted him: "Be direct, man; say *impressed men*."

Claggart made a gesture of subservience, and proceeded. Quite lately he (Claggart) had begun to suspect that on the gun decks some sort of movement prompted by the sailor in question was covertly going on, but he had not thought himself warranted in reporting the suspicion so long as it remained indistinct. But from what he had that afternoon observed in the man referred to, the suspicion of something clandestine going on had advanced to a point less removed from certainty. He deeply felt, he added, the serious responsibility assumed in making a report involving such possible consequences to the individual mainly concerned, besides tending to augment those natural anxieties which every naval commander must feel in view of extraordinary outbreaks so recent as those which, he sorrowfully said it, it needed not to name.

Now at the first broaching of the matter Captain Vere, taken by surprise, could not wholly dissemble his disquietude. But as Claggart went on, the former's aspect changed into restiveness under something in the testifier's manner in giving his testimony. However, he refrained from interrupting him. And Claggart, continuing, concluded with this: "God forbid, your honor, that the *Bellipotent*'s should be the experience of the ———"

"Never mind that!" here peremptorily broke in the superior, his face altering with anger, instinctively divining the ship that the other was about to name, one in which the Nore Mutiny had assumed a singularly tragical character that for a time jeopardized the life of its commander. Under the circumstances he was indignant at the purposed allusion. When the commissioned officers themselves were on all occasions very heedful how they referred to the recent events in the fleet, for a petty officer unnecessarily to allude to them in the presence of his captain, this struck him as a most immodest presumption. Besides, to his quick sense of self-respect it even looked under the circumstances something like an attempt to alarm him. Nor at first was he without some surprise that one who so far as he had hitherto come under his notice had shown considerable tact in his function should in this particular evince such lack of it.

But these thoughts and kindred dubious ones flitting across his mind were suddenly replaced by an intuitional surmise which, though as yet obscure in form, served practically to affect his reception of the ill tidings. Certain it is that, long versed in everything pertaining to the complicated gun-deck life, which like every other form of life has its secret mines and dubious side, the side popularly disclaimed, Captain Vere did not permit himself to be unduly disturbed by the general tenor of his subordinate's report.

Furthermore, if in view of recent events prompt action should be taken at the first palpable sign of recurring insubordination, for all that, not judicious would it be, he thought, to keep the idea of lingering disaffection alive by undue forwardness in crediting an informer, even if his own subordinate and charged among other things with police surveillance of the crew. This feeling would not perhaps have so prevailed with him were it not that upon a prior occasion the patriotic zeal officially evinced by Claggart had somewhat irritated him as appearing rather supersensible and strained. Furthermore, something even in the official's self-possessed and somewhat ostentatious manner in making his specifications strangely reminded him of a bandsman, a perjurious witness in a capital case before a court-martial ashore of which when a lieutenant he (Captain Vere) had been a member.

Now the peremptory check given to Claggart in the matter of the arrested allusion was quickly followed up by this: "You say that there is at least one dangerous man aboard. Name him."

"William Budd, a foretopman, your honor."

"William Budd!" repeated Captain Vere with unfeigned astonishment. "And mean you the man that Lieutenant Ratcliffe took from the merchantman not very long ago, the young fellow who seems to be so popular with the men—Billy, the Handsome Sailor, as they call him?"

"The same, your honor; but for all his youth and good looks, a deep one. Not for nothing does he insinuate himself into the good will of his shipmates, since at the least they will at a pinch say—all hands will—a good word for him, and at all hazards. Did Lieutenant Ratcliffe happen to tell your honor of that adroit fling of Budd's, jumping up in the cutter's bow under the merchantman's stern when he was being taken off? It is even masked by that sort of good-humored air that at heart he resents his impressment. You have but noted his fair cheek. A mantrap may be under the ruddy-tipped daisies."

Now the Handsome Sailor as a signal figure among the crew had naturally enough attracted the captain's attention from the first. Though in general not very demonstrative to his officers, he had congratulated Lieutenant Ratcliffe upon his good fortune in lighting on such a fine specimen of the *genus homo*, who in the nude might have posed for a statue of young Adam before the Fall. As to Billy's adieu to the ship *Rights-of-Man*, which the boarding lieutenant had indeed reported to him, but, in a deferential way, more as a good story than aught else, Captain Vere, though mistakenly understanding it as a satiric sally, had but thought so much the better of the impressed man for it; as a military sailor, admiring the spirit that could take an arbitrary enlistment so merrily and sensibly. The foretopman's conduct, too, so far as it had fallen under the captain's notice, had confirmed the first happy augury, while the new recruit's qualities as a "sailorman" seemed to be such that he had thought of recommending him to the executive officer for promotion to a place that would more frequently bring him under his own observation, namely, the captaincy of the mizzentop,[1] replacing there in the starboard watch a man not so young whom partly for that reason he deemed less fitted for the post. Be it parenthesized here that since the mizzentopmen have not to handle such breadths of heavy canvas as the lower sails on the mainmast and foremast, a young man if of the right stuff not only seems best adapted to duty there, but in fact is generally selected for the captaincy of that top, and the company under him are light hands and often but striplings. In sum, Captain Vere had from the beginning deemed Billy Budd to be what in the naval parlance of the time was called a "King's bargain": that is to say, for His Britannic Majesty's navy a capital investment at small outlay or none at all.

After a brief pause, during which the reminiscences above mentioned passed vividly through his mind and he weighed the import of Claggart's last suggestion conveyed in the phrase "mantrap under the daisies," and the more he weighed it the less reliance he felt in the informer's good faith, suddenly he turned upon him and in a low voice demanded: "Do you come to me, Master-at-arms, with so foggy a tale? As to Budd, cite me an act or spoken word of his confirmatory of what you in general charge against him. Stay," drawing nearer to him; "heed what you speak. Just now, and in a case like this, there is a yardarm-end for the false witness."

"Ah, your honor!" sighed Claggart, mildly shaking his shapely head as in sad deprecation of such unmerited severity of tone.

---

1 Yet another platform on one of the ship's masts, high above the deck.

Then, bridling—erecting himself as in virtuous self-assertion—he circumstantially alleged certain words and acts which collectively, if credited, led to presumptions mortally inculpating Budd. And for some of these averments, he added, substantiating proof was not far.

With gray eyes impatient and distrustful essaying to fathom to the bottom Claggart's calm violet ones, Captain Vere again heard him out; then for the moment stood ruminating. The mood he evinced, Claggart—himself for the time liberated from the other's scrutiny—steadily regarded with a look difficult to render: a look curious of the operation of his tactics, a look such as might have been that of the spokesman of the envious children of Jacob deceptively imposing upon the troubled patriarch the blood-dyed coat of young Joseph.[1]

Though something exceptional in the moral quality of Captain Vere made him, in earnest encounter with a fellow man, a veritable touchstone of that man's essential nature, yet now as to Claggart and what was really going on in him his feeling partook less of intuitional conviction than of strong suspicion clogged by strange dubieties. The perplexity he evinced proceeded less from aught touching the man informed against—as Claggart doubtless opined—than from considerations how best to act in regard to the informer. At first, indeed, he was naturally for summoning that substantiation of his allegations which Claggart said was at hand. But such a proceeding would result in the matter at once getting abroad, which in the present stage of it, he thought, might undesirably affect the ship's company. If Claggart was a false witness—that closed the affair. And therefore, before trying the accusation, he would first practically test the accuser; and he thought this could be done in a quiet, undemonstrative way.

The measure he determined upon involved a shifting of the scene, a transfer to a place less exposed to observation than the broad quarter-deck. For although the few gun-room officers there at the time had, in due observance of naval etiquette, withdrawn to leeward the moment Captain Vere had begun his promenade on the deck's weather side; and though during the colloquy with Claggart they of course ventured not to diminish the distance; and though throughout the interview Captain Vere's

---

1 In Genesis 37, when Joseph's brothers show their father, Jacob, a coat soaked in blood, he is tricked into believing his favourite son has been killed by a wild animal, when in fact the brothers had sold Joseph into slavery.

voice was far from high, and Claggart's silvery and low; and the wind in the cordage and the wash of the sea helped the more to put them beyond earshot; nevertheless, the interview's continuance already had attracted observation from some topmen aloft and other sailors in the waist or further forward.

Having determined upon his measures, Captain Vere forthwith took action. Abruptly turning to Claggart, he asked, "Master-at-arms, is it now Budd's watch aloft?"

"No, your honor."

Whereupon, "Mr. Wilkes!" summoning the nearest midshipman. "Tell Albert to come to me." Albert was the captain's hammock-boy, a sort of sea valet in whose discretion and fidelity his master had much confidence. The lad appeared.

"You know Budd, the foretopman?"

"I do, sir."

"Go find him. It is his watch off. Manage to tell him out of earshot that he is wanted aft. Contrive it that he speaks to nobody. Keep him in talk yourself. And not till you get well aft here, not till then let him know that the place where he is wanted is my cabin. You understand. Go.—Master-at-arms, show yourself on the decks below, and when you think it time for Albert to be coming with his man, stand by quietly to follow the sailor in."

19

Now when the foretopman found himself in the cabin, closeted there, as it were, with the captain and Claggart, he was surprised enough. But it was a surprise unaccompanied by apprehension or distrust. To an immature nature essentially honest and humane, forewarning intimations of subtler danger from one's kind come tardily if at all. The only thing that took shape in the young sailor's mind was this: Yes, the captain, I have always thought, looks kindly upon me. Wonder if he's going to make me his coxswain. I should like that. And may be now he is going to ask the master-at-arms about me.

"Shut the door there, sentry," said the commander; "stand without, and let nobody come in.—Now, Master-at-arms, tell this man to his face what you told of him to me," and stood prepared to scrutinize the mutually confronting visages.

With the measured step and calm collected air of an asylum physician approaching in the public hall some patient beginning to show indications of a coming paroxysm, Claggart deliberately advanced within short range of Billy and, mesmerically looking him in the eye, briefly recapitulated the accusation.

Not at first did Billy take it in. When he did, the rose-tan of his cheek looked struck as by white leprosy. He stood like one impaled and gagged. Meanwhile the accuser's eyes, removing not as yet from the blue dilated ones, underwent a phenomenal change, their wonted rich violet color blurring into a muddy purple. Those lights of human intelligence, losing human expression, were gelidly protruding like the alien eyes of certain uncatalogued creatures of the deep. The first mesmeristic glance was one of serpent fascination; the last was as the paralyzing lurch of the torpedo fish.

"Speak, man!" said Captain Vere to the transfixed one, struck by his aspect even more than by Claggart's. "Speak! Defend yourself!" Which appeal caused but a strange dumb gesturing and gurgling in Billy; amazement at such an accusation so suddenly sprung on inexperienced nonage; this, and, it may be, horror of the accuser's eyes, serving to bring out his lurking defect and in this instance for the time intensifying it into a convulsed tongue-tie; while the intent head and entire form straining forward in an agony of ineffectual eagerness to obey the injunction to speak and defend himself, gave an expression to the face like that of a condemned vestal priestess in the moment of being buried alive, and in the first struggle against suffocation.

Though at the time Captain Vere was quite ignorant of Billy's liability to vocal impediment, he now immediately divined it, since vividly Billy's aspect recalled to him that of a bright young schoolmate of his whom he had once seen struck by much the same startling impotence in the act of eagerly rising in the class to be foremost in response to a testing question put to it by the master. Going close up to the young sailor, and laying a soothing hand on his shoulder, he said, "There is no hurry, my boy. Take your time, take your time." Contrary to the effect intended, these words so fatherly in tone, doubtless touching Billy's heart to the quick, prompted yet more violent efforts at utterance—efforts soon ending for the time in confirming the paralysis, and bringing to his face an expression which was as a crucifixion to behold. The next instant, quick as the flame from a discharged cannon at night, his right arm shot out, and Claggart dropped to the deck. Whether intentionally or but owing to the young athlete's superior height, the blow had taken effect full upon the forehead, so shapely and intellectual-looking a feature in the master-at-arms; so that the body fell over length-wise, like a heavy plank tilted from erectness. A gasp or two, and he lay motionless.

"Fated boy," breathed Captain Vere in tone so low as to be almost a whisper, "what have you done! But here, help me."

The twain raised the felled one from the loins up into a sitting position. The spare form flexibly acquiesced, but inertly. It was like handling a dead snake. They lowered it back. Regaining erectness, Captain Vere with one hand covering his face stood to all appearance as impassive as the object at his feet. Was he absorbed in taking in all the bearings of the event and what was best not only now at once to be done, but also in the sequel? Slowly he uncovered his face; and the effect was as if the moon emerging from eclipse should reappear with quite another aspect than that which had gone into hiding. The father in him, mani-fested towards Billy thus far in the scene, was replaced by the mil-itary disciplinarian. In his official tone he bade the foretopman retire to a stateroom aft (pointing it out), and there remain till thence summoned. This order Billy in silence mechanically obeyed. Then going to the cabin door where it opened on the quarter-deck, Captain Vere said to the sentry without, "Tell somebody to send Albert here." When the lad appeared, his master so contrived it that he should not catch sight of the prone one. "Albert," he said to him, "tell the surgeon I wish to see him. You need not come back till called."

When the surgeon entered—a self-poised character of that grave sense and experience that hardly anything could take him aback—Captain Vere advanced to meet him, thus unconsciously intercepting his view of Claggart, and, interrupting the other's wonted ceremonious salutation, said, "Nay. Tell me how it is with yonder man," directing his attention to the prostrate one.

The surgeon looked, and for all his self-command somewhat started at the abrupt revelation. On Claggart's always pallid com-plexion, thick black blood was now oozing from nostril and ear. To the gazer's professional eye it was unmistakably no living man that he saw.

"Is it so, then?" said Captain Vere, intently watching him. "I thought it. But verify it." Whereupon the customary tests con-firmed the surgeon's first glance, who now, looking up in unfeigned concern, cast a look of intense inquisitiveness upon his superior. But Captain Vere, with one hand to his brow, was stand-ing motionless. Suddenly, catching the surgeon's arm convulsively, he exclaimed, pointing down to the body, "It is the divine judgment on Ananias![1] Look!"

Disturbed by the excited manner he had never before observed in the *Bellipotent*'s captain, and as yet wholly ignorant of the affair, the prudent surgeon nevertheless held his peace, only again looking an earnest interrogatory as to what it was that had resulted in such a tragedy.

But Captain Vere was now again motionless, standing absorbed in thought. Again starting, he vehemently exclaimed, "Struck dead by an angel of God! Yet the angel must hang!"

At these passionate interjections, mere incoherences to the listener as yet unapprised of the antecedents, the surgeon was profoundly discomposed. But now, as recollecting himself, Captain Vere in less passionate tone briefly related the circumstances leading up to the event. "But come; we must dispatch," he added. "Help me to remove him" (meaning the body) "to yonder compartment," designating one opposite that where the foretopman remained immured. Anew disturbed by a request that, as implying a desire for secrecy, seemed unaccountably strange to him, there was nothing for the subordinate to do but comply.

"Go now," said Captain Vere with something of his wonted manner. "Go now. I presently shall call a drumhead court.[2] Tell the lieutenants what has happened, and tell Mr. Mordant" (meaning the captain of marines), "and charge them to keep the matter to themselves."

20

Full of disquietude and misgiving, the surgeon left the cabin. Was Captain Vere suddenly affected in his mind, or was it but a transient excitement, brought about by so strange and extraordinary

---

1 In Acts 4:32–37, Ananias and his wife sell land and keep the profit rather than use it for charity, as dictated by community custom; each is struck dead instantly for lying to God.
2 A field court martial. It is difficult to know whether Melville was unfamiliar with the ins and outs of these regulations, or if he takes artistic license with them, because technically Vere does not follow them to the letter of the law. However, following Robert Milder, "The point, in either case, is not whether Vere's behavior is at variance with the actual law and procedure of the 1790s but whether Melville gives the reader sufficient cause to believe that it is" (*Billy Budd* 408, n336). See Appendix E1.

a tragedy? As to the drumhead court, it struck the surgeon as impolitic, if nothing more. The thing to do, he thought, was to place Billy Budd in confinement, and in a way dictated by usage, and postpone further action in so extraordinary a case to such time as they should rejoin the squadron, and then refer it to the admiral. He recalled the unwonted agitation of Captain Vere and his excited exclamations, so at variance with his normal manner. Was he unhinged?

But assuming that he is, it is not so susceptible of proof. What then can the surgeon do? No more trying situation is conceivable than that of an officer subordinate under a captain whom he suspects to be not mad, indeed, but yet not quite unaffected in his intellects. To argue his order to him would be insolence. To resist him would be mutiny.

In obedience to Captain Vere, he communicated what had happened to the lieutenants and captain of marines, saying nothing as to the captain's state. They fully shared his own surprise and concern. Like him too, they seemed to think that such a matter should be referred to the admiral.

21

Who in the rainbow can draw the line where the violet tint ends and the orange tint begins? Distinctly we see the difference of the colors, but where exactly does the one first blendingly enter into the other? So with sanity and insanity. In pronounced cases there is no question about them. But in some supposed cases, in various degrees supposedly less pronounced, to draw the exact line of demarcation few will undertake, though for a fee becoming considerate some professional experts will. There is nothing namable but that some men will, or undertake to, do it for pay.

Whether Captain Vere, as the surgeon professionally and privately surmised, was really the sudden victim of any degree of aberration, every one must determine for himself by such light as this narrative may afford.

That the unhappy event which has been narrated could not have happened at a worse juncture was but too true. For it was close on the heel of the suppressed insurrections, an aftertime very critical to naval authority, demanding from every English sea commander two qualities not readily interfusable—prudence and rigor. Moreover, there was something crucial in the case.

In the jugglery of circumstances preceding and attending the event on board the *Bellipotent*, and in the light of that martial code whereby it was formally to be judged, innocence and guilt personified in Claggart and Budd in effect changed places. In a legal view the apparent victim of the tragedy was he who had sought to victimize a man blameless; and the indisputable deed of the latter, navally regarded, constituted the most heinous of military crimes. Yet more. The essential right and wrong involved in the matter, the clearer that might be, so much the worse for the responsibility of a loyal sea commander, inasmuch as he was not authorized to determine the matter on that primitive basis.

Small wonder then that the *Bellipotent*'s captain, though in general a man of rapid decision, felt that circumspectness not less than promptitude was necessary. Until he could decide upon his course, and in each detail; and not only so, but until the concluding measure was upon the point of being enacted, he deemed it advisable, in view of all the circumstances, to guard as much as possible against publicity. Here he may or may not have erred. Certain it is, however, that subsequently in the confidential talk of more than one or two gun rooms and cabins he was not a little criticized by some officers, a fact imputed by his friends and vehemently by his cousin Jack Denton to professional jealousy of Starry Vere. Some imaginative ground for invidious comment there was. The maintenance of secrecy in the matter, the confining all knowledge of it for a time to the place where the homicide occurred, the quarter-deck cabin; in these particulars lurked some resemblance to the policy adopted in those tragedies of the palace which have occurred more than once in the capital founded by Peter the Barbarian.[1]

The case indeed was such that fain would the *Bellipotent*'s captain have deferred taking any action whatever respecting it further than to keep the foretopman a close prisoner till the ship rejoined the squadron and then submitting the matter to the judgment of his admiral.

But a true military officer is in one particular like a true monk. Not with more of self-abnegation will the latter keep his vows of monastic obedience than the former his vows of allegiance to martial duty.

---

1 Peter the Great (1672–1725), tsar and emperor who modernized
   Russia, making it into a regional power largely at the expense of the
   Russian people, who through brutal forced labour created the city of St.
   Petersburg out of a swamp in the early 1700s.

Feeling that unless quick action was taken on it, the deed of the foretopman, so soon as it should be known on the gun decks, would tend to awaken any slumbering embers of the Nore among the crew, a sense of the urgency of the case overruled in Captain Vere every other consideration. But though a conscientious disciplinarian, he was no lover of authority for mere authority's sake. Very far was he from embracing opportunities for monopolizing to himself the perils of moral responsibility, none at least that could properly be referred to an official superior or shared with him by his official equals or even subordinates. So thinking, he was glad it would not be at variance with usage to turn the matter over to a summary court of his own officers, reserving to himself, as the one on whom the ultimate accountability would rest, the right of maintaining a supervision of it, or formally or informally interposing at need. Accordingly a drumhead court was summarily convened, he electing the individuals composing it: the first lieutenant, the captain of marines, and the sailing master.

In associating an officer of marines with the sea lieutenant and the sailing master in a case having to do with a sailor, the commander perhaps deviated from general custom. He was prompted thereto by the circumstance that he took that soldier to be a judicious person, thoughtful, and not altogether incapable of grappling with a difficult case unprecedented in his prior experience. Yet even as to him he was not without some latent misgiving, for withal he was an extremely good-natured man, an enjoyer of his dinner, a sound sleeper, and inclined to obesity—a man who though he would always maintain his manhood in battle might not prove altogether reliable in a moral dilemma involving aught of the tragic. As to the first lieutenant and the sailing master, Captain Vere could not but be aware that though honest natures, of approved gallantry upon occasion, their intelligence was mostly confined to the matter of active seamanship and the fighting demands of their profession.

The court was held in the same cabin where the unfortunate affair had taken place. This cabin, the commander's, embraced the entire area under the poop deck. Aft, and on either side, was a small stateroom, the one now temporarily a jail and the other a dead-house, and a yet smaller compartment, leaving a space between expanding forward into a goodly oblong of length coinciding with the ship's beam. A skylight of moderate dimension was overhead, and at each end of the oblong space were two sashed porthole windows easily convertible back into embrasures for short carronades.

All being quickly in readiness, Billy Budd was arraigned, Captain Vere necessarily appearing as the sole witness in the case, and as such temporarily sinking his rank, though singularly maintaining it in a matter apparently trivial, namely, that he testified from the ship's weather side, with that object having caused the court to sit on the lee side. Concisely he narrated all that had led up to the catastrophe, omitting nothing in Claggart's accusation and deposing as to the manner in which the prisoner had received it. At this testimony the three officers glanced with no little surprise at Billy Budd, the last man they would have suspected either of the mutinous design alleged by Claggart or the undeniable deed he himself had done. The first lieutenant, taking judicial primacy and turning toward the prisoner, said, "Captain Vere has spoken. Is it or is it not as Captain Vere says?"

In response came syllables not so much impeded in the utterance as might have been anticipated. They were these: "Captain Vere tells the truth. It is just as Captain Vere says, but it is not as the master-at-arms said. I have eaten the King's bread and I am true to the King."

"I believe you, my man," said the witness, his voice indicating a suppressed emotion not otherwise betrayed.

"God will bless you for that, your honor!" not without stammering said Billy, and all but broke down. But immediately he was recalled to self-control by another question, to which with the same emotional difficulty of utterance he said, "No, there was no malice between us. I never bore malice against the master-at-arms. I am sorry that he is dead. I did not mean to kill him. Could I have used my tongue I would not have struck him. But he foully lied to my face and in presence of my captain, and I had to say something, and I could only say it with a blow, God help me!"

In the impulsive aboveboard manner of the frank one the court saw confirmed all that was implied in words that just previously had perplexed them, coming as they did from the testifier to the tragedy and promptly following Billy's impassioned disclaimer of mutinous intent—Captain Vere's words, "I believe you, my man."

Next it was asked of him whether he knew of or suspected aught savoring of incipient trouble (meaning mutiny, though the explicit term was avoided) going on in any section of the ship's company.

The reply lingered. This was naturally imputed by the court to the same vocal embarrassment which had retarded or obstructed previous answers. But in main it was otherwise here, the question immediately recalling to Billy's mind the interview with the after-guardsman in the forechains. But an innate repugnance to playing a part at all approaching that of an informer against one's own shipmates—the same erring sense of uninstructed honor which had stood in the way of his reporting the matter at the time, though as a loyal man-of-war's man it was incumbent on him, and failure so to do, if charged against him and proven, would have subjected him to the heaviest of penalties; this, with the blind feeling now his that nothing really was being hatched, prevailed with him. When the answer came it was a negative.

"One question more," said the officer of marines, now first speaking and with a troubled earnestness. "You tell us that what the master-at-arms said against you was a lie. Now why should he have so lied, so maliciously lied, since you declare there was no malice between you?"

At that question, unintentionally touching on a spiritual sphere wholly obscure to Billy's thoughts, he was nonplussed, evincing a confusion indeed that some observers, such as can readily be imagined, would have construed into involuntary evidence of hidden guilt. Nevertheless, he strove some way to answer, but all at once relinquished the vain endeavor, at the same time turning an appealing glance towards Captain Vere as deeming him his best helper and friend. Captain Vere, who had been seated for a time, rose to his feet, addressing the interrogator. "The question you put to him comes naturally enough. But how can he rightly answer it?—or anybody else, unless indeed it be he who lies within there," designating the compartment where lay the corpse. "But the prone one there will not rise to our summons. In effect, though, as it seems to me, the point you make is hardly material. Quite aside from any conceivable motive actuating the master-at-arms, and irrespective of the provocation to the blow, a martial court must needs in the present case confine its attention to the blow's consequence, which consequence justly is to be deemed not otherwise than as the striker's deed."

This utterance, the full significance of which it was not at all likely that Billy took in, nevertheless caused him to turn a wistful interrogative look toward the speaker, a look in its dumb expressiveness not unlike that which a dog of generous breed might turn upon his master, seeking in his face some elucidation of a previous gesture ambiguous to the canine intelligence. Nor was the same utterance without marked effect upon the three officers, more especially the soldier. Couched in it seemed to them a meaning unanticipated, involving a prejudgment on the speaker's part. It served to augment a mental disturbance previously evident enough.

The soldier once more spoke, in a tone of suggestive dubiety addressing at once his associates and Captain Vere: "Nobody is present—none of the ship's company, I mean—who might shed lateral light, if any is to be had, upon what remains mysterious in this matter."

"That is thoughtfully put," said Captain Vere; "I see your drift. Ay, there is a mystery; but, to use a scriptural phrase, it is a 'mystery of iniquity,'[1] a matter for psychologic theologians to discuss. But what has a military court to do with it? Not to add that for us any possible investigation of it is cut off by the lasting tongue-tie of—him—in yonder," again designating the mortuary stateroom. "The prisoner's deed—with that alone we have to do."

To this, and particularly the closing reiteration, the marine soldier, knowing not how aptly to reply, sadly abstained from saying aught. The first lieutenant, who at the outset had not unnaturally assumed primacy in the court, now overrulingly instructed by a glance from Captain Vere, a glance more effective than words, resumed that primacy. Turning to the prisoner, "Budd," he said, and scarce in equable tones, "Budd, if you have aught further to say for yourself, say it now."

Upon this the young sailor turned another quick glance toward Captain Vere; then, as taking a hint from that aspect, a hint confirming his own instinct that silence was now best, replied to the lieutenant, "I have said all, sir."

The marine—the same who had been the sentinel without the cabin door at the time that the foretopman, followed by the master-at-arms, entered it—he, standing by the sailor throughout these judicial proceedings, was now directed to take him back to the after compartment originally assigned to the prisoner and his custodian. As the twain disappeared from view, the three officers, as partially liberated from some inward constraint associated with Billy's mere presence, simultaneously stirred in their seats. They exchanged looks of troubled indecision, yet feeling that decide they must and without long delay. For Captain Vere, he for the time stood—unconsciously with his back toward them, apparently in one of his absent fits—gazing out from a sashed porthole to windward upon the monotonous blank of the twilight sea. But the court's silence continuing, broken only at moments by brief

1 See p. 85, note 1.

consultations, in low earnest tones, this served to arouse him and energize him. Turning, he to-and-fro paced the cabin athwart; in the returning ascent to windward climbing the slant deck in the ship's lee roll, without knowing it symbolizing thus in his action a mind resolute to surmount difficulties even if against primitive instincts strong as the wind and the sea. Presently he came to a stand before the three. After scanning their faces he stood less as mustering his thoughts for expression than as one inly deliberating how best to put them to well-meaning men not intellectually mature, men with whom it was necessary to demonstrate certain principles that were axioms to himself. Similar impatience as to talking is perhaps one reason that deters some minds from addressing any popular assemblies.

When speak he did, something, both in the substance of what he said and his manner of saying it, showed the influence of unshared studies modifying and tempering the practical training of an active career. This, along with his phraseology, now and then was suggestive of the grounds whereon rested that imputation of a certain pedantry socially alleged against him by certain naval men of wholly practical cast, captains who nevertheless would frankly concede that His Majesty's navy mustered no more efficient officer of their grade than Starry Vere.

What he said was to this effect: "Hitherto I have been but the witness, little more; and I should hardly think now to take another tone, that of your coadjutor for the time, did I not perceive in you—at the crisis too—a troubled hesitancy, proceeding, I doubt not, from the clash of military duty with moral scruple—scruple vitalized by compassion. For the compassion, how can I otherwise than share it? But, mindful of paramount obligations, I strive against scruples that may tend to enervate decision. Not, gentlemen, that I hide from myself that the case is an exceptional one. Speculatively regarded, it well might be referred to a jury of casuists.[1] But for us here, acting not as casuists or moralists, it is a case practical, and under martial law[2] practically to be dealt with.

---

1 Those who explain events speculatively by trying to deduce causes, such as motive or intention; more specifically, those who believe all actions can be sourced. The reference is similar to Vere's earlier comment that discussions of motive are the province of "psychologic theologians" and not a "military court" (p. 112).

2 The Articles of War, the statutory regulations governing the Royal Navy and the American Navy as well. See Appendices B1, E1, and E3. On the rule of law, see Appendix B. See also Appendix C1a.

"But your scruples: do they move as in a dusk? Challenge them. Make them advance and declare themselves. Come now; do they import something like this: If, mindless of palliating circumstances, we are bound to regard the death of the master-at-arms as the prisoner's deed, then does that deed constitute a capital crime whereof the penalty is a mortal one. But in natural justice is nothing but the prisoner's overt act to be considered? How can we adjudge to summary and shameful death a fellow creature innocent before God, and whom we feel to be so?— Does that state it aright? You sign sad assent. Well, I too feel that, the full force of that. It is Nature. But do these buttons that we wear attest that our allegiance is to Nature? No, to the King. Though the ocean, which is inviolate Nature primeval, though this be the element where we move and have our being as sailors, yet as the King's officers lies our duty in a sphere correspondingly natural? So little is that true, that in receiving our commissions we in the most important regards ceased to be natural free agents. When war is declared are we the commissioned fighters previously consulted? We fight at command. If our judgments approve the war, that is but coincidence. So in other particulars. So now. For suppose condemnation to follow these present proceedings. Would it be so much we ourselves that would condemn as it would be martial law operating through us? For that law and the rigor of it, we are not responsible. Our vowed responsibility[1] is in this: That however pitilessly that law may operate in any instances, we nevertheless adhere to it and administer it.

"But the exceptional in the matter moves the hearts within you. Even so too is mine moved. But let not warm hearts betray heads that should be cool. Ashore in a criminal case, will an upright judge allow himself off the bench to be waylaid by some tender kinswoman of the accused seeking to touch him with her tearful plea? Well, the heart here, sometimes the feminine in man, is as that piteous woman, and hard though it be, she must here be ruled out."

He paused, earnestly studying them for a moment; then resumed.

"But something in your aspect seems to urge that it is not solely the heart that moves in you, but also the conscience, the private conscience. But tell me whether or not, occupying the position we do, private conscience should not yield to that imperial one formulated in the code under which alone we officially proceed?"

---

1 Naval officers sworn to serve the king.

Here the three men moved in their seats, less convinced than agitated by the course of an argument troubling but the more the spontaneous conflict within.

Perceiving which, the speaker paused for a moment; then abruptly changing his tone, went on.

"To steady us a bit, let us recur to the facts.—In wartime at sea a man-of-war's man strikes his superior in grade, and the blow kills. Apart from its effect the blow itself is, according to the Articles of War, a capital crime. Furthermore———"

"Ay, sir," emotionally broke in the officer of marines, "in one sense it was. But surely Budd purposed neither mutiny nor homicide."

"Surely not, my good man. And before a court less arbitrary and more merciful than a martial one, that plea would largely extenuate. At the Last Assizes[1] it shall acquit. But how here? We proceed under the law of the Mutiny Act.[2] In feature no child can resemble his father more than that Act resembles in spirit the thing from which it derives—War. In His Majesty's service—in this ship, indeed—there are Englishmen forced to fight for the King against their will. Against their conscience, for aught we know. Though as their fellow creatures some of us may appreciate their position, yet as navy officers what reck we of it? Still less recks the enemy. Our impressed men he would fain cut down in the same swath with our volunteers. As regards the enemy's naval conscripts, some of whom may even share our own abhorrence of the regicidal French Directory, it is the same on our side. War looks but to the frontage, the appearance. And the Mutiny Act, War's child, takes after the father. Budd's intent or non-intent is nothing to the purpose.

"But while, put to it by those anxieties in you which I cannot but respect, I only repeat myself—while thus strangely we prolong proceedings that should be summary—the enemy may be sighted and an engagement result. We must do; and one of two things must we do—condemn or let go."

"Can we not convict and yet mitigate the penalty?" asked the sailing master, here speaking, and falteringly, for the first.

"Gentlemen, were that clearly lawful for us under the circumstances, consider the consequences of such clemency. The

---

1 Judgment Day.
2 The first Mutiny Act was passed by Parliament in 1689; here Melville uses it as a synonym for the Articles of War, though technically the Mutiny Act referred to land-based forces.

people" (meaning the ship's company) "have native sense; most of them are familiar with our naval usage and tradition; and how would they take it? Even could you explain to them—which our official position forbids—they, long molded by arbitrary discipline, have not that kind of intelligent responsiveness that might qualify them to comprehend and discriminate. No, to the people the foretopman's deed, however it be worded in the announcement, will be plain homicide committed in a flagrant act of mutiny. What penalty for that should follow, they know. But it does not follow. *Why?* they will ruminate. You know what sailors are. Will they not revert to the recent outbreak at the Nore?[1] Ay. They know the well-founded alarm—the panic it struck throughout England. Your clement sentence they would account pusillanimous. They would think that we flinch, that we are afraid of them—afraid of practicing a lawful rigor singularly demanded at this juncture, lest it should provoke new troubles. What shame to us such a conjecture on their part, and how deadly to discipline. You see then, whither, prompted by duty and the law, I steadfastly drive. But I beseech you, my friends, do not take me amiss. I feel as you do for this unfortunate boy. But did he know our hearts, I take him to be of that generous nature that he would feel even for us on whom in this military necessity so heavy a compulsion is laid."

With that, crossing the deck he resumed his place by the sashed porthole, tacitly leaving the three to come to a decision. On the cabin's opposite side the troubled court sat silent. Loyal lieges, plain and practical, though at bottom they dissented from some points Captain Vere had put to them, they were without the faculty, hardly had the inclination, to gainsay one whom they felt to be an earnest man, one too not less their superior in mind than in naval rank. But it is not improbable that even such of his words as were not without influence over them, less came home to them than his closing appeal to their instinct as sea officers: in the forethought he threw out as to the practical consequences to discipline, considering the unconfirmed tone of the fleet at the time, should a man-of-war's man's violent killing at sea of a superior in grade be allowed to pass for aught else than a capital crime demanding prompt infliction of the penalty.

Not unlikely they were brought to something more or less akin to that harassed frame of mind which in the year 1842 actuated the commander of the US brig-of-war *Somers* to resolve, under

---

1 On the Great Mutiny, see Appendix C1.

the so-called Articles of War, Articles modeled upon the English Mutiny Act, to resolve upon the execution at sea of a midshipman and two sailors as mutineers designing the seizure of the brig. Which resolution was carried out though in a time of peace and within not many days' sail of home. An act vindicated by a naval court of inquiry subsequently convened ashore. History, and here cited without comment. True, the circumstances on board the *Somers* were different from those on board the *Bellipotent*. But the urgency felt, well-warranted or otherwise, was much the same.[1]

Says a writer whom few know,[2] "Forty years after a battle it is easy for a noncombatant to reason about how it ought to have been fought. It is another thing personally and under fire to have to direct the fighting while involved in the obscuring smoke of it. Much so with respect to other emergencies involving considerations both practical and moral, and when it is imperative promptly to act. The greater the fog the more it imperils the steamer, and speed is put on though at the hazard of running somebody down. Little ween the snug card players in the cabin of the responsibilities of the sleepless man on the bridge."

In brief, Billy Budd was formally convicted and sentenced to be hung at the yardarm in the early morning watch, it being now night. Otherwise, as is customary in such cases, the sentence would forthwith have been carried out. In wartime on the field or in the fleet, a mortal punishment decreed by a drumhead court— on the field sometimes decreed by but a nod from the general— follows without delay on the heel of conviction, without appeal.

---

1   In 1842, three sailors aboard the USS *Somers* were executed for mutiny. Though authorities later cleared the officers involved—one of whom was Melville's cousin—the *Somers* Affair, as the event became known, caused a scandal ashore because of the manner and haste with which the trial and executions were conducted and because the accused ringleader was the son of a prominent government official. To many, it seemed as if the Captain, Alexander Slidell Mackenzie (1803–49), had rushed to judgment and forced his subordinates to go along. The ship was in the West Indies at the time, less than a two-week sail from its home port of New York. See Appendix C2.
2   Melville himself, though the quotation is invented; another joke at his own expense.

22

It was Captain Vere himself who of his own motion communicated the finding of the court to the prisoner, for that purpose going to the compartment where he was in custody and bidding the marine there to withdraw for the time.

Beyond the communication of the sentence, what took place at this interview was never known. But in view of the character of the twain briefly closeted in that stateroom, each radically sharing in the rarer qualities of our nature—so rare indeed as to be all but incredible to average minds however much cultivated—some conjectures may be ventured.

It would have been in consonance with the spirit of Captain Vere should he on this occasion have concealed nothing from the condemned one—should he indeed have frankly disclosed to him the part he himself had played in bringing about the decision, at the same time revealing his actuating motives. On Billy's side it is not improbable that such a confession would have been received in much the same spirit that prompted it. Not without a sort of joy, indeed, he might have appreciated the brave opinion of him implied in his captain's making such a confidant of him. Nor, as to the sentence itself, could he have been insensible that it was imparted to him as to one not afraid to die. Even more may have been. Captain Vere in end may have developed the passion sometimes latent under an exterior stoical or indifferent. He was old enough to have been Billy's father. The austere devotee of military duty, letting himself melt back into what remains primeval in our formalized humanity, may in end have caught Billy to his heart, even as Abraham may have caught young Isaac on the brink of resolutely offering him up in obedience to the exacting behest.[1] But there is no telling the sacrament, seldom if in any case revealed to the gadding world, wherever under circumstances at all akin to those here attempted to be set forth two of great Nature's nobler order embrace. There is privacy at the time, inviolable to the survivor; and holy oblivion, the sequel to each diviner magnanimity, providentially covers all at last.

The first to encounter Captain Vere in act of leaving the compartment was the senior lieutenant. The face he beheld, for the moment one expressive of the agony of the strong, was to that

---

1 In Genesis 22, God tests Abraham by commanding him to kill his only son, Isaac, but just before Abraham acts to prove his obedience, God stays his hand.

officer, though a man of fifty, a startling revelation. That the condemned one suffered less than he who mainly had effected the condemnation was apparently indicated by the former's exclamation in the scene soon perforce to be touched upon.

23

Of a series of incidents within a brief term rapidly following each other, the adequate narration may take up a term less brief, especially if explanation or comment here and there seem requisite to the better understanding of such incidents. Between the entrance into the cabin of him who never left it alive, and him who when he did leave it left it as one condemned to die; between this and the closeted interview just given, less than an hour and a half had elapsed. It was an interval long enough, however, to awaken speculations among no few of the ship's company as to what it was that could be detaining in the cabin the master-at-arms and the sailor; for a rumor that both of them had been seen to enter it and neither of them had been seen to emerge, this rumor had got abroad upon the gun decks and in the tops, the people of a great warship being in one respect like villagers, taking microscopic note of every outward movement or non-movement going on. When therefore, in weather not at all tempestuous, all hands were called in the second dogwatch, a summons under such circumstances not usual in those hours, the crew were not wholly unprepared for some announcement extraordinary, one having connection too with the continued absence of the two men from their wonted haunts.

There was a moderate sea at the time; and the moon, newly risen and near to being at its full, silvered the white spar deck wherever not blotted by the clear-cut shadows horizontally thrown of fixtures and moving men. On either side the quarter-deck the marine guard under arms was drawn up; and Captain Vere, standing in his place surrounded by all the wardroom officers, addressed his men. In so doing, his manner showed neither more nor less than that properly pertaining to his supreme position aboard his own ship. In clear terms and concise he told them what had taken place in the cabin: that the master-at-arms was dead, that he who had killed him had been already tried by a summary court and condemned to death, and that the execution would take place in the early morning watch. The word *mutiny* was not named in what he said. He refrained too from making the

occasion an opportunity for any preachment as to the maintenance of discipline, thinking perhaps that under existing circumstances in the navy the consequence of violating discipline should
be made to speak for itself.

Their captain's announcement was listened to by the throng of
standing sailors in a dumbness like that of a seated congregation
of believers in hell listening to the clergyman's announcement of
his Calvinistic text.

At the close, however, a confused murmur went up. It began
to wax. All but instantly, then, at a sign, it was pierced and suppressed by shrill whistles of the boatswain and his mates. The
word was given to about ship.

To be prepared for burial Claggart's body was delivered to
certain petty officers of his mess. And here, not to clog the sequel
with lateral matters, it may be added that at a suitable hour, the
master-at-arms was committed to the sea with every funeral
honor properly belonging to his naval grade.

In this proceeding as in every public one growing out of the
tragedy strict adherence to usage was observed. Nor in any point
could it have been at all deviated from, either with respect to
Claggart or Billy Budd, without begetting undesirable speculations in the ship's company, sailors, and more particularly men-
of-war's men, being of all men the greatest sticklers for usage. For
similar cause, all communication between Captain Vere and the
condemned one ended with the closeted interview already given,
the latter being now surrendered to the ordinary routine preliminary to the end. His transfer under guard from the captain's
quarters was effected without unusual precautions—at least no
visible ones. If possible, not to let the men so much as surmise
that their officers anticipate aught amiss from them is the tacit
rule in a military ship. And the more that some sort of trouble
should really be apprehended, the more do the officers keep that
apprehension to themselves, though not the less unostentatious
vigilance may be augmented. In the present instance, the sentry
placed over the prisoner had strict orders to let no one have communication with him but the chaplain. And certain unobtrusive
measures were taken absolutely to insure this point.

24

In a seventy-four of the old order the deck known as the upper
gun deck was the one covered over by the spar deck, which last,

though not without its armament, was for the most part exposed to the weather. In general it was at all hours free from hammocks; those of the crew swinging on the lower gun deck and berth deck, the latter being not only a dormitory but also the place for the stowing of the sailors' bags, and on both sides lined with the large chests or movable pantries of the many messes of the men.

On the starboard side of the *Bellipotent*'s upper gun deck, behold Billy Budd under sentry lying prone in irons in one of the bays formed by the regular spacing of the guns comprising the batteries on either side. All these pieces were of the heavier caliber of that period. Mounted on lumbering wooden carriages, they were hampered with cumbersome harness of breeching and strong side-tackles for running them out. Guns and carriages, together with the long rammers and shorter linstocks lodged in loops overhead—all these, as customary, were painted black; and the heavy hempen breechings, tarred to the same tint, wore the like livery of the undertakers. In contrast with the funereal hue of these surroundings, the prone sailor's exterior apparel, white jumper and white duck trousers, each more or less soiled, dimly glimmered in the obscure light of the bay like a patch of discolored snow in early April lingering at some upland cave's black mouth. In effect he is already in his shroud, or the garments that shall serve him in lieu of one. Over him but scarce illuminating him, two battle lanterns swing from two massive beams of the deck above. Fed with the oil supplied by the war contractors (whose gains, honest or otherwise, are in every land an anticipated portion of the harvest of death), with flickering splashes of dirty yellow light they pollute the pale moonshine all but ineffectually struggling in obstructed flecks through the open ports from which the tampioned cannon protrude. Other lanterns at intervals serve but to bring out somewhat the obscurer bays which, like small confessionals or side-chapels in a cathedral, branch from the long dim-vistaed broad aisle between the two batteries of that covered tier.

Such was the deck where now lay the Handsome Sailor. Through the rose-tan of his complexion no pallor could have shown. It would have taken days of sequestration from the winds and the sun to have brought about the effacement of that. But the skeleton in the cheekbone at the point of its angle was just beginning delicately to be defined under the warm-tinted skin. In fervid hearts self-contained, some brief experiences devour our human tissue as secret fire in a ship's hold consumes cotton in the bale.

But now lying between the two guns, as nipped in the vice of fate, Billy's agony, mainly proceeding from a generous young heart's virgin experience of the diabolical incarnate and effective in some men—the tension of that agony was over now. It survived not the something healing in the closeted interview with Captain Vere. Without movement, he lay as in a trance, that adolescent expression previously noted as his taking on something akin to the look of a slumbering child in the cradle when the warm hearth-glow of the still chamber at night plays on the dimples that at whiles mysteriously form in the cheek, silently coming and going there. For now and then in the gyved[1] one's trance a serene happy light born of some wandering reminiscence or dream would diffuse itself over his face, and then wane away only anew to return.

The chaplain, coming to see him and finding him thus, and perceiving no sign that he was conscious of his presence, attentively regarded him for a space, then slipping aside, withdrew for the time, peradventure feeling that even he, the minister of Christ though receiving his stipend from Mars, had no consolation to proffer which could result in a peace transcending that which he beheld. But in the small hours he came again. And the prisoner, now awake to his surroundings, noticed his approach, and civilly, all but cheerfully, welcomed him. But it was to little purpose that in the interview following, the good man sought to bring Billy Budd to some godly understanding that he must die, and at dawn. True, Billy himself freely referred to his death as a thing close at hand; but it was something in the way that children will refer to death in general, who yet among their other sports will play a funeral with hearse and mourners.

Not that like children Billy was incapable of conceiving what death really is. No, but he was wholly without irrational fear of it, a fear more prevalent in highly civilized communities than those so-called barbarous ones which in all respects stand nearer to unadulterate Nature. And, as elsewhere said, a barbarian Billy radically was—as much so, for all the costume, as his countrymen the British captives, living trophies, made to march in the Roman triumph of Germanicus.[2] Quite as much so as those later barbarians, young men probably, and picked specimens among the earlier British converts to Christianity, at least nominally such,

---

1 Shackled (adjective).
2 Germanicus Caesar (15 BCE–19 CE), Roman general who led successful raids on early England.

taken to Rome (as today converts from lesser isles of the sea may be taken to London), of whom the Pope of that time,[1] admiring the strangeness of their personal beauty so unlike the Italian stamp, their clear ruddy complexion and curled flaxen locks, exclaimed, "Angles" (meaning *English*, the modern derivative), "Angles, do you call them? And is it because they look so like angels?" Had it been later in time, one would think that the Pope had in mind Fra Angelico's seraphs, some of whom, plucking apples in gardens of the Hesperides, have the faint rosebud complexion of the more beautiful English girls.[2]

If in vain the good chaplain sought to impress the young barbarian with ideas of death akin to those conveyed in the skull, dial, and crossbones on old tombstones, equally futile to all appearance were his efforts to bring home to him the thought of salvation and a Savior. Billy listened, but less out of awe or reverence, perhaps, than from a certain natural politeness, doubtless at bottom regarding all that in much the same way that most mariners of his class take any discourse abstract or out of the common tone of the workaday world. And this sailor way of taking clerical discourse is not wholly unlike the way in which the primer of Christianity, full of transcendent miracles, was received long ago on tropic isles by any superior *savage*, so called[3]—a Tahitian, say, of Captain Cook's[4] time or shortly after that time. Out of natural courtesy he received, but did not appropriate. It was like a gift placed in the palm of an outreached hand upon which the fingers do not close.

But the *Bellipotent*'s chaplain was a discreet man possessing the good sense of a good heart. So he insisted not in his vocation here. At the instance of Captain Vere, a lieutenant had apprised him of pretty much everything as to Billy; and since he felt that innocence was even a better thing than religion wherewith to go to Judgment, he reluctantly withdrew; but in his emotion not without first performing an act strange enough in an Englishman, and under the circumstances yet more so in any regular priest.

---

1 Saint Gregory I (c. 540–604).

2 Reference to Italian painter Fra Angelico's (c. 1400–55) work *The Garden of the Hesperides*; in Greek mythology, the Hesperides were nymphs who guarded the golden apples.

3 Sceptical reference to the work of Christian missionaries, whom Melville attacked in print on multiple occasions.

4 English Captain James Cook (1728–79) led a scientific expedition to Tahiti in 1769 to make astronomical observations.

Stooping over, he kissed on the fair cheek his fellow man, a felon in martial law, one whom though on the confines of death he felt he could never convert to a dogma; nor for all that did he fear for his future.

Marvel not that having been made acquainted with the young sailor's essential innocence the worthy man lifted not a finger to avert the doom of such a martyr to martial discipline. So to do would not only have been as idle as invoking the desert, but would also have been an audacious transgression of the bounds of his function, one as exactly prescribed to him by military law as that of the boatswain or any other naval officer. Bluntly put, a chaplain is the minister of the Prince of Peace serving in the host of the God of War—Mars. As such, he is as incongruous as a musket would be on the altar at Christmas. Why, then, is he there? Because he indirectly subserves the purpose attested by the cannon; because too he lends the sanction of the religion of the meek to that which practically is the abrogation of everything but brute Force.[1]

25

The night so luminous on the spar deck, but otherwise on the cavernous ones below, levels so like the tiered galleries in a coal mine—the luminous night passed away. But like the prophet in the chariot disappearing in heaven and dropping his mantle to Elisha,[2] the withdrawing night transferred its pale robe to the breaking day. A meek, shy light appeared in the East, where stretched a diaphanous fleece of white furrowed vapor. That light slowly waxed. Suddenly *eight bells* was struck aft, responded to by one louder metallic stroke from forward. It was four o'clock in the morning. Instantly the silver whistles were heard summoning all

---

1 Over the course of an entire chapter in *White-Jacket*, amid a longer section on the ostensible anti-democratic abuses carried out against sailors on naval ships, Melville points out sarcastically the incongruities of a Christian minister serving the state on a warship: "Nor, upon reflection, was this to be marveled at, seeing how efficacious, in all despotic governments, it is for the throne and altar to go hand-in-hand" (156). In Melville's poem "Bridegroom Dick" (1888), meanwhile, the speaker refers to the minister as "disciplined and dumb" (p. 184). See Appendix D6. See also Appendix E7.

2 In 2 Kings 2:11–13, Elijah ascends to heaven in a "chariot of fire"; his son, Elisha, takes up the mantle he drops.

hands to witness punishment. Up through the great hatchways rimmed with racks of heavy shot the watch below came pouring, overspreading with the watch already on deck the space between the mainmast and foremast including that occupied by the capacious launch and the black booms tiered on either side of it, boat and booms making a summit of observation for the powder-boys and younger tars. A different group comprising one watch of topmen leaned over the rail of that sea balcony, no small one in a seventy-four, looking down on the crowd below. Man or boy, none spake but in whisper, and few spake at all. Captain Vere—as before, the central figure among the assembled commissioned officers—stood nigh the break of the poop deck facing forward. Just below him on the quarter-deck the marines in full equipment were drawn up much as at the scene of the promulgated sentence.

At sea in the old time, the execution by halter of a military sailor was generally from the foreyard. In the present instance, for special reasons the mainyard[1] was assigned. Under an arm of that yard the prisoner was presently brought up, the chaplain attending him. It was noted at the time, and remarked upon afterwards, that in this final scene the good man evinced little or nothing of the perfunctory. Brief speech indeed he had with the condemned one, but the genuine Gospel was less on his tongue than in his aspect and manner towards him. The final preparations personal to the latter being speedily brought to an end by two boatswain's mates, the consummation impended. Billy stood facing aft. At the penultimate moment, his words, his only ones, words wholly unobstructed in the utterance, were these: "God bless Captain Vere!" Syllables so unanticipated coming from one with the ignominious hemp about his neck—a conventional felon's benediction[2] directed aft towards the quarters of honor; syllables too delivered in the clear melody of a singing bird on the point of launching from the twig—had a phenomenal effect, not unenhanced by the rare personal beauty of the young sailor, spiritualized now through late experiences so poignantly profound.

Without volition, as it were, as if indeed the ship's populace were but the vehicles of some vocal current electric, with one voice from alow and aloft came a resonant sympathetic echo:

---

1 A spar extending from the mainmast holding up the mainsail.
2 Though Billy's words and the crew's echo have important figurative implications, it was customary for condemned persons to forgive or bless the authorities, thus vindicating the state's actions and reasoning; hence the phrase "conventional felon's benediction."

"God bless Captain Vere!" And yet at that instant Billy alone must have been in their hearts, even as in their eyes.

At the pronounced words and the spontaneous echo that voluminously rebounded them, Captain Vere, either through stoic self-control or a sort of momentary paralysis induced by emotional shock, stood erectly rigid as a musket in the ship-armorer's rack.

The hull, deliberately recovering from the periodic roll to leeward, was just regaining an even keel when the last signal, a preconcerted dumb one, was given. At the same moment it chanced that the vapory fleece hanging low in the East was shot through with a soft glory as of the fleece of the Lamb of God seen in mystical vision, and simultaneously therewith, watched by the wedged mass of upturned faces, Billy ascended; and, ascending, took the full rose of the dawn.[1]

In the pinioned figure arrived at the yard-end, to the wonder of all no motion was apparent, none save that created by the slow roll of the hull in moderate weather, so majestic in a great ship ponderously cannoned.

26

When some days afterwards, in reference to the singularity just mentioned, the purser, a rather ruddy, rotund person more accurate as an accountant than profound as a philosopher, said at mess to the surgeon, "What testimony to the force lodged in will power," the latter, saturnine, spare, and tall, one in whom a discreet causticity went along with a manner less genial than polite, replied, "Your pardon, Mr. Purser.[2] In a hanging scientifically conducted—and under special orders I myself directed how Budd's was to be effected—any movement following the completed suspension and originating in the body suspended, such movement indicates mechanical spasm in the muscular system. Hence the absence of that is no more attributable to will power, as you call it, than to horsepower—begging your pardon."

"But this muscular spasm you speak of, is not that in a degree more or less invariable in these cases?"

"Assuredly so, Mr. Purser."

---

1   Reminiscent of New Testament language describing Christ's ascension.
2   A ship's financial officer.

"How then, my good sir, do you account for its absence in this instance?"

"Mr. Purser, it is clear that your sense of the singularity in this matter equals not mine. You account for it by what you call will power—a term not yet included in the lexicon of science. For me, I do not, with my present knowledge, pretend to account for it at all. Even should we assume the hypothesis that at the first touch of the halyards the action of Budd's heart, intensified by extraordinary emotion at its climax, abruptly stopped—much like a watch when in carelessly winding it up you strain at the finish, thus snapping the chain—even under that hypothesis how account for the phenomenon that followed?"

"You admit, then, that the absence of spasmodic movement was phenomenal."

"It was phenomenal, Mr. Purser, in the sense that it was an appearance the cause of which is not immediately to be assigned."

"But tell me, my dear sir," pertinaciously continued the other, "was the man's death effected by the halter, or was it a species of euthanasia?"[1]

"*Euthanasia*, Mr. Purser, is something like your *will power:* I doubt its authenticity as a scientific term—begging your pardon again. It is at once imaginative and metaphysical—in short, Greek.—But," abruptly changing his tone, "there is a case in the sick bay that I do not care to leave to my assistants. Beg your pardon, but excuse me." And rising from the mess he formally withdrew.

27

The silence at the moment of execution and for a moment or two continuing thereafter, a silence but emphasized by the regular

---

1   There has been considerable speculation about Melville's use of
     "euthanasia." Melville was working in part from Schopenhauer's *The
     World as Will and Idea* (1818–44), which theorizes euthanasia as noble
     suicide, that is, as a moral admission that the sufferings of life are too
     great and can never be overcome. (See Appendix E4.) This reading
     would be consistent with the overall tenor of philosophical pessimism in
     Melville's late writings. (See Appendix G.) Melville is also likely playing
     on the more conventional Greek sense of euthanasia as the patriotic
     sacrifice of self.

wash of the sea against the hull or the flutter of a sail caused by the helmsman's eyes being tempted astray, this emphasized silence was gradually disturbed by a sound not easily to be verbally rendered. Whoever has heard the freshet-wave of a torrent suddenly swelled by pouring showers in tropical mountains, showers not shared by the plain; whoever has heard the first muffled murmur of its sloping advance through precipitous woods may form some conception of the sound now heard. The seeming remoteness of its source was because of its murmurous indistinctness, since it came from close by, even from the men massed on the ship's open deck. Being inarticulate, it was dubious in significance further than it seemed to indicate some capricious revulsion of thought or feeling such as mobs ashore are liable to, in the present instance possibly implying a sullen revocation on the men's part of their involuntary echoing of Billy's benediction. But ere the murmur had time to wax into clamor it was met by a strategic command, the more telling that it came with abrupt unexpectedness: "Pipe down the starboard watch, Boatswain, and see that they go."

Shrill as the shriek of the sea hawk, the silver whistles of the boatswain and his mates pierced that ominous low sound, dissipating it; and yielding to the mechanism of discipline the throng was thinned by one-half. For the remainder, most of them were set to temporary employments connected with trimming the yards and so forth, business readily to be got up to serve occasion by any officer of the deck.

Now each proceeding that follows a mortal sentence pronounced at sea by a drumhead court is characterized by promptitude not perceptibly merging into hurry, though bordering that. The hammock, the one which had been Billy's bed when alive, having already been ballasted with shot and otherwise prepared to serve for his canvas coffin, the last offices of the sea undertakers, the sailmaker's mates, were now speedily completed. When everything was in readiness a second call for all hands, made necessary by the strategic movement before mentioned, was sounded, now to witness burial.

The details of this closing formality it needs not to give. But when the tilted plank let slide its freight into the sea, a second strange human murmur was heard, blended now with another inarticulate sound proceeding from certain larger seafowl who, their attention having been attracted by the peculiar commotion in the water resulting from the heavy sloped dive of the shotted hammock into the sea, flew screaming to the spot. So near the hull did they come, that the stridor or bony creak of their gaunt double-jointed pinions was audible. As the ship under light airs passed on, leaving the burial spot astern, they still kept circling it low down with the moving shadow of their outstretched wings and the croaked requiem of their cries.

Upon sailors as superstitious as those of the age preceding ours, men-of-war's men too who had just beheld the prodigy of repose in the form suspended in air, and now foundering in the deeps; to such mariners the action of the seafowl, though dictated by mere animal greed for prey, was big with no prosaic significance. An uncertain movement began among them, in which some encroachment was made. It was tolerated but for a moment. For suddenly the drum beat to quarters, which familiar sound happening at least twice every day, had upon the present occasion a signal peremptoriness in it. True martial discipline long continued superinduces in average man a sort of impulse whose operation at the official word of command much resembles in its promptitude the effect of an instinct.

The drumbeat dissolved the multitude, distributing most of them along the batteries of the two covered gun decks. There, as wonted, the guns' crews stood by their respective cannon erect and silent. In due course the first officer, sword under arm and standing in his place on the quarter-deck, formally received the successive reports of the sworded lieutenants commanding the sections of batteries below; the last of which reports being made, the summed report he delivered with the customary salute to the commander. All this occupied time, which in the present case was the object in beating to quarters at an hour prior to the customary one. That such variance from usage was authorized by an officer like Captain Vere, a martinet as some deemed him, was evidence of the necessity for unusual action implied in what he deemed to be temporarily the mood of his men. "With mankind," he would say, "forms, measured forms, are everything; and that is the import couched in the story of Orpheus with his lyre spellbinding the wild denizens of the wood."[1] And this he once applied to the disruption of forms going on across the Channel and the consequences thereof.

---

1   Orpheus, Greek mythological musician and singer capable of calming and controlling all things through song; also perhaps an allusion to Orpheus' failed attempt to rescue his wife from the underworld. The upshot is that eventually even Orpheus' powers fail him, suggesting that the forms Vere believes in so absolutely may also fail.

.At this unwonted muster at quarters, all proceeded as at the regular hour. The band on the quarter-deck played a sacred air, after which the chaplain went through the customary morning service. That done, the drum beat the retreat; and toned by music and religious rites subserving the discipline and purposes of war, the men in their wonted orderly manner dispersed to the places allotted them when not at the guns.

And now it was full day. The fleece of low-hanging vapor had vanished, licked up by the sun that late had so glorified it. And the circumambient air in the clearness of its serenity[1] was like smooth white marble in the polished block not yet removed from the marble-dealer's yard.

28

The symmetry of form attainable in pure fiction cannot so readily be achieved in a narration essentially having less to do with fable than with fact. Truth uncompromisingly told will always have its ragged edges; hence the conclusion of such a narration is apt to be less finished than an architectural finial.

How it fared with the Handsome Sailor during the year of the Great Mutiny has been faithfully given. But though properly the story ends with his life, something in way of sequel will not be amiss. Three brief chapters will suffice.

In the general rechristening under the Directory of the craft originally forming the navy of the French monarchy, the *St. Louis* line-of-battle ship was named the *Athée* (the *Atheist*). Such a name, like some other substituted ones in the Revolutionary fleet, while proclaiming the infidel audacity of the ruling power, was yet, though not so intended to be, the aptest name, if one consider it, ever given to a warship; far more so indeed than the *Devastation*, the *Erebus* (the *Hell*), and similar names bestowed upon fighting ships.

On the return passage to the English fleet from the detached cruise during which occurred the events already recorded, the

---

1 Hayford and Sealts call attention to the recurrence of the vapour imagery from Billy's execution, as well as to the New Testament allusion (James 4:14) that serves as the epigraph to Melville's 1891 poem "Buddha": "For what is your life? It is even a vapor, that approacheth for a little time, and then vanisheth away" (199).

Bellipotent fell in with the *Athée*.[1] An engagement ensued; during which Captain Vere, in the act of putting his ship alongside the enemy with a view of throwing his boarders across her bulwarks, was hit by a musket ball from a porthole of the enemy's main cabin. More than disabled, he dropped to the deck and was carried below to the same cockpit where some of his men already lay. The senior lieutenant took command. Under him the enemy was finally captured, and though much crippled was by rare good fortune successfully taken into Gibraltar, an English port not very distant from the scene of the fight. There, Captain Vere with the rest of the wounded was put ashore. He lingered for some days, but the end came. Unhappily he was cut off too early for the Nile and Trafalgar. The spirit that 'spite its philosophic austerity may yet have indulged in the most secret of all passions, ambition, never attained to the fulness of fame.

Not long before death, while lying under the influence of that magical drug which, soothing the physical frame, mysteriously operates on the subtler element in man, he was heard to murmur words inexplicable to his attendant: "Billy Budd, Billy Budd." That these were not the accents of remorse would seem clear from what the attendant said to the *Bellipotent*'s senior officer of marines, who, as the most reluctant to condemn of the members of the drumhead court, too well knew, though here he kept the knowledge to himself, who Billy Budd was.

29

Some few weeks after the execution, among other matters under the head of "News from the Mediterranean," there appeared in a naval chronicle of the time, an authorized weekly publication, an account of the affair. It was doubtless for the most part written in good faith, though the medium, partly rumor, through which the facts must have reached the writer served to deflect and in part falsify them. The account was as follows:

"On the tenth of the last month a deplorable occurrence took place on board H.M.S. *Bellipotent*. John Claggart, the ship's master-at-arms, discovering that some sort of plot was incipient among an inferior section of the ship's company, and that the

---

1 According to Hayford and Sealts, at one point Melville had called the ship that kills Vere the *Directory*, after the French revolutionary government in power when the story takes place (199).

ringleader was one William Budd; he, Claggart, in the act of arraigning the man before the captain, was vindictively stabbed to the heart by the suddenly drawn sheath knife of Budd.

"The deed and the implement employed sufficiently suggest that though mustered into the service under an English name the assassin was no Englishman, but one of those aliens adopting English cognomens whom the present extraordinary necessities of the service have caused to be admitted into it in considerable numbers.

"The enormity of the crime and the extreme depravity of the criminal appear the greater in view of the character of the victim, a middle-aged man respectable and discreet, belonging to that minor official grade, the petty officers, upon whom, as none know better than the commissioned gentlemen, the efficiency of His Majesty's navy so largely depends. His function was a responsible one, at once onerous and thankless; and his fidelity in it the greater because of his strong patriotic impulse. In this instance as in so many other instances in these days, the character of this unfortunate man signally refutes, if refutation were needed, that peevish saying attributed to the late Dr. Johnson,[1] that patriotism is the last refuge of a scoundrel.

"The criminal paid the penalty of his crime. The promptitude of the punishment has proved salutary. Nothing amiss is now apprehended aboard H.M.S. *Bellipotent*."

The above, appearing in a publication now long ago superannuated and forgotten, is all that hitherto has stood in human record to attest what manner of men respectively were John Claggart and Billy Budd.[2]

30

Everything is for a term venerated in navies. Any tangible object associated with some striking incident of the service is converted into a monument. The spar from which the foretopman was suspended was for some few years kept trace of by the bluejackets.

---

1 Dr. Samuel Johnson (1709–84), famed English writer known, among other things, for his pithy sayings, including this one, which comes from James Boswell's *Life of Johnson* (1791).

2 In her 1889 account of the Somers Affair, Gail Hamilton (Mary Abigail Dodge, 1833–96) similarly plays on media misrepresentations of supposed mutineers. See Appendix C2b.

Their knowledges followed it from ship to dockyard and again from dockyard to ship, still pursuing it even when at last reduced to a mere dockyard boom. To them a chip of it was as a piece of the Cross.[1] Ignorant though they were of the secret facts of the tragedy, and not thinking but that the penalty was somehow unavoidably inflicted from the naval point of view, for all that, they instinctively felt that Billy was a sort of man as incapable of mutiny as of wilful murder. They recalled the fresh young image of the Handsome Sailor, that face never deformed by a sneer or subtler vile freak of the heart within. This impression of him was doubtless deepened by the fact that he was gone, and in a measure mysteriously gone. On the gun decks of the *Bellipotent* the general estimate of his nature and its unconscious simplicity eventually found rude utterance from another foretopman, one of his own watch, gifted, as some sailors are, with an artless *poetic* temperament. The tarry hand made some lines which, after circulating among the shipboard crews for a while, finally got rudely printed at Portsmouth as a ballad. The title given to it was the sailor's.

BILLY IN THE DARBIES[2]

Good of the chaplain to enter Lone Bay
And down on his marrowbones here and pray
For the likes just o' me, Billy Budd.—But, look:
Through the port comes the moonshine astray!
It tips the guard's cutlass and silvers this nook;
But 'twill die in the dawning of Billy's last day.
A jewel-block they'll make of me tomorrow,
Pendant pearl from the yardarm-end
Like the eardrop I gave to Bristol Molly—
O, 'tis me, not the sentence they'll suspend.
Ay, ay, all is up; and I must up too,
Early in the morning, aloft from alow.
On an empty stomach now never it would do.
They'll give me a nibble—bit o' biscuit ere I go.

---

1 The cross on which Jesus was crucified, though Hayford and Sealts note that Melville elsewhere "used the same not uncommon expression with merely casual intent" (201).
2 Slang for handcuffs, which Billy later imagines are "oozy weeds" (seaweed) encircling him after his burial at sea (p. 134). This is the final version of the poem out of which *Billy Budd* originally grew.

Sure, a messmate will reach me the last parting cup;
But, turning heads away from the hoist and the belay,[1]
Heaven knows who will have the running of me up!
No pipe to those halyards.—But aren't it all sham?
A blur's in my eyes; it is dreaming that I am.
A hatchet to my hawser? All adrift to go?
The drum roll to grog, and Billy never know?
But Donald he has promised to stand by the plank;
So I'll shake a friendly hand ere I sink.
But—no! It is dead then I'll be, come to think.
I remember Taff the Welshman when he sank.
And his cheek it was like the budding pink.
But me they'll lash in hammock, drop me deep.
Fathoms down, fathoms down, how I'll dream fast asleep.
I feel it stealing now. Sentry, are you there?
Just ease these darbies at the wrist,
And roll me over fair!
I am sleepy, and the oozy weeds about me twist.

---

1   A rope attached or turned around another object to increase strength
    and stability.

Appendix A: The British Debate over the French Revolution

[When Edmund Burke (1729–97) and Thomas Paine (1737–1809) published their rival interpretations of the French Revolution, each book became a classic of political thought almost overnight. Burke's *Reflections on the Revolution in France* (1790) remains an elegant argument for conservatism, a reasoned defense of what Melville calls in *Clarel* "tradition old and broad" (14). Paine's *Rights of Man* (1791–92) is a canny Enlightenment-style attack on everything that's dangerous about putting tradition on a pedestal. In the big picture of eighteenth-century political thought, Paine and Burke actually weren't so different. Both denounced despotism; they just disagreed about what it looked like. For Burke, it looked like your average revolutionary. For Paine, it looked like your average aristocrat, or king.]

1. From Edmund Burke, *Reflections on the Revolution in France* (1790; repr. in *Burke: Select Works*, vol. 2, ed. E.J. Payne [Oxford: Clarendon, 1883], 4–384), 11, 38–40, 57–58, 61, 69–73, 101–02

[A half-naked Marie Antoinette (1755–93) flees her bed seconds ahead of bloodthirsty revolutionaries. She survives, but only to be paraded through the streets amid "all the unutterable abominations of the furies of hell, in the abused shape of the vilest of women" (Burke 84–85). Marie Antoinette and King Louis XVI (r. 1774–92) actually lost their heads after the publication of British parliamentarian Edmund Burke's *Reflections on the Revolution in France*, but Burke was shocked by what he saw across the Channel even before that. While the excerpts below are less sensationalist than what is quoted above, taken together they give a sense of Burke's outrage and confusion at what he called "this strange chaos of levity and ferocity," the French Revolution (p. 136). How could the French turn their backs on centuries of custom and law? If Burke's argument sounds caustic and reactionary, that's because it is. It's also well-built and poised. And if it sounds familiar, it should. It's Vere's reasoning in *Billy Budd* and has been a pillar of Anglo-American conservatism since its publication.]

It looks to me as if I were in a great crisis, not of the affairs of France alone, but of all Europe, perhaps of more than Europe. All circumstances taken together, the French revolution is the most astonishing that has hitherto happened in the world. The most wonderful things are brought about in many instances by means the most absurd and ridiculous; in the most ridiculous modes; and apparently, by the most contemptible instruments. Every thing seems out of nature in this strange chaos of levity and ferocity, and of all sorts of crimes jumbled together with all sorts of follies. In viewing this monstrous tragi-comic scene, the most opposite passions necessarily succeed, and sometimes mix with each other in the mind: alternate laughter and tears; alternate scorn and horror.

You will observe that from Magna Charta to the Declaration of Right,[1] it has been the uniform policy of our constitution to claim and assert our liberties, as an *entailed inheritance* derived to us from our forefathers, and to be transmitted to our posterity; as an estate specially belonging to the people of this kingdom, without any reference whatever to any other more general or prior right. By this means our constitution preserves an unity in so great a diversity of its parts. We have an inheritable crown; an inheritable peerage; and an house of commons and a people inheriting privileges, franchises, and liberties, from a long line of ancestors.

This policy appears to me to be the result of profound reflection; or rather the happy effect of following nature, which is wisdom without reflection, and above it. A spirit of innovation is generally the result of a selfish temper and confined views. People will not look forward to posterity, who never look backward to their ancestors. Besides, the people of England well know, that the idea of inheritance furnishes a sure principle of conservation, and a sure principle of transmission; without at all excluding a principle of improvement.... By a constitutional policy, working after the pattern of nature, we receive, we hold, we transmit our government and our privileges, in the same manner in which we enjoy and transmit our property and our lives. The institutions of policy, the goods of fortune, the gifts of providence are handed down, to us, and from us, in the same course and order. Our political system is placed in a just correspondence and symmetry with the order of the world, and with the mode of existence decreed to a permanent body composed of transitory parts; wherein,

---

1 Declaration of Right, shorthand for parliamentary acts adopted during the accession of William and Mary to the British throne in 1688–89, acts guaranteeing certain rights and freedoms and imposing restrictions on the powers of the government; John Locke's (1632–1704) theory of social contract provided some of the impetus. Though it was later annulled by the pope, England's Magna Carta (1215), an agreement between King John (r. 1199–1216) and disgruntled nobles, nevertheless serves as a foundation for British and American legal articulations of individual rights.

by the disposition of a stupendous wisdom, moulding together the great mysterious incorporation of the human race, the whole, at one time, is never old, or middle-aged, or young, but in a condition of unchangeable constancy, moves on through the varied tenour of perpetual decay, fall, renovation, and progression. Thus, by preserving the method of nature in the conduct of the state, in what we improve, we are never wholly new; in what we retain we are never wholly obsolete. By adhering in this manner and on those principles to our forefathers, we are guided not by the superstition of antiquarians, but by the spirit of philosophic analogy....

Through the same plan of a conformity to nature in our artificial institutions, and by calling in the aid of her unerring and powerful instincts, to fortify the fallible and feeble contrivances of our reason, we have derived several other, and those no small benefits, from considering our liberties in the light of an inheritance. Always acting as if in the presence of canonized forefathers, the spirit of freedom, leading in itself to misrule and excess, is tempered with an awful gravity. This idea of a liberal descent inspires us with a sense of habitual native dignity, which prevents that upstart insolence almost inevitably adhering to and disgracing those who are the first acquirers of any distinction. By this means our liberty becomes a noble freedom. It carries an imposing and majestic aspect. It has a pedigree and illustrating ancestors. It has its bearings and its ensigns armorial. It has its gallery of portraits; its monumental inscriptions; its records, evidences, and titles. We procure reverence to our civil institutions on the principle upon which nature teaches us to revere individual men; on account of their age; and on account of those from whom they are descended. All your sophisters cannot produce any thing better adapted to preserve a rational and manly freedom than the course that we have pursued, who have chosen our nature rather than our speculations, our breasts rather than our inventions, for the great conservatories and magazines of our rights and privileges.

Believe me, Sir, those who attempt to level, never equalize. In all societies, consisting of various descriptions of citizens, some description must be uppermost. The levellers therefore only change and pervert the natural order of things; they load the edifice of society, by setting up in the air what the solidity of the structure requires to be on the ground. The associations of taylors and carpenters, of which the republic (of Paris, for instance) is composed, cannot be equal to the situation, into which, by the worst of usurpations, an usurpation on the prerogatives of nature, you attempt to force them.

The chancellor of France at the opening of the states, said, in a tone of oratorical flourish, that all occupations were honourable. If he meant only, that no honest employment was disgraceful, he would not have gone beyond the truth. But in asserting, that any thing is honourable, we imply some distinction in its favour. The occupation of an hair-dresser or of a working tallow-chandler, cannot be a matter of honour to any person—to say nothing of a number of other more servile employments. Such descriptions of men ought not to suffer oppression from the state; but the state suffers oppression, if such as they, either individually or collectively, are permitted to rule. In this you think you are combating prejudice, but you are at war with nature.

It is said, that twenty-four millions ought to prevail over two hundred thousand. True; if the constitution of a kingdom be a problem of arithmetic. This sort of discourse does well enough with the lamp-post for its second: to men who *may* reason calmly, it is ridiculous. The will of the many, and their interest, must very often differ; and great will be the difference when they make an evil choice. A government of five hundred country attornies and obscure curates is not good for twenty-four millions of men, though it were chosen by eight and forty millions; nor is it the better for being guided by a dozen of persons of quality, who have betrayed their trust in order to obtain that power. At present, you seem in everything to have strayed out of the high road of nature. The property of France does not govern it. Of course, property is destroyed, and rational liberty has no existence. All you have got for the present is a paper circulation, and a stock-jobbing constitution: and as to the future, do you seriously think that the territory of France, upon the republican system of eighty-three independent municipalities, (to say nothing of the parts that compose them) can ever be governed as one body, or can ever be set in motion by the impulse of one mind? When the National Assembly[1] has completed its work, it will have accomplished its ruin.

Far am I from denying in theory; full as far is my heart from withholding in practice, (if I were of power to give or to withhold,) the *real* rights of men. In denying their false claims of right, I do not mean to injure those which are real, and are such as their pretended rights would totally destroy. If civil society be made for the advantage of man, all the advantages for which it is made become his right. It is an institution of beneficence; and law itself is only beneficence acting by a rule. Men have a right to live by that rule; they have a right to do justice; as between their fellows, whether their fellows are in public function or in ordinary occupation. They have a right to the fruits of their industry; and to the means of making their industry fruitful. They

---

1 The first government of the French Revolution.

have a right to the acquisitions of their parents; to the nourishment and improvement of their offspring; to instruction in life, and to consolation in death. Whatever each man can separately do, without trespassing upon others, he has a right to do for himself; and he has a right to a fair portion of all which society, with all its combinations of skill and force, can do in his favour. In this partnership all men have equal rights; but not to equal things. He that has but five shillings in the partnership, has as good a right to it, as he that has five hundred pounds has to his larger proportion. But he has not a right to an equal dividend in the product of the joint stock; and as to the share of power, authority, and direction which each individual ought to have in the management of the state, that I must deny to be amongst the direct original rights of man in civil society; for I have in my contemplation the civil social man, and no other. It is a thing to be settled by convention.

If civil society be the offspring of convention, that convention must be its law. That convention must limit and modify all the descriptions of constitution which are formed under it. Every sort of legislative, judicial, or executory power are its creatures. They can have no being in any other state of things; and how can any man claim, under the conventions of civil society, rights which do not so much as suppose its existence? Rights which are absolutely repugnant to it? One of the first motives to civil society and which becomes one of its fundamental rules, is, *that no man should be judge in his own cause.* By this each person has at once divested himself of the first fundamental right of uncovenanted man, that is, to judge for himself and to assert his own cause. He abdicates all right to be his own governor. He inclusively, in a great measure, abandons the right of self-defence, the first law of nature. Men cannot enjoy the rights of an uncivil and of a civil state together. That he may obtain justice he gives up his right of determining what it is in points the most essential to him. That he may secure some liberty, he makes a surrender in trust of the whole of it.

Government is not made in virtue of natural rights, which may and do exist in total independence of it; and exist in much greater clearness, and in a much greater degree of abstract perfection: but their abstract perfection is their practical defect. By having a right to every thing they want every thing. Government is a contrivance of human wisdom to provide for human *wants.* Men have a right that these wants should be provided for by this wisdom. Among these wants is to be reckoned the want, out of civil society, of a sufficient restraint upon their passions. Society requires not only that the passions of individuals should be subjected, but that even in the mass and body, as well as in the individuals, the inclinations of men should frequently be thwarted, their will controlled, and their passions brought into subjection. This can only be done *by a power out of themselves*; and not, in the exercise of its function, subject to that will and to those passions which it is its office to bridle and subdue. In this sense the restraints on men, as well as their liberties, are to be reckoned among their rights. But as the liberties and the restrictions vary with times and circumstances, and admit of infinite modifications, they cannot be settled upon any abstract rule; and nothing is so foolish as to discuss them upon that principle.

The moment you abate anything from the full rights of men, each to govern himself, and suffer any artificial positive limitation upon those rights, from that moment the whole organization of government becomes a consideration of convenience. This it is which makes the constitution of a state, and the due distribution of its powers, a matter of the most delicate and complicated skill. It requires a deep knowledge of human nature and human necessities, and of the things which facilitate or obstruct the various ends which are to be pursued by the mechanism of civil institutions. The state is to have recruits to its strength, and remedies to its distempers. What is the use of discussing a man's abstract right to food or to medicine? The question is upon the method of procuring and administering them. In that deliberation I shall always advise to call in the aid of the farmer and the physician rather than the professor of metaphysics.

The science of constructing a commonwealth, or renovating it, or reforming it, is, like every other experimental science, not to be taught *à priori*. Nor is it a short experience that can instruct us in that practical science; because the real effects of moral causes are not always immediate; but that which in the first instance is prejudicial may be excellent in its remoter operation; and its excellence may arise even from the ill effects it produces in the beginning. The reverse also happens; and very plausible schemes, with very pleasing commencements, have often shameful and lamentable conclusions. In states there are often some obscure and almost latent causes, things which appear at first view of little moment, on which a very great part of its prosperity or adversity may most essentially depend. The science of government being therefore so practical in itself, and intended for such practical purposes ... it is with infinite caution that any man ought to venture upon pulling down an edifice which has answered in any tolerable degree for ages the common purposes of society, or on building it up again, without having models and patterns of approved utility before his eyes....

The pretended rights of these theorists are all extremes; and in proportion as they are metaphysically true, they are morally and politically false. The rights of men are in a sort of *middle*, incapable of definition, but not impossible to be discerned. The rights of men in governments are their advantages; and these are often in balances between differences of good, in compromises sometimes between good and evil, and sometimes between evil and evil. Political reason is a computing principle: adding, subtracting, multiplying, and dividing, morally and not metaphysically or mathematically, true moral denominations.

Thanks to our sullen resistance to innovation, thanks to the cold sluggishness of our national character, we will bear the stamp of our forefathers. We have not, as I conceive, lost the generosity and dignity of thinking of the fourteenth century; nor as yet have we subtilized ourselves into savages. We are not the converts of Rousseau; we are not the disciples of Voltaire; Helvetius has made no progress amongst us.[1] Atheists are not our preachers; madmen are not our lawgivers. We know that *we* have made no discoveries, and we think that no discoveries are to be made, in morality; nor many in the great principles of government, nor in the ideas of liberty, which were understood long before we were born, altogether as well as they will be after the grave has heaped its mold upon our presumption, and the silent tomb shall have imposed its law on our pert loquacity. In England we have not yet been completely embowelled of our natural entrails; we still feel within us, and we cherish and cultivate, those inbred sentiments which are the faithful guardians, the active monitors of our duty, the true supporters of all liberal and manly morals. We have not been drawn and trussed, in order that we may be filled, like stuffed birds in a museum, with chaff and rags, and paltry blurred shreds of paper about the rights of man. We preserve the whole of our feelings still native and entire, unsophisticated by pedantry and infidelity. We have real hearts of flesh and blood beating in our bosoms. We fear God; we look up with awe to kings; with affection to parliaments; with duty to magistrates; with reverence to priests; and with respect to nobility. Why? Because when such ideas are brought before our minds, it is *natural* to be so affected; because all other feelings are false and spurious, and tend to corrupt our minds, to vitiate our primary morals, to render us unfit for rational liberty; and by teaching us a servile, licentious, and abandoned insolence, to be our low sport for a few holidays, to make us perfectly fit for, and justly deserving of slavery, through the whole course of our lives.

You see, Sir, that in this enlightened age I am bold enough to confess that we are generally men of untaught feelings; that, instead of

---

1 Jean-Jacques Rousseau (1712–78), Voltaire (François-Marie Arouet, 1694–1778), and Claude Adrien Helvétius (1715–71) were Enlightenment philosophers whose writings helped inspire the Revolution and its governments.

casting away all our old prejudices, we cherish them to a very considerable degree, and, to take more shame to ourselves, we cherish them because they are prejudices; and the longer they have lasted, and the more generally they have prevailed, the more we cherish them.

2. From Thomas Paine, *Rights of Man* (1791–92; repr. in *The Writings of Thomas Paine*, vol. 2, ed. Moncure Daniel Conway [New York: G.P. Putnam's Sons, 1894], 264–523), 277–79, 284–85, 306–07, 366, 385–86, 426

[If it hadn't been for Burke's *Reflections* we wouldn't have Paine's *Rights of Man*. Burke was taken aback by the "levity and ferocity" of the events in France. With barely restrained anger, Paine explains where that levity and ferocity came from: a society that is unfailingly unfair. "Every place has its Bastille," Paine writes in prose every bit as elegant, if punchier, than Burke's, "and every Bastille its despot" (p. 143). Where Burke's logic underwrites Vere's, Paine's underwrites the logic of readers who believe that Vere overreaches with his authority and disregards his humanity.]

There never did, there never will, and there never can, exist a Parliament, or any description of men, or any generation of men, in any country, possessed of the right or the power of binding and controuling posterity ... or of commanding for ever how the world shall be governed, or who shall govern it; and therefore all such clauses, acts or declarations by which the makers of them attempt to do what they have neither the right nor the power to do, nor the power to execute, are in themselves null and void. Every age and generation must be as free to act for itself in all cases as the age and generations which preceded it. The vanity and presumption of governing beyond the grave is the most ridiculous and insolent of all tyrannies. Man has no property in man; neither has any generation a property in the generations which are to follow. The Parliament or the people of 1688,[1] or of any other period, had no more right to dispose of the people of the present day, or to bind or to control them in any shape whatever, than the parliament or the people of the present day have to dispose of, bind or control those who are to live a hundred or a thousand years hence. Every generation is, and must be, competent to all the purposes which its occasions require. It is the living, and not the dead, that are to be accommodated. When man ceases to be, his power and his wants cease with him; and having no longer any participation in

---

1 See Appendix A1, p. 136, note 1.

the concerns of this world, he has no longer any authority in directing who shall be its governors, or how its government shall be organised, or how administered.

I am not contending for nor against any form of government, nor for nor against any party, here or elsewhere. That which a whole nation chooses to do it has a right to do. Mr. Burke says, No. Where, then, does the right exist? I am contending for the rights of the living, and against their being willed away and controuled and contracted for by the manuscript assumed authority of the dead, and Mr. Burke is contending for the authority of the dead over the rights and freedom of the living. There was a time when kings disposed of their crowns by will upon their death-beds, and consigned the people, like beasts of the field, to whatever successor they appointed. This is now so exploded as scarcely to be remembered, and so monstrous as hardly to be believed. But the Parliamentary clauses upon which Mr. Burke builds his political church are of the same nature.

Those who have quitted the world, and those who have not yet arrived at it, are as remote from each other as the utmost stretch of mortal imagination can conceive.

When despotism has established itself for ages in a country, as in France, it is not in the person of the king only that it resides. It has the appearance of being so in show, and in nominal authority; but it is not so in practice and in fact. It has its standard everywhere. Every office and department has its despotism, founded upon custom and usage. Every place has its Bastille, and every Bastille its despot. The original hereditary despotism resident in the person of the king, divides and sub-divides itself into a thousand shapes and forms, till at last the whole of it is acted by deputation. This was the case in France; and against this species of despotism, proceeding on through an endless labyrinth of office till the source of it is scarcely perceptible, there is no mode of redress. It strengthens itself by assuming the appearance of duty, and tyrannises under the pretence of obeying.

Hitherto we have spoken only (and that but in part) of the natural rights of man. We have now to consider the civil rights of man, and to show how the one originates from the other. Man did not enter into society to become worse than he was before, nor to have fewer rights than he had before, but to have those rights better secured. His natural rights are the foundation of all his civil rights....

... Natural rights are those which appertain to man in right of his existence. Of this kind are all the intellectual rights, or rights of the mind, and also all those rights of acting as an individual for his own comfort and happiness, which are not injurious to the natural rights of others. Civil rights are those which appertain to man in right of his being a member of society. Every civil right has for its foundation some natural right pre-existing in the individual, but to the enjoyment of which his individual power is not, in all cases, sufficiently competent. Of this kind are all those which relate to security and protection.

The natural rights which [the individual] retains are all those in which the power to execute is as perfect in the individual as the right itself. Among this class, as is before mentioned, are all the intellectual rights, or rights of the mind; consequently religion is one of those rights. The natural rights which are not retained, are all those in which, though the right is perfect in the individual, the power to execute them is defective. They answer not his purpose. A man, by natural right, has a right to judge in his own cause; and so far as the right of the mind is concerned, he never surrenders it. But what availeth it him to judge, if he has not power to redress? He therefore deposits this right in the common stock of society, and takes the arm of society, of which he is a part, in preference and in addition to his own. Society *grants* him nothing. Every man is a proprietor in society, and draws on the capital as a matter of right.

But, after all, what is this metaphor called a crown, or rather what is monarchy? Is it a thing, or is it a name or is it a fraud? Is it a "contrivance of human wisdom," or of human craft to obtain money from a nation under specious pretences? Is it a thing necessary to a nation? If it is, in what does that necessity consist, what service does it perform, what is its business, and what are its merits? Does the virtue consist in the metaphor, or in the man? Doth the goldsmith that makes the crown, make the virtue also? ... In fine, what is it?

What is government more than the management of the affairs of a Nation? It is not, and from its nature cannot be, the property of any particular man or family, but of the whole community, at whose expence it is supported; and though by force and contrivance it has been usurped into an inheritance, the usurpation cannot alter the right of things. Sovereignty, as a matter of right, appertains to the Nation only, and not to any individual; and a Nation has at all times an inherent indefeasible right to abolish any form of Government it finds inconvenient, and to establish such as accords with its interest, disposition and happiness. The romantic and barbarous distinction of men into Kings and subjects, though it may suit the condition of courtiers, cannot [be] that of citizens; and is exploded by the principle upon which Governments are now founded. Every citizen is a member of the Sovereignty, and, as such, can acknowledge no personal subjection; and his obedience can be only to the laws....

What were formerly called Revolutions, were little more than a change of persons, or an alteration of local circumstances. They rose and fell like things of course, and had nothing in their existence or their fate that could influence beyond the spot that produced them. But what we now see in the world, from the Revolutions of America and France, are a renovation of the natural order of things, a system of principles as universal as truth and the existence of man, and combining moral with political happiness and national prosperity.

[W]hat is called monarchy, always appears to me a silly, contemptible thing. I compare it to something kept behind a curtain, about which there is a great deal of bustle and fuss, and a wonderful air of seeming solemnity; but when, by any accident, the curtain happens to be open—and the company see what it is, they burst into laughter.

In the representative system of government, nothing of this can happen. Like the nation itself, it possesses a perpetual stamina, as well of body as of mind, and presents itself on the open theatre of the world in a fair and manly manner. Whatever are its excellences or defects, they are visible to all. It exists not by fraud and mystery; it deals not in cant and sophistry; but inspires a language that, passing from heart to heart, is felt and understood.

Appendix B: The Rule of Law

[Rephrased, this section might be called "Duty *v.* Conscience." It follows from the Burke–Paine debate excerpted in Appendix A, but the clash is as old as human society. In political philosophy, it's at the root of social contract theory, which means it's also at the root of the very idea of democracy, something Melville calls attention to in the first excerpt below. If we give up our conscience to the state, shouldn't we be assured that the state is going to act in our best interest? Is law the final arbiter of right and wrong? Do we want to live in a world where law trumps conscience? To what do we owe duty? These questions were anything but academic in Melville's America, where slavery and industrialization made philosophical disagreements painfully, sometimes fatally real, just as they are on Vere's *Bellipotent*. And they were anything but easy. "Duty?" Melville's speaker asks in "Bridegroom Dick" (1888) (*Published Poems* 204). "[I]t pulled with more than one string, / This way and that, and anyhow a sting."]

1. **From Herman Melville, *White-Jacket; or The World in a Man-of-War* (New York: Harper and Brothers, 1850; repr. New York: A.L. Burt Company, 1892), 278–79, 284–85**

[*White-Jacket*'s account of life in the American navy is based largely on Melville's experience in the mid-1840s. Its cynicism is conspicuous. Through its eponymous narrator, Melville asks whether naval codes of conduct are commensurate with the nation's philosophical and political ideals. How can a nation's military law supersede the principles it ostensibly safeguards?]

As the Articles of War[1] form the ark and constitution of the penal laws of the American Navy, in all sobriety and earnestness it may be well to glance at their origin. Whence came they? And how is it that one arm of the national defences of a Republic comes to be ruled by a Turkish code,[2] whose every section almost, like each of the tubes of a revolving pistol, fires nothing short of death into the heart of an offender? How comes it that, by virtue of a law solemnly ratified by a Congress of freemen, the representatives of freemen, thousands of Americans are subjected to the most despotic usages, and, from the dockyards of a republic, absolute monarchies are launched, with the "glorious stars

---

1 On the Articles of War, see Appendices E1 and E3. See also p. 113, note 2.
2 In context, the narrator means a ruthless form of law.

and stripes" for an ensign? By what unparalleled anomaly, by what monstrous grafting of tyranny upon freedom did these Articles of War ever come to be so much as heard of in the American Navy?

Whence came they? They cannot be the indigenous growth of those political institutions, which are based upon that arch-democrat Thomas Jefferson's Declaration of Independence?[1] No; they are an importation from abroad, even from Britain, whose laws we Americans hurled off as tyrannical, and yet retained the most tyrannical of all.

But we stop not here; for these Articles of War had their congenial origin in a period of the history of Britain when the Puritan Republic had yielded to a monarchy restored; when a hangman Judge Jeffreys sentenced a world's champion like Algernon Sidney to the block; when one of a race by some deemed accursed of God—even a Stuart, was on the throne; and a Stuart, also, was at the head of the Navy, as Lord High Admiral. One, the son of a King beheaded for encroachments upon the rights of his people, and the other, his own brother, afterward a king, James II., who was hurled from the throne for his tyranny.[2] This is the origin of the Articles of War; and it carries with it an unmistakable clew to their despotism.

In final reference to all that has been said in previous chapters touching the severity and unusualness of the laws of the American Navy, and the large authority vested in its commanding officers, be it here observed, that White-Jacket is not unaware of the fact, that the responsibility of an officer commanding at sea—whether in the merchant service or the national marine—is unparalleled by that of any other

---

1   Thomas Jefferson (1743–1826), primary author of the Declaration of Independence (1776), which dissolved, at least from the American perspective, relations between Great Britain and its thirteen American colonies. In the document, Jefferson's debts to Enlightenment-era philosophies of individual rights are conspicuous, especially those of John Locke.

2   In 1685, James Scott (b. 1649), the illegitimate son of Charles II (r. 1660–85), led a failed revolt against James II (r. 1685–88), the Roman Catholic king of England, last of the male Stuart line, and Scott's uncle. The trials that followed, known as the Bloody Assizes and presided over by George Jeffreys (1645–89), were infamously brutal and resulted in the execution of hundreds of people and the torture of scores more. Jeffreys was earlier responsible for the death sentence of Algernon Sidney (1622–83), a British politician whose posthumous treatise *Discourses Concerning Government* was widely considered a handbook of revolution, especially in the American colonies—hence Melville's reference to Sidney as a republican martyr. Melville locates the "origin" of the Articles of War in a period of English history notorious for its intolerance, state-sanctioned savagery, and paranoia.

relation in which man may stand to man. Nor is he unmindful that both wisdom and humanity dictate that, from the peculiarity of his position, a sea-officer in command should be clothed with a degree of authority and discretion inadmissible in any master ashore. But, at the same time, these principles—recognised by all writers on maritime law—have undoubtedly furnished warrant for clothing modern sea-commanders and naval courts-martial with powers which exceed the due limits of reason and necessity. Nor is this the only instance where right and salutary principles, in themselves almost self-evident and infallible, have been advanced in justification of things, which in themselves are just as self-evidently wrong and pernicious.

Be it here, once and for all, understood, that no sentimental and theoretic love for the common sailor; no romantic belief in that peculiar noble-heartedness and exaggerated generosity of disposition fictitiously imputed to him in novels; and no prevailing desire to gain the reputation of being his friend, have actuated me in anything I have said, in any part of this work, touching the gross oppression under which I know that the sailor suffers. Indifferent as to who may be the parties concerned, I but desire to see wrong things righted, and equal justice administered to all.

Nor, as has been elsewhere hinted, is the general ignorance or depravity of any race of men to be alleged as an apology for tyranny over them. On the contrary, it cannot admit of a reasonable doubt, in any unbiased mind conversant with the interior life of a man-of-war, that most of the sailor iniquities practised therein are indirectly to be ascribed to the morally debasing effects of the unjust, despotic, and degrading laws under which the man-of-war's-man lives.

2. From Ralph Waldo Emerson, "The Fugitive Slave Law" (1851; repr. in *Miscellanies* [Boston: Houghton Mifflin, 1906], 177–214), 186, 188–89

[The Fugitive Slave Law of 1850 made it a crime for anyone in a free state to assist runaway slaves. In one fell swoop, Congress made acting according to one's conscience a crime. It also put Northern judges who opposed slavery in a tight spot. One was Lemuel Shaw (1781–1861), Chief Justice of the Massachusetts Supreme Court and Melville's father-in-law. In *Billy Budd*'s trial scene, in Chapter 21, Vere abridges the logic that Shaw and other judges found themselves defending, and thus intentionally or unintentionally validating, when they ordered slaves returned to the South under the terms of the law: "For that law and the rigor of it, we are not responsible," Vere reminds the officers sitting in judgment of Billy. "Our vowed responsibility is in this: That however pitilessly that law may operate in any instances, we nevertheless adhere to it and administer it" (p. 114). Ralph Waldo Emerson (1803–82), New England's most prominent public intellectual, delivered his response to that logic in the speech below in May 1851. His thesis, that "If our resistance to this law is not right, there is no right," expresses the belief that law must have an ethical footing (187).]

An immoral law makes it a man's duty to break it, at every hazard. For virtue is the very self of every man. It is therefore a principle of law that an immoral contract is void, and that an immoral statute is void. For, as laws do not make right, and are simply declaratory of a right which already existed, it is not to be presumed that they can so stultify themselves as to command injustice.

[The Fugitive Slave Law] is contrary to the primal sentiment of duty, and therefore all men that are born are, in proportion to their power of thought and their moral sensibility, found to be the natural enemies of this law. The resistance of all moral beings is secured to it. I had thought, I confess, what must come at last would come at first, a handing of all men against the authority of this statute. I thought it a point on which all sane men were agreed, that the law must respect the public morality. I thought that all men of all conditions had been made sharers of a certain experience, that in certain rare and retired moments they had been made to see how man is man, or what makes the essence of rational beings, namely, that whilst animals have to do with eating the fruits of the ground, men have to do with rectitude, with benefit, with truth, with something which *is*, independent of appearances: and that this tie makes the substantiality of life, this, and not their ploughing, or sailing, their trade or the breeding of families. I thought that every time a man goes back to his own thoughts, these angels receive him, talk with him, and that, in the best hours, he is uplifted in virtue of this essence, into a peace and into a power which the material world cannot give: that these moments counterbalance the years of drudgery, and that this owning of a law, be it called morals, religion, or godhead, or what you will, constituted the explanation of life, the excuse and indemnity for the errors and calamities which sadden it.

3. From Henry David Thoreau, "Slavery in Massachusetts" (1854; repr. in *The Writings of Henry David Thoreau*, vol. 4 [Boston: Houghton Mifflin: 1906], 388–408), 392–93, 394, 401

[Thoreau (1817–62) delivered the lecture on which this essay is based in Massachusetts on 4 July 1854. The occasion was the capture in Boston of an escaped slave, Anthony Burns (1834–62), and the debate over whether he ought to be remanded to his master in Virginia in accordance with the Fugitive Slave Law. Like Emerson, and like Melville, Thoreau wondered what role conscience ought to play in civil society. Is Vere, according to Thoreau's logic here, just another tool?]

Three years ago ... just a week after the authorities of Boston assembled to carry back a perfectly innocent man, and one whom they knew to be innocent, into slavery, the inhabitants of Concord caused the bells to be rung and the cannons to be fired, to celebrate their liberty,—and the courage and love of liberty of their ancestors who fought at the bridge.[1] As if *those* three millions had fought for the right to be free themselves, but to hold in slavery three million others. Nowadays, men wear a fool's-cap, and call it a liberty-cap. I do not know but there are some who, if they were tied to a whipping-post, and could but get one hand free, would use it to ring the bells and fire the cannons to celebrate *their* liberty. So some of my townsmen took the liberty to ring and fire. That was the extent of their freedom; and when the sound of the bells died away, their liberty died away also; when the powder was all expended, their liberty went off with the smoke.

The joke could be no broader if the inmates of the prisons were to subscribe for all the powder to be used in such salutes, and hire the jailers to do the firing and ringing for them, while they enjoyed it through the grating.

I wish my countrymen to consider, that whatever the human law may be, neither an individual nor a nation can ever commit the least act of injustice against the obscurest individual without having to pay the penalty for it. A government which deliberately enacts injustice, and persists in it, will at length even become the laughing-stock of the world.

I am sorry to say that I doubt if there is a judge in Massachusetts who is prepared to resign his office, and get his living innocently, whenever it is required of him to pass sentence under a law which is merely contrary to the law of God. I am compelled to see that they put themselves, or rather are by character, in this respect, exactly on a level with the marine who discharges his musket in any direction he is ordered to. They are just as much tools, and as little men. Certainly, they are not the more to be respected, because their master enslaves their understandings and consciences, instead of their bodies.

---

1   The Battle of Concord, in 1775, was the first skirmish of the American Revolutionary War.

4. From Henry David Thoreau, "A Plea for Captain John Brown" (1859; repr. in *The Writings of Henry David Thoreau*, vol. 4 [Boston: Houghton Mifflin: 1906], 409–40), 437–38

[In 1859, abolitionist John Brown (1800–59) led an attack on the federal armoury at Harpers Ferry, Virginia (now West Virginia) in hopes of sparking a slave rebellion. He was captured, tried, and executed for treason. Though Brown was a polarizing figure even among abolitionists, the failed raid pushed the United States closer to civil war. Among those who called for the state to spare his life was Thoreau, for whom Brown was a figure of righteousness in the face of unjust laws and yet another reason to be suspicious of the efficacy of law.]

The murderer always knows that he is justly punished: but when a government takes the life of a man without the consent of his conscience, it is an audacious government, and is taking a step towards its own dissolution. Is it not possible that an individual may be right and a government wrong? Are laws to be enforced simply because they were made? or declared by any number of men to be good, if they are *not* good? Is there any necessity for a man's being a tool to perform a deed of which his better nature disapproves? Is it the intention of lawmakers that *good* men shall be hung ever? Are judges to interpret the law according to the letter, and not the spirit? What right have *you* to enter into a compact with yourself that you *will* do thus or so, against the light within you? Is it for *you* to *make up* your mind,—to form any resolution whatever,—and not accept the convictions that are forced upon you, and which ever pass your understanding? I do not believe in lawyers, in that mode of attacking or defending a man, because you descend to meet the judge on his own ground, and, in cases of the highest importance, it is of no consequence whether a man breaks a human law or not. Let lawyers decide trivial cases. Business men may arrange that among themselves. If they were the interpreters of the everlasting laws which rightfully bind man, that would be another thing.

5. Herman Melville, "The Portent. (1859.)," *Battle-Pieces and Aspects of the War* (New York: Harper and Brothers, 1866), 12

["The Portent" opens Melville's first published collection of poetry, *Battle-Pieces*. It depicts the hanging of John Brown (see Appendix B4) by the Commonwealth of Virginia in December 1859. How the speaker feels about Brown's execution, and the law that requires it, is difficult to gauge. Melville seems to have wanted it that way. Was Brown's violence ultimately more righteous than the law requiring his death?]

Hanging from the beam,
    Slowly swaying (such the law),
Gaunt the shadow on your green,
    Shenandoah!
The cut is on the crown   5
(Lo, John Brown),
And the stabs shall heal no more.

Hidden in the cap
    Is the anguish none can draw;
So your future veils its face,   10
    Shenandoah!
But the streaming beard is shown
(Weird John Brown),
The meteor of the war.

6. Herman Melville, "The House-top. A Night Piece. (July, 1863.)," *Battle-Pieces and Aspects of the War* (New York: Harper and Brothers, 1866), 86–87

[The context for this widely reprinted poem is the New York City Draft Riot of 1863, when economic, ethnic, and racial tensions boiled over in reaction to the first federal military draft. As in "The Portent," Melville's speaker's mixed emotions are historically accurate. Though many New Yorkers were shocked by the violence of the riot, they nevertheless cautioned against cracking down too hard on those responsible. That caution would all but disappear a decade later, when the railroad strike of 1877 took civil unrest to a whole new level (see Appendix B8). "The House-top" is also about the ethics of war. On the one hand, the North's scorched-earth tactics at the end of the Civil War seemed to many a disproportionate response to the threat posed by the South. On the other hand, what should we expect when "The Town"—i.e., the nation—"is taken by its rats"?]

No sleep. The sultriness pervades the air
And binds the brain—a dense oppression, such
As tawny tigers feel in matted shades,
Vexing their blood and making apt for ravage.
Beneath the stars the roofy desert spreads   5
Vacant as Libya. All is hushed near by.

Yet fitfully from far breaks a mixed surf
Of muffled sound, the Atheist roar of riot.
Yonder, where parching Sirius set in drought,[1]
Balefully glares red Arson—there—and there.   10
The Town is taken by its rats—ship-rats
And rats of the wharves. All civil charms
And priestly spells which late held hearts in awe—
Fear-bound, subjected to a better sway
Than sway of self; these like a dream dissolve,   15
And man rebounds whole æons back in nature.
Hail to the low dull rumble, dull and dead,
And ponderous drag that shakes the wall.
Wise Draco[2] comes, deep in the midnight roll
Of black artillery; he comes, though late;   20
In code corroborating Calvin's creed[3]
And cynic tyrannies of honest kings;
He comes, nor parlies; and the Town, redeemed,
Gives thanks devout; nor, being thankful, heeds
The grimy slur on the Republic's faith implied,   25
Which holds that Man is naturally good,
And—more—is Nature's Roman, never to be scourged.

7. Sarah Piatt, "The Palace-Burner. A Picture in a Newspaper," *The Independent* (28 November 1872): 2

[American poet Sarah Piatt (1836–1919) based this dramatic monologue about a mother and her young son on a picture that appeared in *Harper's Weekly* in July 1871. It depicts the execution of an impoverished woman, a Pétroleuse, accused of aiding the Paris Commune, the revolutionary government which ruled briefly that year. Like the British in the 1790s, Americans in the 1870s worried that the political upheavals in France would find their way across the water. The poem also reflects, however, the conflicted feelings that many Americans experienced in

---

1 Sirius, the Dog Star, is the brightest star in the night sky, believed by ancient Egyptians to cause the Nile to flood and associated by the Romans with summer heat.

2 Draco was a seventh-century BCE Athenian legislator responsible for the first written laws, laws so merciless that they gave rise to the adjective *draconian*; the speaker's use of his name may be read as affirmation or criticism of the state's response to the rioters.

3 A reference to the Calvinist doctrine of predestination, which many late-nineteenth-century Americans considered oppressive and which here serves as a metaphor for fate. See p. 84, note 4.

"The End of the Commune—Execution of a Pétroleuse," *Harper's Weekly* (8 July 1871), 628.

response to social unrest at home and abroad. Piatt's speaker equivocates when she suggests that she respects both the law and those who break it, probably because many Americans felt the same.]

She has been burning palaces.[1] "To see
  The sparks look pretty in the wind?" Well, yes—
And something more. But women brave as she
  Leave much for cowards such as I to guess.

---

1 At the time it was believed that the Pétroleuses, poor women in Paris who sympathized with the ideals of the revolution, had set fire to the city; historians have since discredited that story.

But this is old, so old that everything   5
   Is ashes here—the woman and the rest.
Two years are oh! so long. Now you may bring
   Some newer pictures. You like this one best?

You wish that you had lived in Paris then?
   You would have loved to burn a palace, too?   10
But they had guns in France, and Christian men
   Shot wicked little Communists, like you.

You would have burned the palace? Just because
   You did not live in it yourself? Oh! why?
Have I not taught you to respect the laws?   15
   You would have burned the palace. Would not *I*?

Would I? Go to your play. Would I, indeed?
   I? Does the boy not know my soul to be
Languid and worldly, with a dainty need
   For light and music? Yet he questions me.   20

Can he have seen my soul more near than I?
   Ah! in the dusk and distance sweet she seems,
With lips to kiss away a baby's cry,
   Hands fit for flowers, and eyes for tears and dreams.

Can he have seen my soul? And could she wear   25
   Such utter life upon a dying face,
Such unappealing, beautiful despair,
   Such garments—soon to be a shroud—with grace?

Has she a charm so calm that it could breathe
   In damp, low places, till some frightened hour;   30
Then start, like a fair, subtle snake, and wreathe
   A stinging poison with a shadowy power?

Would *I* burn palaces? The child has seen
   In this fierce creature of the Commune here,
So bright with bitterness and so serene,   35
   A being finer than my soul, I fear.

8. From L.H. Atwater, "The Great Railroad Strike," *Presbyterian Quarterly and Princeton Review* 23 (October 1877): 719, 720, 729–30

[One of the largest civil disturbances in American history took place in 1877, when railroad employees stopped working and effectively shut down the nation's transportation system. Though the labour action was not coordinated, it quickly gained traction with other disaffected workers. The unrest was met with violence in cities like Pittsburgh, where militia troops used Gatling guns on demonstrators. Critics wondered aloud whether French revolutionaries were seeding discontent among the working classes. Strikers and sympathizers, on the other hand, argued that the labour situation had become untenable and abusive, that the government was in the pocket of big business, and that the violent suppression of citizens in places proved, as Melville argues in *White-Jacket* and perhaps in *Billy Budd*, that the nation was becoming a little too adept at profaning the ideals on which it was founded (see Appendix B1). The article below, by Lyman Hotchkiss Atwater (1813–83), a Calvinist theologian and professor at Princeton, represents the feeling of social conservatives who saw in the strike nothing more than the work of "a few desperate and infuriated men."]

[The railroad strike] partially uncapped the crater of a social volcano over which we have been sleeping, nearly all of us without suspicion or alarm, while a few have been aware of its existence. These were the less surprised when it burst forth, because they had long seen its smouldering fires, ready to rage on the slightest gust of provocation, and come forth in fury and devastation in a time unlooked for, even as a thief cometh in the night. They have seen this to be the inevitable danger of the so-called trades-unions into which nearly all the skilled laborers, or manual laborers in special occupations, are organized. How and why they stand related as cause and effect will be made to appear in its proper place. The vast increase of tramps, idlers, and the scum of Old World communism lately cast among us, enhances the danger.

The knowledge that a few desperate and infuriated men could in this manner lay their hand upon the throat of the country, and griping [*sic*] it almost to the very point of strangulation, keep its hold for days and weeks, was indeed a revelation of direst portent to those who, having thought they foresaw the impending evil, were thus rudely taught that they had only imagined the speck, in the sky which spread, and thickened, and lowered, until it discharged itself far and wide in lightning, thunder, tempest and tornado. No event since the bombardment of Sumter[1] has struck the country with such startling and ominous dismay, or been accepted as so loud a summons to rally to the defence of our altars and firesides as the mobocratic reign of terror in the latter part of July under the lead of railroad strikers. The periodical press of the country, almost without exception, has felt called to the duty of contributing its quota of light upon the causes and cure of the portentous social phenomena, of which these events, unless rightly improved for the prevention of their recurrence, or evils equivalent, if not worse, are not the end, but only the beginning.

... [I]s a free people about to sit tamely under such a despotism, and allow their persons, property, liberty, government to be dependent on the beck, the caprice of a junto[2] of men, who stand ready to strike in the dark, from their secret conclave, at everything we hold dear, our very altars and our firesides, no one knows when? ... [S]hould we rest until this monstrous usurpation, and fomenting cause of social disorganization, of mobs and riots, of evils, of which the experience of last summer gave us a fearful lesson, be abated and abolished?

9. From Clement, "Let Law Violated Be Vindicated," *New York Evangelist* (26 August 1886): 1

[In May 1886, during a rally for an eight-hour work day in Chicago's Haymarket Square, a bomb was detonated amid advancing police. Despite confusion over who threw the device, eight anarchists were convicted in what seemed to many a show trial. As in the railroad strike of 1877 (see Appendix B8), supporters of the convictions argued that the American way of life was under assault by forces of the political left, while critics of the authorities proposed that that ideal had already been coopted by big business, which was more interested in profit than rights. The opening sentence refers to the idea behind the article's title: that law is the arbiter of right and wrong in America, which is to say that law is always right because it is the law (see Appendix C2a).]

This is the meaning of the verdict of the jury in the Anarchist case at Chicago. That verdict, is, as all our readers know, that seven of the eight defendants shall be hung, and that the eighth ... shall be confined in the penitentiary for fifteen years. Save only a little handful of now

---

1 The Confederate bombardment of Fort Sumter, in Charleston harbour, on 12 April 1861, was the first battle of the American Civil War (1861–65).
2 A faction.

frightened persons who are of kindred spirit with the Anarchists, that verdict commands universal approval in this region. Not only men of wealth, but equally with them, the laboring men, the toiling masses, who are made up of honest and law-abiding citizens, give their united and hearty sanction to the verdict of this courageous and faithful jury. It was a tremendous responsibility which was laid upon them. On the one hand, they must have shrunk, as humane men desiring to spare rather than to take life, from uniting in a verdict which dooms seven men to die. It would be a dreadful error if, through mistake or prejudice, they should condemn to die men who had done nothing deserving of death. On the other hand, the majesty of the law had been insulted and defied by the brutal murder of seven of its sworn and heroic defenders, and by the cruel maiming and mangling of scores of others.... If these men were among the conspirators, whether as leaders or followers, who had brought about these terrible results, then they ought to die. Mercy to them would be vengeance to society. Not to throttle them, would be to "throttle the law" as one of them, on that fatal night at the Haymarket, fiercely called upon his fellow-conspirators to do. The peril was great. The interests at stake were of unspeakable magnitude and importance, involving not the order and welfare of one city only, but the welfare of the whole country, and to some extent doubtless, of other countries besides our own.

10. From Arthur Edwards, "Chicago's Experience with Anarchy," *Chautauquan* 7 (December 1886): 70

[This article expresses a way of thinking that was common at the time Melville was writing *Billy Budd* and that is reflected in the book's newspaper account of the events aboard the *Bellipotent* (Chapter 29): that Haymarket was a local skirmish in a worldwide conflict between the forces of democracy and communism, conservatism and liberalism, good and evil.]

It is not extravagant to say that this Chicago anarchist trial and verdict, mark an era whose significance was felt in every European capital on the twentieth day of August, 1886. It was a test case for all modern civilization. The jury's awful response paralyzed every anarchist who had landed in this country, and we doubt not that it modified the emigrant plans of thousands who contemplated their vulture-like flight to our shores....

Enough has been done to demonstrate that society will not suffer such monsters to teach—much less, put into force—these suicidal doctrines. It seems possible to plot against and terrorize even a czar so that life should be a burden to him, but a free country is a power against which license cannot prevail. Kings must fight their open and secret foes; but liberty by virtue of the free choice of enlightened citizens is invincible. It is far more easy to imagine Russia subjugated by Nihilists, and Herr Most on the throne of Peter the Great,[1] than to conceive of a decade of American chaos as the result of a crusade by all the anarchists of all continents.

---

1   Johann Most (1846–1906), German-American anarchist, writer, and newspaper publisher. Czar Peter I (1672–1725), founder of modern Russia. See p. 108, note 1.

Appendix C: Naval Mutiny

["Who in the rainbow can draw the line where the violet tint ends and the orange tint begins?," the narrator asks in one of *Billy Budd*'s most famous passages (p. 107). "Distinctly we see the difference of the colors, but where exactly does the one first blendingly enter into the other?" The narrator is talking about Vere's sanity. However, he could just as easily be talking about revolution, or mutiny, which are in principle the same thing. In his 1830 novel *The King's Own*, which opens during the Nore mutiny, the popular British novelist Frederick Marryat (1792–1848) struck a similar note: "Doubtless there is a point at which endurance of oppression ceases to be a virtue, and rebellion can no longer be considered as a crime, but it is a dangerous and intricate problem, the solution of which had better not be attempted" (see below, pp. 164–65). *Billy Budd* is about the "dangerous and intricate problem" of mutiny and sedition generally. Whether the book endorses a course of action—tolerate revolt or crush it—is still debated.]

1. The Spithead and Nore Mutinies, 1797

[The Great Mutiny of 1797 was actually two munities, Spithead and Nore. It's the Nore that haunts Vere, because it was there that rebellious British sailors threatened to give the French the keys to the kingdom just when the British navy was at its weakest. In their classic account *The Floating Republic* (1935), G.E. Manwaring and Bonamy Dobrée suggest that for Britain, suddenly without its first line of defense, the Great Munity "was like the crack of doom" (7).]

a. From Robert Southey, *The Life of Nelson* (1813; London: Bickers and Son, 1883), 247

[The Horatio Nelson that nineteenth-century British and Americans knew was the one Robert Southey (1774–1843) described in this revered 1813 biography of England's most revered naval hero. Southey's Nelson is a born admiral: brilliant, impetuous, honest, selfless, and beloved by his crews, if not always appreciated by his superiors. His impatience with rules and regulations and mostly his romantic heroism are used by Melville in Chapters 4 and 5 of *Billy Budd* as counterpoints to Vere's pragmatism.]

Never was any commander more beloved. He governed men by their reason and their affections: they knew that he was incapable of caprice or tyranny; and they obeyed him with alacrity and joy, because he possessed their confidence as well as their love.... Severe discipline he detested, though he had been bred in a severe school: he never inflicted corporal punishment, if it were possible to avoid it; and when compelled to enforce it, he, who was familiar with wounds and death, suffered like a woman. In his whole life Nelson was never known to act unkindly towards an officer. If he was asked to prosecute one for ill behaviour, he used to answer: "That there was no occasion for him to ruin a poor devil, who was sufficiently his own enemy to ruin himself." But in Nelson there was more than the easiness and humanity of a happy nature: he did not merely abstain from injury; his was an active and watchful benevolence, ever desirous not only to render justice, but to do good.

b. From Douglas Jerrold, *Black-Eyed Susan* (1829; Boston: William V. Spencer, 1856), 30–31

[British playwright Douglas Jerrold (1803–57) wrote a play explicitly about the events of 1797, *The Mutiny of the Nore* (1830), and Melville likely drew on it for *Billy Budd*. However, his popular melodrama *Black-Eyed Susan* (1829) is a fuller portrayal of the political, legal, and economic forces behind Spithead and Nore, even if only by analogy. The play's hero, William, who has already suffered various indignities that are part and parcel of life in the Royal Navy, is court-martialled after striking his captain, Crosstree. Like Billy, William is guilty of mutiny but only technically: he stumbled upon the captain preparing to sexually assault his wife, Susan, and attacked him. The trial scene reprinted here is particularly acute in its depiction of a rule of law that eclipses the sympathy of judges, the same dilemma in which Vere and his officers find themselves. William's belief that "the gilt swabs on the shoulders can't alter the heart that swells beneath" (p. 163) mirrors the feelings of readers critical of Vere's argument that in donning the uniform he and his officers "ceased to be natural free agents" (p. 114).]

Adm[iral]. Remove the prisoner. [*Exeunt Master-at-Arms, with William*][1] Gentlemen, nothing more remains for us than to consider the justice of our verdict. Although the case of the unfortunate man admits of many pa'liatives, still for the upholding of a necessary discipline, any commiseration would afford a dangerous precedent, and I fear, cannot be indulged—Gentlemen, are you all determined on your verdict? Guilty, or not guilty? (*After a pause, the Captains bow assent.*) It remains then for me to pass the sentence of the law? (*Captains bow.*)

---

1 Some stage directions are abbreviated or omitted.

Bring back the prisoner. [*Re-enter William and Master-at-Arms*] ... Prisoner—after a patient and impartial investigation of your case, this court has unanimously pronounced you *Guilty*—(*pause.*) If you have anything to say in arrest of judgment,—now is your time to speak.

Wil[liam].　...Your honors, I had been three years at sea, and had never looked upon or heard from my wife—as sweet a little craft as was ever launched—I had come ashore, and I was as lively as a petrel[1] in a storm—I found Susan, that's my wife, your honors, all her gilt taken by the land-sharks;[2] but yet all taut, with a face as red and as rosy as the king's head on the side of a fire-bucket. Well, your honors, when we were as merry as a ship's crew on a pay-day, there comes an order to go aboard [our vessel]—I left Susan, and went with the rest of the liberty-men to [ask] leave of the first-lieutenant. I hadn't been gone the turning of an hour-glass, when I heard Susan giving signals of distress, I out with my cutlass, made all sail, and came up to my craft—I found her battling with a pirate[3]—I never looked at his figure head, never stopped—would any of your honors? long live you and your wives, say I! would any of your honors have rowed alongside as if you'd been going aboard a royal yacht?—no, you wouldn't; for the gilt swabs on the shoulders can't alter the heart that swells beneath; you would have done as I did; and what did I; why, I cut him down like a piece of old junk—had he been the first lord of the Admiralty, I had done it. [*Overcome with emotion.*]

Adm.　　Prisoner, we keenly feel for your situation; yet you, as a good sailor, must know that the course of justice cannot be evaded.

Wil.　　Your honors, let me be no bar to it; I do not talk for my life. Death! why, if I 'scaped it here—the next capfull of wind might blow me from the yard-arm. All I would strive for, is to show I had no malice: all I wish whilst you pass sentence, is your pity. That, your honors, whilst it is your duty to condemn the sailor, may, as having wives your honor and children you love, respect the husband.

Adm.　　Have you any thing further to advance?

Wil.　　All my cable is run out.—I'm brought too.

Adm.　　(*All the Captains rise.*) Prisoner! it is now my most painful duty to pass the sentence of the Court upon you. The Court commis-

---

1　A seabird.
2　Susan is bankrupted by creditors and landlords.
3　That is, her assaulter. William speaks almost entirely in nautical metaphors.

erates your situation! and, in consideration of your services, will see that every care is taken of your wife when deprived of your protection.

Wil.   Poor Susan!

Adm.   Prisoner! your case falls under the twenty-second article of war. (*Reads.*) "If any man in, or belonging to the Fleet, shall draw, or offer to draw, or lift up his hand against his superior officer, he shall suffer death."[1] (*Putting on his hat.*) The sentence of the Court is, that you be hanged at the foreyard-arm of this his Majesty's ship, at the hour of 10 o'clock: Heaven pardon your sins, and have mercy on your soul! This Court is now dissolved.

c. From Captain [Frederick] Marryat, *The King's Own and the Pirate* (1830; London: J.M. Dent, 1895), 1–2

[The opening of Frederick Marryat's bestselling novel *The King's Own*, likely one of Melville's sources, loosely fictionalizes the mutinies at Spithead and Nore with a mixture of sympathy for, and dismay with, almost everyone involved, sailors and officers alike. Only the actions of the admiralty and crown come in for unequivocal criticism. Like Melville, Marryat makes mutiny into a problem for philosophers, sociologists, and psychologists.]

There is perhaps no event in the annals of our history which excited more alarm at the time of its occurrence, or has since been the subject of more general interest, than the Mutiny at the Nore, in the year 1797. Forty thousand men, to whom the nation looked for defence from its surrounding enemies, and in steadfast reliance upon whose bravery it lay down every night in tranquillity,—men who had dared everything for their king and country, and in whose breasts patriotism, although suppressed for the time, could never be extinguished,—irritated by ungrateful neglect on the one hand, and by seditious advisers on the other, turned the guns which they had so often manned in defence of the English flag against their own countrymen and their own home, and, with all the acrimony of feeling ever attending family quarrels, seemed determined to sacrifice the nation and themselves, rather than listen to the dictates of reason and of conscience.

Doubtless there is a point at which endurance of oppression ceases to be a virtue, and rebellion can no longer be considered as a crime; but it is a dangerous and intricate problem, the solution of which had

---

1   This is the same article under which Billy is condemned.

better not be attempted. It must, however, be acknowledged, that the seamen, on the occasion of the first mutiny, had just grounds of complaint, and that they did not proceed to acts of violence until repeated and humble remonstrance had been made in vain.

Whether we act in a body or individually, such is the infirmity and selfishness of human nature, that we often surrender to importunity that which we refuse to the dictates of gratitude,—yielding for our own comfort, to the demands of turbulence, while quiet unpretending merit is overlooked and oppressed, until, roused by neglect, it demands, as a right, what policy alone should have granted as a favour.

Such was the behaviour, on the part of government, which produced the mutiny at the Nore.

2. The *Somers* Mutiny, 1842

[The mutiny at Nore troubles Vere, but another mutiny troubles *Billy Budd*'s narrator. In 1842, three sailors were executed for treason aboard the US warship *Somers*. The case became a sensation for a few reasons: it was the first time American sailors were executed at sea for treason under the Articles of War; from the outside, it looked as though the captain had abused his authority; the accused ringleader, Philip Spencer (1823–42), was the son of the Secretary of War, John C. Spencer (1788–1855); moreover, the procedural inquiries into the trial and execution seemed less than rigorous. It mattered to Melville for other reasons, too. His cousin, Guert Gansevoort (1812–68), was a junior officer on the ship and seemed never to recover from the role he played in the events. In the late 1880s, after Melville had begun writing *Billy Budd*, the *Somers* was back in the news. Given the timing, the event could not have inspired Melville to write the novella, but the reference in Chapter 21 shows that it was on his mind.]

a. From [Charles Sumner,] "The Mutiny of the Somers," *North American Review* 57 (July 1843): 195, 214, 225, 228–29

[Years before being caned on the Capital floor by a fellow Senator, Charles Sumner (1811–74) was a respected orator, writer, reformer, and lawyer. It was this latter role that likely prompted his defense of *Somers* captain Alexander Slidell Mackenzie (1803–48) and exposition of the rule of law, reprinted below (see also Appendix B). Melville likely based elements of Vere's argument in Chapter 21 on Sumner's rationalization of Mackenzie's actions in the heat of the moment. Prior to the section reprinted here, Sumner directly ties the *Somers* to the Spithead and Nore mutinies.]

The highest crime known to the law is treason; it is higher than other crimes, because it draws in its train the perpetration of all others. It is an endeavour to overturn the government of the country. To accomplish its end, it unlooses the bands of social order, it subverts the authority of law, and inflames the worst passions of men. It is wise, therefore, for nations to guard against this crime, by jealous laws and stern punishments.

For the present, we leave all the considerations suggested by this historical examination, and hasten to the immediate subject before us. The affair of the *Somers* will stand out conspicuously in the naval history of the country, as well for the singular atrocity of the conception of the mutiny, as from the character of its chief instigator, and the summary and painful way in which it was suppressed. The annals of the world do not afford a more impressive scene than that of the young commander of a small ship, away from his country, at sea, in the exercise of what he believed to be a solemn duty, ordering the execution, at the yard-arm, of a brother officer, the son of a distinguished Minister of State. At the risk of repeating a more than thrice-told tale, we proceed at once to give a narrative of this event, which we shall make as brief as possible, endeavouring simply to present the facts that are essential to enable us to determine the responsibility of Commander Mackenzie for an act, in many respects, without precedent in naval history.

After the prompt and decided opinion of the Court of Inquiry, the honorable acquittal [of Mackenzie] by the Court-martial, and the confirmation thereof by the President, it may seem superfluous for us to undertake to add another word, even by way of explanation. The country has spoken through its constituted organs, and their justice cannot be rejudged. But the hardihood of public opinion, and the voice of slander, disregard the formal judgments of courts; and there are not a few, who, with audacious hands, would venture to lift these "anchors" of the law.

What were the duties imposed upon the commander by this event? Of course, to suppress the mutiny, protect the lives of his officers and crew, and save the ship which had been committed to his charge. But the law does not impose extraordinary duties, without conferring at the same time, coextensive powers, or means for the performance of the duties. It does not enjoin upon its servants arduous exertions, without, from its ample armory, intrusting them with weapons adequate to the difficult purpose. These will differ much from the powers to be exercised on ordinary occasions. We will not undertake to decide the question, whether a national ship, on the high seas, in time of peace, and in the absence of mutiny or disturbance, is under the rule of the municipal law or of the martial law. But, however this may be in ordinary circumstances, we cannot doubt that, by the mutiny on board the *Somers*, this ship was placed, for the time being, in a state of war. It was as if the enemy were at the gates, or rather already within the walls, of the city.... Amid the sound of arms, the ordinary municipal law, which might before have controlled the duties and responsibilities of officers, became silent. Martial law prevailed. By the course of events, the commander was invested with a duty not unlike that of the dictator, to see that the ship received no detriment. The law, that laid on his shoulders the burden of these transcendent powers, required in his case, as in many other instances where it imposes duties, only their honest and conscientious exercise to the best of his abilities. In the flagrant proof of the existence of the mutiny, and the melancholy circumstances by which he was surrounded, he might read legibly, as in a warrant of the law the customary formula of that instrument—"*for which these shall be your warrant*"—and proceed, without fear of the future, to the execution of a citizen.

b. From Gail Hamilton, "The Murder of Philip Spencer," *Cosmopolitan* 7 (June–August 1889): 133, 134–35, 354

[In her sad and sarcastic 1889 analysis of the transcripts from the inquiry into the *Somers* Affair, Gail Hamilton (Mary Abigail Dodge, 1833–96) argues that Commander Mackenzie, suffering from paranoid and "malignant idiocy," murdered innocent men and that the navy's own inquiries missed, misunderstood, and ignored evidence to that effect (348). Hamilton expends a fair amount of vitriol on Mackenzie, but at the end of her long article she turns her attention to a different target: Charles Sumner. In the passages below, Hamilton plays Thomas Paine to Sumner's Edmund Burke. "Better to be despised for too anxious apprehensions, than ruined by too confident a security," Burke said in 1790 (11). What if it's the other way around, Hamilton asks? What if it's better to be despised for too confident a belief in civil liberties than ruined by too anxious an obsession with national security? She is confident that's the case. Melville seems less sure in *Billy Budd*, or at least questions whether we can ever really answer the question either way.]

When, in December, 1842, the United States man-of-war *Somers* arrived off the harbor of New York, for some unexplained reason a mystery hung over her arrival. She remained outside for two days, but sent on shore an officer of the vessel, a nephew of the commander, a boy of seventeen, who at once hastened to Washington, bearing a sealed report to the Secretary of the Navy, but giving out also on his way ominous hints of fearful tidings.

Arrived in Washington, the report was immediately printed, and thence flew over the land. It was of a nature to fly.

Its purport was that a wide and most murderous mutiny had been stirred up on board the ship by Philip Spencer, son of the Secretary of War, and a midshipman of the Somers, and that the commander had met the emergency with the most-courageous promptness by hanging young Spencer at the yard-arm. Two associates of lower rank but of equal guilt had suffered the same penalty. With their dying breath they had confessed their guilt and owned their punishment just.[1]

More dreadful tidings never wrung a father's heart or convulsed a nation's capital. The completeness and the suddenness left love not a ray of hope. The men were hanged; there was no [reprieve]. They had confessed their guilt; there was no defense. "You have read," wrote W[illiam] H. Seward,[2] then governor of NewYork, "the awful calamity that has befallen the Spencers. Was ever a blow more appalling? I, of course, knew Philip only as friends know our children. I should as soon have expected a deer to ravage a sheepfold. There are all manner of reports from Washington concerning the manner in which the parents receive this last sad blow, but I have no curiosity on the subject. I know that nature has shock to the mother; but time may heal and obliterate the wound. The card which Mr. Spencer has published (or rather his communication) shows that his iron nerves were proof."

His nerves had need be of iron. The horrible news broke upon him and upon all the world at once. It was only on Saturday that the messenger brought it. There were no telegrams, no premonitory, preparatory hints. His boy was hanged—had been a fortnight dead. That was the first hint as well as the first announcement. Under the shadow of this ghastly fact, the father examined the papers presented by the man who had hung him. His iron nerves did not fail. His clear mind caught the case instantly. ByTuesday he had mastered the legal points leading up to the execution at sea; he had discerned the carefully laid machinery to justify that execution, on shore; he had heard the rising of public opinion, rising responsive to the keynote given by the commander; and he was ready to speak, and did speak, for his lost son. Nor did he forget that son's humble companions. With a calmness which, under the circumstances, was marvelous; with a trust in his country's sense

---

1   Similar to Billy's approbation of Vere's sentence. On this tradition, see p. 125, note 2.

2   William H. Seward (1801–72), Governor of NewYork, US Senator, and US Secretary of State during and after the Civil War.

of right which, considering the issue, is most pathetic; with a self command which can not be too much commended,—he sought, not to pervert or to prejudice the truth, but to stem the current of falsehood; not to prevent a severe, but to stay a hasty judgment; not to avert, but to secure justice.

The appeal—I know not why—was vain. The examination, strange to say, was fruitless. Was it that there was something so captivating to the American people in the idea of hanging the son of a Cabinet officer, that they utterly refused to be balked by so unimportant a question as whether he deserved hanging?

In the name of truth, which is eternal; of justice to the dead, which is the highest duty that can devolve upon the living; the verdict of history should be reversed, and everywhere it should be told and known that Philip Spencer and his two companions were illegally and unjustifiably put to death, absolutely innocent of the crimes wherewith they were charged.

The proof of this is contained in the public and printed records of the court-martial, where it lives, vital and irrefragable, to confound the unjust judgment that defied its witness nearly fifty years ago.

By the appalling power of rant and cunning, stimulated to untiring ingenuity at the stern demand of self-preservation, appealing to religious sentiment and democratic principle, appropriating judicial machinery, and applying the public press, the American people were induced to adopt this murder as their own.

Some voices were raised against it, but they were cried down as being raised for political purposes and against a Christian gentleman. Colonel Benton and Fenimore Cooper wrote clear and conclusive treatises, examining and condemning the commander's course.[1] Charles Sumner—alas!—with a disregard of facts discreditable either to his intelligence or to his integrity, eulogized the commander in *The North American Review*. The New York *Tribune* went astray speaking lies as soon as the *Somers* came into port, and the multitude of newspapers followed it to do evil, till poor Spencer's character was as foully murdered on shore as his body had been at sea.[2] Never was the wrong-

---

1 Thomas Hart Benton (1782–1858), Missouri senator who argued that the captain had murdered the sailors and that the problem with the navy was officers' belief in their own absolute authority (Leeman 183); author James Fenimore Cooper (1789–1851) was no more impressed by the evidence given at the court martial.

2 The presumed newspaper misrepresentations mirror the misrepresentation of the events on the *Bellipotent*. See pp. 131–32.

headedness of the press more signally and grievously, illustrated. The name and fame of Spencer was indeed as irretrievable as his life.

To the high-bred boy, to the two lowly men whose lives were destroyed, whose reputation was stabbed, whose memory was desecrated, this country owes what partial amends the rolling years have left. Forever and forever, as long as America has a history, will those three [bodies] swing and sway from the creaking cordage, an accursed weight before the world, sad ghosts upon the seas, until a juster age shall remove them with sorrowful, sympathetic hands, to lay them in the consecrated sail of a nation's penitence.

Appendix D: Corporal Punishment

[For many sailors-turned-writers, including Melville and Richard Henry Dana Jr., the problem with flogging wasn't that it happened. Even mutineers bought into the necessity of the system. The problem was officers' abuse of punishment and what that said about human nature and the laws governing it. Nor was the problem a new one: when Melville complains in *White-Jacket* that naval officers at all ranks, but especially petty officers, treated sailors like so much cattle, he voiced a complaint that the mutineers at Nore and Spithead had voiced loudly over half a century before.]

1. From Captain [Frederick] Marryat, *The King's Own and the Pirate* (1830; London: J.M. Dent, 1895), 3–7

[Marryat's fictional creation Edward Peters in *The King's Own* is based in part on Nore ringleader Richard Parker (1767–97), though Parker is (confusingly) also a character in the story. At the beginning of the excerpt below, Peters, an honest sailor, is falsely accused of stealing a watch. Marryat's discussion of Parker's flogging through the fleet may seem like the stuff of fiction, but it was quite real. Marryat, himself a former Royal Navy officer in the early 1800s, wondered at the ways in which the navy dehumanized its sailors.]

Summoned on the quarter-deck—cross-examined, and harshly inter-rogated—called a scoundrel by the captain before conviction,—the proud blood mantled in the cheeks of one [Edward Peters] who, at that period, was incapable of crime. The blush of virtuous indignation was construed into presumptive evidence of guilt. The captain,—a superficial, presuming, pompous, yet cowardly creature, whose conduct assisted in no small degree to excite the mutiny on board of his own ship,—declared himself quite convinced of Peters's guilt, because he blushed at the bare idea of being suspected; and punish-ment ensued, with all the degradation allotted to an offence which is never forgiven on board of a man-of-war.

There is, perhaps, no crime that is attended with such serious con-sequences on board a ship as theft.... After positive conviction, no punishment can be too severe for a crime that produces such mischief; but to degrade a man by corporal punishment, to ruin his character, and render him an object of abhorrence and contempt, in the absence of even bare presumptive evidence, was an act of cruelty and injustice, which could excite but one feeling; and, from that day, the man who would have gloried in dying for his country, became a discontented, gloomy, and dangerous subject.

The above effect would have been produced in any man; but to Peters, whose previous history we have yet to narrate, death itself would have been preferable. His heart did not break, but it swelled with contending passions, till it was burst and riven with wounds never to be cicatrised.[1] Suffering under the most painful burthen that can oppress a man who values reputation, writhing with the injustice of accusation when innocent, of conviction without proof, and of punishment unmerited, it is not to be wondered at that Peters took the earliest opportunity of deserting from the ship.

... [T]he man who was selected by Peters as his most intimate friend, the man with whom he had consulted, and to whom he had confided his plans for desertion, gave information of the retreat of his wife and child, from which place Peters was not likely to be very distant; and thus, with the assistance of this, his dearest friend, the master-at-arms and party in quest of him succeeded in his capture.

It so happened, that on the very day on which Peters was brought on board and put into irons, the purser's servant was discovered to have in his possession the watch that had been lost. Thus far the character of Peters was reinstated; and as he had declared, at the time of his capture, that the unjust punishment which he had received had been the motive of his desertion, the captain was strongly urged by the officers to overlook an offence which had everything to be offered in its extenuation. But Captain A— was fond of courts-martial; he imagined that they added to his consequence, which certainly required to be upheld by adventitious aid.... A court-martial was held, and Peters was sentenced to death; but, in consideration of circumstances, the sentence was mitigated to that of being "flogged round the fleet."

Mitigated! Strange vanity in men, that they should imagine their own feelings to be more sensible and acute than those of others; that they should consider that a mitigation in favour of the prisoner, which, had they been placed in his situation, they would have declared an accumulation of the punishment. Not a captain who sat upon that court-martial but would have considered, as Peters did, that death was by far the more lenient sentence of the two. Yet they meant well—they felt kindly towards him, and acknowledged his provocations; but they fell into the too common error of supposing that the finer feelings, which induce a man to prefer death to dishonour, are only to be recognised among the higher classes; and that, because circumstances may have placed a man before the mast, he will undergo punishment,

---

1 Healed by inducing scar tissue.

however severe, however degrading,—in short, every "ill that flesh is heir to,"—in preference to death....

A man sentenced to be flogged round the fleet receives an equal part of the whole number of lashes awarded, alongside each ship composing that fleet. For instance, if sentenced to three hundred lashes, in a fleet composed of ten sail, he will receive thirty alongside of each ship.

A launch is fitted up with a platform and shears. It is occupied by the unfortunate individual, the provost-marshal, the boatswain, and his mates, with their implements of office, and armed marines stationed at the bow and stern. When the signal is made for punishment, all the ships in the fleet send one or two boats each, with crews cleanly dressed, the officers in full uniform, and marines under arms. These boats collect at the side of the ship where the launch is lying, the hands are turned up, and the ship's company are ordered to mount the rigging, to witness that portion of the whole punishment which, after the sentence has been read, is inflicted upon the prisoner. When he has received the allotted number of lashes, he is, for the time, released, and permitted to sit down, with a blanket over his shoulders, while the boats, which attend the execution of the sentence, make fast to the launch, and tow it to the next ship in the fleet, where the same number of lashes are inflicted with corresponding ceremonies;—and thus he is towed from one ship to another until he has received the whole of his punishment.

The severity of this punishment consists not only in the number of lashes, but in the peculiar manner in which they are inflicted; as, after the unfortunate wretch has received the first part of his sentence alongside of one ship, the blood is allowed to congeal, and the wounds partially to close, during the interval which takes place previously to his arrival alongside of the next, when the cat[1] again subjects him to renewed and increased torture. During the latter part of the punishment, the suffering is dreadful; and a man who has undergone this sentence is generally broken down in constitution, if not in spirits, for the remainder of his life.

Such was the punishment inflicted upon the unfortunate Peters; and it would be difficult to decide, at the moment when it was completed, and the blanket thrown over his shoulders, whether the heart or the back of the fainting man were the more lacerated of the two.

Time can heal the wounds of the body, over which it holds its empire; but those of the soul, like the soul itself, spurn his transitory sway.

---

1 In this usage, slang for a cat-o'-nine-tails, a kind of lash.

2. From Richard Henry Dana Jr., *Two Years before the Mast* (1840; New York: Harper and Brothers, 1842), 123–30, 461–62

[Richard Henry Dana Jr. (1815–82), who would go from being a half-hearted sailor to a respected lawyer, never did forgive the abuses of power described below. At the same time, however, he had as little patience for abuse of the law as he did with those who failed to understand why the law existed in the first place. In *White-Jacket*, Melville agreed. *Billy Budd* is more ambivalent.]

[The captain's] displeasure was chiefly turned against a large, heavy-moulded fellow from the Middle States, who was called Sam.... The captain found fault with everything this man did, and hazed him for dropping a marline-spike from the main-yard, where he was at work. This, of course, was an accident, but it was set down against him. We worked late Friday night, and were turned-to early Saturday morning. About ten o'clock the captain ordered our new officer, Russell, who by this time had become thoroughly disliked by all the crew, to get the gig ready to take him ashore. John, the Swede, was sitting in the boat alongside, and Russell and myself were standing by the main hatchway, waiting for the captain, who was down in the hold, where the crew were at work, when we heard his voice raised in violent dispute with somebody, whether it was with the mate, or one of the crew, I could not tell; and then came blows and scuffling. I ran to the side and beckoned to John, who came up, and we leaned down the hatchway; and though we could see no one, yet we knew that the captain had the advantage, for his voice was loud and clear—

"You see your condition! You see your condition! Will you ever give me any more of your jaw?" No answer; and then came wrestling and heaving, as though the man was trying to turn him. "You may as well keep still, for I have got you," said the captain. Then came the question, "Will you ever give me any more of your jaw?"

"I never gave you any, sir," said Sam; for it was his voice that we heard, though low and half choked.

"That's not what I ask you. Will you ever be impudent to me again?"

"I never have been, sir," said Sam.

"Answer my question, or I'll make a spread eagle of you! I'll flog you, by G—d."

"I'm no negro slave," said Sam.

"Then I'll make you one," said the captain; and he came to the hatchway, and sprang on deck, threw off his coat, and rolling up his sleeves, called out to the mate—"Seize that man up, Mr. A——! Seize him up! Make a spread eagle of him! I'll teach you all who is master aboard!"

The crew and officers followed the captain up the hatchway, and after repeated orders the mate laid hold of Sam, who made no resistance, and carried him to the gangway.

"What are you going to flog that man for, sir?" said John, the Swede, to the captain.

Upon hearing this, the captain turned upon him, but knowing him to be quick and resolute, he ordered the steward to bring the irons, and calling upon Russell to help him, went up to John.

"Let me alone," said John. "I'm willing to be put in irons. You need not use any force"; and putting out his hands, the captain slipped the irons on, and sent him aft to the quarter-deck. Sam by this time was *seized up*, as it is called, that is, placed against the shrouds, with his wrists made fast to the shrouds, his jacket off, and his back exposed. The captain stood on the break of the deck, a few feet from him, and a little raised, so as to have a good swing at him, and held in his hand the bight of a thick, strong rope. The officers stood round, and the crew grouped together in the waist. All these preparations made me feel sick and almost faint, angry and excited as I was. A man—a human being, made in God's likeness—fastened up and flogged like a beast! A man, too, whom I had lived with and eaten with for months, and knew almost as well as a brother. The first and almost uncontrollable impulse was resistance. But what was to be done? The time for it had gone by. The two best men were fast, and there were only two beside myself, and a small boy of ten or twelve years of age. And then there were (beside the captain) three officers, steward, agent and clerk. But beside the numbers, what is there for sailors to do? If they resist, it is mutiny; and if they succeed, and take the vessel, it is piracy. If they ever yield again, their punishment must come; and if they do not yield, they are pirates for life. If a sailor resist his commander, he resists the law, and piracy or submission are his only alternatives. Bad as it was, it must be borne. It is what a sailor ships for. Swinging the rope over his head, and bending his body so as to give it full force, the captain brought it down upon the poor fellow's back. Once, twice,—six times. "Will you ever give me any more of your jaw?" The man writhed with pain, but said not a word. Three times more. This was too much, and he muttered something which I could not hear; this brought as many more as the man could stand; when the captain ordered him to be cut down, and to go forward.

"Now for you," said the captain, making up to John and taking his irons off. As soon as he was loose, he ran forward to the forecastle. "Bring that man aft," shouted the captain. The second mate, who had been a shipmate of John's, stood still in the waist, and the mate walked slowly forward; but our third officer, anxious to show his zeal, sprang forward over the windlass, and laid hold of John; but he soon threw him from him.... The captain stood on the quarter-deck, bare-headed, his eyes flashing with rage, and his face as red as blood, swinging the rope, and calling out to his officers, "Drag him aft!—Lay hold of him! I'll *sweeten* him!" &c. &c. ... When he was made fast, he turned to the captain, who stood turning up his sleeves and getting ready for the blow, and asked him what he was to be flogged for. "Have I ever refused my duty, sir? Have you ever known me to hang back, or to be insolent, or not to know my work?"

"No," said the captain, "it is not that that I flog you for; I flog you for your interference—for asking questions."

"Can't a man ask a question here without being flogged?"

"No," shouted the captain; "nobody shall open his mouth aboard this vessel, but myself"; and began laying the blows upon his back, swinging half round between each blow, to give it full effect. As he went on, his passion increased, and he danced about the deck, calling out as he swung the rope,—"If you want to know what I flog you for, I'll tell you. It's because I like to do it!—because I like to do it!—It suits me! That's what I do it for!"

The man writhed under the pain, until he could endure it no longer, when he called out, with an exclamation more common among foreigners than with us—"Oh, Jesus Christ! Oh, Jesus Christ!"

"Don't call on Jesus Christ," shouted the captain; "*he can't help you. Call on Captain T——*. He's the man! He can help you! Jesus Christ can't help you now!"

At these words, which I never shall forget, my blood ran cold. I could look on no longer. Disgusted, sick, and horror-struck, I turned away and leaned over the rail, and looked down into the water. A few rapid thoughts of my own situation, and of the prospect of future revenge, crossed my mind; but the falling of the blows and the cries of the man called me back at once.... Every one else stood still at his post, while the captain, swelling with rage and with the importance of his achievements, walked the quarter-deck, and at each turn, as he came forward, calling out to us,—"You see your condition! You see where I've got you all, and you know what to expect!"—"You've been mistaken in me—you didn't know what I was! Now you know what I am!"—"I'll make you toe the mark, every soul of you, or I'll flog you all, fore and aft, from the boy, up!"—"You've got a driver over you! Yes, a *slave-driver—a negro-driver!* I'll see who'll tell me he isn't a negro slave!" ...

After the day's work was done, we went down into the forecastle, and ate our plain supper; but not a word was spoken.... I thought of our situation, living under a tyranny; of the character of the country we were in; of the length of the voyage, and of the uncertainty attending our return to America; and then, if we should return, of the prospect of obtaining justice and satisfaction for these poor men; and vowed that if God should ever give me the means, I would do something to redress the grievances and relieve the sufferings of that poor class of beings, of whom I then was one.

... I have no fancies about equality on board ship. It is a thing out of the question, and certainly, in the present state of mankind, not to be desired. I never knew a sailor who found fault with the orders and ranks of the service; and if expected to pass the rest of my life before the mast, I would not wish to have the power of the captain diminished an iota. It is absolutely necessary that there should be one head and one voice, to control everything, and be responsible for everything. There are emergencies which require the instant exercise of extreme power. These emergencies do not allow of consultation; and they who would be the captain's constituted advisers might be the very men over whom he would be called upon to exert his authority. It has been found necessary to vest in every government, even the most democratic, some extraordinary, and, at first sight, alarming powers; trusting in public opinion, and subsequent accountability to modify the exercise of them. These are provided to meet exigencies, which all hope may never occur, but which yet by possibility may occur, and if they should, and there were no power to meet them instantly, there would be an end put to the government at once. So it is with the authority of the shipmaster. It will not answer to say that he shall never do this and that thing, because it does not seem always necessary and advisable that it should be done. He has great cares and responsibilities; is answerable for everything; and is subject to emergencies which perhaps no other man exercising authority among civilized people is subject to. Let him, then, have powers commensurate with his utmost possible need; only let him be held strictly responsible for the exercise of them. Any other course would be injustice, as well as bad policy.

3. **From Herman Melville, *White-Jacket; or The World in a Man-of-War* (New York: Harper and Brothers, 1850; repr. New York: A.L. Burt Company, 1892), 127–28, 132, 137–38, 139–40**

[The passages below illustrate why *White-Jacket* is a precursor of *Billy Budd*. While there is little flogging in the latter, the critique of authority in both books overlaps considerably. When does discipline cross the line into brutality? Should the state or military be in the business of brutalizing its citizens? Melville's screed against the abuse of corporal punishment in the American navy was so effective that it helped convince Congress to ban the practice, though he was far from its only critic. The efficacy of flogging on US naval and merchant vessels was hotly debated long before it was outlawed in 1850.]

The same evening ... four [sailors] found themselves prisoners in the "brig," with a sentry standing over them. They were charged with violating a well-known law of the ship—having been engaged in one of those tangled, general fights sometimes occurring among sailors. They had nothing to anticipate but a flogging, at the captain's pleasure.

Toward evening of the next day, they were startled by the dread summons of the boatswain and his mates at the principal hatchway— a summons that ever sends a shudder through every manly heart in a frigate:

"*All hands witness punishment, ahoy!*"

The hoarseness of the cry, its unrelenting prolongation, its being caught up at different points, and sent through the lowermost depths of the ship; all this produces a most dismal effect upon every heart not calloused by long habituation to it.

However much you may desire to absent yourself from the scene that ensues, yet behold it you must; or, at least, stand near it you must; for the regulations enjoin the attendance of the entire ship's company, from the corpulent Captain himself to the smallest boy who strikes the bell.

"*All hands witness punishment, ahoy!*"

To the sensitive seaman that summons sounds like a doom. He knows that the same law which impels it—the same law by which the culprits of the day must suffer; that by that very law he also is liable at any time to be judged and condemned. And the inevitableness of his own presence at the scene; the strong arm that drags him in view of the scourge, and holds him there till all is over; forcing upon his loathing eye and soul the sufferings and groans of men who have familiarly consorted with him, eaten with him, battled out watches with him—men of his own type and badge—all this conveys a terrible hint of the omnipotent authority under which he lives. Indeed, to such a man the naval summons to witness punishment carries a thrill, somewhat akin to what we may impute to the quick and the dead, when they shall hear the Last Trump [*sic*], that is to bid them all arise in their ranks, and behold the final penalties inflicted upon the sinners of our race.

But it must not be imagined that to all men-of-war's-men this summons conveys such poignant emotions; but it is hard to decide whether one should be glad or sad that this is not the case; whether it is grateful to know that so much pain is avoided, or whether it is far sadder to think that, either from constitutional hard-heartedness or the multiplied searings of habit, hundreds of men-of-war's-men have been made proof against the sense of degradation, pity, and shame.

Let us have the charity to believe them—as we do—when some Captains in the Navy say, that the thing of all others most repulsive to them, in the routine of what they consider their duty, is the administration of corporal punishment upon the crew; for, surely, not to feel scarified to the quick at these scenes would argue a man but a beast.

You see a human being, stripped like a slave; scourged worse than a hound. And for what? For things not essentially criminal, but only made so by arbitrary laws.

In the American Navy there is an everlasting suspension of the Habeas Corpus.[1] Upon the bare allegation of misconduct there is no law to restrain the Captain from imprisoning a seaman, and keeping him confined at his pleasure....

Certainly the necessities of navies warrant a code for their government more stringent than the law that governs the land; but that code should conform to the spirit of the political institutions of the country that ordains it. It should not convert into slaves some of the citizens of a nation of free-men.... Our institutions claim to be based upon broad principles of political liberty and equality. Whereas, it would hardly affect one iota the condition on shipboard of an American man-of-war's-man, were he transferred to the Russian navy and made a subject of the Czar.

As a sailor, he shares none of our civil immunities; the law of our soil in no respect accompanies the national floating timbers grown thereon, and to which he clings as his home. For him our Revolution was in vain; to him our Declaration of Independence[2] is a lie.

It is not sufficiently borne in mind, perhaps, that though the naval code comes under the head of the martial law, yet, in time of peace, and in the thousand questions arising between man and man on board ship, this code, to a certain extent, may not improperly be deemed municipal. With its crew of 800 or 1,000 men, a three-decker is a city on the sea. But in most of these matters between man and man, the

---

1 Legal right to contest detention. This is a particularly telling reference, given that after the Fugitive Slave Law went into effect in 1850, Northern imprisonment of escaped slaves was loudly contested on the grounds of unlawful detention. One of the most famous cases involved Thomas Sims, an escaped slave who was ordered returned to Georgia after Melville's father-in-law, Lemuel Shaw, refused a challenge on these grounds. See Appendices B2 and B3.

2 See p. 148, note 1.

Captain instead of being a magistrate, dispensing what the law promulgates, is an absolute ruler, making and unmaking law as he pleases.

It will be seen that the XXth of the Articles of War provides, that if any person in the Navy negligently perform the duties assigned him, he shall suffer such punishment as a court-martial shall adjudge; but if the offender be a private (common sailor) he may, at the discretion of the Captain, be put in irons or flogged. It is needless to say, that in cases where an officer commits a trivial violation of this law, a court-martial is seldom or never called to sit upon his trial; but in the sailor's case, he is at once condemned to the lash. Thus, one set of sea-citizens is exempted from a law that is hung in terror over others. What would landsmen think, were the State of New York to pass a law against some offence, affixing a fine as a penalty, and then add to that law a section restricting its penal operation to mechanics and day laborers, exempting all gentlemen with an income of one thousand dollars? Yet thus, in the spirit of its practical operation, even thus, stands a good part of the naval laws wherein naval flogging is involved.

We plant the question, then, on the topmost argument of all. Irrespective of incidental considerations, we assert that flogging in the navy is opposed to the essential dignity of man, which no legislator has a right to violate; that it is oppressive, and glaringly unequal in its operations; that it is utterly repugnant to the spirit of our democratic institutions; indeed, that it involves a lingering trait of the worst times of a barbarous feudal aristocracy; in a word, we denounce it as religiously, morally, and immutably *wrong*.

No matter, then, what may be the consequences of its abolition; no matter if we have to dismantle our fleets, and our unprotected commerce should fall a prey to the spoiler, the awful admonitions of justice and humanity demand that abolition without procrastination; in a voice that is not to be mistaken, demand that abolition today. It is not a dollar-and-cent question of expediency; it is a matter of *right and wrong*. And if any man can lay his hand on his heart, and solemnly say that this scourging is right, let that man but once feel the lash on his own back, and in his agony you will hear the apostate call the seventh heavens to witness that it is wrong. And, in the name of immortal manhood, would to God that every man who upholds this thing were scourged at the gangway till he recanted.

4. From Solomon Northup, *Twelve Years a Slave* (1853; New York: Miller, Orton, and Mulligan, 1855), 255–60

[In the US both before and after the Civil War, the slave was the obvious symbol of degradation, a situation Melville represents masterfully in his 1855 novella *Benito Cereno*. Indeed, according to historians, chattel slavery was a kind of degradation laboratory. Many of the techniques for punishment developed and used in the slave states found their way into the treatment of other disenfranchised groups, including sailors (Whitman 176). Solomon Northup's account of flogging is not the most famous depiction of corporal punishment in the slave-owning South—better known is that of Harriet Jacobs, which follows—but Steve McQueen's 2013 film *12 Years a Slave* makes it one of the most resonant today. Northup's life dates are unknown: probably born in 1807 or 1808, he disappeared in Canada in 1857, and most historians believe he died soon thereafter, or perhaps as late as the early 1860s.]

... [T]he most cruel whipping that ever I was doomed to witness—one I can never recall with any other emotion than that of horror—was inflicted on the unfortunate Patsey.

It has been seen that the jealousy and hatred of Mistress Epps made the daily life of her young and agile slave completely miserable. I am happy in the belief that on numerous occasions I was the means of averting punishment from the inoffensive girl. In Epps' absence the mistress often ordered me to whip her without the remotest provocation. I would refuse, saying that I feared my master's displeasure, and several times ventured to remonstrate with her against the treatment Patsey received. I endeavored to impress her with the truth that the latter was not responsible for the acts of which she complained, but that she being a slave, and subject entirely to her master's will, he alone was answerable.

At length "the green-eyed monster" crept into the soul of Epps also, and then it was that he joined with his wrathful wife in an infernal jubilee over the girl's miseries.

On a Sabbath day in hoeing time, not long ago, we were on the bayou bank, washing our clothes, as was our usual custom. Presently Patsey was missing.... Patsey found her master in a fearful rage on her return. His violence so alarmed her that at first she attempted to evade direct answers to his questions, which only served to increase his suspicions. She finally, however, drew herself up proudly, and in a spirit of indignation boldly denied his charges.

"Missus don't give me soap to wash with, as she does the rest," said Patsey, "and you know why. I went over to Harriet's to get a piece," and saying this, she drew it forth from a pocket in her dress and exhibited it to him. "That's what I went to Shaw's for, Massa Epps," continued she; "the Lord knows that was all."

"You lie, you black wench!" shouted Epps.

"I *don't* lie, massa. If you kill me, I'll stick to that."

"Oh! I'll fetch you down. I'll learn you to go to Shaw's. I'll take the starch out of ye," he muttered fiercely through his shut teeth.

Then turning to me, he ordered four stakes to be driven into the ground, pointing with the toe of his boot to the places where he wanted them. When the stakes were driven down, he ordered her to be stripped of every article of dress. Ropes were then brought, and the naked girl was laid upon her face, her wrists and feet each tied firmly to a stake. Stepping to the piazza, he took down a heavy whip, and placing it in my hands, commanded me to lash her. Unpleasant as it was, I was compelled to obey him. Nowhere that day, on the face of the whole earth, I venture to say, was there such a demoniac exhibition witnessed as then ensued.

Mistress Epps stood on the piazza among her children, gazing on the scene with an air of heartless satisfaction. The slaves were huddled together at a little distance, their countenances indicating the sorrow of their hearts. Poor Patsey prayed piteously for mercy, but her prayers were vain. Epps ground his teeth, and stamped upon the ground, screaming at me, like a mad fiend, to strike *harder*.

"Strike harder, or *your* turn will come next, you scoundrel," he yelled.

"Oh, mercy, massa!—oh! have mercy, do. Oh, God! pity me," Patsey exclaimed continually, struggling fruitlessly, and the flesh quivering at every stroke.

When I had struck her as many as thirty times, I stopped, and turned round toward Epps, hoping he was satisfied; but with bitter oaths and threats, he ordered me to continue. I inflicted ten or fifteen blows more. By this time her back was covered with long welts, intersecting each other like net work. Epps was yet furious and savage as ever, demanding if she would like to go to Shaw's again, and swearing he would flog her until she wished she was in h—l. Throwing down the whip, I declared I could punish her no more. He ordered me to go on, threatening me with a severer flogging than she had received, in case of refusal. My heart revolted at the inhuman scene, and risking the consequences, I absolutely refused to raise the whip. He then seized it himself, and applied it with ten-fold greater force than I had. The painful cries and shrieks of the tortured Patsey, mingling with the loud and angry curses of Epps, loaded the air. She was terribly lacerated— I may say, without exaggeration, literally flayed. The lash was wet with blood, which flowed down her sides and dropped upon the ground. At length she ceased struggling. Her head sank listlessly on the ground. Her screams and supplications gradually decreased and died away into a low moan. She no longer writhed and shrank beneath the lash when it bit out small pieces of her flesh.

5. From [Harriet Ann Jacobs,] *Incidents in the Life of a Slave Girl*, ed. L[ydia] Maria Child (Boston: [Thayer and Eldridge,] 1861), 23

[Though for many years it was believed that writer and abolitionist Lydia Maria Child (1802–80) composed *Incidents in the Life of a Slave Girl*, we now know that it was in fact written by Harriet Ann Jacobs (1813–97), a slave who escaped from North Carolina in 1842.]

When I had been in the family a few weeks, one of the plantation slaves was brought to town, by order of his master. It was near night when he arrived, and Dr. Flint[1] ordered him to be taken to the work house, and tied up to the joist, so that his feet would just escape the ground. In that situation he was to wait till the doctor had taken his tea. I shall never forget that night. Never before, in my life, had I heard hundreds of blows fall, in succession, on a human being. His piteous groans, and his "O, pray don't, massa," rang in my ear for months afterwards. There were many conjectures as to the cause of this terrible punishment. Some said master accused him of stealing corn; others said the slave had quarrelled with his wife, in presence of the overseer, and had accused his master of being the father of her child. They were both black, and the child was very fair.

I went into the work house next morning, and saw the cowhide still wet with blood, and the boards all covered with gore.

6. From Herman Melville, "Bridegroom Dick. 1876" (1888; repr. in *John Marr and Other Poems* [Princeton, NJ: Princeton UP, 1922] 18–42)

[Sociologists suggest that when corporal punishment is used to demean an individual, it crosses the line from discipline to degradation, something Melville calls attention to in the dramatic monologue below, published in 1888. Note that in this poem the captain, like God in the story of Abraham, does not follow through on the threatened discipline. For him, unlike Vere, "Submission is enough" (p. 186).]

But Captain Turret, *"Old Hemlock"* tall,
(A leaning tower when his tank brimmed all,)
Manoeuvre out alive from the war did he?
Or, too old for that, drift under the lee?   250
Kentuckian colossal, who, touching at Madeira,
The huge puncheon shipped o' prime *Santa-Clara;*

---

1   Flint owns Jacobs, who is narrating.

Then rocked along the deck so solemnly!
No whit the less though judicious was enough
In dealing with the Finn who made the great huff;   255
Our three-decker's giant, a grand boatswain's mate,
Manliest of men in his own natural senses;
But driven stark mad by the devil's drugged stuff,
Storming all aboard from his run-ashore late,
Challenging to battle, vouchsafing no pretenses,   260
A reeling King Ogg,[1] delirious in power,
The quarter-deck carronades he seemed to make cower.
"Put him in *brig* there!" said Lieutenant Marrot.
"Put him in *brig*!" back he mocked like a parrot;
"Try it, then!" swaying a fist like Thor's sledge,[2]   265
And making the pigmy constables hedge—
Ship's corporals and the master-at-arms.
"In *brig* there, I say!"—They dally no more;
Like hounds let slip on a desperate boar,
Together they pounce on the formidable Finn,   270
Pinion and cripple and hustle him in.
Anon, under sentry, between twin guns,
He slides off in drowse, and the long night runs.

Morning brings a summons. Whistling it calls,
Shrilled through the pipes of the boatswain's four aids;   275
Trilled down the hatchways along the dusk halls:
Muster to the Scourge!—Dawn of doom and its blast!
As from cemeteries raised, sailors swarm before the mast,
Tumbling up the ladders from the ship's nether shades.

Keeping in the background and taking small part,   280
Lounging at their ease, indifferent in face,
Behold the trim marines uncompromised in heart;
Their Major, buttoned up, near the staff finds room—
The staff o' lieutenants standing grouped in their place.
All the Laced Caps o' the ward-room come,   285
The Chaplain among them, disciplined and dumb.[3]
The blue-nosed boatswain, complexioned like slag,

---

1 One of the few giants to survive the flood, Og, king of Bashan, is killed by
   Moses, according to Deuteronomy 3:1–11.
2 Heavy, two-handed hammer wielded by the deity Thor of Germanic and
   Norse myth.
3 On the complicity of religious officials with military discipline, see p. 124,
   note 1 and Appendix E7.

Like a blue Monday lours[1]—his implements in bag.
Executioners, his aids, a couple by him stand,
At a nod there the thongs to receive from his hand.   290
Never venturing a caveat whatever may betide,
Though functionally here on humanity's side,
The grave Surgeon shows, like the formal physician
Attending the rack o' the Spanish Inquisition.

The angel o' the "brig" brings his prisoner up;   295
Then, steadied by his old *Santa-Clara*, a sup,
Heading all erect, the ranged assizes there,
Lo, Captain Turret, and under starred bunting,
(A florid full face and fine silvered hair,)
Gigantic the yet greater giant confronting.   300

Now the culprit he liked, as a tall captain can
A Titan subordinate and true *sailor-man*;
And frequent he'd shown it—no worded advance,
But flattering the Finn with a well-timed glance.
But what of that now? In the martinet-mien[2]   305
Read the *Articles of War*,[3] heed the naval routine;
While, cut to the heart a dishonor there to win,
Restored to his senses, stood the Anak Finn;
In racked self-control the squeezed tears peeping,
Scalding the eye with repressed inkeeping.   310
Discipline must be; the scourge is deemed due.
But ah for the sickening and strange heart-benumbing,
Compassionate abasement in shipmates that view;
Such a grand champion shamed there succumbing!
"Brown, tie him up."—The cord he brooked: 315
How else?—his arms spread apart—never threaping;
No, never he flinched, never sideways he looked,
Peeled to the waistband, the marble flesh creeping,
Lashed by the sleet the officious winds urge.
In function his fellows their fellowship merge—   320
The twain standing nigh—the two boatswain's mates,
Sailors of his grade, ay, and brothers of his mess.

---

1 Gloomy weather.
2 The captain's expression (mien) is that of a strict disciplinarian (martinet). In
   The Floating Republic, Manwaring and Dobrée note that "[i]t was far better to
   serve under a martinet, a 'smart' captain, than under a slack one, for in the
   former case there was less unrestrained brutality; punishment might be severe,
   but it was regulated and had some show of justice" (63).
3 On the Articles of War, see Appendices B1, E1, and E3. See also p. 113,
   note 2.

With sharp thongs adroop the junior one awaits
The word to uplift.
              "Untie him—so!
Submission is enough, Man, you may go."   325
Then, promenading aft, brushing fat Purser Smart,
"Flog? Never meant it—hadn't any heart.
Degrade that tall fellow?"

Appendix E: Capital Punishment

[*Billy Budd* is set during what H. Bruce Franklin calls "the most appalling moment in the history of capital punishment" (338) in modernity: England under execution-happy George III (r. 1760–1820). During the years when Melville was writing *Billy Budd*, the US entered another "appalling moment": the introduction of state-sanctioned electrocution. "Appalling" is really not the most accurate word, however. At the time many observers, not to mention the courts, believed that death by electric current was the most conscientious form of execution available. Because of Melville's criticisms of capital punishment in *Typee* and *White-Jacket* (reprinted below), many critics assume that *Billy Budd* also falls into the category of "anti-gallows" literature. Yet, as with so many other contemporaneous issues addressed in the text, it's difficult to tell what the text, much less Melville, is arguing.]

1. From *The Statutes Relating to the Admiralty, Navy, Shipping, and Navigation of the United Kingdom* (1749; London: George Eyre and Andrew Strahan, 1823), 234

[While the statute under which Billy is executed dates to a 1661 Act of Parliament, he is tried under a 1749 amendment notorious for the lack of latitude it allowed in conducting courts martial and for its rigidness of punishment, a fact sometimes overlooked by readers eager to condemn Vere's rush to trial. Still, it's an open question whether Vere had to convene a court martial immediately.]

"If any Officer, Mariner, Soldier or other Person in the Fleet, shall strike any of his Superior Officers, or draw or offer to draw, or lift up any Weapon against him, being in the execution of his Office, on any Pretence whatsoever, every such Person being convicted of any such Offence, by the Sentence of a Court Martial, shall suffer Death; and if any Officer, Mariner, Soldier or other Person in the Fleet, shall presume to quarrel with any of his Superior Officers, being in the execution of his Office, or shall disobey any lawful Command of any of his Superior Officers; every such Person being convicted of any such Offence by the Sentence of a Court Martial, shall suffer Death, or such other Punishment as shall, according to the Nature and Degree of his Offence, be inflicted upon him by the Sentence of a Court Martial."

2. From Herman Melville, *Typee: A Peep at Polynesian Life* (New York: Wiley and Putnam, 1846; repr. as *Typee: A Real Romance of the South Seas* [Boston: St. Botolph Society, 1893]), 181–82

[In Melville's ethnographic account of the weeks he spent among indigenous—and reputedly cannibalistic—peoples, he frequently turns the tables on definitions of civilization and savagery, as in this discussion of the European history of capital punishment.]

In a primitive state of society, the enjoyments of life, though few and simple, are spread over a great extent, and are unalloyed; but Civilisation, for every advantage she imparts, holds a hundred evils in reserve;—the heart-burnings, the jealousies, the social rivalries, the family dissensions, and the thousand self-inflicted discomforts of refined life, which make up in units the swelling aggregate of human misery, are unknown among these unsophisticated people.

But it will be urged that these shocking unprincipled wretches are cannibals. Very true; and a rather bad trait in their character it must be allowed. But they are such only when they seek to gratify the passion of revenge upon their enemies; and I ask whether the mere eating of human flesh so very far exceeds in barbarity that custom which only a few years since was practised in enlightened England:—a convicted traitor, perhaps a man found guilty of honesty, patriotism, and such-like heinous crimes, had his head lopped off with a huge axe, his bowels dragged out and thrown into a fire; while his body, carved into four quarters, was with his head exposed upon pikes, and permitted to rot and fester among the public haunts of men!

The fiend-like skill we display in the invention of all manner of death-dealing engines, the vindictiveness with which we carry on our wars, and the misery and desolation that follow in their train, are enough of themselves to distinguish the white civilized man as the most ferocious animal on the face of the earth.

3. From Herman Melville, *White-Jacket; or The World in a Man-of-War* (New York: Harper and Brothers, 1850; repr. New York: A.L. Burt Company, 1892), 273–74, 276–77

Besides general quarters, and the regular morning and evening quarters for prayers on board the *Neversink*, on the first Sunday of every month we had a grand "*muster round the capstan,*" when we passed in solemn review before the Captain and officers, who closely scanned our frocks and trowsers, to see whether they were according to the

Navy cut. In some ships, every man is required to bring his bag and hammock along for inspection.

This ceremony acquires its chief solemnity, and, to a novice, is rendered even terrible, by the reading of the Articles of War by the Captain's clerk before the assembled ship's company, who in testimony of their enforced reverence for the code, stand bareheaded till the last sentence is pronounced.

To a mere amateur reader the quiet perusal of these Articles of War would be attended with some nervous emotions. Imagine, then, what *my* feelings must have been, when, with my hat deferentially in my hand, I stood before my lord and master, Captain Claret, and heard these Articles read as the law and gospel, the infallible, unappealable dispensation and code, whereby I lived, and moved, and had my being on board of the United States ship *Neversink*.

Of some twenty offences—made penal—that a seaman may commit, and which are specified in this code, thirteen are punishable by death.

"*Shall suffer death!*" This was the burden of nearly every Article read by the Captain's clerk; for he seemed to have been instructed to omit the longer Articles, and only present those which were brief and to the point.

"*Shall suffer death!*" The repeated announcement falls on your ear like the intermitting discharge of artillery. After it has been repeated again and again, you listen to the reader as he deliberately begins a new paragraph; you hear him reciting the involved, but comprehensive and clear arrangement of the sentence, detailing all possible particulars of the offence described, and you breathlessly await, whether *that* clause also is going to be concluded by the discharge of the terrible minute-gun. When, lo! it again booms on your ear—*shall suffer death*! No reservations, no contingencies; not the remotest promise of pardon or reprieve; not a glimpse of commutation of the sentence; all hope and consolation is shut out—*shall suffer death*! that is the simple fact for you to digest; and it is a tougher morsel, believe White-Jacket when he says it, than a forty-two-pound cannon-ball.

[I]n a time of profound peace, I am subject to the cut-throat martial law. And when my own brother, who happens to be dwelling ashore, and does not serve his country as I am now doing—when *he* is at liberty to call personally upon the President of the United States, and express his disapprobation of the whole national administration, here am *I*, liable at any time to be run up at the yard-arm, with a necklace, made by no jeweler, round my neck!

A hard case, truly, White-Jacket; but it cannot be helped. Yes; you live under this same martial law. Does not everything around you din the fact in your ears? Twice every day do you not jump to your quarters at the sound of a drum? Every morning, in port, are you not roused from your hammock by the *reveille*, and sent to it again at nightfall by the *tattoo*?[1] Every Sunday are you not commanded in the mere matter of the very dress you shall wear through that blessed day? Can your shipmates so much as drink their "tot of grog?" nay, can they even drink but a cup of water at the scuttle-butt, without an armed sentry standing over them? Does not every officer wear a sword instead of a cane? You live and move among twenty-four-pounders. White-Jacket; the very cannon-balls are deemed an ornament around you, serving to embellish the hatchways; and should you come to die at sea, White-Jacket, still two cannon-balls would bear you company when you would be committed to the deep. Yea, by all methods, and devices, and inventions, you are momentarily admonished of the fact that you live under the Articles of War. And by virtue of them it is, White-Jacket, that, without a hearing and without a trial, you may, at a wink from the Captain, be condemned to the scourge.

Speak you true? Then let me fly!

Nay, White-Jacket, the landless horizon hoops you in.

Some tempest, then, surge all the sea against us! hidden reefs and rocks, arise and dash the ships to chips! I was not born a serf, and will not live a slave! Quick! corkscrew whirlpools, suck us down! world's end whelm us!

Nay, White-Jacket, though this frigate laid her broken bones upon the Antarctic shores of Palmer's Land; though not two planks adhered; though all her guns were spiked by sword-fish blades, and at her yawning hatchways mouth-yawning sharks swam in and out; yet, should you escape the wreck and scramble to the beach, this Martial Law would meet you still, and snatch you by the throat. Hark! ...

... I tell you there is no escape. Afloat or wrecked the Martial Law relaxes not its gripe [*sic*]. And though, by that self-same warrant, for some offence therein set down, you were indeed to "suffer death," even then the Martial Law might hunt you straight through the other world, and out again at its other end, following you through all eternity, like an endless thread on the inevitable track of its own point, passing unnumbered needles through.

---

1 The *reveille* and the *tattoo* are musical signals used respectively to awaken soldiers and to return them to their barracks (or, in this case, bunks) in the evening.

4. From Arthur Schopenhauer, "On Suicide" (1851; repr. in *Studies in Pessimism: A Series of Essays*, trans. T. Bailey Saunders [London: Swan Sonnenschein and Co., 1893]), 49–50

[In *Billy Budd*, Melville gestures to the debate over humane execution discussed in the excerpt below. He does this by making Billy's death so peaceful that the purser wonders if it was less an execution than euthanasia—ending life to relieve suffering—or perhaps even suicide. Melville is likely nodding here, in Chapter 26, to the philosophy of Arthur Schopenhauer (1788–1860), who argued that suicide is a form of self-euthanasia, an acknowledgement that suffering is inescapable.]

It will generally be found that, as soon as the terrors of life reach the point at which they outweigh the terrors of death, a man will put an end to his life. But the terrors of death offer considerable resistance; they stand like a sentinel at the gate leading out of this world. Perhaps there is no man alive who would not have already put an end to his life, if this end had been of a purely negative character, a sudden stoppage of existence. There is something positive about it; it is the destruction of the body; and a man shrinks from that, because his body is the manifestation of the will to live.

However, the struggle with that sentinel is, as a rule, not so hard as it may seem from a long way off, mainly in consequence of the antagonism between the ills of the body and the ills of the mind. If we are in great bodily pain, or the pain lasts a long time, we become indifferent to other troubles; all we think about is to get well. In the same way great mental suffering makes us insensible to bodily pain; we despise it; nay, if it should outweigh the other, it distracts our thoughts, and we welcome it as a pause in mental suffering. It is this feeling that makes suicide easy; for the bodily pain that accompanies it loses all significance in the eyes of one who is tortured by an excess of mental suffering. This is especially evident in the case of those who are driven to suicide by some purely morbid and exaggerated ill-humor. No special effort to overcome their feelings is necessary, nor do such people require to be worked up in order to take the step; but as soon as the keeper into whose charge they are given leaves them for a couple of minutes, they quickly bring their life to an end.

When, in some dreadful and ghastly dream, we reach the moment of greatest horror, it awakes us; thereby banishing all the hideous shapes that were born of the night. And life is a dream: when the moment of greatest horror compels us to break it off, the same thing happens.

5. From E.S. Nadal, "The Rationale of the Opposition to Capital Punishment," *North American Review* 116 (January 1873): 139–40, 145–46

[The campaign against capital punishment was topical prior to the Civil War, but the war made it practically a moot point. By the 1870s capital punishment was back in the news, thanks in part to articles such as this one by Ehrman Syme Nadal (1843–1922), a respected literary critic.]

The opponents of the death penalty, knowing it to be ... useless, and necessarily slovenly and capricious in its administration, have a right to take its horribleness into account as a reason for its immediate discontinuance. The great mass of people, the country through, I suppose, hold the question in abeyance; most men who have strong opinions upon the subject are opposed to executions. And yet we go on hanging people in this absent-minded, mechanical manner, because we seem to find no appropriate place to stop. We condone the few executions that take place with the reflection that these are to be the last of them. But this does not make it a bit better for the men who are hanged. On the contrary, it must be particularly trying to be executed under the present state of things. An intelligent culprit must reflect bitterly that all this altered public sentiment goes for naught.

It is well that the reader should remind himself of how strange a thing it is to put a man to death. If one's gardener were going to be hanged, he would discover that he had all his lifetime been very ignorant of hanging.... Immemorial custom and tradition have deprived him of the sense of how strange a thing it is to put a perfectly well man to death. Darius once asked some Athenians, who were living at his court, what they thought of the practice of sons eating their dead fathers. The Athenians said they could conceive of nothing worse than to eat their dead fathers. He then asked some Scythians, who were there also, what they thought upon this point. They said they could conceive nothing worse than not to eat their dead fathers. We can get used to anything.[1]

---

1   Herodotus (c. 484–425 BCE) recounts this story of Persian king Darius I (550–485 BCE) in the *Histories* (c. 450–420 BCE). The final line is a paraphrase of the Greek poet Pindar (c. 522–443 BCE).

6. From Elbridge T. Gerry, "Capital Punishment by Electricity," *North American Review* 149 (September 1889): 321, 324–25

[Billy isn't executed by electric current, but Melville describes the scene as though he were, or, really, as though everyone else is. When Melville was writing, electrocution was in the air, so to speak. In August 1890, New York became the first state to execute someone using electricity. It would have happened earlier, but authorities had to wait for a court ruling on whether the process was cruel and unusual punishment. In the end, the courts agreed with proponents who said it was more humane than hanging and easily more humane than the harrowing methods employed in previous centuries. The following two articles represent the tenor of arguments for and against electrocution. Elbridge Thomas Gerry (1837–1927) was a New York lawyer and social reformer.]

The penalty of death for the commission of crime had its origin in the mandate uttered by the Creator after the world had witnessed the first murder. The divine authority to terminate human life for the illegal shedding of blood, enlarged by the subsequent enunciation of the law from Mount Sinai in its application to other offences,[1] appears to have been exercised ever since by every nation on the earth, barbarous as well as civilized, in some form or other, in punishment of offences more or less heinous in their character. Under the Mosaic code[2] there were no less than thirty-three capital crimes, and the mode of execution, that by stoning to death, made the people themselves the instruments for its infliction. For a long period human ingenuity exhausted itself in efforts to devise means of death by which the latter should only be the final result of prolonged physical pain and agony. The vengeance of the law, as it was popularly termed, was sought to be made as terrible as possible, first in retaliation for the crime committed, and, secondly, in order to produce, by the horrible tortures which it inflicted, a deterrent effect, in the language of the old law-books, on other evilly-minded persons disposed in like manner to offend. The sickening details still preserved of executions by impalement, sawing under, boiling, burning, and flaying alive, crushing by weights, breaking on the wheel, tearing asunder by wild horses, and the like, create a doubt in the mind of the student of history, especially of the law, whether such punishments, so far from deterring, did not both suggest

---

1 That is, in the Ten Commandments given to Moses and the Israelites at Mount Sinai. See Exodus 20:1–17.
2 The five initial books of the Old Testament.

and stimulate the commission of the very crimes they were designed to prevent.

Of all the potent forces capable of producing death, there is none known to science more nearly instantaneous than electricity. In the ordinary occurrence in nature, where a person struck by lightning falls dead, nothing can be more sudden or rapid. And where—to give what has already proved to be a practical and fatal illustration—electricity is generated artificially for illuminating purpose, the interruption of the current by the intervention of or contact with any portion of the human body is invariably followed by the most serious consequences to the latter. Over ninety cases of accidental death by such contacts during the past two years are recorded, and in every case the action of the current was so instantaneous as to leave not the shadow of a doubt that death was literally quicker than thought. The body was not mutilated; there were no indications of any death-struggle; none of physical pain. The Constitution of the State of New York ... wisely prohibits the infliction of "cruel *and* unusual punishments." Hanging, for the reasons shown, while not unusual, may be, and too often is, cruel. Electricity, on the other hand, while not yet usual, has yet to be proven to be cruel; and as death whenever produced by it has been instantaneous, it is difficult to see how it can be shown to be cruel. That burns and injuries do result from contact with the electric current does not disprove its instantaneous lethal power.

7. From Hugh O. Pentecost, "The Crime of Capital Punishment," *The Arena* 1 (January 1890): 175–76, 177, 178, 180, 181

[Minister, lawyer, reformer, and all-around radical Hugh O. Pentecost (1848–1907) was well known for his outspoken views on everything from anarchism to organized religion. He spoke out against the hangings of the supposed Haymarket conspirators, against electrocution, and against capital punishment generally, as the following article illustrates. In strikingly modern terms, Pentecost rails against the political uses to which capital punishment is put—he calls it "judicial murder" (p. 196)—and in a move reminiscent of *Billy Budd*'s Chapter 24— where the narrator notes that the minister attending Billy in his cell collects "his stipend from Mars" (p. 122)—Pentecost decries "the State doing deeds of violence and blood in the name of law and order, and with the sanction and concurrence of religion" (p. 195).]

Capital punishment is an offence to enlightened thought and well-educated conscience because it is a measure of revenge, a sentiment which no person or people should harbor. It is said by apologists, that the theory of legal killing is not that of revenge, but that the killing is done merely as a warning to evil-doers and for the safety of society. But this is an afterthought, an explanation which the growing humane sentiment of the people is forcing from the barbarians who defend and practise murder by law. The real reason for capital punishment is that it is commonly supposed that one who commits murder "deserves to die." When the idea of revenge is eliminated from our habits of thought with regard to criminals, capital punishment will be esteemed an act of brutality which no community would think of permitting....

Every judge who sentences a fellow being to death, every juryman who votes for a verdict of death against a fellow being, every sheriff who carries out the sentence, every hang man who actually springs the drop, every priest or minister who assists at an execution, preparing the criminals for death by teaching them that in submitting to the crime about to be committed upon them they are conforming themselves to that which God approves, is a murderer; none the less so because they act in accordance with the statute law and social custom. Some of the most horrible crimes against humanity are committed according to statute law and common custom.

From the moment a murder is committed, society, in the person of its policemen and prosecuting attorney, becomes a pitiless bloodhound. Clubs, handcuffs, and prison bars fill the criminal's horizon.... Society becomes solely an avenger; pitiless, remorseless, thirsting for blood. The human heart turns to ice. The human hand is withheld. The human eye is averted. The human voice grows hard and dry. Society turns into an engine of death, with no more feeling than the cold blade of a guillotine.

One of the worst phases of capital punishment, to my mind, is the invariable presence upon the scaffold, as the general assistant of the hangman, of a Christian priest or minister. At every scaffold there is a strange and significant union of Church and State. The State is there in the person of the hangman. The Church is there in the person of the priest or minister. It is the old familiar scene of the State doing deeds of violence and blood in the name of law and order, and with the sanction and concurrence of religion. It is the old combination of the secular arm doing that of which the representative of an ignoble hypothetical God approves. It is a junction of two terrible engines of unhappiness and tyranny—superstition and physical force.

It may be said that to speak of the ministers of religion in this connection and in these terms is unfair, but I think not. Most ministers of the Christian religion are upholders of capital punishment, as they are of every respectable infamy. They cooperate with the "machinery of justice" in preparing the victim of revenge for the slaughter. They are very useful coadjutors, too, because they quiet the victim's mind and, no doubt, prevent many distressing exhibitions of fear which would help to bring legal killing into disrepute.

In New York State killing by electricity has been adopted, and one man is already condemned to die in that manner. This certainly seems to be more in keeping with the scientific spirit of the age in which we live, and it has an air of respectability about it that hanging has not, but, in my opinion, it is a more ghastly method of judicial murder than hanging. It is, in fact, a killing device that rivals in horror the worst tortures of the worst ages of the world.

This new system of judicial murder seems to me worse than the roastings of the savages, worse than the burnings, and pinchings, and stretchings of the Inquisition; worse than these if for no other reason than that it is to be practised by those who claim to be enlightened, civilized beings. Nevertheless, there are some favorable points about it, one of which is that it is the result of a demand that there shall be a change in the manner of our killing; and another is that henceforth in one State judicial killing will be done in secret. This is a tacit confession that it must be done hereafter in secret or not much longer at all. When the State begins to be ashamed of what it does the practice is doomed, you may be sure.

8. From Frederick Douglass, "Lynch Law in the South," *North American Review* 155 (July 1892): 17–18

[Another history is conjured by Billy's hanging: that of racial violence. Recent critics have paid especial attention to the ways in which Billy's execution is largely symbolic, intended to impress upon the crew the fact that the officers will countenance no violation of law, even if that means killing a man who never intended to violate the law in the first place. Sociologists refer to such acts as "social control." Following the Civil War, the hanging of African Americans by whites was a way of controlling the black public and reinforcing racial hierarchy through terror. Lynching was a ritual of exclusion, a way "to purify the ship of state by excluding from it the taint of darkness, revolt, and illegitimacy" (Jay 390). Even if only by analogy, lynching is one of the "forms, measured forms" that Vere lauds: the routines and sometimes the punishments that remind the individual of his or her place in the system (p. 129). Former slave Frederick Douglass (1812?–95) was one of the foremost abolitionists and orators in the US; for many Americans, his 1845 and 1855 autobiographies were the standard first-hand account of slavery.]

When all lawful remedies for the prevention of crime have been employed and have failed; when criminals administer the law in the interest of crime; when the government has become a foul and damning conspiracy against the welfare of society; when men guilty of the most infamous crimes are permitted to escape with impunity; when there is no longer any reasonable ground upon which to base a hope of reformation, there is at least an apology for the application of lynch law;[1] but, even in this extremity, it must be regarded as an effort to neutralize one poison by the employment of another. Certain it is that in no tolerable condition of society can lynch law be excused or defended. Its presence is either an evidence of governmental depravity, or of a demoralized state of society. It is generally in the hands of the worst class of men in the community, and is enacted under the most degrading and blinding influences. To break down the doors of jails, wrench off the iron bars of the cells, and in the dark hours of midnight drag out alleged criminals, and to shoot, hang, or burn them to death, requires preparation imparted by copious draughts of whiskey, which leave the actors without inclination or ability to judge of the guilt or innocence of the victims of their wrath.

... [T]here is, in the nature of the act [of lynching] itself, the essence of a crime more far-reaching, dangerous, and deadly than the crime it is intended to punish. Lynch law violates all of those merciful maxims of law and order which experience has shown to be wise and necessary for the protection of liberty, the security of the citizen, and the maintenance of justice for the whole people. It violates the principle which requires, for the conviction of crime, that a man shall be confronted in open court by his accusers. It violates the principle that it is better that ten guilty men shall escape than that one innocent man shall be punished. It violates the rule that presumes innocence until guilt is proven. It compels the accused to prove his innocence and denies him a reasonable doubt in his favor. It simply constitutes itself not a court of

---

1 Extralegal violence carried out in the absence of due process, used especially by nineteenth- and twentieth-century white Americans to terrorize African Americans.

trial, but a court of execution. It comes to its work in a storm of passion and thirsting for human blood, ready to shoot, stab, or burn its victim, who is denied a word of entreaty or explanation. Like the gods of the heathen these mobs have eyes, but see not, ears, but hear not, and they rush to their work of death as pitilessly as the tiger rushes upon his prey.

Appendix F: Sexuality

[Melville didn't know it, of course, but he was writing *Billy Budd* at the dawn of what historian George Chauncey calls the "Modern Gay World." One of Melville's late correspondents, Havelock Ellis (1859–1939), did as much as anyone to usher in that world. In 1896 Ellis co-authored with John Addington Symonds *Sexual Inversion*, a ground-breaking study of sexuality that faulted normative ideas about the "rightness" of heterosexuality, albeit too late for Claggart. Melville's "man of sorrows" can only want from afar and then, as W.H. Auden said in the 1930s, destroy the thing he wants because he wants what society won't let him have (p. 95). Modern adaptations of *Billy Budd* make much of this predicament. Claire Denis's 1999 film *Beau Travail*, for example, lifts Billy, Claggart, and Vere off their British warship patrolling the eighteenth-century Mediterranean and sets them in a French Foreign Legion detachment in twentieth-century East Africa. Denis's portrayal of the male dynamic is highly erotic. Recent productions of Benjamin Britten's (1913–76) oft-staged 1951 opera are erotic as well, so much so that, like Denis's film, the opera can feel like a barely muted mash-up of the descriptions of same-sex physical acts in *Typee* and the politics governing those acts in *Billy Budd*. Surprisingly, however, reviewers of these adaptations sometimes act as though questions about sexuality weren't *already* in *Billy Budd*. For too many people, Melville's final fiction is a fable of good versus evil and not much else. Such flattening of the book's sexual tension doesn't do it or its readers any favours. Nor does it help us understand Melville's overall body of work. The male–male sexual dynamics of early novels like *Typee* and *Moby-Dick* have long been a topic of conversation, but his poetry, including "Bridegroom Dick," also considers the politics and "fate" of same-sex desire, and does so as pointedly and productively as anything Melville wrote prior to 1857.]

1. **From *The Statutes Relating to the Admiralty, Navy, Shipping, and Navigation of the United Kingdom* (1749; London: George Eyre and Andrew Strahan, 1823)**

[Under the 1749 amendment to the 1661 British parliamentary act establishing the Articles of War, same-sex physical acts were outlawed.]

If any Person in the Fleet shall commit the unnatural and detestable Sin of Buggery or Sodomy with Man or Beast, he shall be punished with Death by the Sentence of a Court Martial.

2. Walt Whitman, "In Paths Untrodden," *Leaves of Grass* (1860; Boston: James R. Osgood and Company, 1881–82)

["In Paths Untrodden" was first published in the 1860 edition of *Leaves of Grass* in "Calamus," Walt Whitman's (1819–92) grouping of poems about same-sex love and physical affection.]

In paths untrodden,
In the growth by margins of pond-waters,
Escaped from the life that exhibits itself,
From all the standards hitherto publish'd, from the pleasures,
    profits, conformities,
Which too long I was offering to feed my soul,   5
Clear to me now standards not yet publish'd, clear to me that
    my soul,
That the soul of the man I speak for rejoices in comrades,
Here by myself away from the clank of the world,
Tallying and talk'd to here by tongues aromatic,
No longer abash'd, (for in this secluded spot I can respond as
    I would not dare elsewhere,)   10
Strong upon me the life that does not exhibit itself, yet contains all
    the rest,
Resolv'd to sing no songs to-day but those of manly attachment,
Projecting them along that substantial life,
Bequeathing hence types of athletic love,
Afternoon this delicious Ninth-month in my forty-first year,   15
I proceed for all who are or have been young men,
To tell the secret of my nights and days,
To celebrate the need of comrades.

3. From John Addington Symonds, *A Problem in Greek Ethics* (1883; London, 1901), 1

[British writer, historian, and critic John Addington Symonds (1840–93) was an open advocate of same-sex love, theorizing and historicizing it in works such as *A Problem in Greek Ethics*, first published in a very small edition in 1883, and in *Sexual Inversion* (1897), co-authored with Havelock Ellis.]

For the student of sexual Inversion, ancient Greece offers a wide field for observation and reflection. Its importance has hitherto been underrated by medical and legal writers on the subject, who do not seem to be aware that here along in history have we the example of a great and highly-developed race not only tolerating homosexual passions, but deeming them of spiritual value, and attempting to utilise them for the benefit of society. Here, also, through the copious stores of literature at our disposal, we can arrive at something definite regarding the various forms assumed by these passions, when allowed free scope for development in the midst of a refined and intellectual civilisation. What the Greeks called paiderastia, or boy-love, was a phenomenon of one of the most brilliant periods of human culture, in one of the most highly organised and nobly active nations.... To trace the history of so remarkable a custom in their several communities, and to ascertain, so far as this is possible, the ethical feeling of the Greeks upon this subject, must be of service to the scientific psychologist. It enables him to approach the subject from another point of view than that usually adopted by modern jurists, psychiatrists, writers on forensic medicine.

4. From Herman Melville, "Bridegroom Dick. 1876" (1888; *John Marr and Other Poems* [Princeton, NJ: Princeton UP, 1922], 18–42)

[Melville's 1888 dramatic monologue featuring an old sailor and his wife is awash in sexual innuendo. The sailor, who is speaking, looks back fondly on his younger days as a coxswain, "the Commodore's pet," though a little too eagerly for his wife's comfort (*Published Poems* 206). The bawdy, sometimes scatological insinuations of the passages below aside, "Bridegroom Dick" is a considered meditation on homo- and heterosexuality within the confines of both shipboard and married life. The innuendo and punning are part of what make the poem so effective, if light-hearted, a public discussion of nineteenth-century sexual norms. Melville was a master of sexual innuendo, writing, for example, of Hawthorne in 1850: "But already I feel that this Hawthorne has dropped germanous seeds into my soul. He expands and deepens down, the more I contemplate him; and further, and further, shoots his strong New-England roots into the hot soil of my Southern soul" (*Piazza Tales* 250).]

The troublous colic o' intestine war
It sets the bowels o' affection ajar.   170
But, lord, old dame, so spins the whizzing world,
A humming-top, ay, for the little boy-gods
Flogging it well with their smart little rods,
Tittering at time and the coil uncurled.

Now, now, sweetheart, you sidle away,   175
No, never you like *that* kind o' *gay*;[1]
But sour if I get, giving truth her due,
Honey-sweet forever, wife, will Dick be to you!

...

Don't fidget so, wife; an old man's passion   426
Amounts to no more than this smoke that I puff;
There, there, now, buss[2] me in good old fashion;
A died-down candle will flicker in the snuff.

...

My pipe is smoked out, and the grog runs slack;
But bowse away, wife, at your blessed Bohea;[3]   435
This empty can here must needs solace me—
Nay, sweetheart, nay; I take that back;
Dick drinks from your eyes and he finds no lack!

5. From John Addington Symonds, *Walt Whitman: A Study* (London: John C. Nimmo, 1893), 66, 74–76

[In 1890 John Addington Symonds wrote to Whitman, asking him to acknowledge his sexuality and possibly even help campaign for tolerance. Whitman denied that he or his work could be read on such terms. Melville probably would have denied it, too. Perhaps both men were feeling less sanguine that conditions ever would improve for orientations that were not traditionally heterosexual. Here, Symonds acknowledges Whitman's denial but also points out that Whitman's work can't help but be read as a commentary on all forms of love and physical affection. He could easily have said the same of Melville's.]

If we are to have sex handled openly in literature—and I do not see why we should not have it, or how we are to avoid it—surely it is better to be in the company of poets like Æschylus[4] and Whitman, who place human love among the large and universal mysteries of nature, than to

---

1 The term "gay" here likely refers generally to sexually unrestricted or sexually liberated behaviour, not necessarily to same-sex physical acts, though in this context the two would be one and the same. The word acquired the latter connotation in the early twentieth century.
2 Kiss.
3 Bowse, to drink; Bohea is a tea.
4 Greek playwright (c. 523–c. 456 BCE).

dwell with theologians who confound its simple truth with sinfulness, or with self-dubbed "psychologues" who dabble in its morbid pruriencies....

It is clear then that, in his treatment of comradeship [in his "Calamus" poems], or the impassioned love of man for man, Whitman has struck a keynote, to the emotional intensity of which the modern world is unaccustomed.... Studying his works by their own light, and by the light of their author's character, interpreting each part by reference to the whole and in the spirit of the whole, an impartial critic will, I think, be drawn to the conclusion that what he calls the "adhesiveness" of comradeship is meant to have no interblending with the "amativeness" of sexual love. Personally, it is undeniable that Whitman possessed a specially keen sense of the fine restraint and continence, the cleanliness and chastity, that are inseparable from the perfectly virile and physically complete nature of healthy manhood. Still we have the right to predicate the same ground-qualities in ... those founders of the martial institution of Greek love; and yet it is notorious to students of Greek civilisation that the lofty sentiment of their masculine chivalry was intertwined with much that is repulsive to modern sentiment. Whitman does not appear to have taken some of the phenomena of contemporary morals into due account, although he must have been aware of them. Else he would have foreseen that, human nature being what it is, we cannot expect to eliminate all sensual alloy from emotions raised to a high pitch of passionate intensity, and that permanent elements within the midst of our society will imperil the absolute purity of the ideal he attempts to establish. It is obvious that those unenviable mortals who are the inheritors of sexual anomalies, will recognise their own emotion in Whitman's "superb friendship, exalté, previously unknown," which "waits, and has been always waiting, latent in all men," the "something fierce in me, eligible to burst forth," "ethereal comradeship," "the last athletic reality." Had I not the strongest proof in Whitman's private correspondence with myself that he repudiated any such deductions from his "Calamus," I admit that I should have regarded them as justified; and I am not certain whether his own feelings upon this delicate topic may not have altered since the time when "Calamus" was first composed. These considerations do not, however, affect the spiritual quality of his ideal. After acknowledging, what Whitman omitted to perceive, that there are inevitable points of contact between sexual anomaly and his doctrine of comradeship, the question now remains whether he has not suggested the way whereby abnormal instincts may be moralised and raised to higher value.

6. W.H. Auden, "Herman Melville" (1939; repr. in *Another Time* [London: Faber and Faber, 1940], 33–34)

[Anglo-American poet W.H. Auden (1907–73) looked back on two Melvilles: the aging writer who wrote *Billy Budd* and the young writer who, it would seem, loved Hawthorne. Reminiscent of Melville's late poems, which are practically case studies in retrospection, Auden's "Herman Melville" is at once an account of Melville's career, his life, and his work, including *Moby-Dick* and especially *Billy Budd*, which Auden understands as a story of sexuality, evil, innocence, judgment, and forgiveness.]

Towards the end he sailed into an extraordinary mildness,
And anchored in his home and reached his wife
And rode within the harbour of her hand,
And went across each morning to an office
As though his occupation were another island.   5

Goodness existed: that was the new knowledge
His terror had to blow itself quite out
To let him see it; but it was the gale had blown him
Past the Cape Horn of sensible success
Which cries: 'This rock is Eden. Shipwreck here.'   10

But deafened him with thunder and confused with lightning:
—The maniac hero hunting like a jewel
The rare ambiguous monster that had maimed his sex,
The unexplained survivor breaking off the nightmare—
All that was intricate and false; the truth was simple.   15

Evil is unspectacular and always human,
And shares our bed and eats at our own table,
And we are introduced to Goodness every day,
Even in drawing-rooms among a crowd of faults;
He has a name like Billy and is almost perfect   20
But wears a stammer like decoration:
And every time they meet the same thing has to happen;
It is the Evil that is helpless like a lover
And has to pick a quarrel and succeeds,
And both are openly destroyed before our eyes.   25

For now he was awake and knew
No one is ever spared except in dreams;

But there was something else the nightmare had distorted—
Even the punishment was human and a form of love:
The howling storm had been his father's presence   30
And all the time he had been carried on his father's breast.

Who now had set him gently down and left him.
He stood upon the narrow balcony and listened:
And all the stars above him sang as in his childhood
'All, all is vanity,'[1] but it was not the same;   35
For now the words descended like the calm of mountains—
—Nathaniel had been shy because his love was selfish—
But now he cried in exultation and surrender
'The Godhead is broken like bread. We are the pieces.'[2]

And sat down at his desk and wrote a story.   40

---

1 From Ecclesiastes (1:2), one of Melville's favourite books of the Bible.
2 In a November 1851 letter to Nathaniel Hawthorne, Melville responded to
   Hawthorne's praise for *Moby-Dick*: "Whence come you, Hawthorne? By what
   right do you drink from my flagon of life? And when I put it to my lips—lo,
   they are yours and not mine. I feel that the Godhead is broken up like the
   bread at the [Last] Supper, and that we are the pieces" (*Correspondence* 212).

Appendix G: Pessimism

[As formalized by philosopher Arthur Schopenhauer, pessimism holds that life consists entirely and meaninglessly of striving and suffering. Pessimism stood in stark contrast to the brand of optimism that ran through much Anglo-American Victorian culture, typified by Tennyson's fist-pumping conclusion to his 1842 poem "Ulysses": "To strive, to seek, to find, and not to yield" (56). Pessimists like English novelist Thomas Hardy (1840–1928) and Scottish poet James Thomson would want it this way: "To strive, to seek, to yield." We don't know Melville's opinion of Hardy, but we do know he began reading Thomson intensely late in life. In Thomson and later in Schopenhauer, Melville found fellow travellers. Sceptical of the optimism of his era(s), he saw in pessimist writings a sense of the world that seems to have accorded with his own, not to mention a sense of the world that "testament of acceptance" readings see in *Billy Budd*. It's important to note, however, that he never got too comfortable in any one philosophical couch any more than he ever settled too snugly into a political one. Writing in 1885 of Thomson's work, Melville explained that "altho' neither pessimist nor optimist myself, nevertheless I relish it in the verse if for nothing else than as a counterpoise to the exorbitant hopefulness, juvenile and shallow, that makes so much bluster in these days" (*Correspondence* 486). While in most of his poems pessimism reigns, the final work, "The Enthusiast," equivocates powerfully.]

1. From Arthur Schopenhauer, *The World as Will and Idea* (1819–44; repr. trans. R.B. Haldane and J. Kemp, vol. 1 [London: Trübner and Co., 1883]), 398–99

[In this section from his magnum opus, Schopenhauer sets out succinctly the philosophy of pessimism: that the will of all life, which he defines as its "inmost nature," is to thrive and suffer when that thriving is inevitably arrested (*World* 398).]

[The will] always strives, for striving is its sole nature, which no attained goal can put an end to. Therefore it is not susceptible of any final satisfaction, but can only be restrained by hindrances, while in itself it goes on for ever. We see this in the simplest of all natural phenomena, gravity, which does not cease to strive and press towards a mathematical centre to reach which would be the annihilation both of itself and matter, and would not cease even if the whole universe were already rolled into one ball.... No body is without relationship, *i.e.*, without tendency or without desire and longing, as Jacob Böhme[1] would say. Electricity transmits its inner self-repulsion to infinity, though the mass of the earth absorbs the effect. Galvanism is certainly, so long as the pile is working, an aimless, unceasingly repeated act of repulsion and attraction. The existence of the plant is just such a restless, never satisfied striving, a ceaseless tendency through ever-ascending forms, till the end, the seed, becomes a new starting-point; and this repeated *ad infinitum*—nowhere an end, nowhere a final satisfaction, nowhere a resting-place. It will also be remembered ... that the multitude of natural forces and organised forms everywhere strive with each other for the matter in which they desire to appear, for each of them only possesses what it has wrested from the others; and thus a constant internecine war is waged, from which, for the most part, arises the resistance through which that striving, which constitutes the inner nature of everything, is at all points hindered; struggles in vain, yet, from its nature, cannot leave off; toils on laboriously till this phenomenon dies, when others eagerly seize its place and its matter.

We have long since recognised this striving, which constitutes the kernel and in-itself of everything, as identical with that which in us, where it manifests itself most distinctly in the light of the fullest consciousness, is called *will*. Its hindrance through an obstacle which places itself between it and its temporary aim we call *suffering*, and, on the other hand, its attainment of the end satisfaction, wellbeing, happiness. We may also transfer this terminology to the phenomena of the unconscious world, for though weaker in degree, they are identical in nature. Then we see them involved in constant suffering, and without any continuing happiness. For all effort springs from defect—from discontent with one's estate—is thus suffering so long as it is not satisfied; but no satisfaction is lasting, rather it is always merely the starting-point of a new effort. The striving we see everywhere hindered in many ways, everywhere in conflict, and therefore always under the form of suffering. Thus, if there is no final end of striving, there is no measure and end of suffering.

2. From James Thomson, *The City of Dreadful Night* (1870–74; repr. in *The City of Dreadful Night and Other Poems* [Portland, ME: Thomas B. Mosher, 1903], 3–57)

[At first blush, the tone of James Thomson's (1834–82) pessimist masterpiece seems thoroughly gloomy. What would one expect from the

---

1 Jakob Böhme (1575–1624), German mystic who influenced European Romantic thought.

writer who, according to the editors of an old anthology of English literature, "led the most miserable life of any Victorian poet" (Bloom 1476)? However, to Thomson, and to Melville, what some saw as doom and gloom was just the way things are, or, in Thomson's words, "the bitter old and wrinkled truth / Stripped naked." "When one casts off" the hope that things will ever improve, there is release from the "burden" that hope entails (p. 211).]

... [A] cold rage seizes one at whiles
    To show the bitter old and wrinkled truth
Stripped naked of all vesture that beguiles,   10
    False dreams, false hopes, false masks and modes of youth;
Because it gives some sense of power and passion
In helpless impotence to try to fashion
    Our woe in living words howe'er uncouth.

Surely I write not for the hopeful young,   15
    Or those who deem their happiness of worth,
Or such as pasture and grow fat among
    The shows of life and feel nor doubt nor dearth,
Or pious spirits with a God above them
To sanctify and glorify and love them,   20
    Or sages who foresee a heaven on earth.

For none of these I write, and none of these
    Could read the writing if they deigned to try:
So may they flourish, in their due degrees,
    On our sweet earth and in their unplaced sky.   25
If any cares for the weak words here written,
It must be some one desolate, Fate-smitten,
    Whose faith and hope are dead, and who would die.

Yes, here and there some weary wanderer
    In that same city of tremendous night,   30
Will understand the speech, and feel a stir
    Of fellowship in all-disastrous fight;
"I suffer mute and lonely, yet another
Uplifts his voice to let me know a brother
    Travels the same wild paths though out of sight."   35

...

I sat forlornly by the river-side,
    And watched the bridge-lamps glow like golden stars

Above the blackness of the swelling tide,
    Down which they struck rough gold in ruddier bars;   340
And heard the heave and plashing of the flow
Against the wall a dozen feet below.

Large elm-trees stood along that river-walk;
    And under one, a few steps from my seat,
I heard strange voices join in stranger talk,   345
    Although I had not heard approaching feet:
These bodiless voices in my waking dream
Flowed dark words blending with the sombre stream:—

And you have after all come back; come back.
I was about to follow on your track.   350
And you have failed: our spark of hope is black.

That I have failed is proved by my return:
The spark is quenched, nor ever more will burn.
But listen; and the story you shall learn.

I reached the portal common spirits fear,   355
And read the words above it, dark yet clear,
"Leave hope behind, all ye who enter here":[1]

And would have passed in, gratified to gain
That positive eternity of pain,
Instead of this insufferable inane.   360

A demon warder clutched me, Not so fast;
First leave your hopes behind!—But years have passed
Since I left all behind me, to the last:

You cannot count for hope, with all your wit,
This bleak despair that drives me to the Pit: 365
How could I seek to enter void of it?

He snarled, What thing is this which apes a soul,
And would find entrance to our gulf of dole
Without the payment of the settled toll?

Outside the gate he showed an open chest: 370

---

1 The inscription at the entrance to hell in Dante's (1265–1321) *Inferno* (1320),
   Canto III.

Here pay their entrance fees the souls unblest;
Cast in some hope, you enter with the rest.

This is Pandora's box;[1] whose lid shall shut,
And Hell-gate too, when hopes have filled it; but
They are so thin that it will never glut.   375

I stood a few steps backwards, desolate;
And watched the spirits pass me to their fate,
And fling off hope, and enter at the gate.

When one casts off a load he springs upright,
Squares back his shoulders, breathes with all his might,   380
And briskly paces forward strong and light:

But these, as if they took some burden, bowed;
The whole frame sank; however strong and proud
Before, they crept in quite infirm and cowed.

And as they passed me, earnestly from each   385
A morsel of his hope I did beseech,
To pay my entrance; but all mocked my speech.

No one would cede a tittle of his store,
Though knowing that in instants three or four
He must resign the whole for evermore.   390

So I returned. Our destiny is fell;
For in this Limbo we must ever dwell,
Shut out alike from Heaven and Earth and Hell.

The other sighed back, Yea; but if we grope
With care through all this Limbo's dreary scope,   395
We yet may pick up some minute lost hope;

And, sharing it between us, entrance win,
In spite of fiends so jealous for gross sin:
Let us without delay our search begin.

...

---

1   In Greek mythology, a jar containing all manner of evil. When Pandora
    opened it, out of curiosity, evil went into the world. Inside the jar, only hope
    remained.

The sense that every struggle brings defeat
   Because Fate holds no prize to crown success;
That all the oracles are dumb or cheat   1105
   Because they have no secret to express;
That none can pierce the vast black veil uncertain
Because there is no light beyond the curtain;
   That all is vanity and nothingness.

Titanic from her high throne in the north,   1110
   That City's sombre Patroness and Queen,
In bronze sublimity she gazes forth
   Over her Capital of teen and threne,[1]
Over the river with its isles and bridges,
The marsh and moorland, to the stern rock-ridges,   1115
   Confronting them with a coëval mien.[2]

The moving moon and stars from east to west
   Circle before her in the sea of air;
Shadows and gleams glide round her solemn rest.
   Her subjects often gaze up to her there: 1120
The strong to drink new strength of iron endurance,
The weak new terrors; all, renewed assurance
   And confirmation of the old despair.

3. Herman Melville, "The Berg. A Dream" (1888; repr. in *John Marr and Other Poems* [Princeton, NJ: Princeton UP, 1922], 78–79)

["The Berg," published in 1888's *John Marr*, is one of Melville's most successful pessimist experiments. The poem originally ended with the line "Along thy dead indifference of walls," but afterward, in his own copy, Melville changed the line to "Along thy dense stolidity of walls," an emendation that better encapsulates the stoicism of pessimistic thought (*Poems*, ed. Robillard 27).]

I saw a ship of martial build
(Her standards set, her brave apparel on)
Directed as by madness mere
Against a stolid iceberg steer,
Nor budge it, though the infatuate ship went down.   5

---

1 Teen: woe or hurt; threne: a dirge.
2 With a contemporaneous, or perhaps similar, aspect.

The impact made huge ice-cubes fall
Sullen, in tons that crashed the deck;
But that one avalanche was all—
No other movement save the foundering wreck.

Along the spurs of ridges pale,   10
Not any slenderest shaft and frail,
A prism over glass—green gorges lone,
Toppled; nor lace of traceries fine,
Nor pendant drops in grot or mine
Were jarred, when the stunned ship went down.   15
Nor sole the gulls in cloud that wheeled
Circling one snow-flanked peak afar,
But nearer fowl the floes that skimmed
And crystal beaches, felt no jar.
No thrill transmitted stirred the lock   20
Of jack-straw needle-ice at base;
Towers undermined by waves—the block
Atilt impending—kept their place.
Seals, dozing sleek on sliddery ledges
Slipt never, when by loftier edges   25
Through very inertia overthrown,
The impetuous ship in bafflement went down.
Hard Berg (methought), so cold, so vast,
With mortal damps self-overcast;
Exhaling still thy dankish breath—   30
Adrift dissolving, bound for death;
Though lumpish thou, a lumbering one—
A lumbering lubbard loitering slow,
Impingers rue thee and go down,
Sounding thy precipice below,   35
Nor stir the slimy slug that sprawls
Along thy dense stolidity of walls.

4. Herman Melville, "The Enthusiast" (1891; repr. in *John Marr and Other Poems* [Princeton, NJ: Princeton UP, 1922], 94–95)

["The Enthusiast," published in *Timoleon* in 1891, is a tour-de-force example of Melville's art of equivocation, a poem that somehow counsels both surrender and resistance. It shows that as much as Melville was drawn to the thought of Thomson and Schopenhauer, he never could find comfort in a single way of thinking.]

"Though He slay me yet will I trust in Him."[1]

Shall hearts that beat no base retreat
   In youth's magnanimous years—
Ignoble hold it, if discreet
   When interest tames to fears;
Shall spirits that worship light   5
   Perfidious deem its sacred glow,
   Recant, and trudge where worldlings go,
Conform and own them right?

Shall Time with creeping influence cold
   Unnerve and cow? the heart   10
Pine for the heartless ones enrolled
   With palterers of the mart?[2]
Shall faith abjure her skies,
   Or pale probation blench her down
   To shrink from Truth so still, so lone   15
Mid loud gregarious lies?

Each burning boat in Caesar's rear,
   Flames—No return through me![3]
So put the torch to ties though dear,
   If ties but tempters be.   20
Nor cringe if come the night:
   Walk through the cloud to meet the pall,
   Though light forsake thee, never fall
From fealty to light.

5. From William James, *The Varieties of Religious Experience* (New York: Longman's, Green and Company, 1902), 41–42

[Pessimism had its critics, among them the American philosopher William James (1842–1910), who addressed it in his ground-breaking 1902 empiricist examination of faith, *The Varieties of Religious Experience*. In the passages below, James associates the pessimism of thinkers like Schopenhauer with the classical stoicism of Marcus Aurelius (121–180

---

1 Melville left off the rest of this quotation of Job 13:15: "but I will maintain mine own ways before him" (*Published Poems* 795). See Appendix G5, where William James comments on this passage.

2 Using trickery to get ahead financially.

3 Plutarch (c. 50–c. 125 CE) relates how Julius Caesar (100–44 BCE) burned his boats at Alexandria to avoid the enemy capturing them; perhaps also a reference to Caesar burning his boats to prevent his own soldiers from retreating.

CE). For James, as intellectually interesting and in some senses attractive as pessimism is, it's ultimately little more than a "pinched and mumping sick-room attitude" (46). Don't mistake James's annoyance: he's not proselytizing on behalf of religion. He's unimpressed by pessimism as a cognitive strategy for dealing with the unknown.]

"I accept the universe" is reported to have been a favorite utterance of our New England transcendentalist, Margaret Fuller; and when some one repeated this phrase to Thomas Carlyle, his sardonic comment is said to have been: "Gad! she'd better!" At bottom the whole concern of both morality and religion is with the manner of our acceptance of the universe.[1] Do we accept it only in part and grudgingly, or heartily and altogether? Shall our protests against certain things in it be radical and unforgiving, or shall we think that, even with evil, there are ways of living that must lead to good? If we accept the whole, shall we do so as if stunned into submission,—as Carlyle would have us—"Gad! we'd better!"—or shall we do so with enthusiastic assent? Morality pure and simple accepts the law of the whole which it finds reigning, so far as to acknowledge and obey it, but it may obey it with the heaviest and coldest heart, and never cease to feel it as a yoke. But for religion, in its strong and fully developed manifestations, the service of the highest never is felt as a yoke. Dull submission is left far behind, and a mood of welcome, which may fill any place on the scale between cheerful serenity and enthusiastic gladness, has taken its place.

It makes a tremendous emotional and practical difference to one whether one accept the universe in the drab discolored way of stoic resignation to necessity, or with the passionate happiness of Christian saints. The difference is as great as that between passivity and activity, as that between the defensive and the aggressive mood. Gradual as are the steps by which an individual may grow from one state into the other, many as are the intermediate stages which different individuals represent, yet when you place the typical extremes beside each other for comparison, you feel that two discontinuous psychological universes confront you, and that in passing from one to the other a 'critical point' has been overcome.

If we compare stoic with Christian ejaculations we see much more than a difference of doctrine; rather is it a difference of emotional mood that parts them. When Marcus Aurelius[2] reflects on the eternal

---

1   Margaret Fuller (1810–50), American author, editor, and Transcendentalist; Thomas Carlyle (1795–1881), famed British author and social critic.
2   Marcus Aurelius (121–180 CE), Roman emperor and author of *Meditations* (170–180), a key text in the philosophy of Stoicism in its Greek and then Roman heyday.

reason that has ordered things, there is a frosty chill about his words which you rarely find in a Jewish, and never in a Christian piece of religious writing. The universe is 'accepted' by all these writers; but how devoid of passion, or exultation the spirit of the Roman Emperor is! Compare his fine sentence: "If gods care not for me or my children, here is a reason for it," with Job's cry: "Though he slay me, yet will I trust in him!"[1] and you immediately see the difference I mean. The *anima mundi*,[2] to whose disposal of his own personal destiny the Stoic consents, is there to be respected and submitted to, but the Christian God is there to be loved; and the difference of emotional atmosphere is like that between an arctic climate and the tropics, though the outcome in the way of accepting actual conditions uncomplainingly may seem in abstract terms to be much the same.

---

1 See the epigraph to Melville's poem "The Enthusiast," above.
2 World soul (Latin), the Platonic idea of the connection between the human soul and the planet; it was fundamental to Stoic philosophy.

Works Cited and Select Bibliography

This bibliography is geared especially toward readers new to Melville or to *Billy Budd*.

Key Editions of *Billy Budd*

Billy Budd, and Other Prose Pieces. Ed. Raymond Weaver. London: Constable, 1924.

The Shorter Novels of Herman Melville. Ed. Raymond Weaver. New York: Horace Liveright, 1928.

Billy Budd. Ed. F. Barron Freeman. Cambridge, MA: Harvard UP, 1948.

Billy Budd, Sailor (An Inside Narrative). Ed. Harrison Hayford and Merton M. Sealts Jr. Chicago: U of Chicago P, 1962.

Relevant Writings by Melville

Clarel: A Poem and Pilgrimage in the Holy Land. 1876. Ed. Harrison Hayford and Walter E. Bezanson. Evanston and Chicago: Northwestern UP and the Newberry Library, 1991.

Correspondence. Ed. Lynn Horth. Evanston and Chicago: Northwestern UP and the Newberry Library, 1991.

Journals. Ed. Howard C. Horsford and Lynn Horth. Evanston and Chicago: Northwestern UP and the Newberry Library, 1989.

Moby-Dick; or, The Whale. 1851. Ed. Harrison Hayford, Hershel Parker, and G. Thomas Tanselle. Evanston and Chicago: Northwestern UP and the Newberry Library, 1988.

The Piazza Tales, and Other Prose Pieces, 1838–1860. Ed. Harrison Hayford, Alma A. MacDougall, and G. Thomas Tanselle. Evanston and Chicago: Northwestern UP and the Newberry Library, 1987.

Pierre; or, The Ambiguities. 1852. Ed. Harrison Hayford, Hershel Parker, and G. Thomas Tanselle. Evanston and Chicago: Northwestern UP and the Newberry Library, 1971.

Published Poems. Ed. Robert Charles Ryan and Hershel Parker. Evanston and Chicago: Northwestern UP and the Newberry Library, 1971.

Redburn, His First Voyage. 1849. Evanston and Chicago: Northwestern UP and the Newberry Library, 1969.

Tales, Poems, and Other Writings. Ed. John Bryant. New York: Modern Library, 2001.

White-Jacket; or, The World in a Man-of-War. 1850. Ed. Harrison
  Hayford, Hershel Parker, and G. Thomas Tanselle. Evanston and
  Chicago: Northwestern UP and the Newberry Library, 1970.

Biographical Sources

Delbanco, Andrew. *Melville: His World and Work.* New York: Knopf,
  2005.
Gale, Robert L. *A Herman Melville Encyclopedia.* Westport, CT:
  Greenwood P, 1995.
Garner, Stanton. *The Civil War World of Herman Melville.* Lawrence:
  U of Kansas P, 1993.
——. "Herman Melville and the Customs Service." *Melville's Ever-
  moving Dawn: Centennial Essays.* Ed. John Bryant and Robert
  Milder. Kent, OH: Kent State UP, 1997. 276–93.
Hardwick, Elizabeth. *Herman Melville: A Penguin Life.* New York:
  Viking, 2000.
Kennedy, Frederick James, and Joyce Daveau Kennedy. "Archibald
  MacMechan and the Melville Revival." *Leviathan* 1.2 (1999):
  5–37.
Leyda, Jay, ed. *The Melville Log: A Documentary Life of Herman
  Melville, 1819–1891.* 2 vols. 1951. New York: Gordion P, 1969.
Marovitz, Sanford E. "The Melville Revival." *A Companion to
  Herman Melville.* Ed. Wyn Kelley. Malden, MA: Blackwell, 2006.
  515–31.
Metcalf, Eleanor. *Herman Melville: Cycle and Epicycle.* Cambridge,
  MA: Harvard UP, 1953.
Miller, Edwin Haviland. *Herman Melville: A Biography.* New York:
  Braziller, 1975.
Parker, Hershel. *Herman Melville: A Biography.* 2 vols. Baltimore:
  Johns Hopkins UP, 1996–2002.
Robertson-Lorant, Laurie. *Melville: A Biography.* New York: Clarkson
  Potter, 1996.
Rogin, Michael Paul. *Subversive Genealogy: The Politics and Art of
  Herman Melville.* Berkeley: U of California P, 1983.

Bibliographies and Guides to Criticism

Bercaw, Mary K. *Melville's Sources.* Evanston: Northwestern UP,
  1987.
Cowen, Walker, ed. *Melville's Marginalia.* 2 vols. 1965. Reprint. New
  York: Garland, 1987. (See also *Melville's Marginalia Online,* under
  "Melville on the Web," below.)

Hayes, Kevin J., and Hershel Parker. *Checklist of Melville Reviews*. Evanston: Northwestern UP, 1991.

Higgins, Brian. *Herman Melville: An Annotated Bibliography*. Boston: G.K. Hall, 1979.

——. *Herman Melville: A Reference Guide, 1931–1960*. Boston: G.K. Hall, 1987.

Higgins, Brian, and Hershel Parker, eds. *Herman Melville: The Contemporary Reviews*. Cambridge: Cambridge UP, 1995.

Lauter, Paul. "Melville Climbs the Canon." *American Literature* 66.1 (1994): 1–24.

Sealts, Merton M., Jr. *Melville's Reading*. Revised and enlarged ed. Columbia: U of South Carolina P, 1988.

Yothers, Brian. *Melville's Mirrors: Literary Criticism and America's Most Elusive Author*. Rochester, NY: Camden House, 2011.

Studies of Melville's Work

Arvin, Newton. *Herman Melville*. [New York]: William Sloane Associates, 1950.

Berthoff, Werner. *The Example of Melville*. Princeton, NJ: Princeton UP, 1962.

Bryant, John. "Herman Melville: A Writer in Process." *Tales, Poems, and Other Writings* by Herman Melville. New York: Modern Library, 2001. xvii–l.

Chase, Richard. *Herman Melville: A Critical Study*. New York: Macmillan, 1949.

——. "Introduction." *Melville: A Collection of Critical Essays*. Englewood Cliffs, NJ: Prentice-Hall, 1962. 1–10.

Coffler, Gail H. *Melville's Allusions to Religion: A Comprehensive Index and Glossary*. Westport, CT: Praeger, 2004.

Dillingham, William B. *Melville and His Circle: The Last Years*. Athens: U of Georgia P, 1996.

Dryden, Edgar A. *Monumental Melville: The Formation of a Literary Career*. Stanford, CA: Stanford UP, 2004.

Gunn, Giles, ed. *A Historical Guide to Herman Melville*. New York: Oxford UP, 2005.

Hayes, Kevin J. *The Cambridge Introduction to Herman Melville*. New York: Cambridge UP, 2007.

Kelley, Wyn. *Herman Melville: An Introduction*. Malden, MA: Blackwell, 2008.

Milder, Robert. *Exiled Royalties: Melville and the Life We Imagine*. New York: Oxford UP, 2006.

Olson, Charles. *Call Me Ishmael: A Study of Melville*. 1947. New York: Grove P, 1967.

Otter, Samuel. *Melville's Anatomies*. Berkeley: U of California P, 1999.

Percy, Walker. "Herman Melville." 1987. *Signposts in a Strange Land*. New York: Farrar, Straus and Giroux, 1991. 197–203.

Wood, James. "The All and the If: God and Metaphor in Melville." 1999. *The Broken Estate: Essays on Literature and Belief*. New York: Picador, 2010. 42–56.

Wright, Nathalia. *Melville's Use of the Bible*. Durham, NC: Duke UP, 1949.

Studies of *Billy Budd*

The scholarship on *Billy Budd* is extensive. The following list prioritizes work published since 2000, though it includes seminal older treatments.

Alweiss, Lilian. "On Moral Dilemmas: Winch, Kant, and *Billy Budd*." *Philosophy* 78.2 (2003): 205–18.

Arendt, Hannah. "The Social Question." *On Revolution*. 1963. New York: Penguin, 1965. 59–114.

Arjomand, Minou. "E.M. Forster's *Billy Budd* and the Collaborative Work of Opera." *Theatre Survey* 51.2 (2010): 225–45.

Barton, John Cyril. "Melville, MacKenzie, and Military Executions." *Literary Executions: Capital Punishment and American Culture, 1820–1925*. Baltimore: Johns Hopkins UP, 2014. 174–224.

Cameron, Sharon. "'Lines of Stones': The Unpersonified Impersonal in Melville's *Billy Budd*." *Impersonality: Seven Essays*. Baltimore: Johns Hopkins UP, 2007. 181–204.

Castiglia, Christopher. "Cold War Allegories and the Politics of Criticism." *The New Cambridge Companion to Herman Melville*. Ed. Robert S. Levine. New York: Cambridge UP, 2014. 219–32.

Claviez, Thomas. "Rainbows, Fogs, and Other Smokescreens: *Billy Budd* and the Question of Ethics." *Arizona Quarterly* 62.4 (2006): 31–46.

Coffler, Gail. "Classical Iconography in the Aesthetics of *Billy Budd, Sailor*." *Savage Eye: Melville and the Visual Arts*. Ed. Christopher Sten. Kent, OH: Kent State UP, 1991. 257–76.

Colatrella, Carol. "Summary Judgment in *Billy Budd*." *Literature and Moral Reform: Melville and the Discipline of Reading*. Gainesville: U of Florida P, 2002. 226–45.

Crain, Caleb. "Melville's Palinode." *American Sympathy: Men, Friend-*

ship and Literature in the New Nation. New Haven, CT: Yale UP, 2001. 238–70.

Crane, Gregg. "Judgment in *Billy Budd.*" *The New Cambridge Companion to Herman Melville.* Ed. Robert S. Levine. New York: Cambridge UP, 2014. 142–54.

Culbert, Jennifer L. "Melville's Law." *A Political Companion to Herman Melville.* Ed. Jason Frank. Lexington: UP of Kentucky, 2013. 386–412.

Dimock, Wai-Chee. "A Theory of Resonance." *PMLA* 112.5 (1997): 1060–71.

Drysdale, David J. "Melville's Motley Crew: History and Constituent Power in *Billy Budd.*" *Nineteenth-Century Literature* 67.3 (2012): 312–36.

Fogle, Richard. "*Billy Budd*—Acceptance of Irony." 1958. *Twentieth Century Interpretations of* Billy Budd. Ed. Howard P. Vincent. Englewood Cliffs, NJ: Prentice-Hall, 1971. 41–47.

Franklin, H. Bruce. "*Billy Budd* and Capital Punishment: A Tale of Two Centuries." *American Literature* 69.2 (1997): 337–59.

Gilmore, Michael T. "'Speak, man!': *Billy Budd* in the Crucible of Reconstruction." *American Literary History* 21.3 (2009): 492–517.

Glick, Wendell. "Expediency and Absolute Morality in *Billy Budd.*" *PMLA* 68.1 (1953): 103–10.

Goodheart, Eugene. "*Billy Budd* and the World's Imperfection." *Sewanee Review* 114.1 (2006): 81–92.

Hayford, Harrison, and Merton M. Sealts Jr. "Editor's Introduction." *Billy Budd, Sailor (An Inside Narrative).* By Herman Melville. Chicago: U of Chicago P, 1962. 1–39.

Hunt, Lester H. "*Billy Budd*: Melville's Dilemma." *Philosophy and Literature* 26.2 (2002): 273–95.

Ives, Charles. "*Billy Budd* and the Articles of War." *American Literature* 34.1 (1963): 31–39.

Jay, Gregory. "Douglass, Melville, and the Lynching of Billy Budd." *Frederick Douglass and Herman Melville: Essays in Relation.* Ed. Robert S. Levine and Samuel Otter. Chapel Hill: U of North Carolina P, 2008. 369–95.

Johnson, Barbara. "Melville's Fist: The Execution of Billy Budd." *Studies in Romanticism* 18.4 (1979): 567–99.

Jones, Paul Christian. "Herman Melville's *Billy Budd*: The Legacy of Antebellum Anti-Gallows Literature." *Against the Gallows: Antebellum American Writers and the Movement to Abolish Capital Punishment.* Iowa City: U of Iowa P, 2011. 160–81.

Loosemore, Philip. "Revolution, Counterrevolution, and Natural Law in *Billy Budd, Sailor.*" *Criticism* 53.1 (2011): 99–126.

Martin, Robert K. "Losing Hope." *Hero, Captain, and Stranger: Male Friendship, Social Critique, and Literary Form in the Sea Novels of Herman Melville*. Chapel Hill: U of North Carolina P, 1986. 95–124.

——. "Saving Captain Vere: *Billy Budd* from Melville's Novella to Britten's Opera." *Studies in Short Fiction* 23.1 (1986): 49–56.

Milder, Robert. "Introduction." *Billy Budd, Sailor and Selected Tales*. By Herman Melville. New York: Oxford UP, 2009. vii–xxxix.

Mizruchi, Susan L. "The Return to Sacrifice in Melville and Others." *Science of Sacrifice: American Literature and Modern Social Theory*. Princeton, NJ: Princeton UP, 1998. 89–188.

Parker, Hershel. *Reading* Billy Budd. Evanston: Northwestern UP, 1990.

Reynolds, Larry J. "*Billy Budd* and American Labor Unrest: The Case for Striking Back." *New Essays on* Billy Budd. Ed. Donald Yanella. New York: Cambridge UP, 2002. 21–48.

——. "The Revolutionary Times of Melville's *Billy Budd*." *Righteous Violence: Revolution, Slavery, and the American Renaissance*. Athens: U of Georgia P, 2010. 182–200.

Rowe, Joyce A. "The King's Buttons: The Language of Law in *Billy Budd*." *Prospects* 27 (2003): 271–301.

Samet, Elizabeth D. "A Singular Absence of Heroic Poses." *Willing Obedience: Citizens, Soldiers, and the Progress of Consent in America, 1776–1898*. Stanford, CA: Stanford UP, 2004. 178–221.

Schiffman, Joseph. "Melville's Final Stage: Irony: A Re-Examination of *Billy Budd* Criticism." *American Literature* 22.2 (1950): 128–36.

Scorza, Thomas J. *In the Time before Steamships:* Billy Budd, *the Limits of Politics, and Modernity*. DeKalb: Northern Illinois UP, 1979.

Sedgwick, Eve Kosofsky. "Some Binarisms (I): *Billy Budd*: After the Homosexual." *Epistemology of the Closet*. Berkeley: U of California P, 1990. 91–130.

Shaw, Peter. "The Fate of a Story." *American Scholar* 62.4 (1993): 591–600.

Solove, Daniel J. "Melville's *Billy Budd* and Security in a Time of Crisis." *Cardozo Law Review* 26.6 (2005): 2443–70.

Spanos, William V. *The Exceptionalist State and the State of Exception: Herman Melville's* Billy Budd, Sailor. Baltimore: Johns Hopkins UP, 2011.

Sten, Christopher W. "Vere's Use of the 'Forms': Means and Ends in *Billy Budd*." *American Literature* 47.1 (1975): 37–51.

Stern, Milton R. "Introduction." *Billy Budd, Sailor: An Inside Narrative* by Herman Melville. Indianapolis: Bobbs-Merrill, 1975. vii–xliv.

Thomas, Brook. "*Billy Budd* and the Untold Story of the Law."
Cardozo Studies in Law and Literature 1.1 (1989): 49–69.
———. "Measured Forms" and "Ragged Edges." *Cross-Examinations in Law and Literature: Cooper, Hawthorne, Stowe, and Melville.* New York: Cambridge UP, 1987. 201–50.

Umphrey, Martha Merrill. "Law's Bonds: Eros and Identification in *Billy Budd*." *American Imago* 64.3 (2007): 413–31.

Updike, John. "Introduction." *The Complete Shorter Fiction.* By Herman Melville. New York: Knopf, 1987. xi–xxxiv.

Watson, E.L. Grant. "Melville's Testament of Acceptance." *New England Quarterly* 6.2 (1933): 319–27.

Weisburg, Richard. "Accepting the Inside Narrator's Challenge: *Billy Budd* and the 'Legalistic' Reader." *Cardozo Studies in Law and Literature* 1.1 (1989): 27–48.

Wenke, John. "Complicating Vere: Melville's Practice of Revision in *Billy Budd*." *Leviathan* 1.2 (1999): 83–88

———. "Melville's Indirection: *Billy Budd*, the Genetic Text, and 'the deadly space between.'" *New Essays on* Billy Budd. Ed. Donald Yanella. New York: Cambridge UP, 2002. 114–44.

Studies of Melville's Poetry

Melville's poetry is essential to understanding his late career, including *Billy Budd*. What follows is a selective list of helpful sources on that poetry, including editions by Hennig Cohen, Douglas Robillard, and Robert Penn Warren, all of which have excellent introductions to, and notes on, Melville's work. See also *Published Poems*, ed. Ryan and Parker, and *Tales, Poems, and Other Writings*, ed. Bryant, cited above under "Relevant Writings by Melville." The forthcoming Northwestern-Newberry edition of *Billy Budd* will also contain all of Melville's unpublished poetry and commentaries thereon.

Buell, Lawrence. "Melville the Poet." *The Cambridge Companion to Herman Melville.* Ed. Robert S. Levine. New York: Cambridge UP, 1998. 135–56.

Donahue, Jane. "Melville's Classicism: Law and Order in His Poetry." *Papers on Language and Literature* 5 (1969): 63–72.

Jackson, Virginia. "Who Reads Poetry?" *PMLA* 123.1 (2008): 181–87.

Lee, Maurice S. "Melville, Douglass, the Civil War, Pragmatism." *Frederick Douglass and Herman Melville: Essays in Relation.* Ed. Robert S. Levine and Samuel Otter. Chapel Hill: U of North Carolina P, 2008. 396–415.

Marrs, Cody. "A Wayward Art: *Battle-Pieces* and Melville's Poetic

Turn." *American Literature* 82.1 (2010): 91–119.

Melville, Herman. *The Poems of Herman Melville*. Ed. Douglas Robillard. Rev. ed. Kent, OH: Kent State UP, 2000.

——. *Selected Poems of Herman Melville*. Ed. Hennig Cohen. New York: Fordham UP, 1991.

——. *Selected Poems of Herman Melville: A Reader's Edition*. Ed. Robert Penn Warren. New York: Random House, 1970.

Nabers, Deak. "Victory of LAW: Melville and Reconstruction." *Victory of Law: The Fourteenth Amendment, the Civil War, and American Literature, 1852–1867*. Baltimore: Johns Hopkins UP, 2006. 19–46.

Parker, Hershel. *Melville: The Making of the Poet*. Evanston: Northwestern UP, 2008.

Renker, Elizabeth. "Melville the Poet in the Postbellum World." *The New Cambridge Companion to Herman Melville*. Ed. Robert S. Levine. New York: Cambridge UP, 2014. 127–41.

——. "Melville the Realist Poet." *A Companion to Herman Melville*. Ed. Wyn Kelley. Malden, MA: Blackwell, 2006. 482–96.

Shurr, William. *The Mystery of Iniquity: Melville as Poet, 1857–1891*. Lexington: UP of Kentucky, 1972.

Spengemann, William C. *Three American Poets: Walt Whitman, Emily Dickinson, and Herman Melville*. Notre Dame, IN: U of Notre Dame P, 2010.

Stein, William B. *The Poetry of Melville's Late Years: Time, History, Myth, and Religion*. Albany: State U of New York P, 1970.

Vendler, Helen. "Melville and the Lyric of History." *Southern Review* 35.3 (1999): 579–94.

Contextual Sources

Aaron, Daniel. *The Unwritten War: American Writers and the Civil War*. New York: Oxford UP, 1973.

Adams, Henry. *The Education of Henry Adams*. 1907. New York: Modern Library, 1931.

Beatty, Jack. *Age of Betrayal: The Triumph of Money in America*. New York: Vintage, 2007.

Beckert, Sven. *The Monied Metropolis: New York City and the Consolidation of the American Bourgeoisie, 1850–1906*. Cambridge: Cambridge UP, 2001.

Burke, Edmund. *Reflections on the Revolution in France. Burke: Select Works*. Ed. E.J. Payne. Vol. 2. Oxford: Clarendon P, 1883. 4–384.

Castiglia, Christopher, and Christopher Looby. "Come Again? New Approaches to Sexuality in Nineteenth-Century Literature." *ESQ* 55.3–4 (2009): 195–209.

Chauncey, George. *Gay New York: Gender, Urban Culture, and the Making of the Modern Gay World, 1890–1940*. New York: Basic Books, 1994.

Dana, Richard Henry, Jr. *Two Years before the Mast*. 1840. New York: Harper and Brothers, 1842.

D'Emilio, John, and Estelle B. Freedman. *Intimate Matters: A History of Sexuality in America*. 3rd ed. Chicago: U of Chicago P, 2012.

Dugan, James. *The Great Mutiny*. New York: Putnam, 1965.

Foner, Philip S. *The Great Labor Uprising of 1877*. New York: Monad P, 1977.

Green, James R. *Death in the Haymarket: A Story of Chicago, the First Labor Movement, and the Bombing that Divided Gilded Age America*. New York: Pantheon, 2006.

Hamilton, Gail. "The Murder of Philip Spencer." *Cosmopolitan* 7 (Jun.–Aug. 1889): 133–40, 248–55, 345–54.

Howe, Daniel Walker. *What Hath God Wrought: The Transformation of America, 1815–1848*. New York: Oxford UP, 2007.

Hutchinson, Anthony. *Writing the Republic: Liberalism and Morality in American Political Fiction*. New York: Columbia UP, 2007.

Jerrold, Douglas. *The Mutiny at the Nore. A Nautical Drama, in Two Acts*. 1830. London: Thomas Hailes Lacy, n.d. Chadwyck-Healey English Prose Drama Full-Text Database.

Maciag, Drew. *Edmund Burke in America: The Contested Career of the Father of Modern Conservatism*. New York: Columbia UP, 2013.

Manwaring, G.E., and Bonamy Dobrée. 1935. *The Floating Republic*. New York: Augustus M. Kelley, 1966.

Marr, Timothy. *The Cultural Roots of American Islamicism*. New York: Cambridge UP, 2006.

Matthiessen, F.O. *American Renaissance: Art and Expression in the Age of Emerson and Whitman*. New York: Oxford UP, 1941.

Menand, Louis. *The Metaphysical Club: A Story of Ideas in America*. New York: Farrar, Straus and Giroux, 2001.

Paine, Thomas. *Rights of Man. The Writings of Thomas Paine*. Vol. 2. Ed. Moncure Daniel Conway. New York: G.P. Putnam's Sons, 1894. 264–523.

Painter, Nell Irvin. *Standing at Armageddon: The United States 1877–1919*. New York: Norton, 1987.

Parini, Jay. *The Passages of H. M.* New York: Anchor, 2011.

Parrington, Vernon Lewis. *Main Currents in American Thought*. 1927. Vol. 2. New York: Harcourt Brace, 1930.

Trachtenberg, Alan. *The Incorporation of America: Culture and Society in the Gilded Age*. New York: Hill and Wang, 1982.

Whitman, James Q. *Harsh Justice: Criminal Punishment and the Widening Divide between America and Europe*. New York: Oxford UP, 2003.

Melville on the Web

[Billy Budd Manuscript.] Melville, Herman, 1819–1891. Herman
  Melville Papers, 1761–1964. Billy Budd. A.Ms.; [n.p., n.d.]. MS
  Am 188 (363). Houghton Library, Harvard University, Cambridge,
  MA. http://nrs.harvard.edu/urn-3:FHCL.Hough:4686413.
Bryant, John and Wyn Kelley. *Melville Electronic Library.*
  http://mel.hofstra.edu/index.html.
The Melville Society. http://melvillesociety.org/.
Olson-Smith, Steven, Peter Norberg, and Dennis C. Marmon.
  Melville's Marginalia Online.
  http://melvillesmarginalia.org/front.php. (See also Walker Cowen,
  ed., *Melville's Marginalia*, in "Bibliographies and Guides to Criti-
  cism," above.)
Wright American Fiction. www.dlib.indiana.edu/collections/wright.

Other Texts Cited in This Edition

Auden, W.H. "Herman Melville." *Another Time*. London: Faber and
  Faber, 1940. 33–34.
Bloom, Harold, et al. "Other Victorian Poets." *The Oxford Anthology
  of English Literature.* Vol. 2. New York: Oxford UP, 1973. 1475–76.
Edwards, Jonathan. "Sinners in the Hands of an Angry God." *A
  Jonathan Edwards Reader*. Ed. John E. Smith, Harry S. Stout, and
  Kenneth P. Minkema. New Haven, CT: Yale UP, 1995. 89–105.
Emerson, Ralph Waldo. "The Fugitive Slave Law." 1851. Reprint.
  Miscellanies. Boston: Houghton Mifflin, 1906. 177–214.
Hawthorne, Nathaniel. *The English Notebooks: 1856–1860*. Ed.
  Thomas Woodson and Bill Ellis. Columbus: The Ohio State UP,
  1997.
James, William. *The Varieties of Religious Experience*. New York:
  Longman's, Green and Co., 1902.
Kierkegaard, Søren. *Fear and Trembling; Repetition*. Trans. and ed.
  Howard V. Hong and Edna H. Hong. Princeton, NJ: Princeton
  UP, 1983.
Leeman, William P. *The Long Road to Annapolis: The Founding of the
  Naval Academy and the Emerging American Republic*. Chapel Hill: U
  of North Carolina P, 2010.
Montaigne, Michel de. *The Complete Essays of Montaigne*. Trans.
  Donald M. Frame. Stanford, CA: Stanford UP, 1958.
Renouard, Jean-Philippe, and Lise Wajeman. "The Weight of Here
  and Now: Conversation with Claire Denis, 2001." *Journal of Euro-
  pean Studies* 34.1–2 (2004): 19–32.

Schopenhauer, Arthur. *Studies in Pessimism: A Series of Essays.* Trans. T. Bailey Saunders. London: Swan Sonnenschein and Co., 1893.

——. *The World as Will and Idea.* 1819–44. Reprint. Trans. R.B. Haldane and J. Kemp. Vol. 1. London: Trübner and Co., 1883.

Taylor, Charles. *The Sources of the Self: The Making of the Modern Identity.* Cambridge, MA: Harvard UP, 1898.

Tennyson, Alfred Lord. *Selections from Tennyson.* Toronto: Copp, Clark, 1891.

Thomson, James. *The City of Dreadful Night and Other Poems.* Portland, ME: Thomas B. Mosher, 1903.

Thoreau, Henry David. *The Writings of Henry David Thoreau.* Vol. 4. Boston: Houghton Mifflin: 1906.

Twain, Mark. *The Adventures of Huckleberry Finn.* 1884. Ed. Victor Fischer and Lin Salamo. Berkeley: U of California P, 2003.

Webster, Noah. *Letters of Noah Webster.* Ed. Harry R. Warfel. New York: Library Publishers, 1953.